The Addams Family
An Evilution

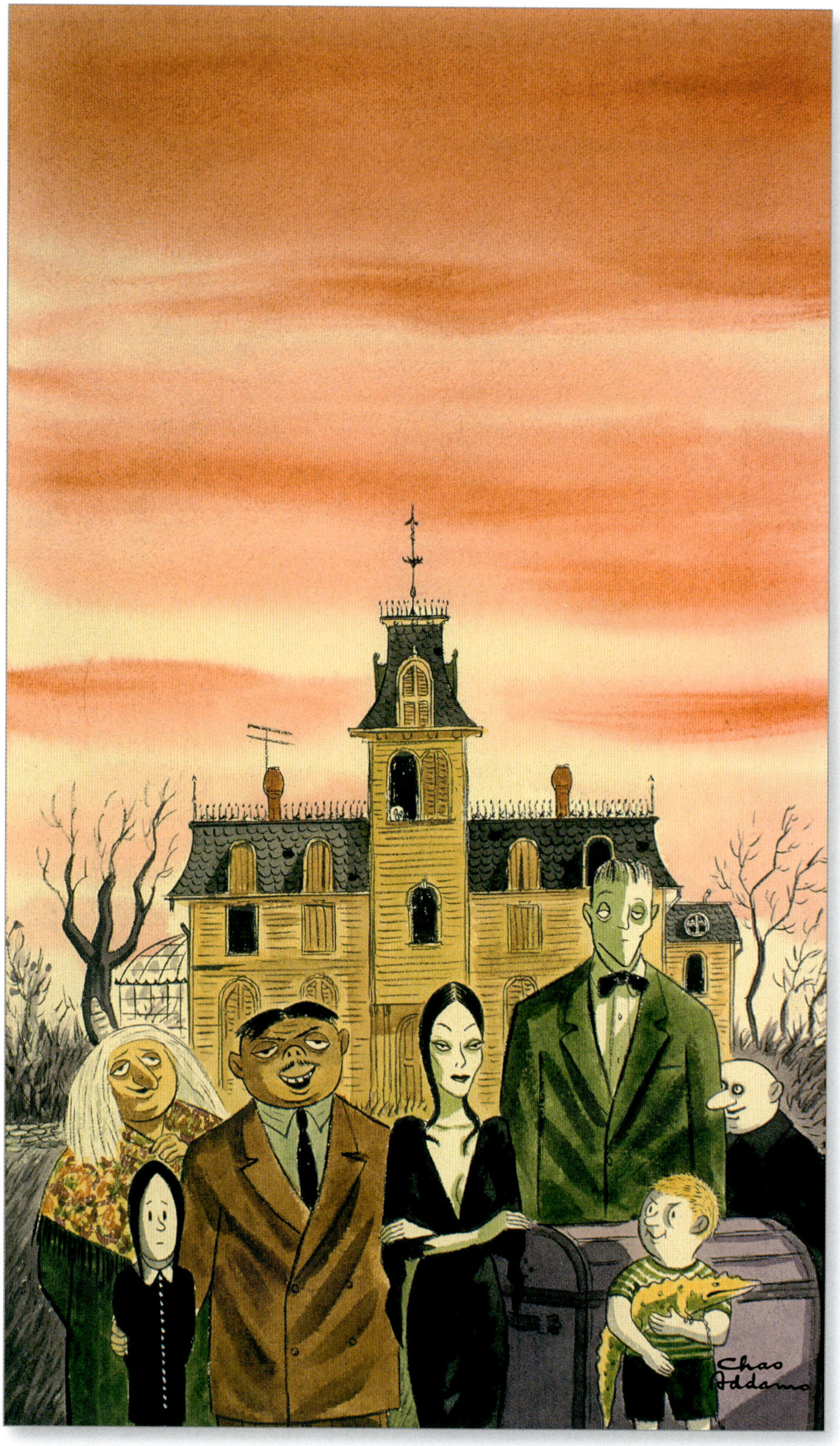
Chas
Addams

THE ADDAMS FAMILY
AN EVILUTION

Chas Addams

H. Kevin Miserocchi

Pomegranate
PORTLAND, OREGON

Pomegranate Communications, Inc.
105 SE 18th Ave., Portland, OR 97214
800-227-1428   pomegranate.com
sales@pomegranate.com

Copyright © 2010 by Tee and Charles Addams Foundation. All rights reserved.
No part of this publication may be reproduced or transmitted in any form or by any means, electronic or mechanical, including photocopying, recording, or by any information storage or retrieval system, without permission in writing from the copyright holders.

Chas Addams's name and signature are trademarks of the Tee and Charles Addams Foundation. All rights reserved.

Library of Congress Cataloging-in-Publication Data
Miserocchi, H. Kevin.
 Charles Addams : the Addams Family, an evilution / by H. Kevin Miserocchi.
     p. cm.
 Includes index.
 ISBN 978-0-7649-5388-0
 1. Addams, Charles, 1912–1988—Themes, motives. 2. Addams family (Fictitious characters) I. Title. II. Title: Addams Family, an evilution.
 NC1429.A25A4 2010
 741.5'6973—dc22
                    2009038338

Pomegranate Item No. A180

Designed by Shannon Lemme

Printed in China
33 32 31 30 29 28 27 26 25 24   19 18 17 16 15 14 13 12 11 10

DEDICATION

This book is dedicated to the memory of

Charles Samuel Addams

and

Tee Matthews Addams

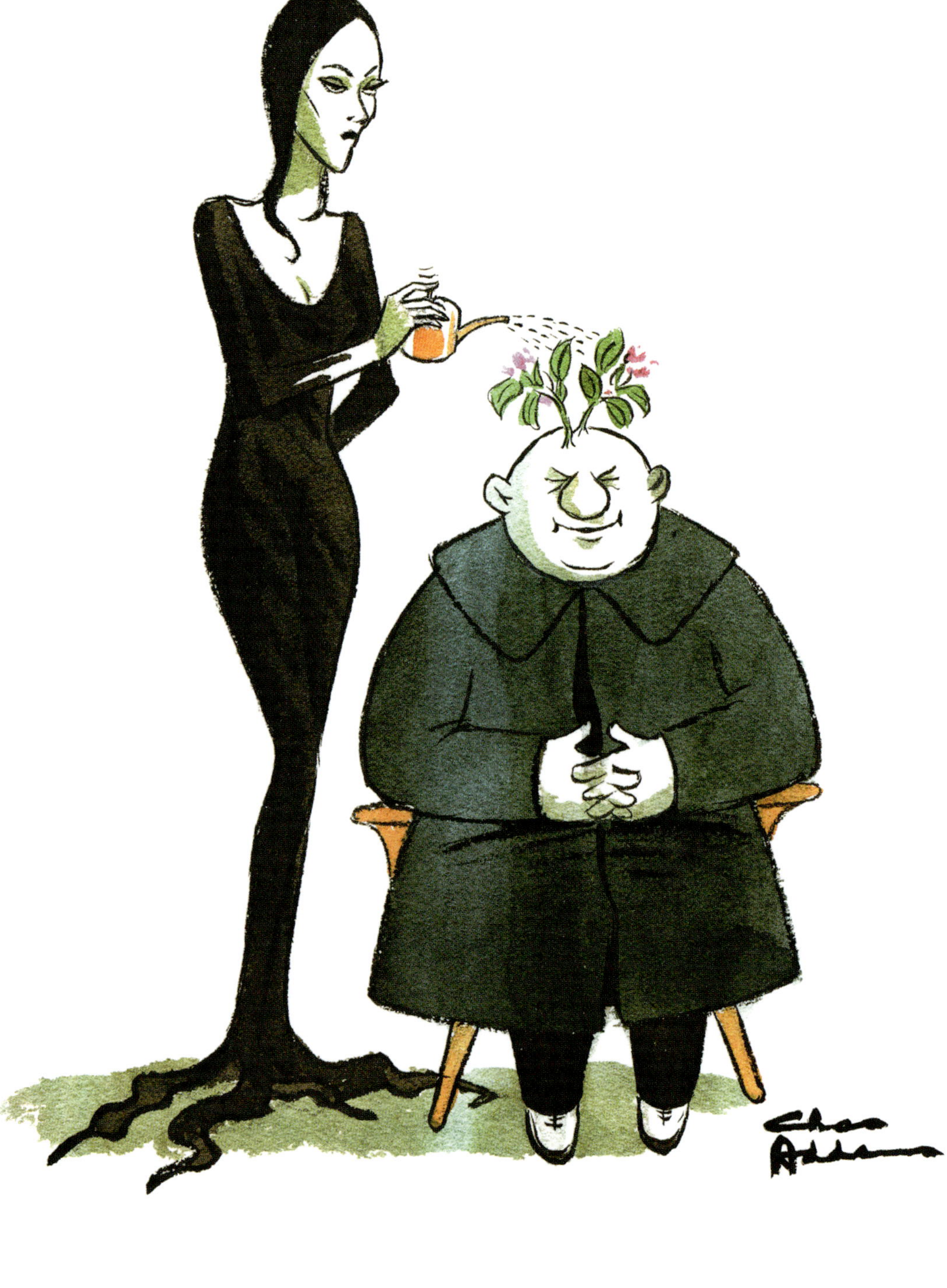

CONTENTS

Preface 9

Introduction 13

The Family 16

Morticia 42

Gomez 62

Wednesday and The Boy Pugsley 80

Lurch, the Butler 118

Granny Frump (a.k.a. Grandma Frump) 128

Uncle Fester 146

The Thing 182

Relatives & Family Friends 192

A House to Die For 210

Index of Illustrations 222

Bibliography: Compilations of Charles Addams Cartoons 224

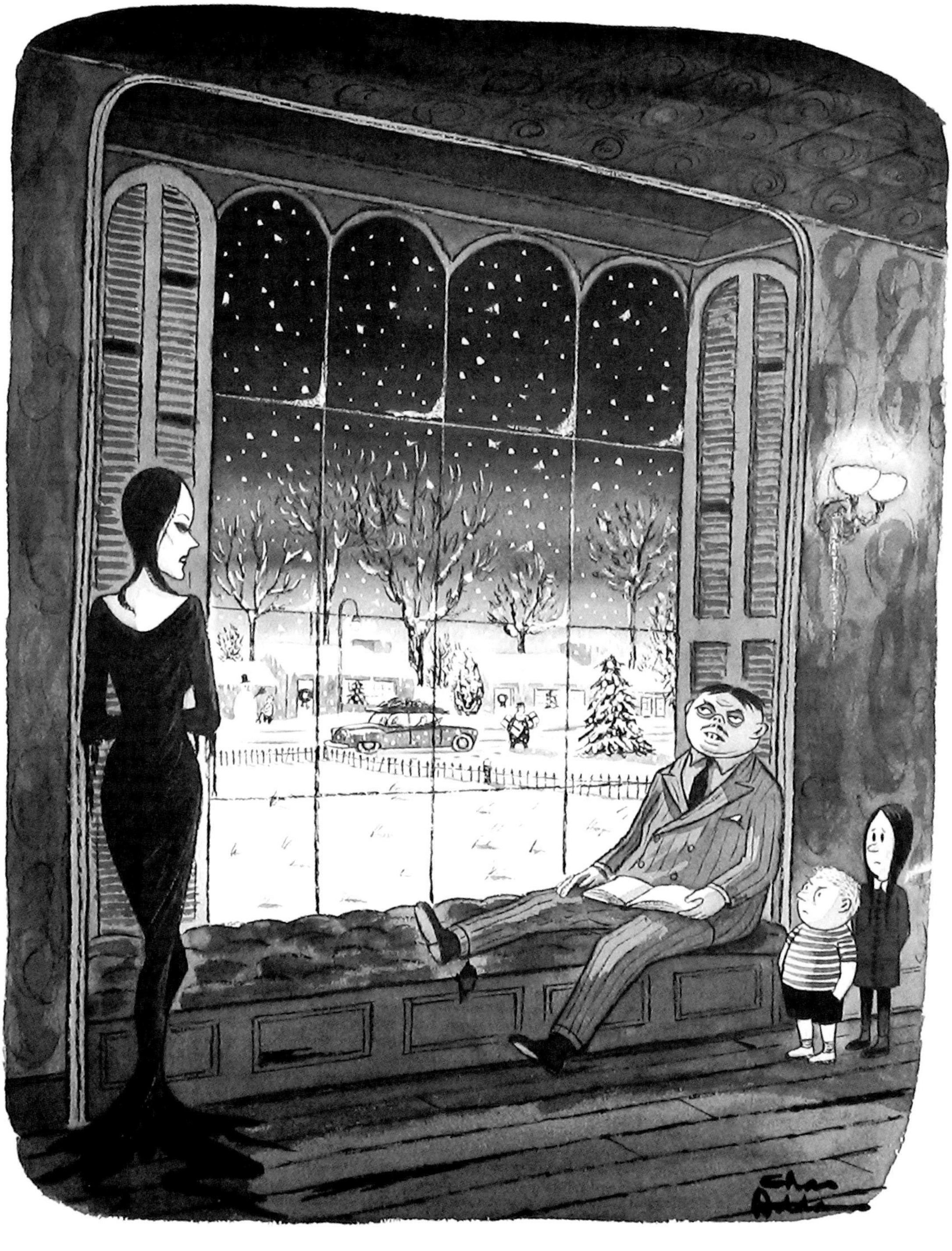

"Suddenly, I have a dreadful urge to be merry."

PREFACE

THE Tee and Charles Addams Foundation has had the great fortune to be the recipient of the entire Charles Addams archive through an endowment by his widow, Marilyn "Tee" Matthews Addams (1926–2002), who formed the Foundation in 1999. This archive includes about half of the nearly 1,600 published works by Charles Addams (1912–1988)—the other half resides in institutional and private collections worldwide—and an enormous body of previously unpublished work, photographs, correspondence, and interview materials in all media.

This compilation is the first complete look at the development of The Addams Family characters, through both the published and the never-before-published work. The character descriptions introducing most of the chapters are the words of Charles Addams exactly as he wrote them for inclusion as Exhibit A in the Filmways TV Productions, Inc., agreement dated September 11, 1963, a contract that produced the sixty-four episodes of *The Addams Family* televised from 1964 until 1966. Filmways producer David Levy asked Addams to create this document to be used as a template for each character's demeanor or possible behavioral traits. Addams primarily relied on his drawings to describe the substance of their actions, although in a few instances he suggests intimate psychological and emotional qualities perhaps not portrayed in the actual works, but evidently brewing in the creator's imagination.

As in nearly all families, the whole comprises various parts, each one unique. This unusual group developed gradually and did not appear as a true family until many years after each character's initial appearance. Some of the eventual members were absorbed into The Addams Family even though they had first appeared elsewhere or as slightly different characters within the Addams oeuvre. Once the clan had attained national and international recognition, all Family members, in toto and individually, appeared in the marketplace. They sold perfumes, typewriters, international telephone services, magazines, and even Japanese scotch. They appeared on the covers of *Business Week* and *Show* magazines, *TV Guide* and *MAD*. They were the advertising spokespersons for Decorators Walk and both the *New Yorker* magazine and at least one of that magazine's exhibitions. They appeared on the pages and covers of journals and invitations to social events and charitable fund-raising benefits. They were even immortalized as a 4 x 13–foot wall mural at the Dune Deck, a hotel cocktail lounge and restaurant in Westhampton Beach, New York. When the Dune Deck was demolished, the panel was cut out from the wall and donated to the Pattee Library, Pennsylvania State University, where it resides today.

Charles Addams set out not to create a family but rather to suggest how society as a whole might interpret characters bent on the darker side while living lives similar to those embracing the light. After years of witnessing their delightful wickedness on the pages of magazines and Addams books and advertisements of all types, the press began referring to the characters as "Addams' family of ghouls" and the exquisite home in which they performed their one-act plays as "the Addams house." Charles Addams's name became synonymous with all aspects of his work and the world he created. Addams himself began to refer to his characters as "Addams' Evils."

Always described as strange, eerie, odd, and spooky, the Family nevertheless had many of the same joys and woes that all families experience—for example, keeping the house in order and seeing that the children take responsibility for the welfare of their pets. How delightfully refreshing that they had a trapdoor and a secret panel for the carpenter to fix, that the children arrived home from camp in pet carriers, and that at least one pet was a small dragon! They celebrated Christmas as eagerly as they did Halloween, just with their own traditions. What would an Addams Family Christmas be without lighting a fire in the fireplace in anticipation of Santa's arrival down the chimney, or pouring boiling oil down on the neighborhood carolers? They really weren't that different after all.

On behalf of a great percentage of the Addams audience, John Calloway revealed to Charles Addams in his 1981 interview for Chicago Educational Television that he was haunted by his work, to which Addams replied, "If it haunts you that much, you remember it and that's what we want. That's what I want you to be." Charles Addams was the engineer of a trademark sinister edge, and he knew how to inject that edge into themes, situations, and experiences basically considered the "normal way of life." He only asked us to consider the side less visited.

This book celebrates the joy of fitting in, even if you appear inexplicably different and make those around you uncomfortable. Charles Addams was true to himself, and his cartoon characters emulate that honesty through the purity of their evil intent.

H. Kevin Miserocchi, Director
Tee and Charles Addams Foundation

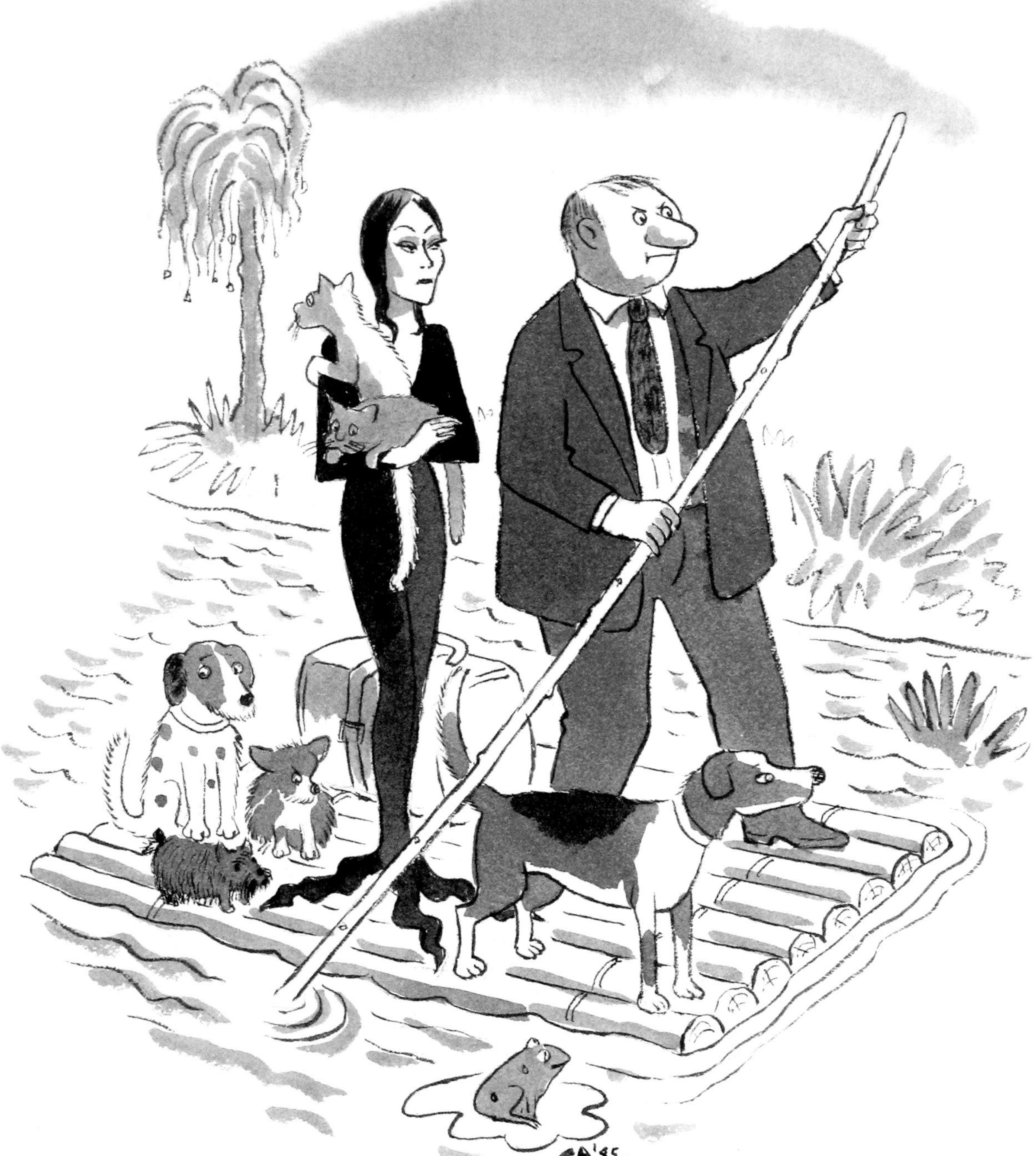
CA'85

The Addams Family is moving to The Swamp

INTRODUCTION

It was dead on, yet alarmingly off center. It was so simple, but so rife with sophistication. It set a marker for decades to come. It was not compromised. It was completely honest. It made us think and laugh and "beg for another one, Sir," all at the same time. It spawned cult adoration. It was clean and brilliant, yet it dared to lean into the darkness. And it had an unusual birth, never before witnessed on Earth. It was The Addams Family. And it continues to live.

Perhaps it is not the version you know. The threads of its naissance arose an entire generation before Filmways TV Productions' black-and-white program debuted on ABC on the evening of September 18, 1964, and more than two generations before Raul Julia and Anjelica Huston introduced it to the big screen in two slickly amusing films from Orion Pictures and Paramount Pictures. What these nearly forty-six years of viewing audiences may not know is that the Family was born in print, a medium that, not long from now, may evolve out of our realm. And that this Family, though not actually named thusly until its transformation by live actors into television, bore the moniker of The Addams Family via the natural lineage of its true father, Charles Samuel Addams—or Chas Addams, as was his lifetime signature, first used with the publication of his second full cartoon for the *New Yorker* on March 18, 1933. This quiet man employed a deft pen line, a beautiful brushstroke, and pungent wit to create the painterly cartoons in which his characters charmed the reading public through the *New Yorker,* McClure Syndicate newspapers, and countless publications around the world, as well as on the pages of his own anthologies, eight of which had been published by 1964.

The Addams Family characters were not the sole denizens of the world of Charles Addams, nor were they born together, though chronological order is nearly irrelevant to their union. However unintentional, they became a phenomenon, and no one was more surprised by this than Charles Addams himself. The enormous worldwide following his television Family spawned was something Addams never anticipated, but he maintained sole control of his creation. He designed and painted the sets, wrote the scripts, cast each story, and costumed his characters in clothing of his own design. On occasion, dialogue or story line could and would be suggested, but Addams's interpretations, right down to camera angles, were uniquely his own.

Charles Addams was born in Westfield, New Jersey, in 1912. After the *New Yorker* first published his work, when Addams was just twenty-one years old, he became one of the magazine's marquee contributors, a relationship that lasted until his death. His body of work spans almost sixty years of output and is estimated to contain several thousand works. The Addams Family characters appear in only about 150 of his original works, about half of which were first published in the *New Yorker*.

Addams himself was often described as ghoulish, macabre, bizarre, and depraved, on the basis of his wicked sense of humor. He was known by friends and acquaintances as charming, tender, and captivating. He was in near-perfect balance, juggling the three loves of his life: women, cartooning, and vintage cars, in no order of preference. His pheromone levels were enormous, as his women friends neared eighty in number, and his strong male bonds were nearly as numerous. He owned some twenty vintage and deluxe automobiles in his lifetime, repairing many himself.

Marilyn "Tee" Matthews Addams was Charles Addams's third and final spouse, as was he for her. Having been photographically immortalized by Alfred Eisenstaedt in *Life* magazine as a Florida teen in 1943, Tee became an international pinup girl during the last two years of World War II, during which time she modeled with the John Robert Powers agency in Manhattan. Tee and Charlie were very close friends for nearly forty years before they were married, in her pet cemetery in Water Mill, New York, in 1980. He memorialized the occasion with a drawing of Morticia and Uncle Fester exchanging vows, witnessed by an unidentified fiend, among others. He also recorded their relocation to "The Swamp," the name affectionately bestowed upon their home in Sagaponack, New York, with an announcement card illustrating the happy couple rafting home with their family of animals. They were the love of each other's life.

Charles Addams was keenly interested in all life around him. He lived comfortably within the boundaries of "the norm" while he investigated the "other side" with his art. He was classy and disarmingly droll in both districts. As well, Addams loved plotting a good prank as much as rendering a devious deed.

What greater tribute could be paid to such an unassuming member of the creative elite than for his adoring audience to embrace the Addams world as still a part of this world, seventy years after its first character appeared in print. More than twenty years following his death in 1988, and in celebration of the Broadway opening of *The Addams Family* musical, Charles Addams's gift continues to entice its established audience while it snares the next. His genius remains timeless amid a world that constantly changes its focus.

Charles Addams and Wednesday doll made by Aboriginals, Ltd.

THE FAMILY

Gomez and Pugsley are enthusiastic. Morticia is even in disposition, muted, witty, sometimes deadly. Grandma Frump is foolishly good-natured. Wednesday is her mother's daughter. A closely knit family, the real head being Morticia—although each of the others is a definite character—except for Grandma, who is easily led. Many of the troubles they have as a family are due to Grandma's fumbling, weak character. The house is a wreck, of course, but this is a house-proud family just the same and every trap door is in good repair. Money is no problem.

Chas Addams

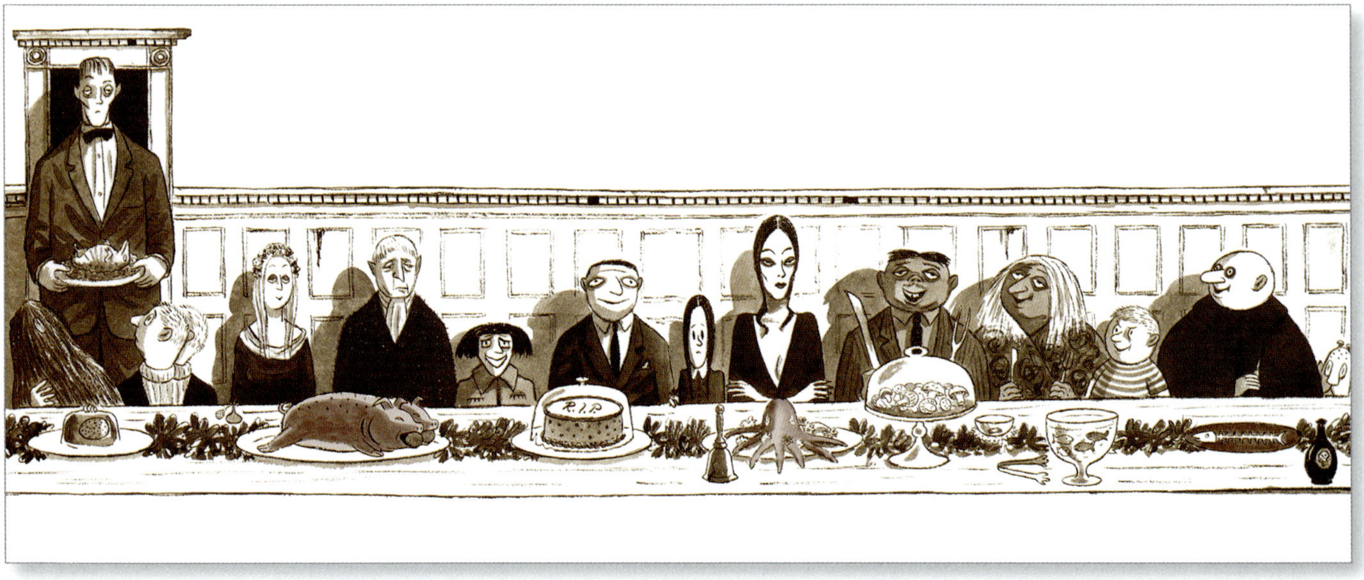
R.I.P.

STRONG family values are evident throughout Charles Addams's depictions of the family from the dark side. They hang together; they feel secure with one another; they have rules and morals that keep the family unit intact. Sure, the logs they burn in their fireplace are carved to look like men; they moonbathe instead of sunbathe; they prefer gazing at the sweeping vista of a cemetery rather than sunlit rolling hills; they take their outings in Central Park in the dead of night. The point is, they do these things together. They might be scary, weird, creepy, and macabre, but The Addams Family is our secret envy. If only our family dinners could be so much fun!

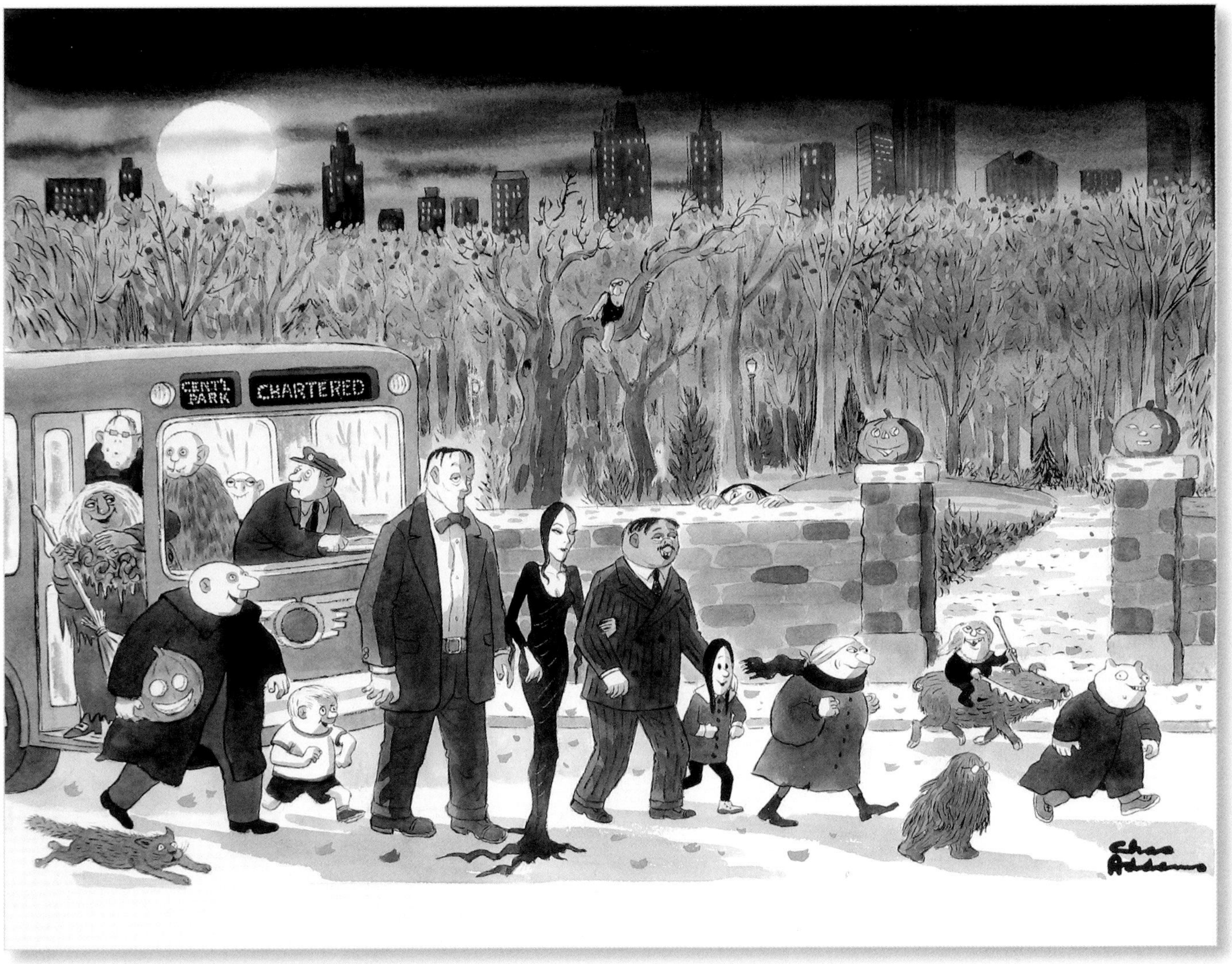
CENT'L PARK
CHARTERED
Chas Addams

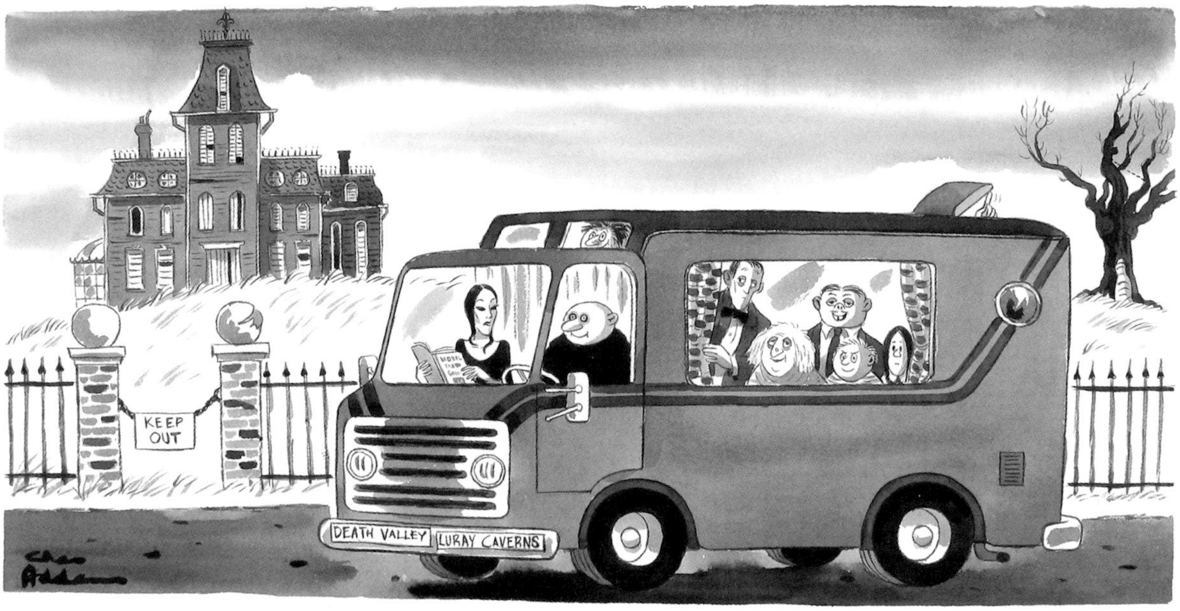
KEEP OUT
DEATH VALLEY
LURAY CAVERNS

"We'll feel right at home: The travel guide says there are bats in the belfry."

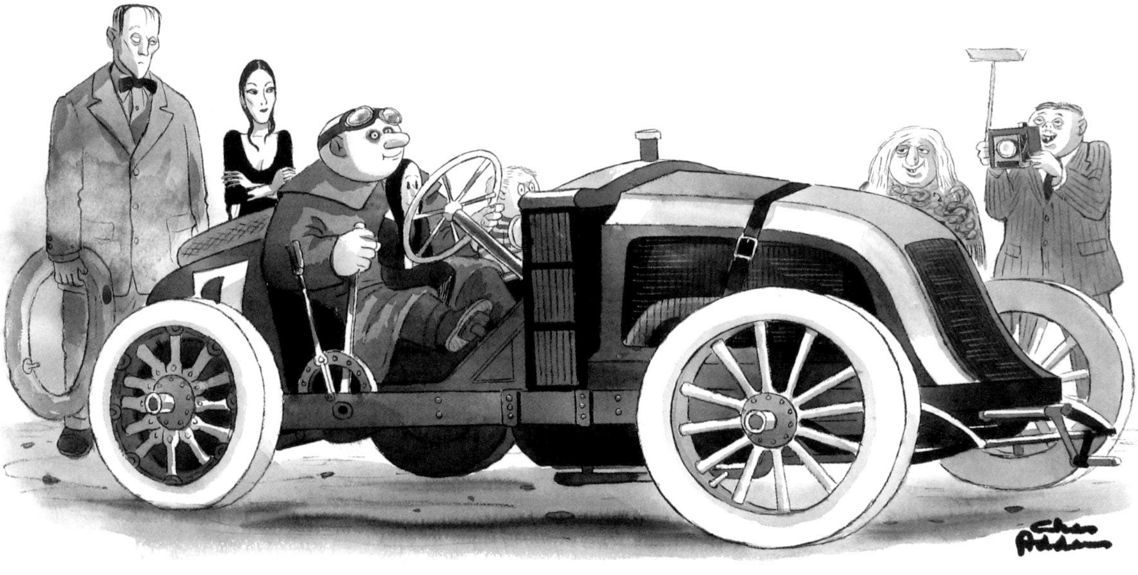

The Family Goes Racing

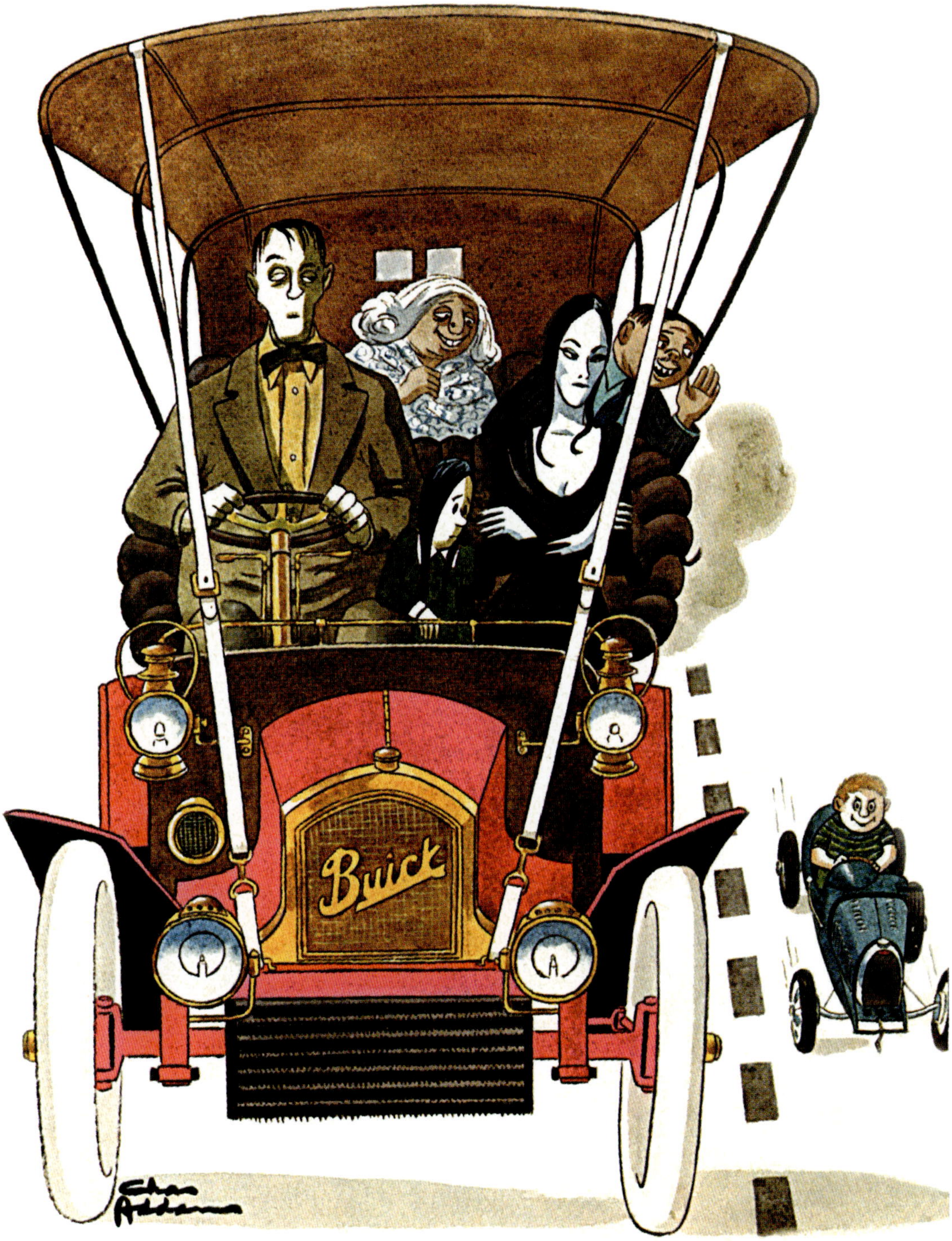
Buick

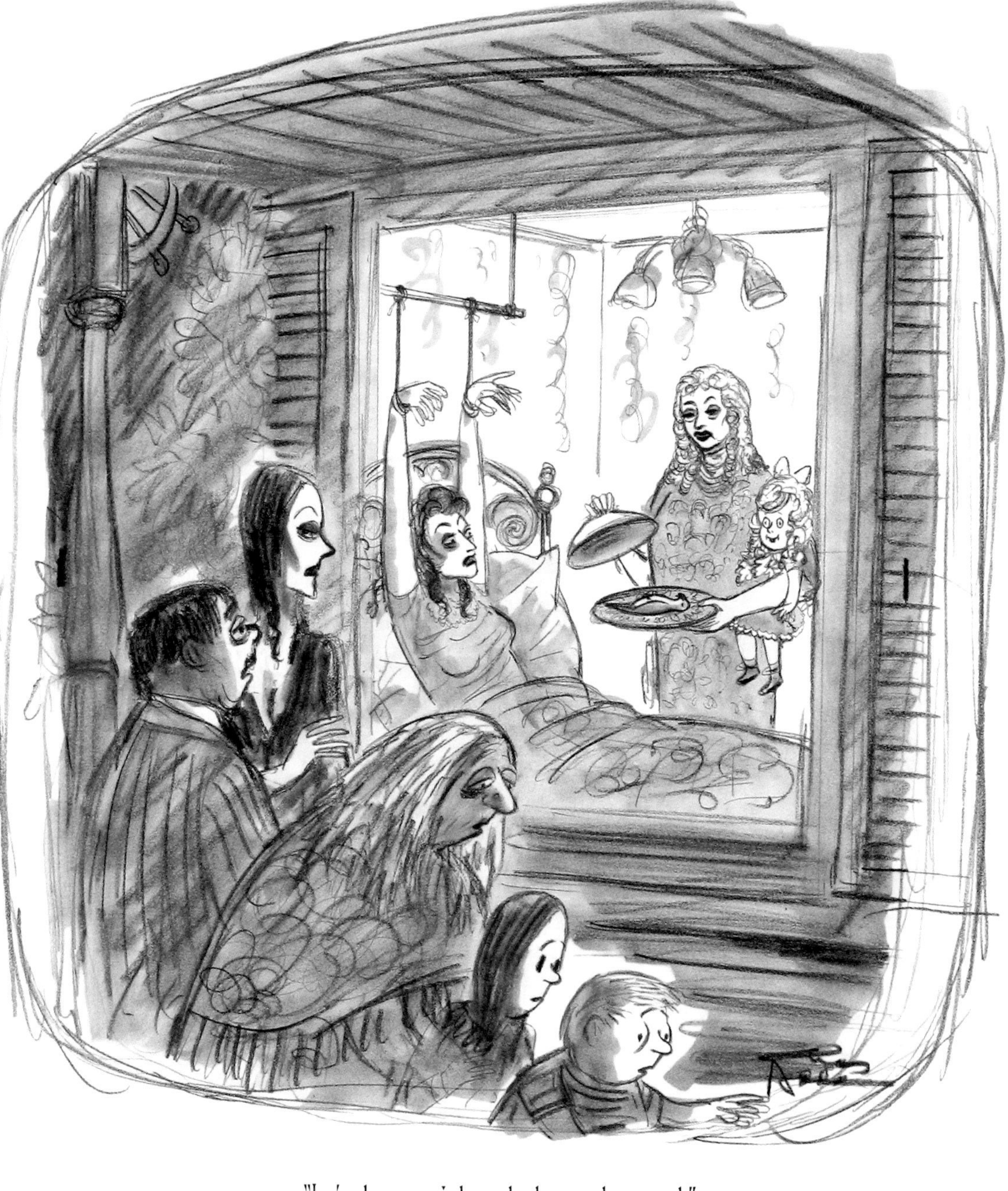

"Let's clear out. I draw the line at this crowd."

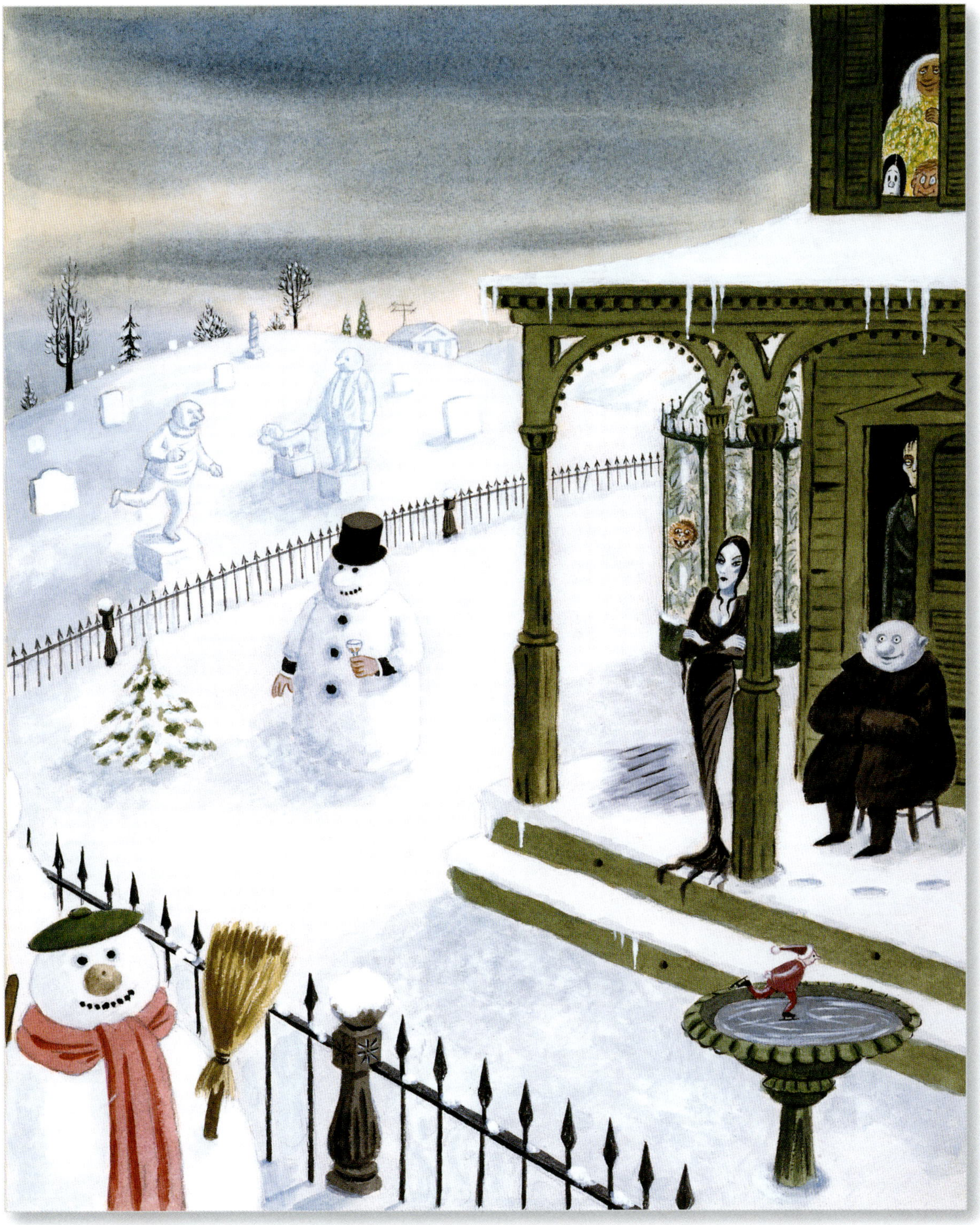

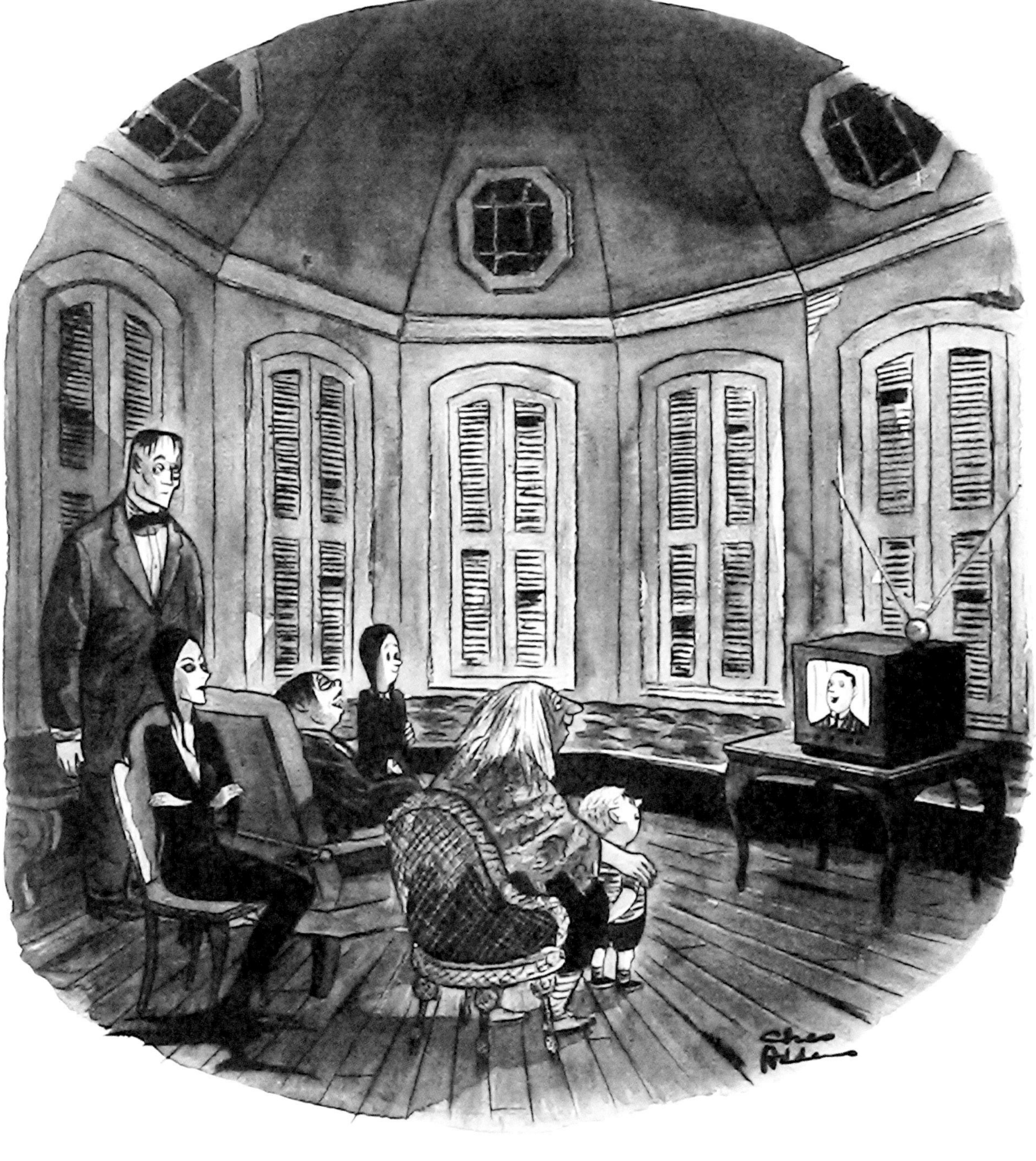

"And now we present 'Mary and Bill,' the story of a family that might be your next-door neighbors, and of their everyday life among everyday people just like yourselves . . ."

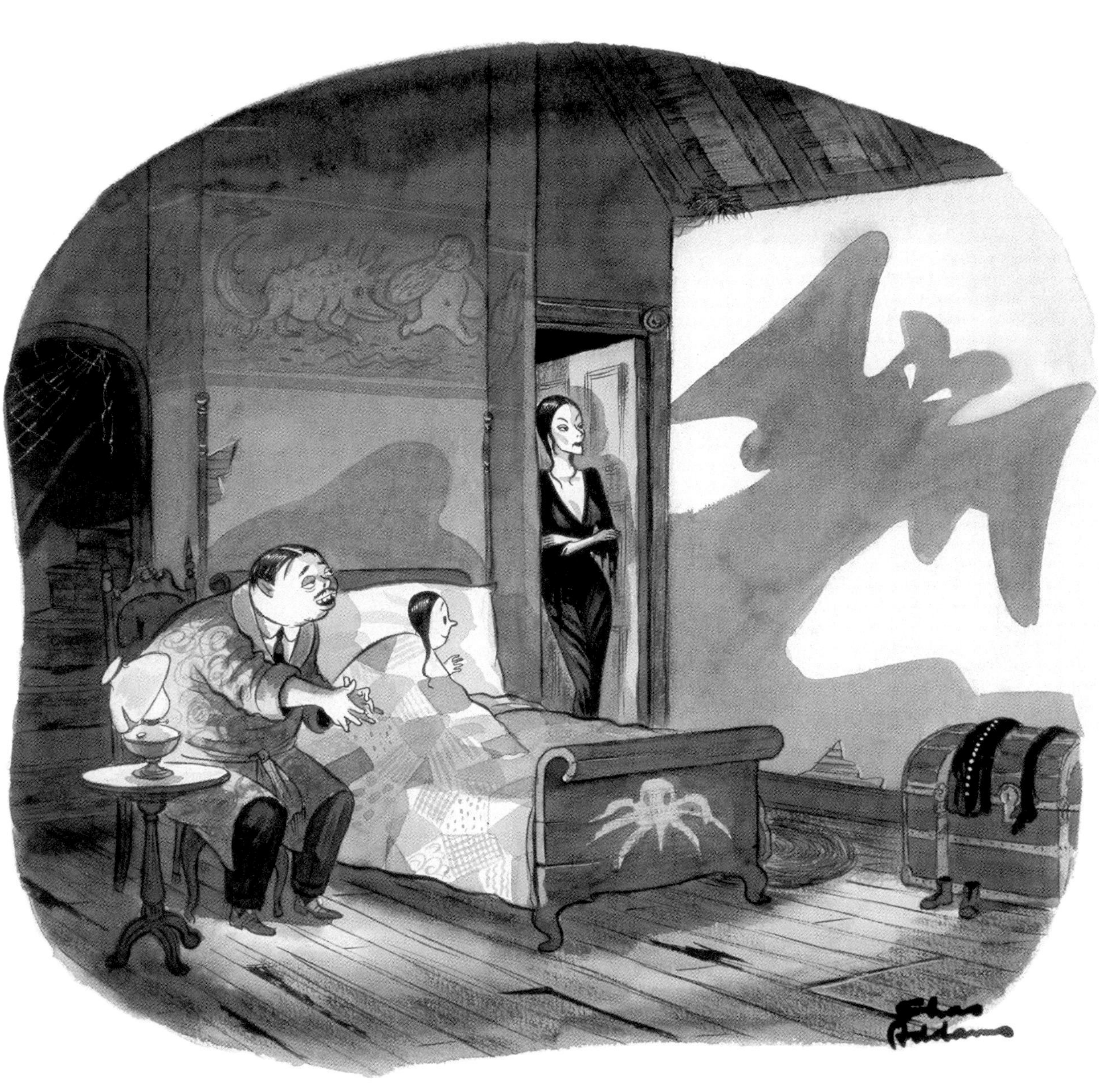

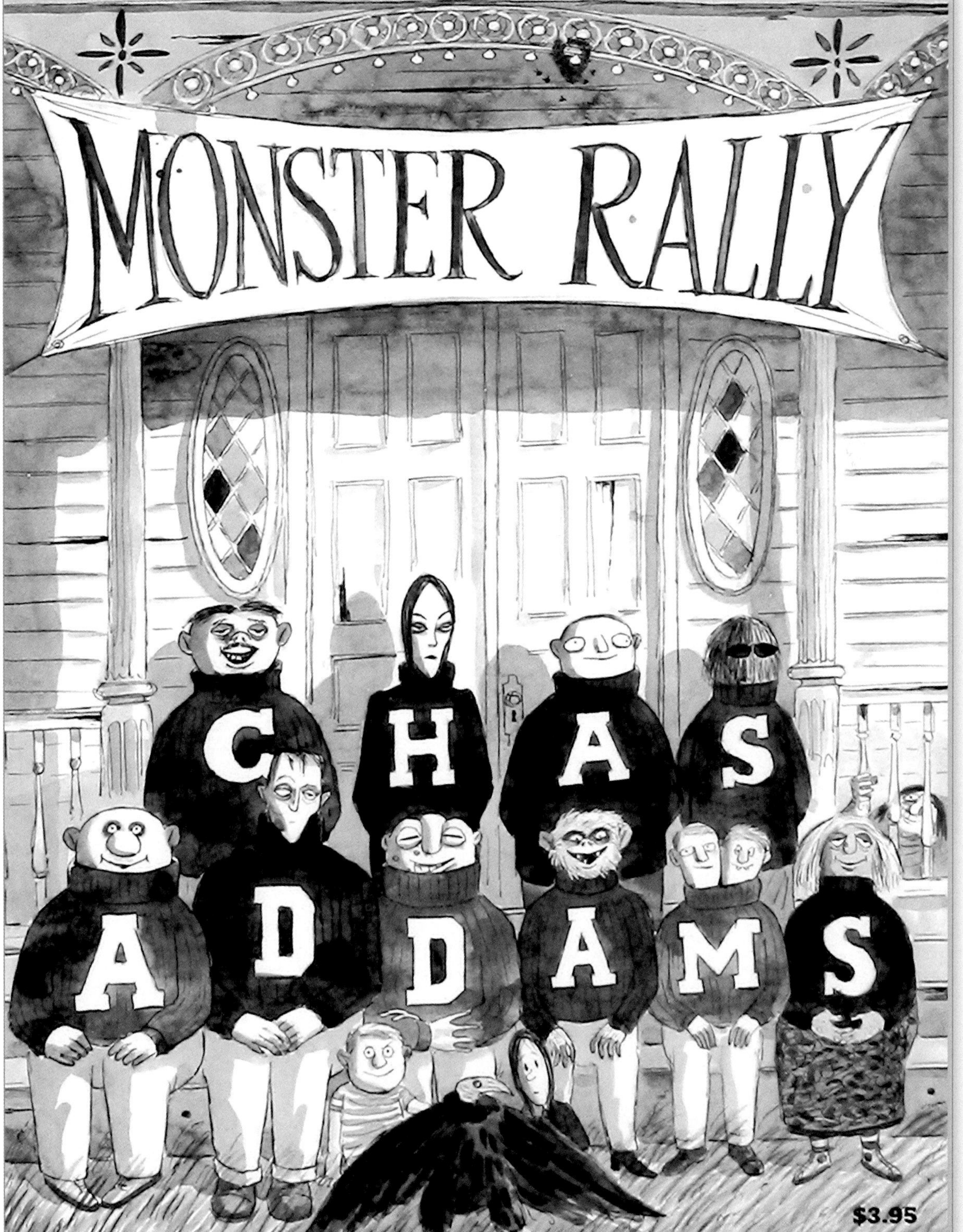
MONSTER RALLY
CHAS
ADDAMS
$3.95

"I've told you a hundred times. Don't feed Grandma at the table."

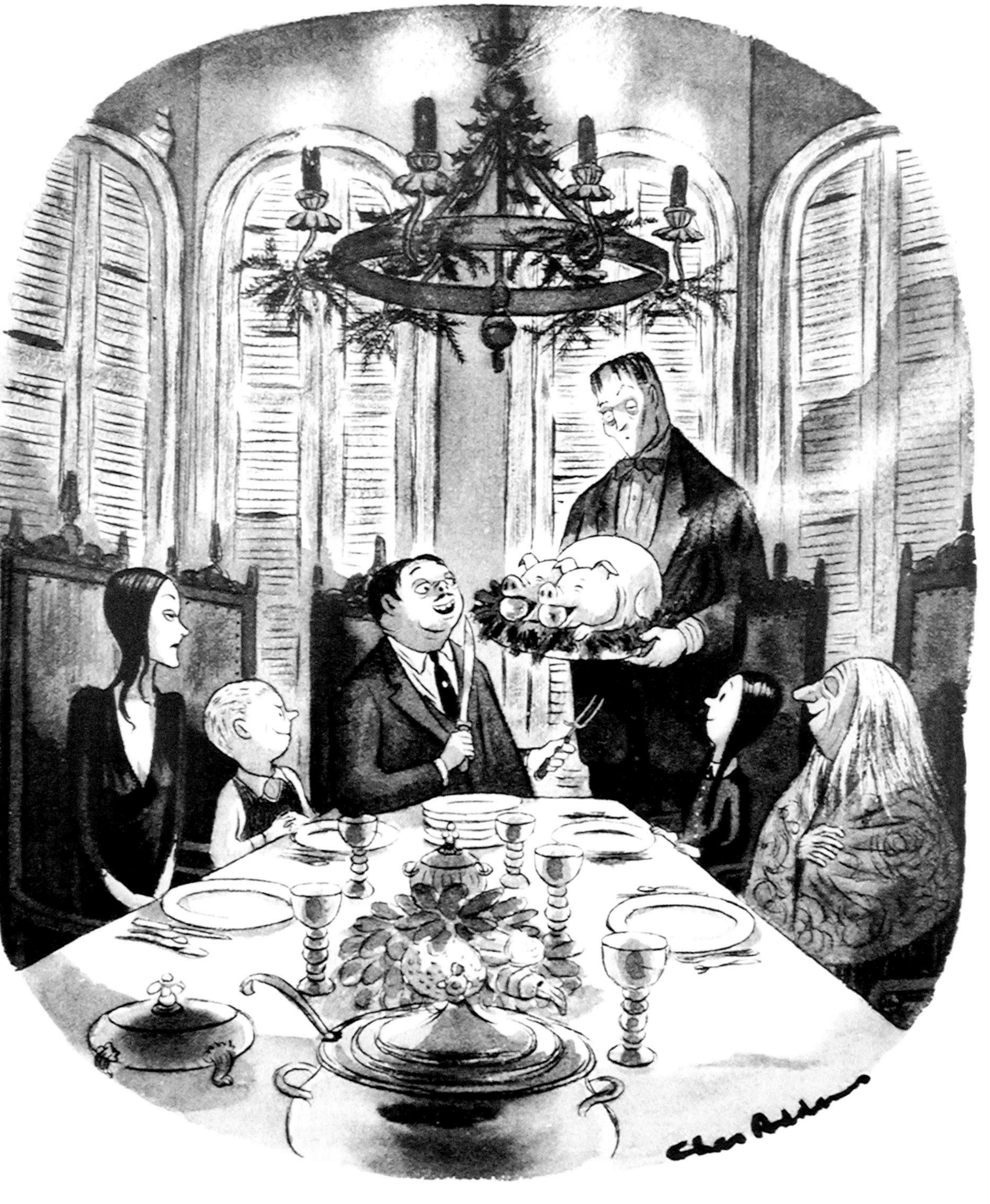
Chas Addams

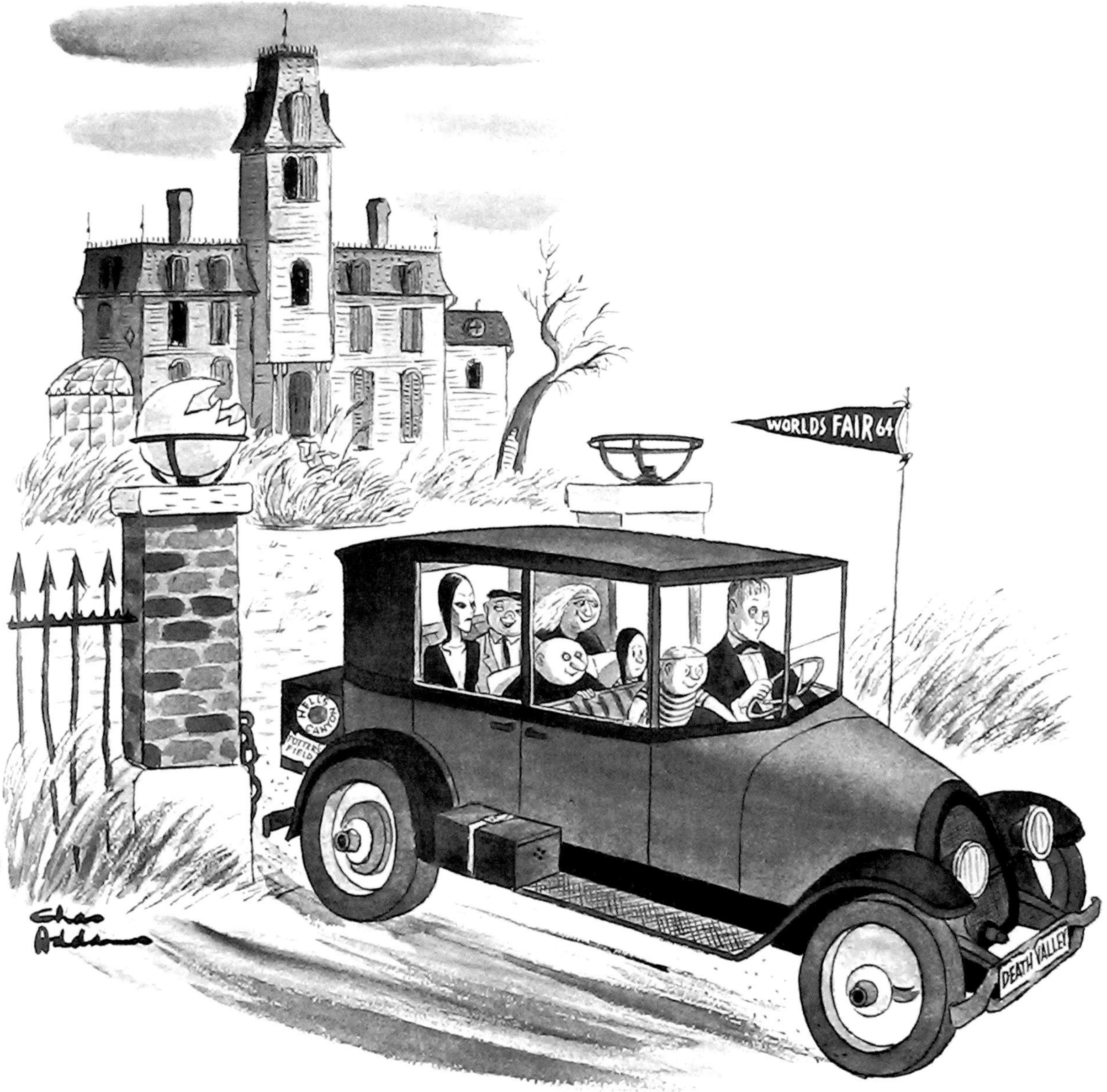
WORLDS FAIR 64
HELL'S CANYON
POTTERS FIELD
DEATH VALLEY
Chas Addams

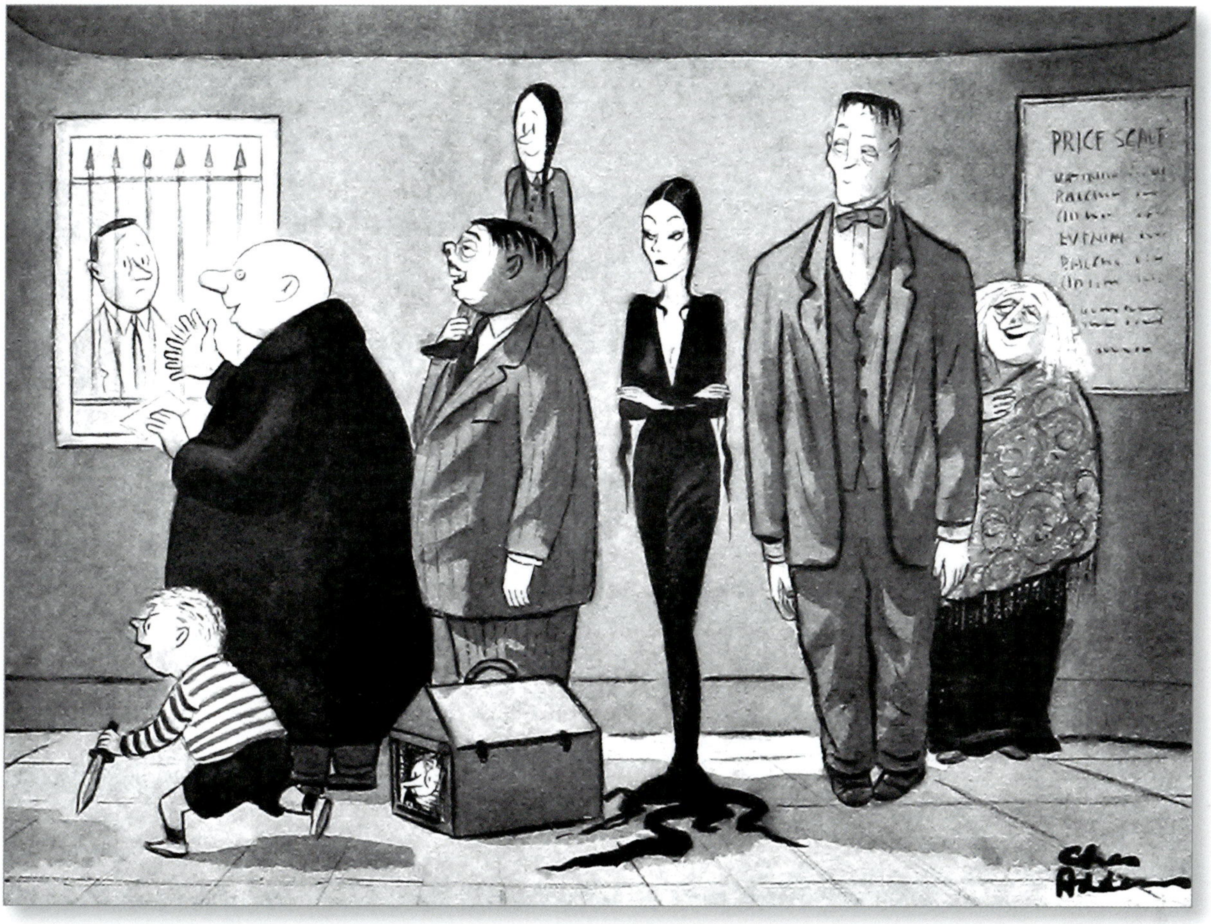
PRICE SCALE
Chas Addams

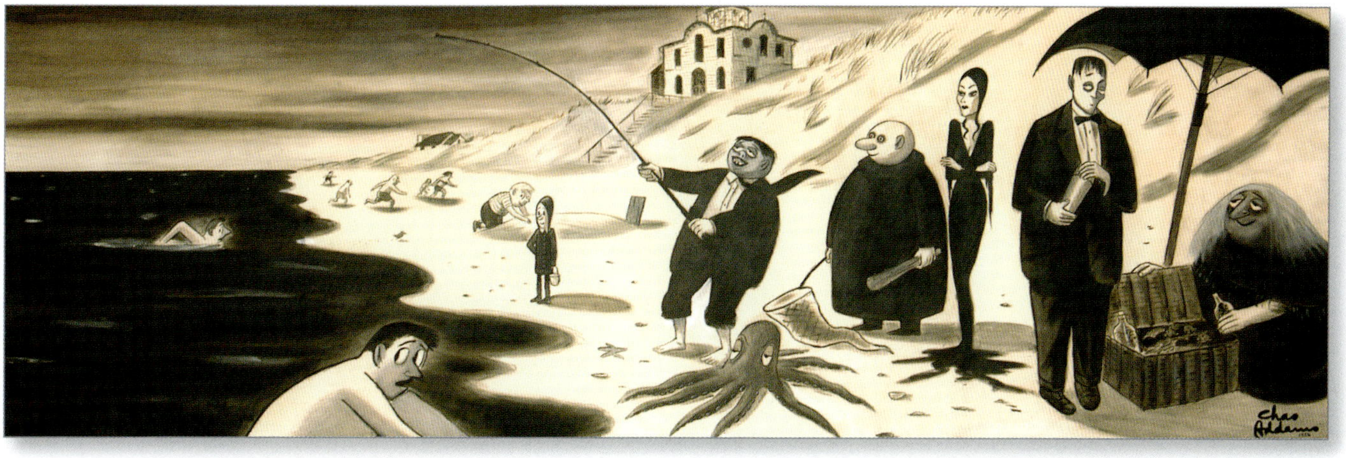
Chas Addams

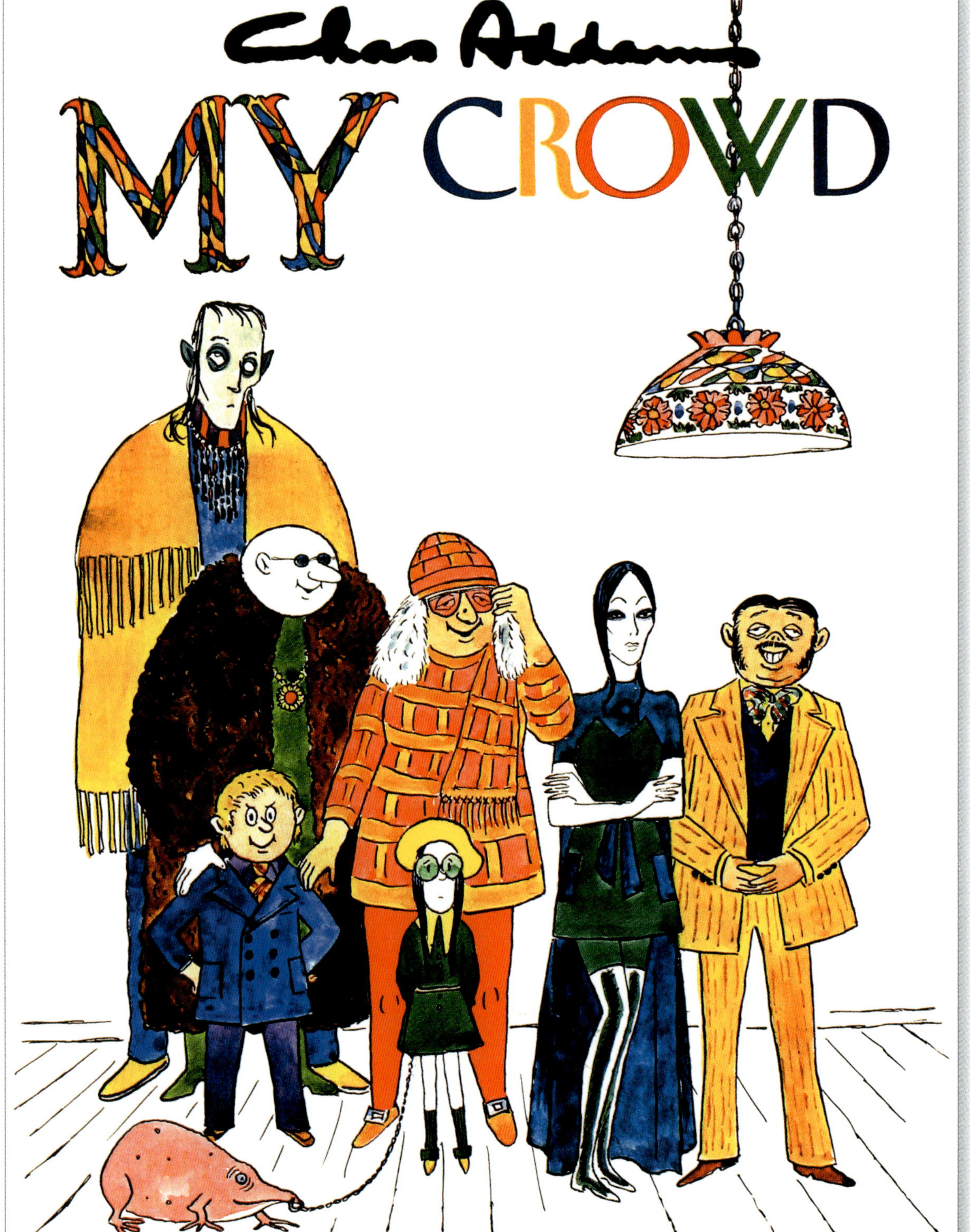
Chas Addams
MY CROWD

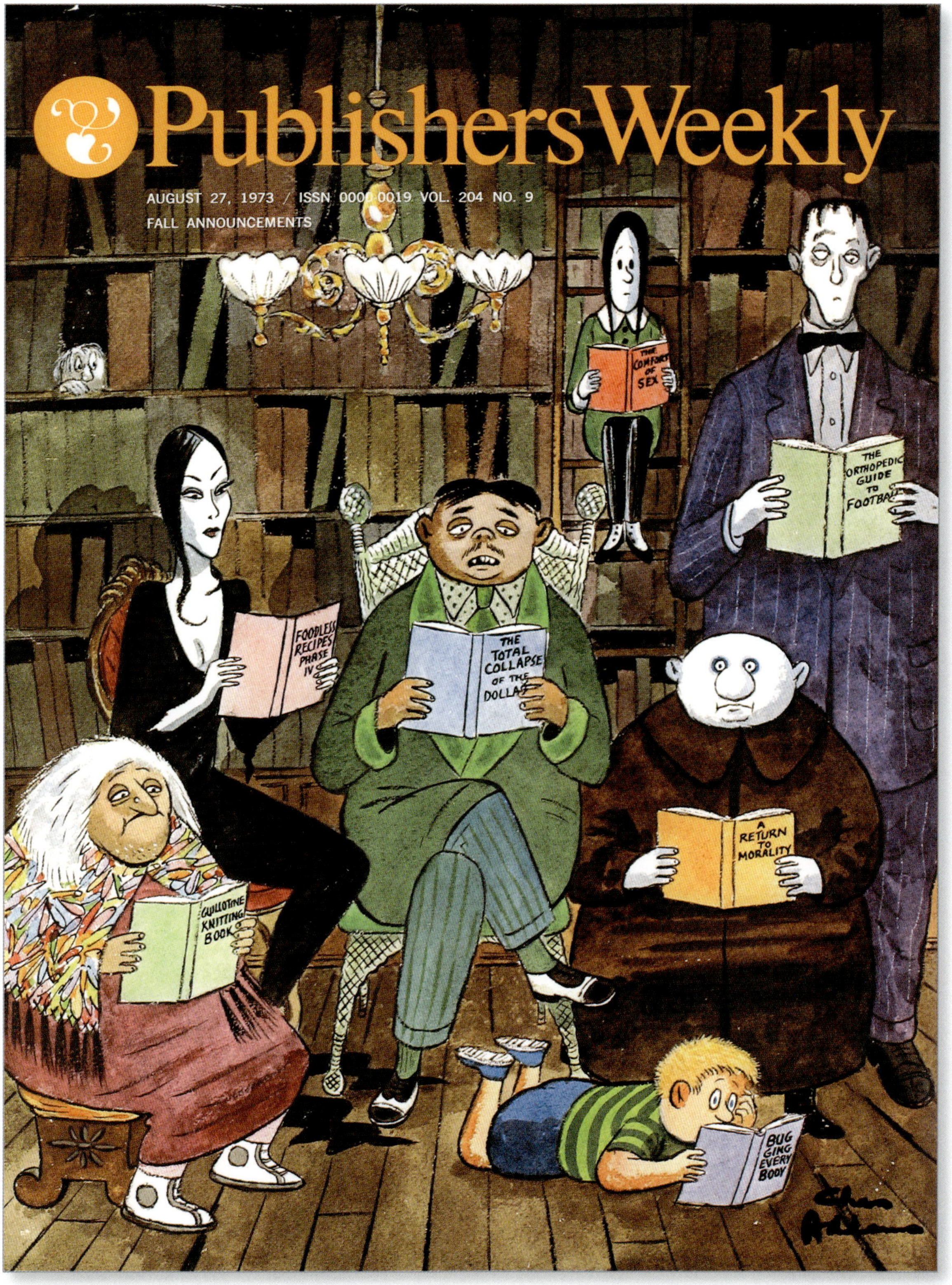
Publishers Weekly
AUGUST 27, 1973 / ISSN 0000-0019 VOL. 204 NO. 9
FALL ANNOUNCEMENTS
THE COMFORTS OF SEX
THE ORTHOPEDIC GUIDE TO FOOTBALL
FOODLESS RECIPES PHASE IV
THE TOTAL COLLAPSE OF THE DOLLAR
A RETURN TO MORALITY
GUILLOTINE KNITTING BOOK
BUG GING EVERY BODY

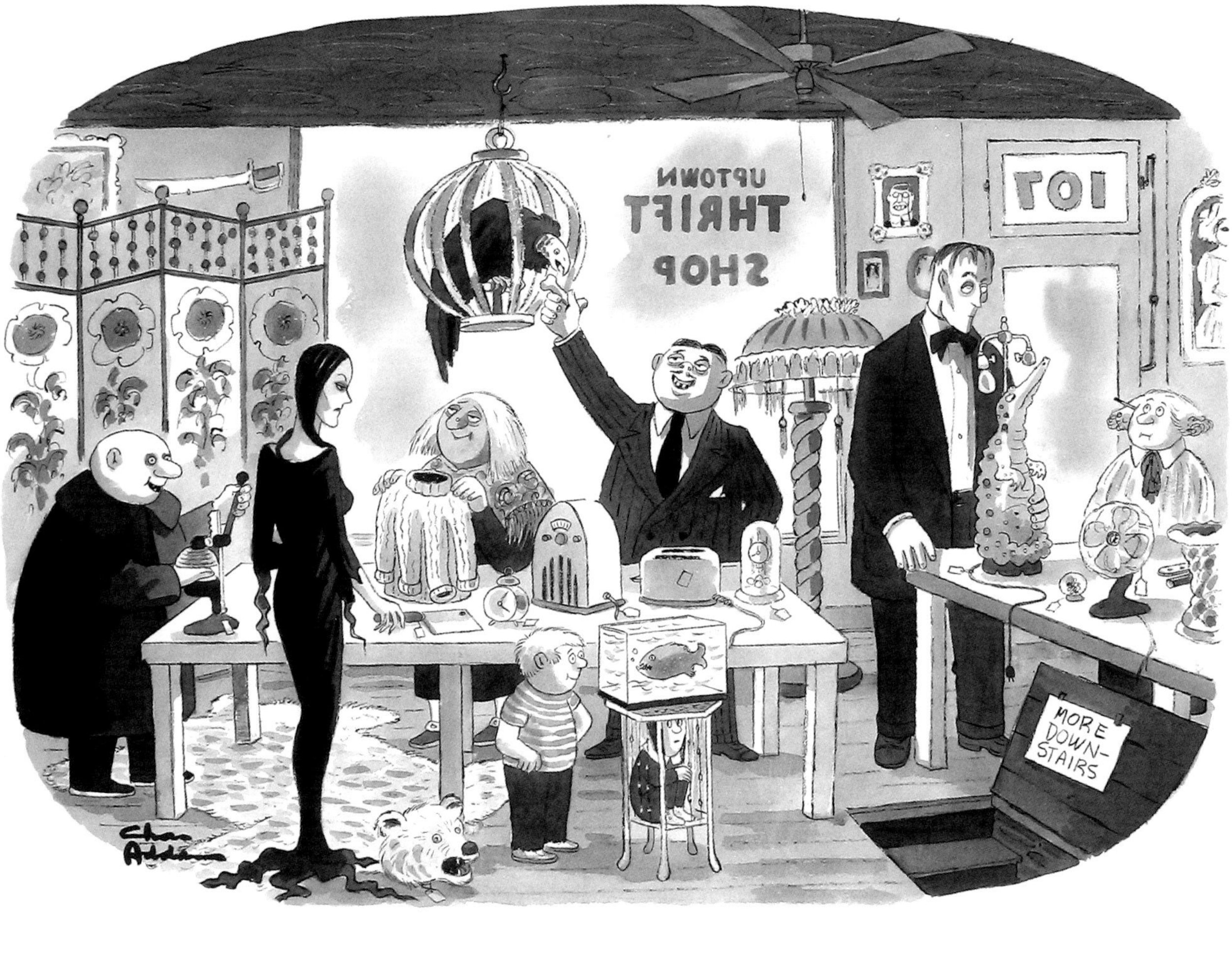
UPTOWN
THRIFT
SHOP
107
MORE
DOWN-
STAIRS
Chas Addams

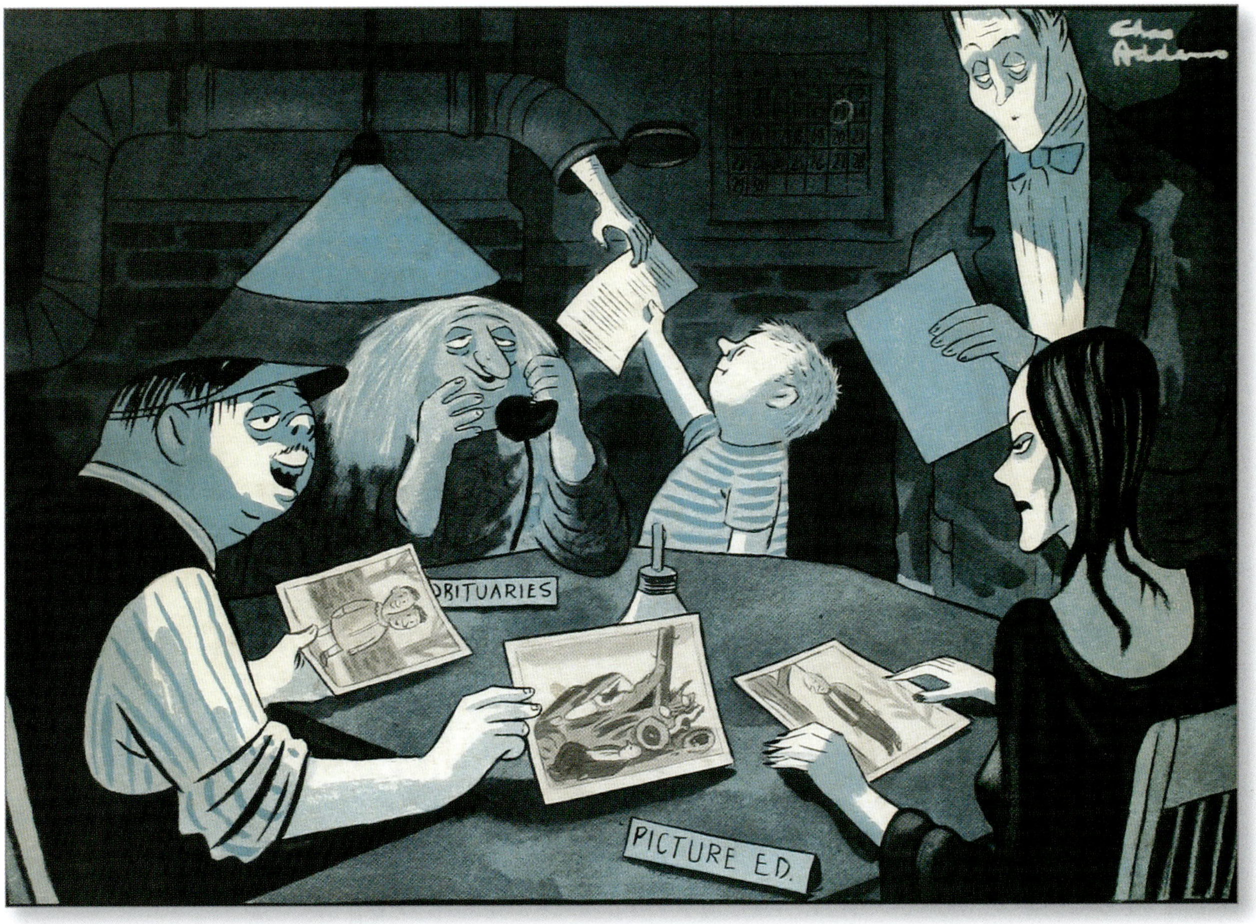
OBITUARIES
PICTURE ED.
Chas Addams

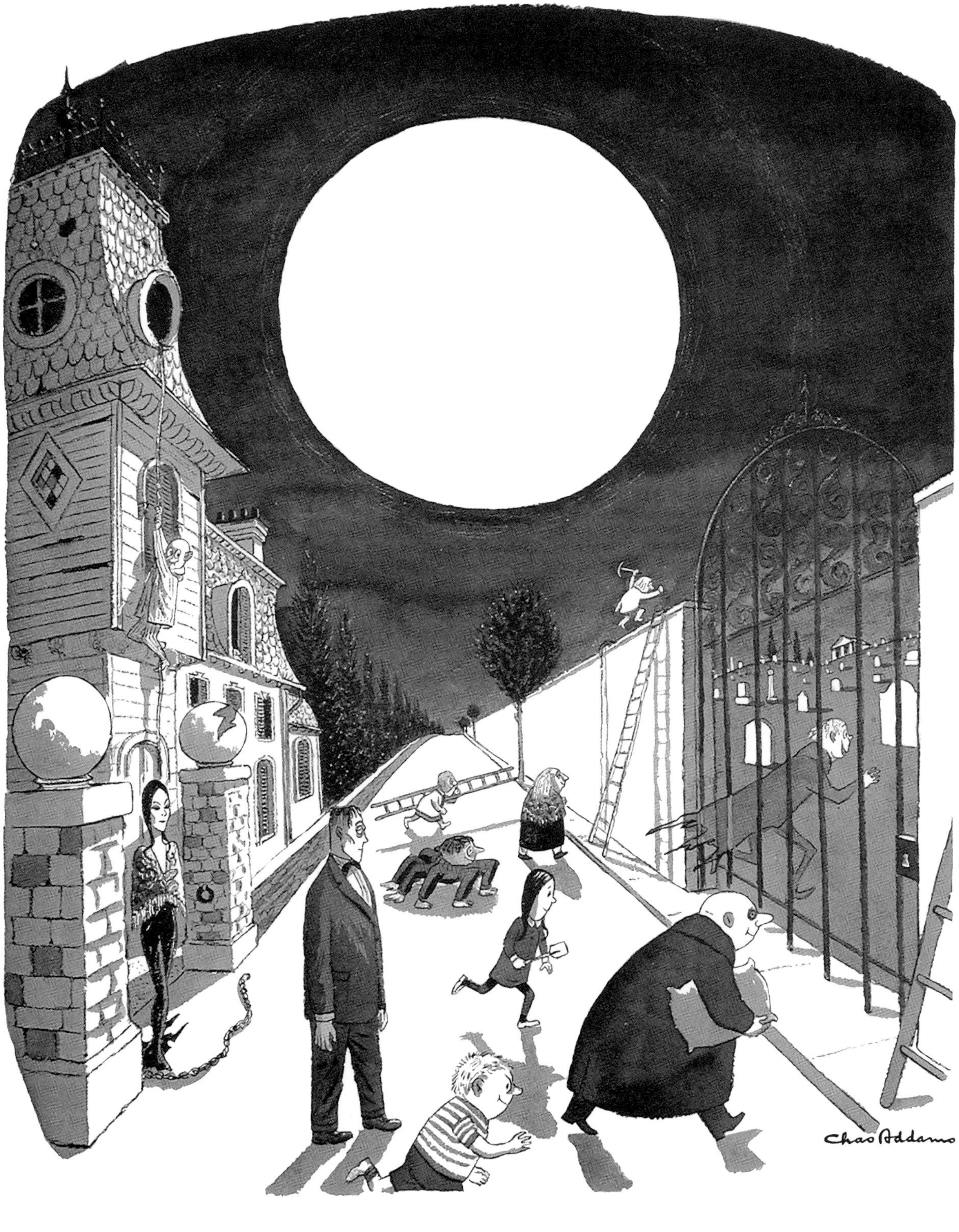
Chas Addams

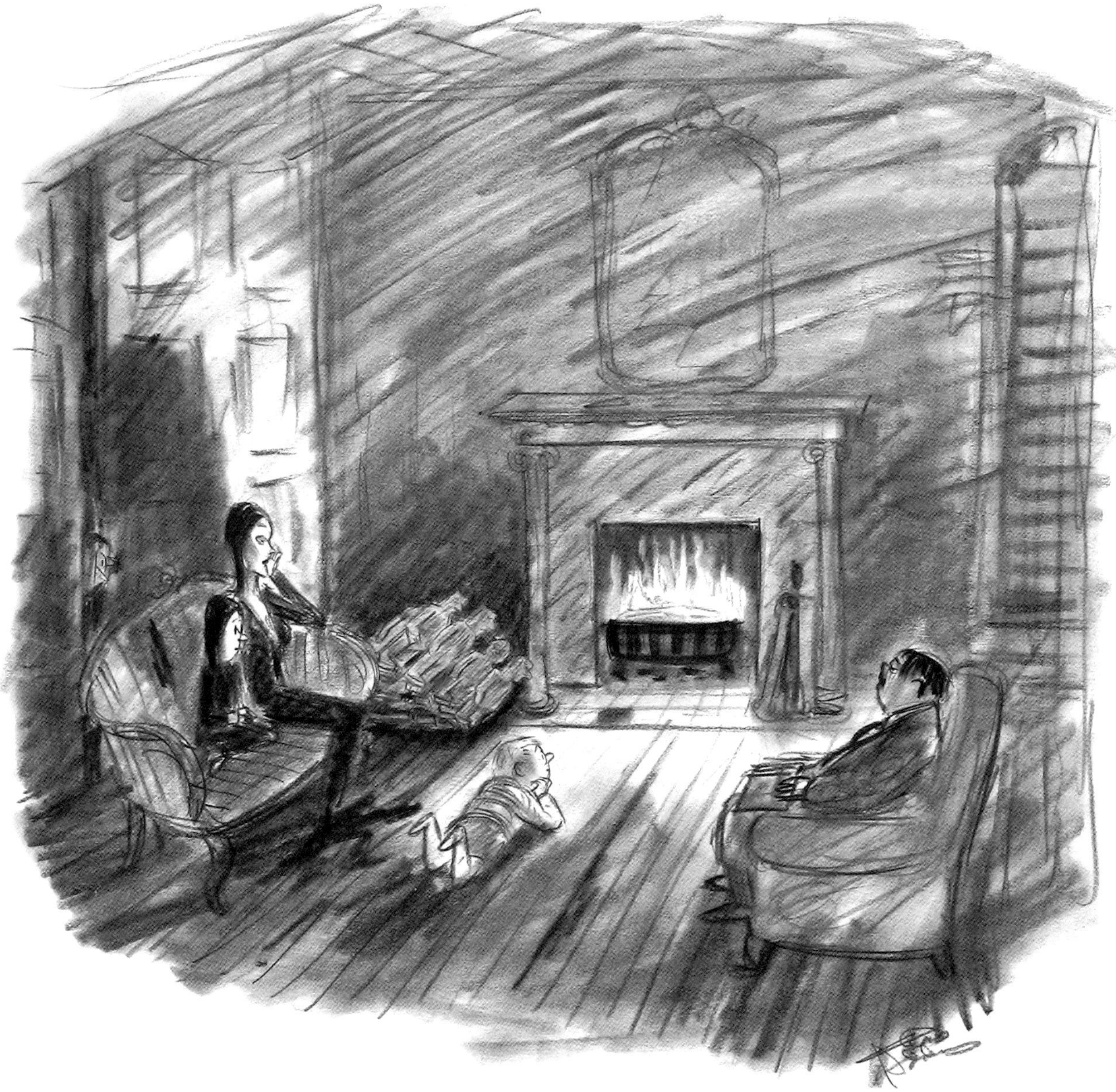

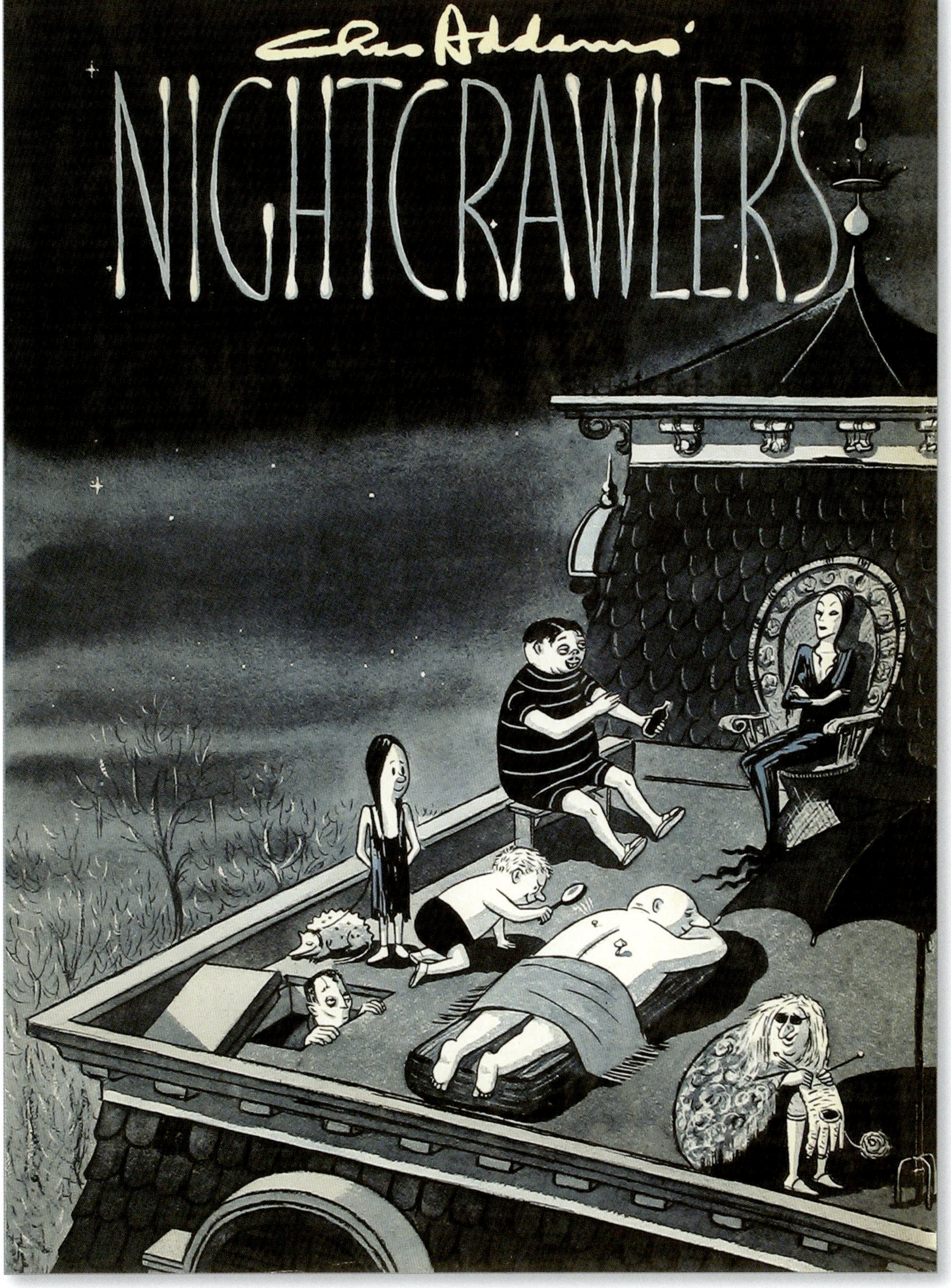
Chas Addams'
NIGHTCRAWLERS

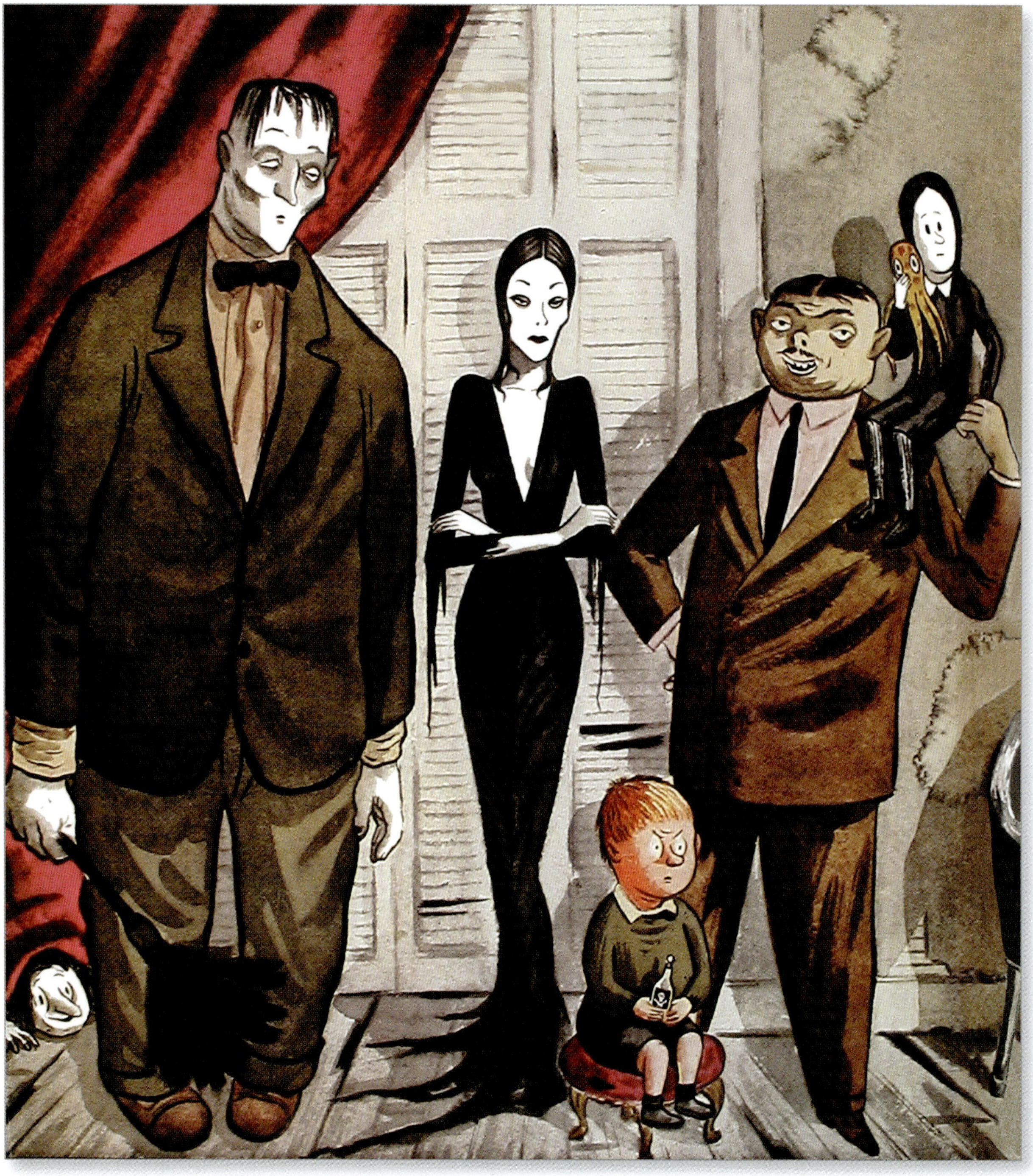

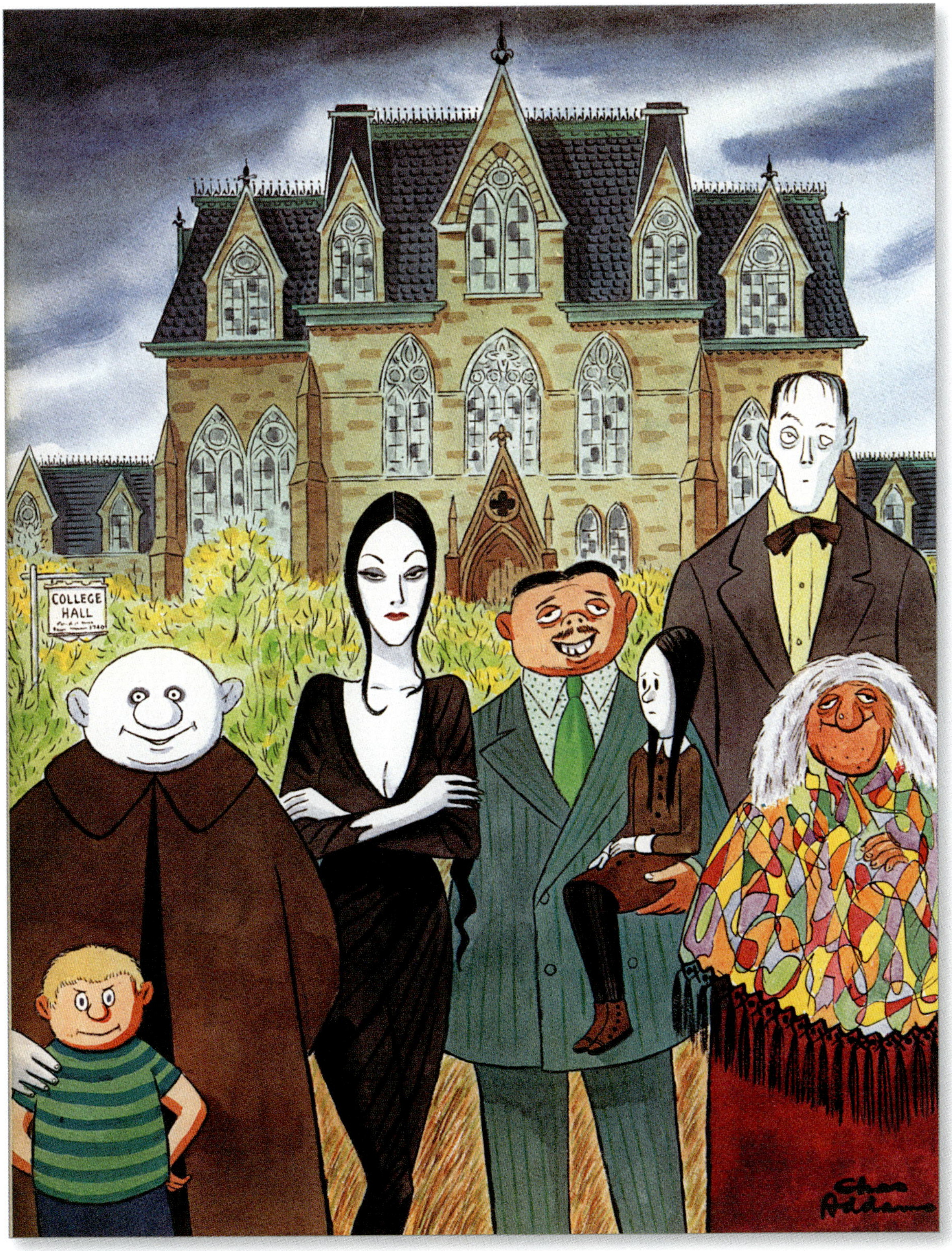
COLLEGE
HALL
Chas Addams

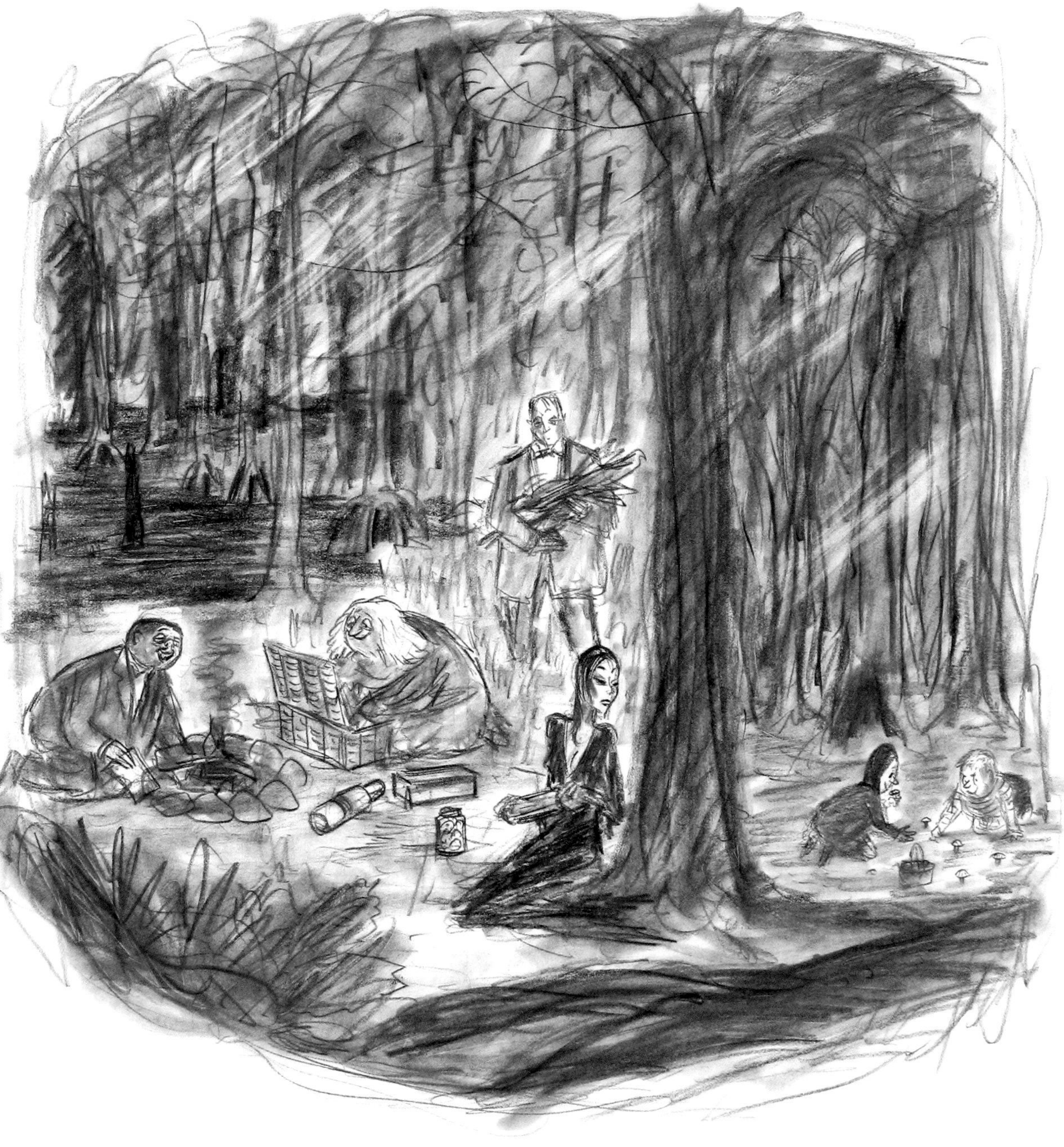

"Now don't spoil your appetites, kiddies."

MORTICIA

The real head of the family and the critical and moving force behind it. Low-voiced, incisive, and subtle; smiles are rare. This ruined beauty has a romantic side, too, and is given to low-keyed rhapsodies about her garden of deadly nightshade, henbane and dwarf's hair. Generally indulgent [of] the often sinister activities of the children, but feels that Uncle Fester has to be held in check. Her costume is always the same—the form-fitting black gown, tattered or cut to ribbons at the elbows and feet. Occasionally, she will wear a shawl. Her voice is never raised, but has great range. Contemptuous and original and with a fierce family loyalty. She never uses a cliché except to be funny. She is a thoughtful hostess in her way and, if a guest needs anything, he is advised to scream for it. The children are instructed to observe the amenities and always kick Daddy good night.

Chas Addams

MORTICIA shares in the official debut as the first Addams Family character in print—with Lurch, the butler, and The Thing—in a cartoon published in the *New Yorker* on August 6, 1938. A vacuum cleaner salesman makes a pitch to the lady of the house and her servant against the backdrop of the glorious dilapidation of the entrance foyer and stairwell, with the caption "Vibrationless, noiseless, and a great time and back saver. No well-appointed home should be without it" (page 119). With the exceptions of his Medusa at the beauty shop (1936) or his Lady Godiva riding at the horse show (1938), Charles Addams tended to portray his leading women as wives who were shrews, heavier-set women who bossed their diminutive husbands with sour faces and a complete lack of style or sophistication. Morticia, then, was an anomaly: she was a beauty with a youthful, curvaceous figure sheathed in a romantically tattered and flowing gown of black gauze.

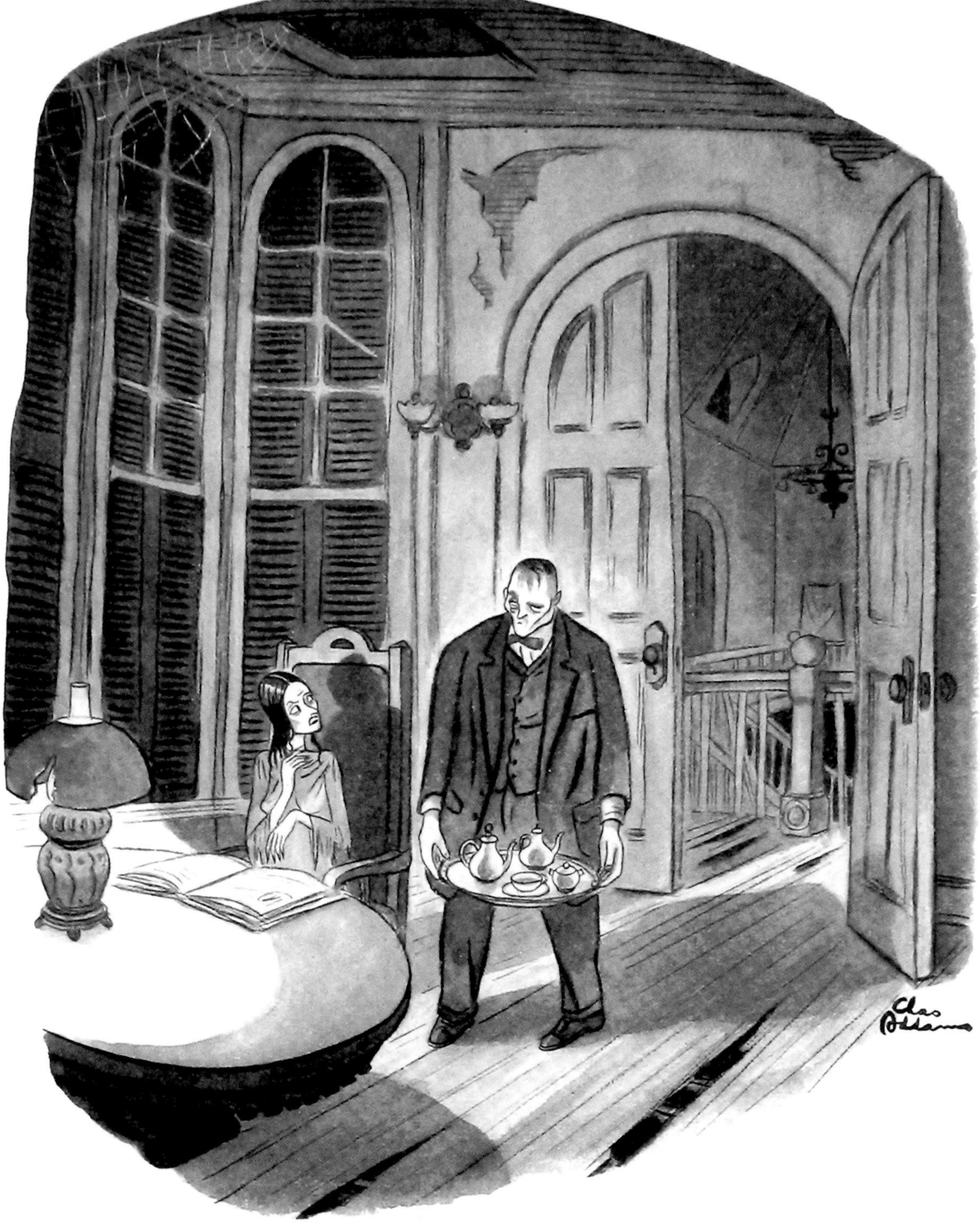
Chas Addams

"Oh, it's *you!* For a moment you gave me quite a start."

A year later, Addams's second version of Morticia is less glamorous. As she sits reading in an upper-floor drawing room, she is startled by her butler serving tea. "Oh, it's *you!*" she exclaims. "For a moment you gave me quite a start." Next, the April 6, 1940, cartoon from the *New Yorker* shows a shocked and possibly disappointed dandy who has walked his date, Addams's third Morticia incarnation, home—which happens to be a manhole with a ladder, complete with a lantern, leading down into it. His date flatly states, "Well, here's where I say good night." It appears that Addams was trying out this dark, slim beauty in a few different locations and circumstances: at first she might be alone with just a butler to make ends meet; later she might be dressed for the opera, with a similarly gaunt face, styled dark hair, and an untattered black gown, but clearly living in equally dire straits. Another version turns up in February 1941 as a barefoot, willowy neighbor holding a teacup and asking the hag next door (an early version of Granny Frump) for a cup of cyanide (page 129).

Charles Addams claimed to have named Morticia by leafing through the Yellow Pages and, quite naturally, stumbling upon the lengthy section titled "Morticians." He often mentioned that there was a bit of Gloria Swanson, the alluring film star of both the silent and silver screens, in his design of Morticia. In the August 2, 1941, *New Yorker* publication of his drawing captioned "While you're here, there's a squeaky trap-door I'd like you to look at," Morticia is back with her butler, now having a carpenter repair a secret-paneled bookcase door. This time she is very glamorous, with her hair still parted in the middle, a few matted tendrils at each side, but a fashionable gathering at the back of her neck; her gown is more stylishly tattered and quite low-cut, revealing a prominent collarbone and ample bust atop a statuesque figure. She has the appearance of a flamenco dancer but, nevertheless, a strong woman in complete control of a domestic situation.

From then on Morticia's appearance was firmly established, as described by Addams for the 1963 television contract, and her living circumstances were clearly that of the matriarch of the Addams mansion. Into the fifties, Morticia evolved into a truly glamorous femme fatale—no more circles under the eyes, new eye shadow, and stylized hair tendrils.

The Addams matriarch was nothing like Yvonne De Carlo's character Lily Munster, the voluptuous vampire wife of Herman, from the CBS television series *The Munsters*, which aired at the same time as *The Addams Family*. Morticia was a weathered, even withered, beauty with no interest in ghoulish practices. She may have loved bats, but that did not make her one.

Practically every interview with Charles Addams eventually got around to the interviewer questioning his sources, as though he might have based this bizarre creature on a specific female. He once proffered that Morticia was "an ideal, a kind of good looks, with eyes slightly up center and dark, snakelike hair." Was this

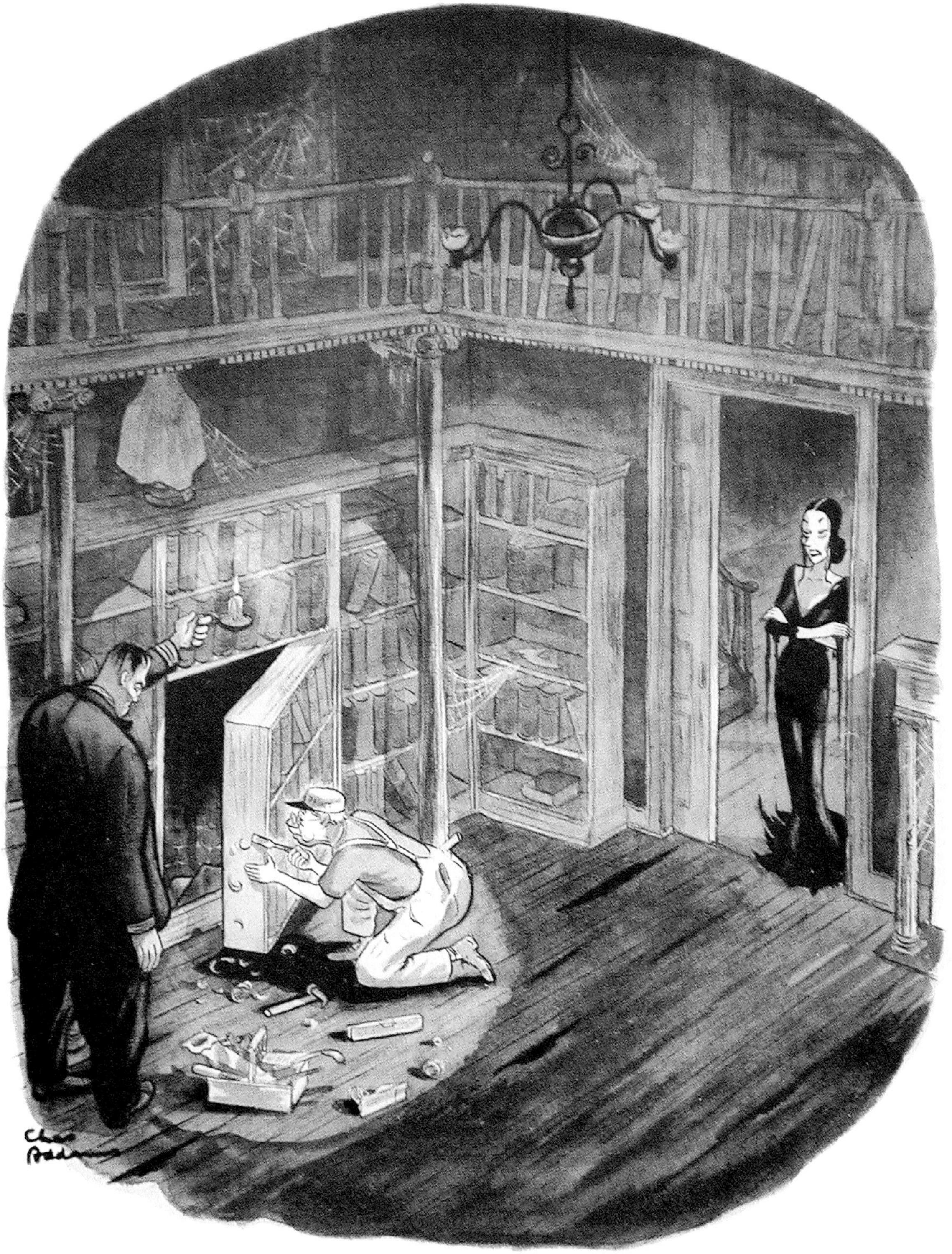

"While you're here, there's a squeaky trap-door I'd like you to look at."

wife number one or two or three, or just a skeletal enchantress from his past? True, he had married three raven-haired beauties in his lifetime, and, true, they all were slim and statuesque, though not necessarily tall. (Actually, Morticia's angular, cadaverous physique may have caused her to seem taller than she was.)

The truth, however, as Addams told it, is that he created what he adored. He was just plain lucky to have married his heavenly fantasy three times.

"Dearest: How I wish you were here with me now to see how lovely our little garden has become! The black nightshade is in full bloom, and the death camass we planted last fall is coming along beautifully. The henbane seems to have shot up overnight. You will be glad to know that the dwarf's hair was not affected by the dry spell, as we feared, after all. A myriad [of] delightful little slugs appeared, as if from nowhere, on the rotten stump by the belladonna patch, and this morning I noticed snake eggs hatching near the pool. Do finish up that business, darling, and hurry home."

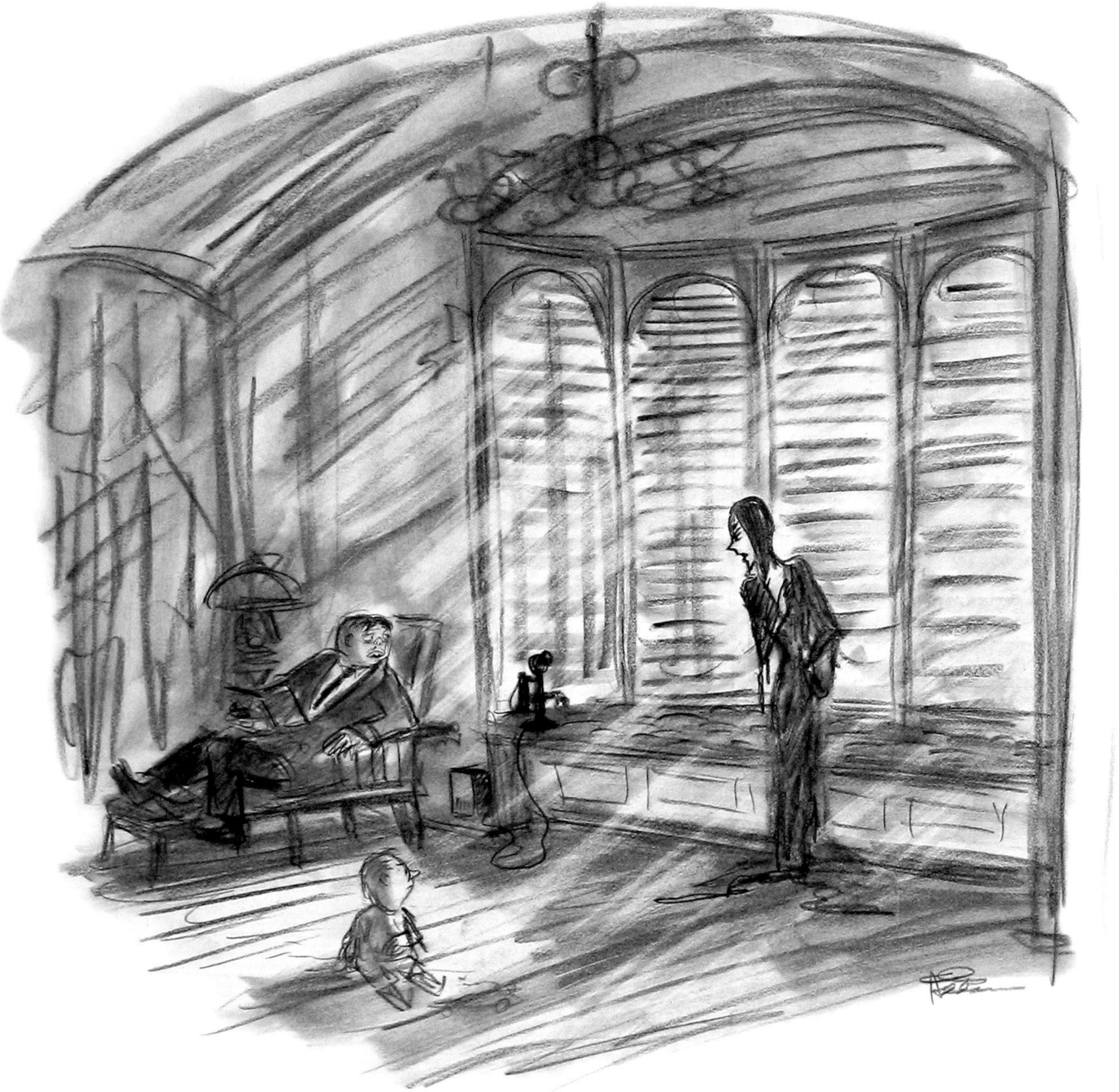

"Heavens! Who could be ringing us at this hour?"

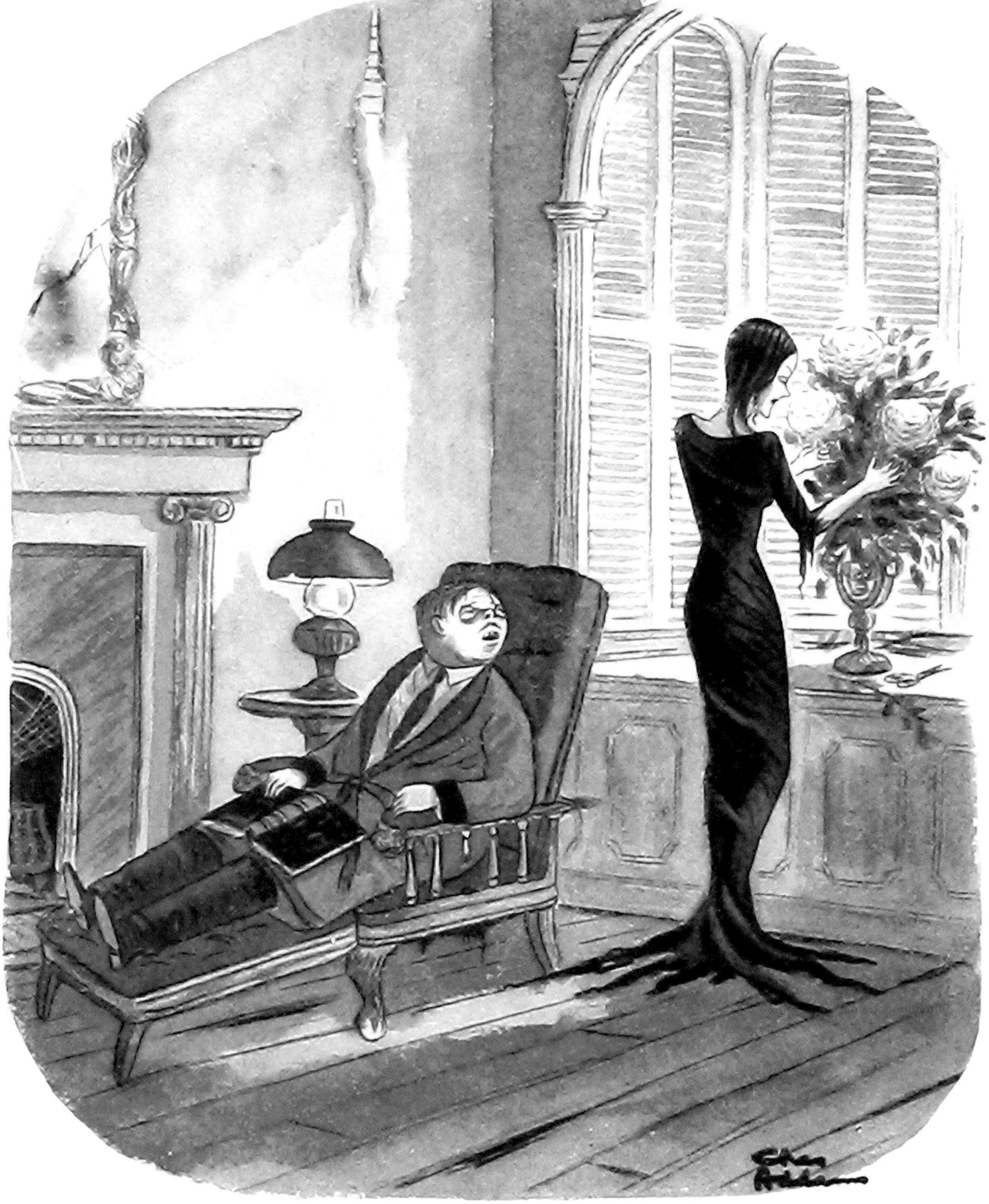

"You're in a strange mood today, I must say."

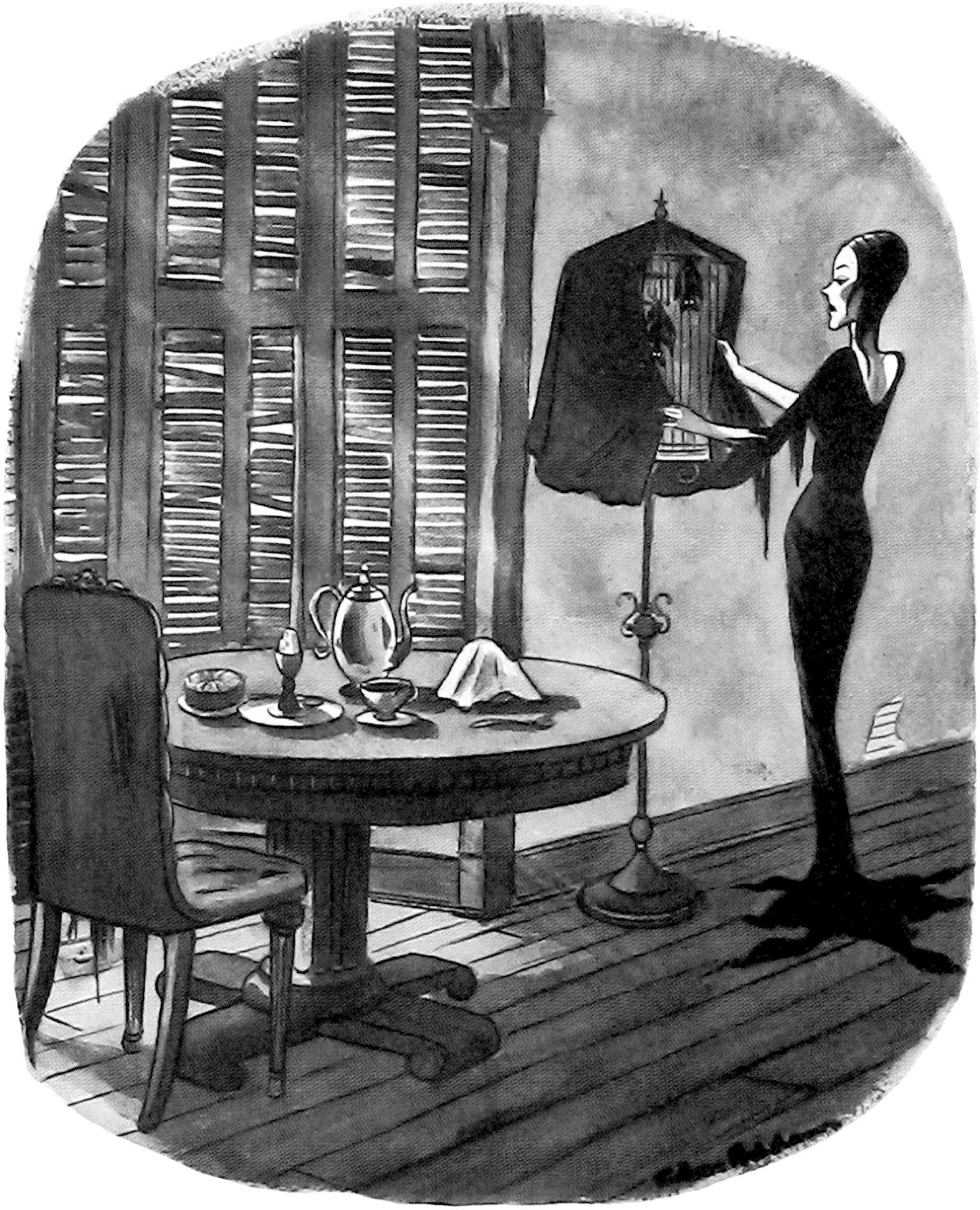

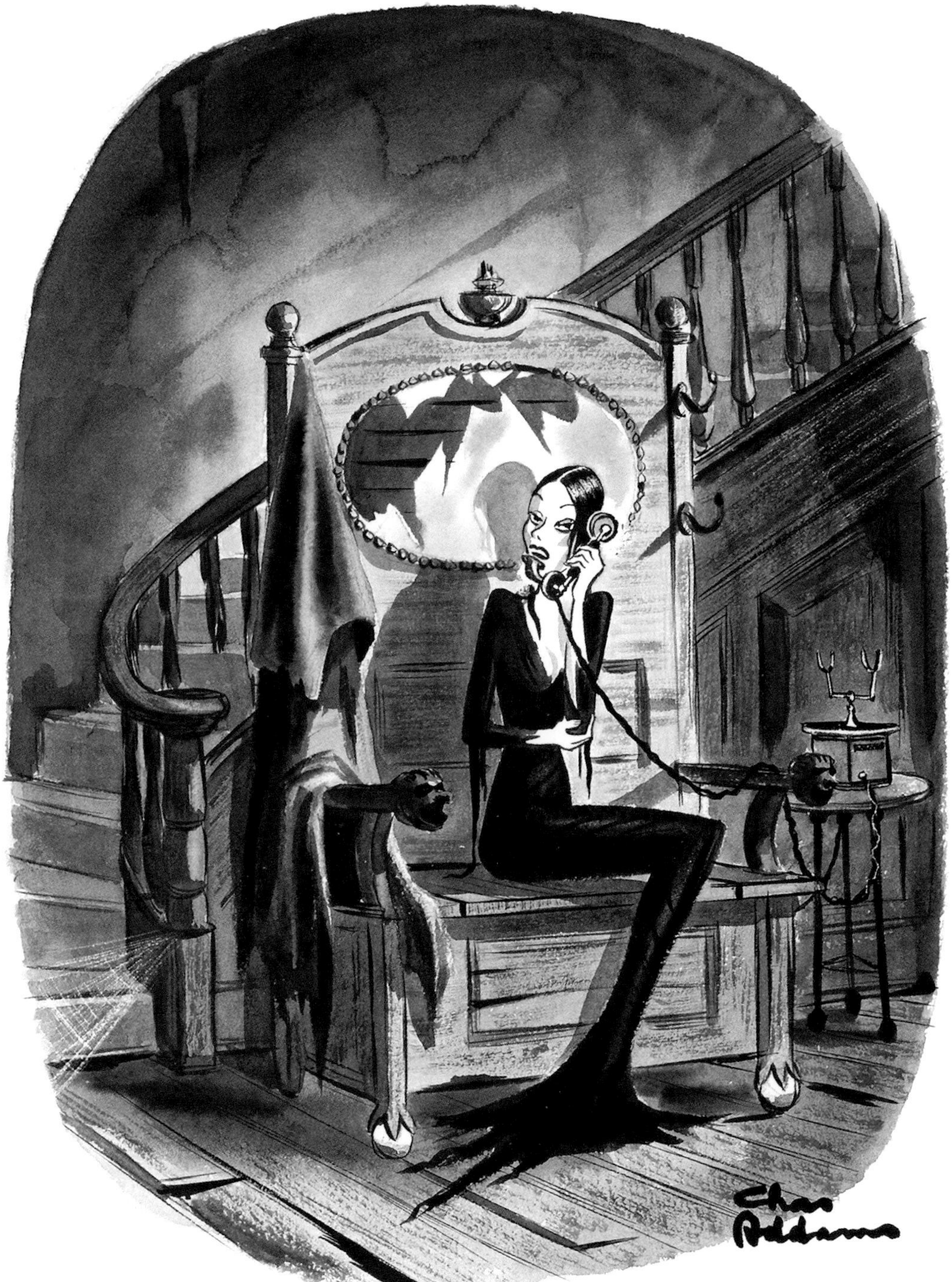
Chas Addams

"Oh, I couldn't make it Friday—I've so many things to do. It's the thirteenth, you know."

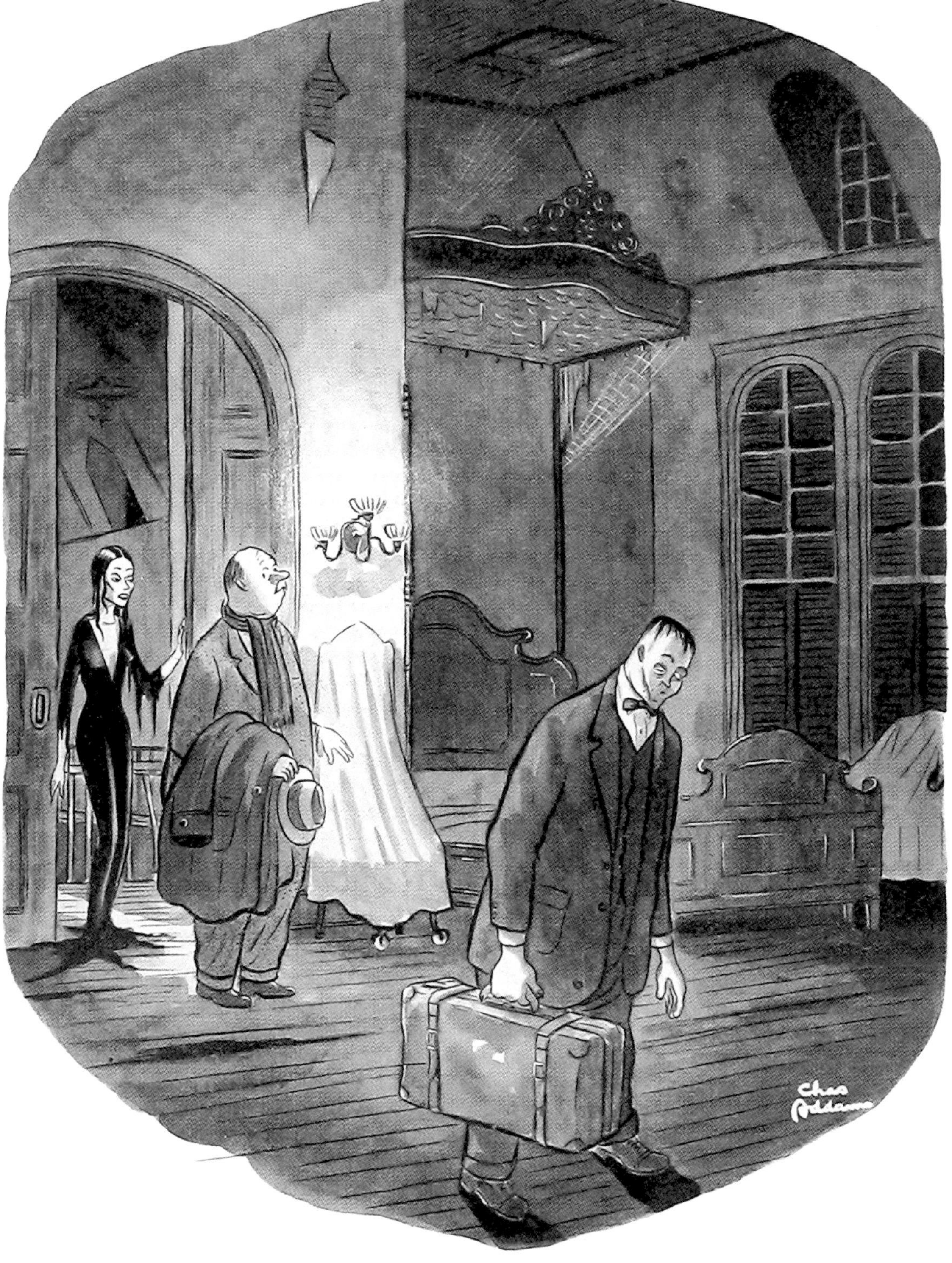
Chas Addams

"This is your room. If you should need anything, just scream."

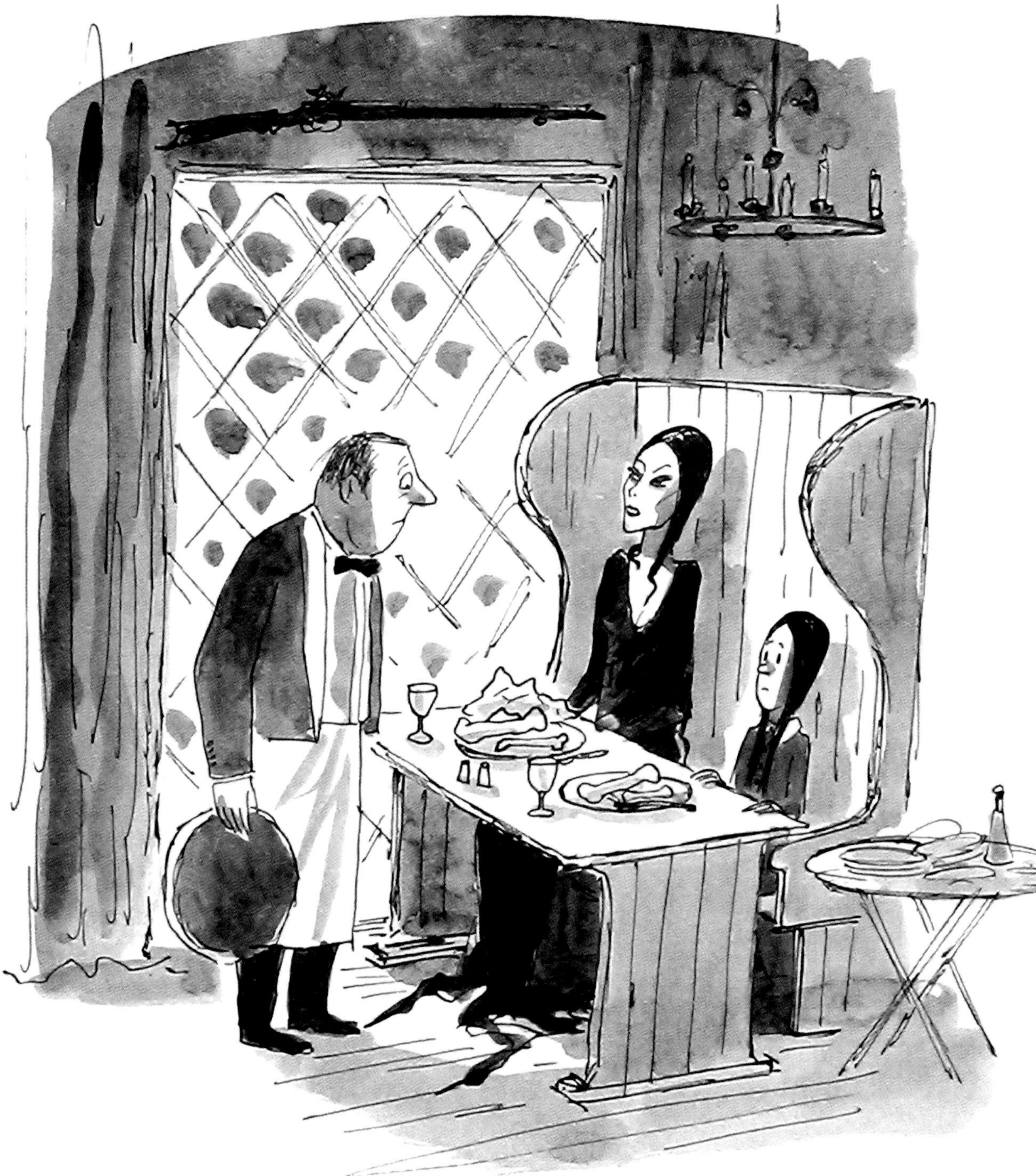

"Put them in a bag, please. We're taking them home for the bird."

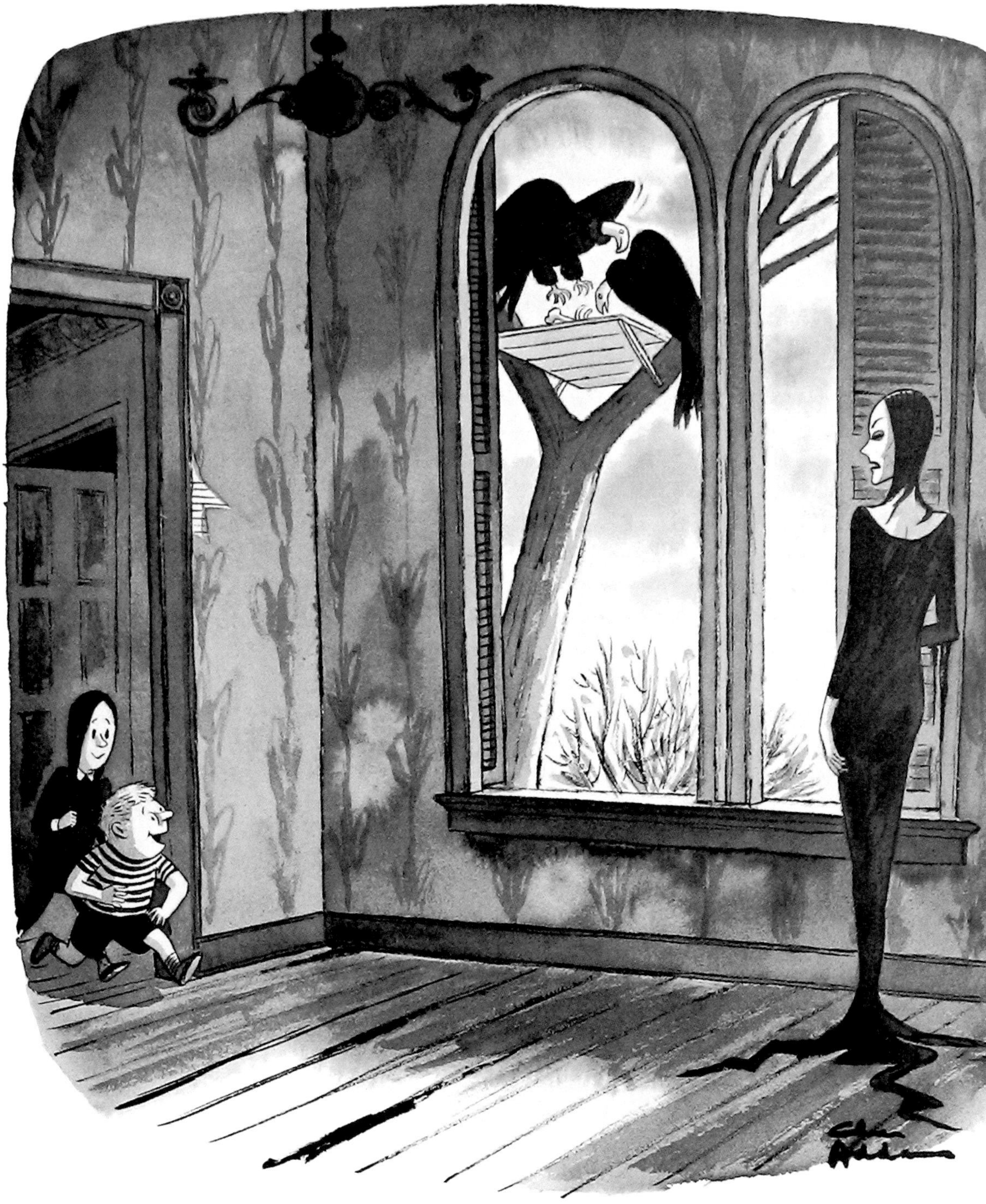

"Hurry, kiddies, they're coming into the feeding station now."

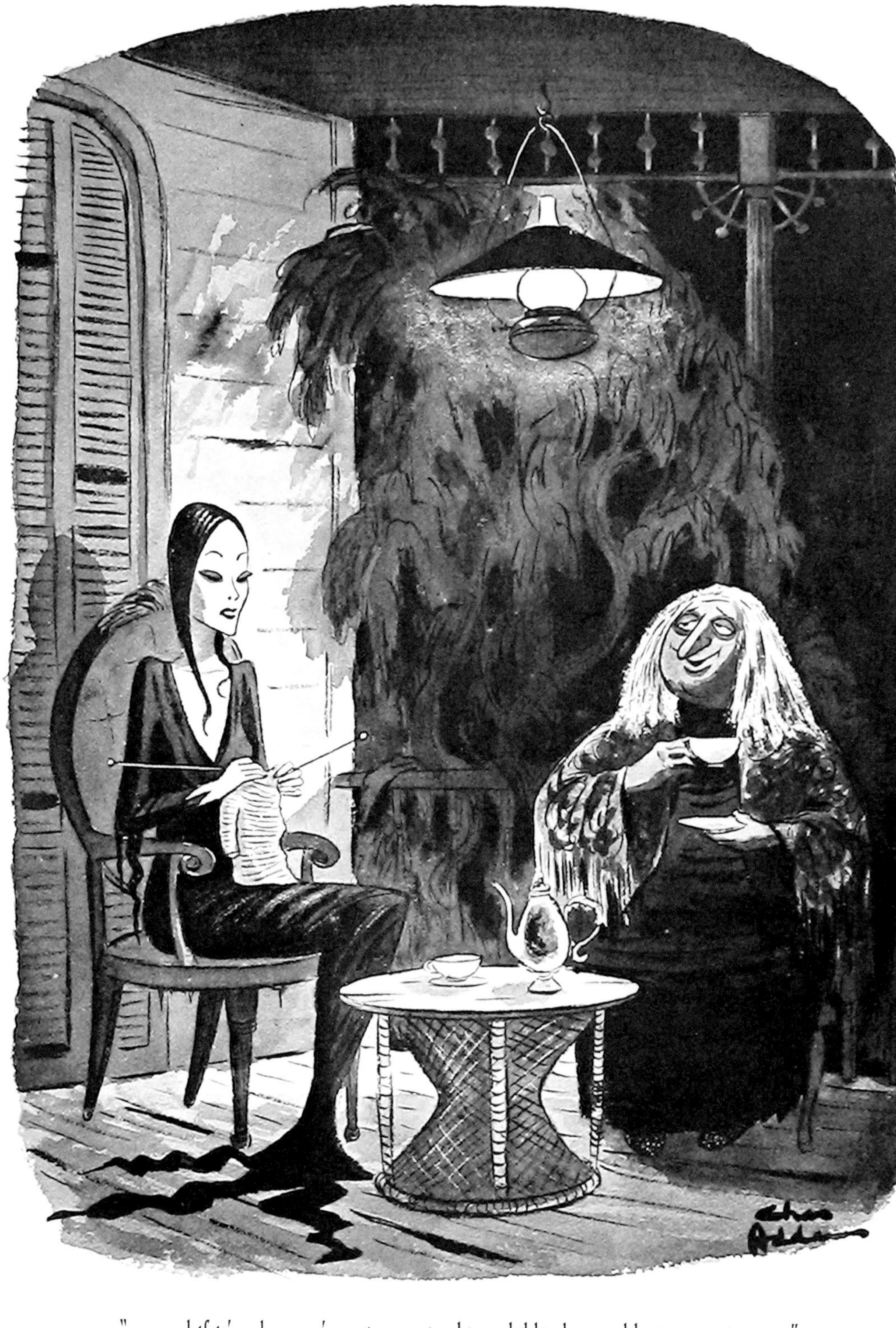

"... and if it's a boy, we're going to give him a biblical name like Cain or Ananias."

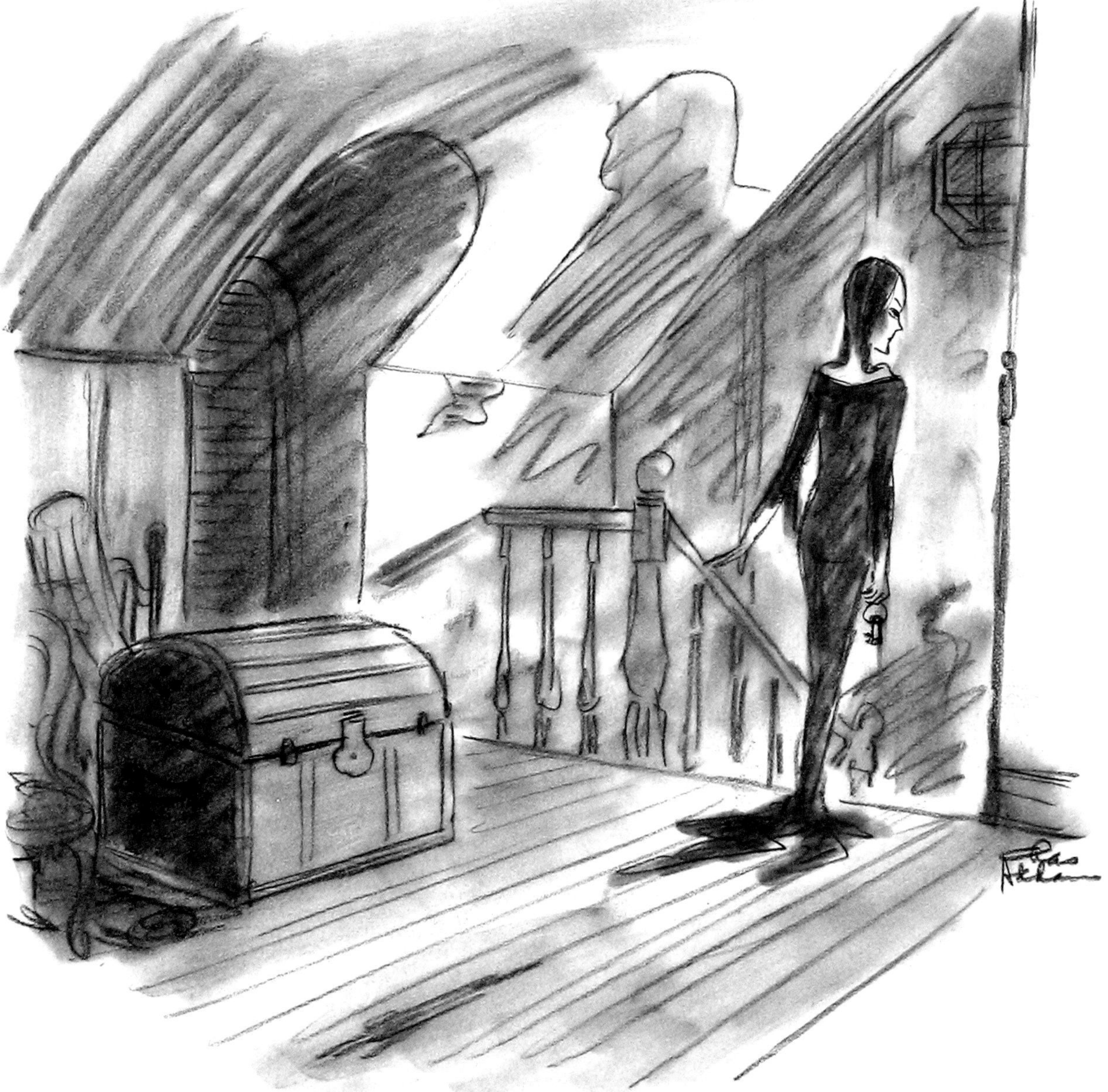

"Why can't you just spank us like other mommies?"

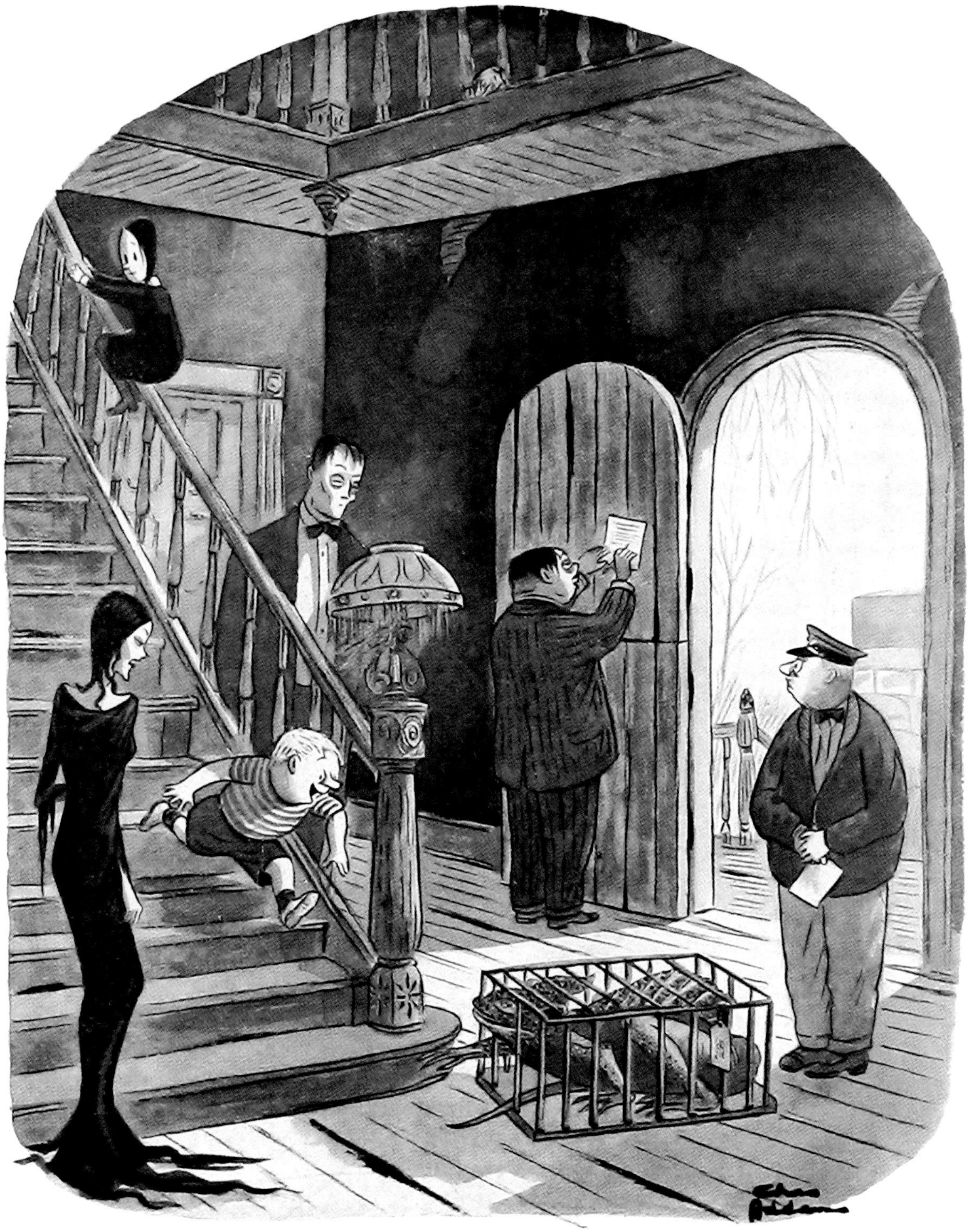

"Now, remember, you can have him as long as you feed him and take good care of him. When you don't, back he goes."

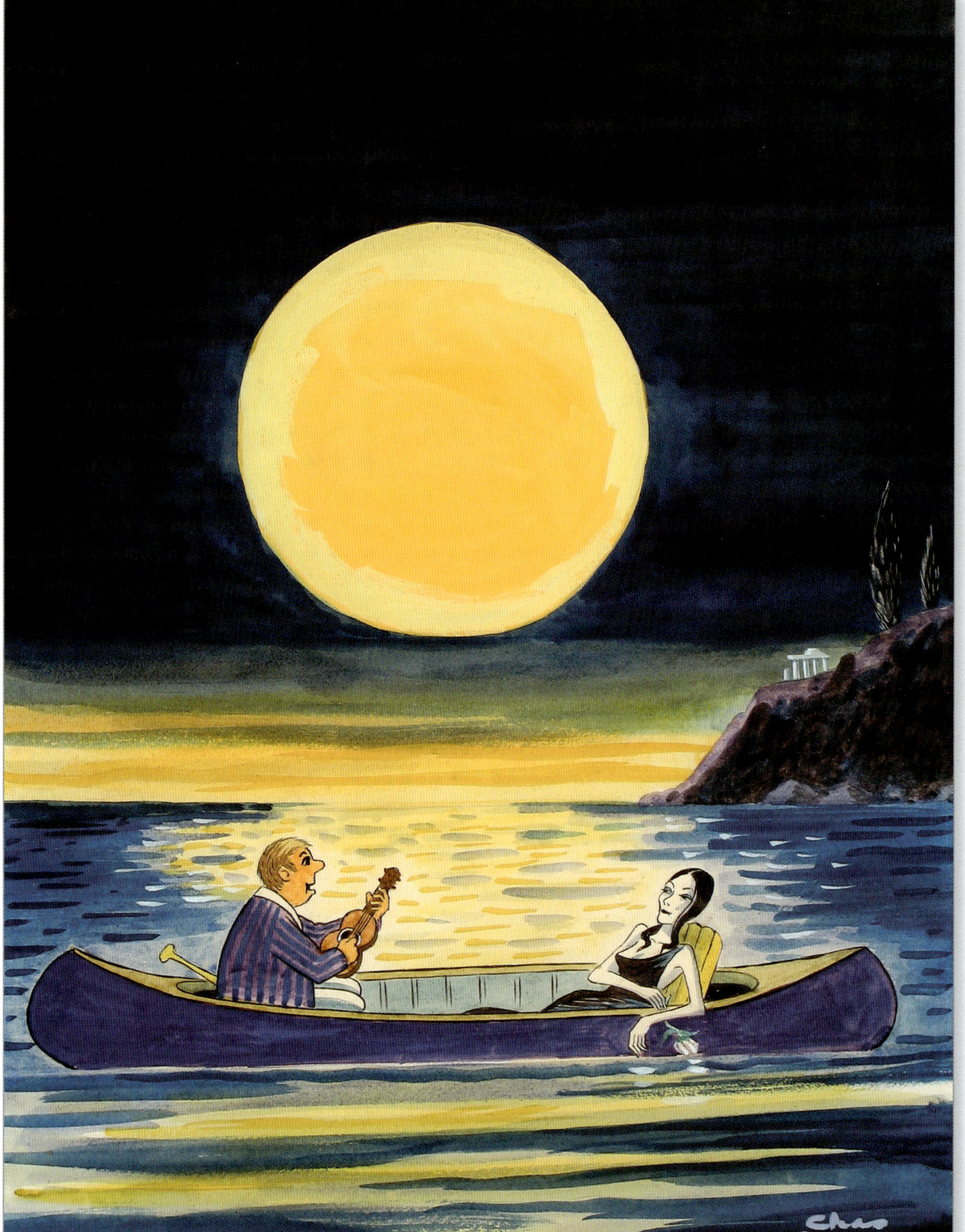
Chas Addams

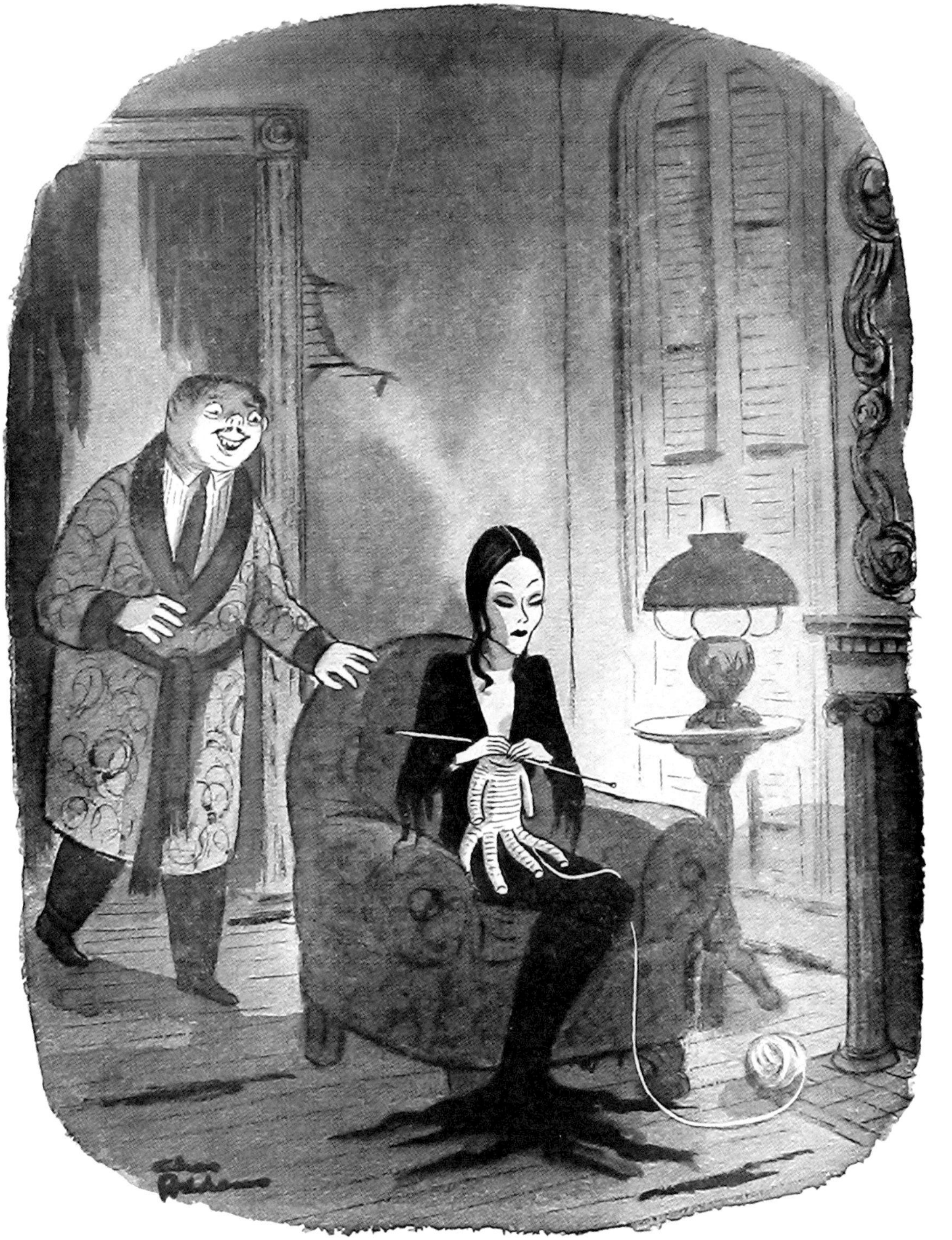

"Darling!"

GOMEZ

Husband of Morticia (if indeed they are married at all), a crafty schemer, but also a jolly man in his own way. Tries hard to be father and teacher to the children, though sometimes misguided—we can depend on Morticia to straighten him out. Sentimental and often puckish—optimistic, he is full of enthusiasm for his dreadful plots. He is dressed in a tight double-breasted striped suit and is sometimes seen in a rather formal dressing gown. The only one who smokes—though Pugsley can be allowed an occasional cigar.

Chas Addams

NAMED after an old family friend, Gomez is a rube, a dark and scruffy, even a bit greasy, little man with a turned-up nose and a lot more money than wit or brains, so he can have whatever he wants. And what he wants is the likes of his complete opposite, the white and lissome and sinuous Morticia.

He is not the swashbuckling, bon vivant matinee idol conceived in Scott Rudin's two Addams Family feature films starring Raul Julia as the debonair Gomez. (Of note, however, is the previously unpublished drawing in which Addams tried a handsome, erudite Gomez, seated at the bar of the Addams home amid his surprised family, as Morticia whispers to Grandma, "It must have been Moonglow"; see page 71.) And, although the physical types and the chemistry between television's John Astin and Carolyn Jones were closer to those of Addams's Gomez and Morticia, the artist preferred to avoid any cliché of the handsome prince and princess riding off into the sunset by having these two perfectly mismatched miscreants find each other completely alluring. It was a more interesting story than the old fairy tale, and it was rather extraordinary that the magazine and newspaper readership of the early forties ever found them intriguing. Of course, the art was so hauntingly beautiful, and so different from any style that had appeared before, that the public may not have considered the pairing as unbelievably odd—they were a cartoon, after all.

Gomez had no earlier incarnations; he was born in the *New Yorker* on November 14, 1942. In a tight embrace with Morticia, seated on a Victorian settee in their dilapidated living room, Gomez asks, "Are you unhappy, darling?" To which Morticia replies, "Oh, yes, yes! Completely."

Although this couple shares a love of ancient torture devices, no Addams drawing refers to swordplay between them. Nor does any cartoon show them dancing or refer to Morticia's ability to speak French. Although Addams smoked cigars and he suggested that Gomez did, he never drew Gomez smoking. These traits have all been fostered by media interpreters of The Addams Family, but they do make sense within the semi-sophisticated approach to life that Charles Addams claims Morticia and Gomez embrace. Of course, Gomez is of a Latin temperament, which, according to tradition, is likely to heat up Morticia's cool demeanor. Dancing or dueling aside, we understand they are devoted to each other.

While the couple spends much time together without the children or other Family members, most of Addams's drawings indicate that Morticia is a doer while Gomez is a participator. Aside from building a torture rack in the basement with the children (*New Yorker,* May 27, 1950), with Gomez advising, "You'll see, chicks, that half the fun is in making it yourself," or taking Pugsley out behind the old woodshed for wearing a YMCA sweatshirt, in the previously unpublished work from about 1960, Addams's Gomez behaved precisely as "normal" fathers have historically been characterized, by leaving most of the parenting to the mother. But Morticia and Gomez genuinely revel in the experience of watching their children learn from them, and it is clear that Charles Addams intended this odd pair to present themselves as good parents. They offer a slightly different set of rules and lessons to steer their children of the darker side, but they guide them nonetheless.

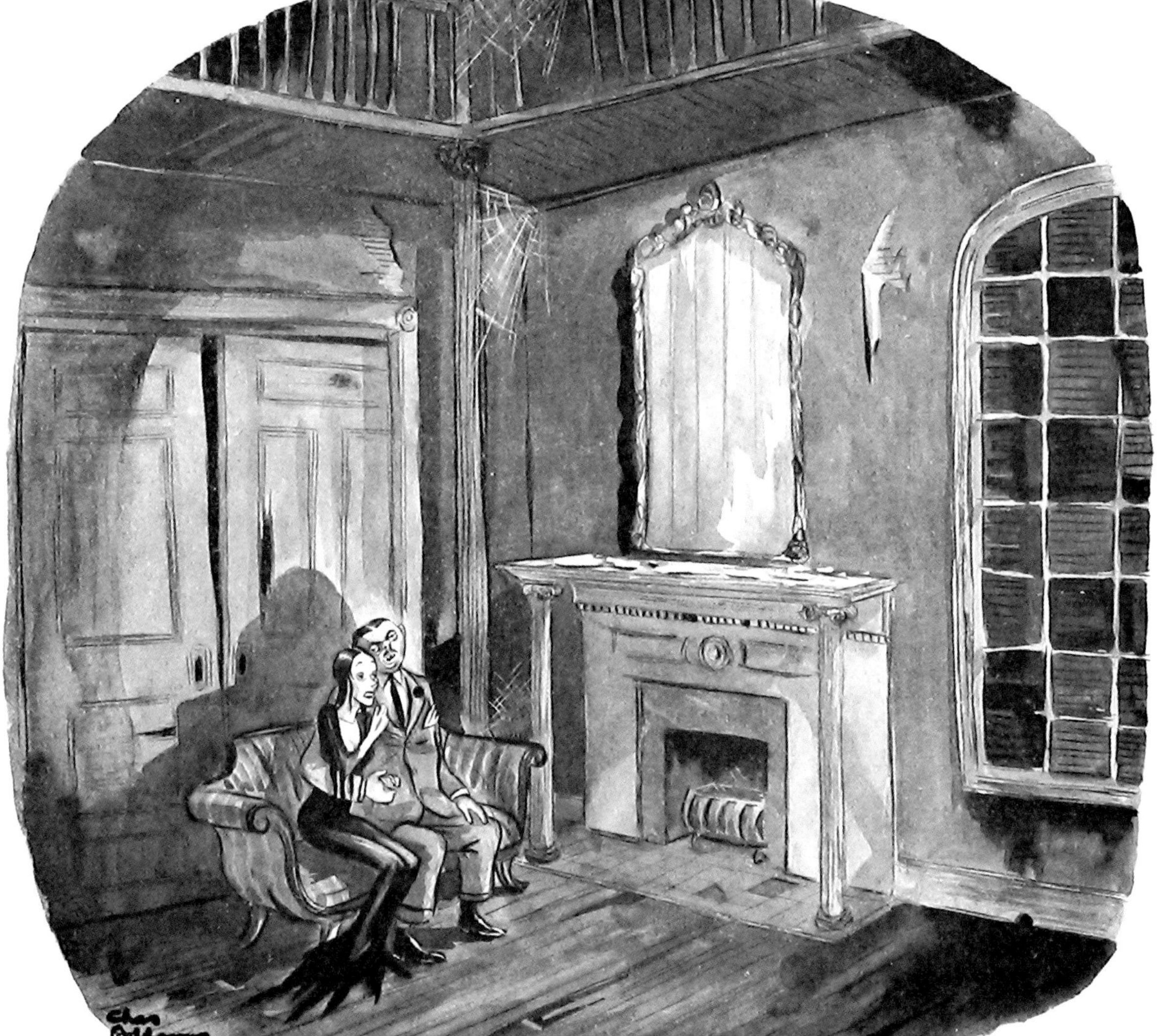
Chas Addams

"Are you unhappy, darling?" "Oh, yes, yes! Completely."

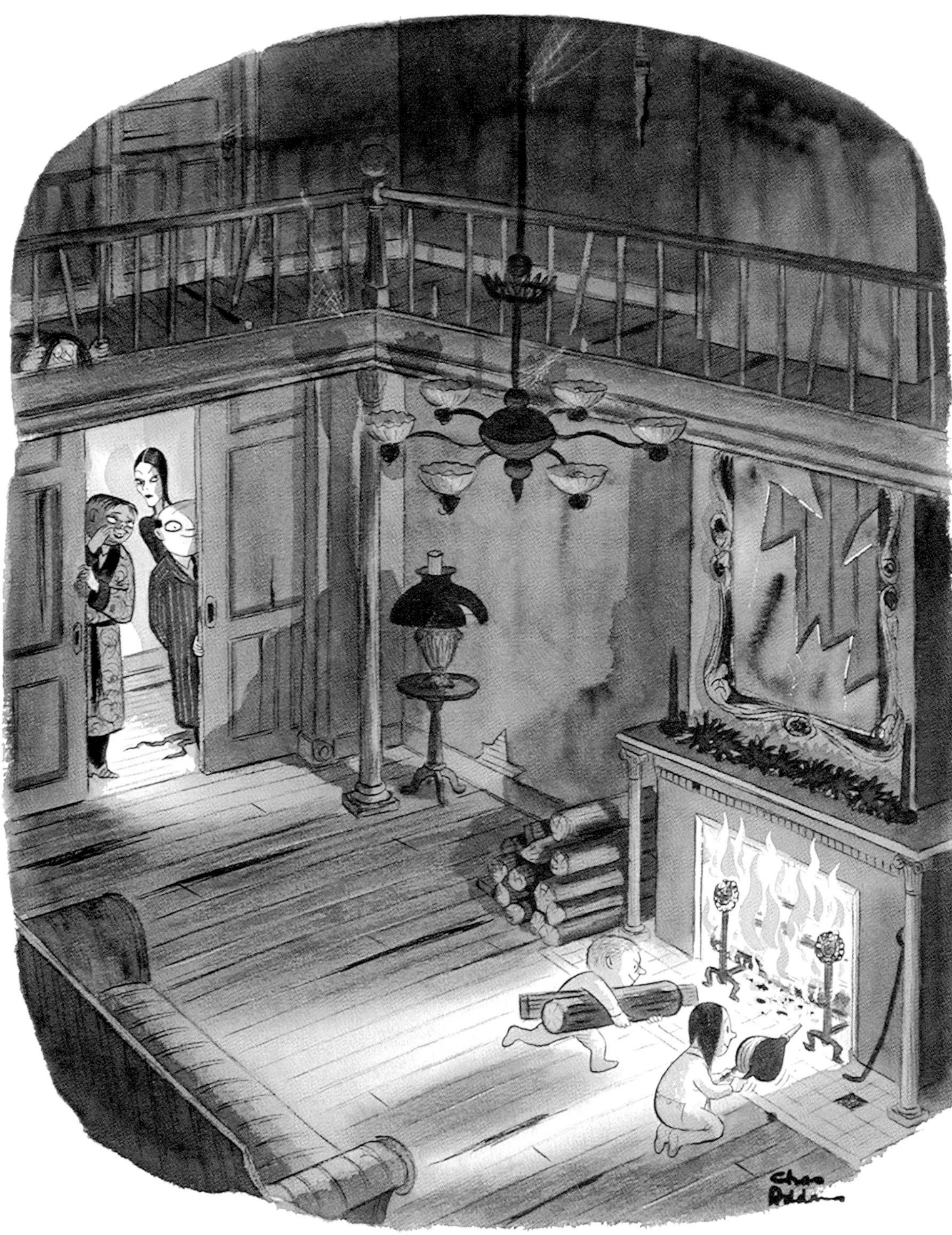

"The little dears! They still believe in Santa Claus."

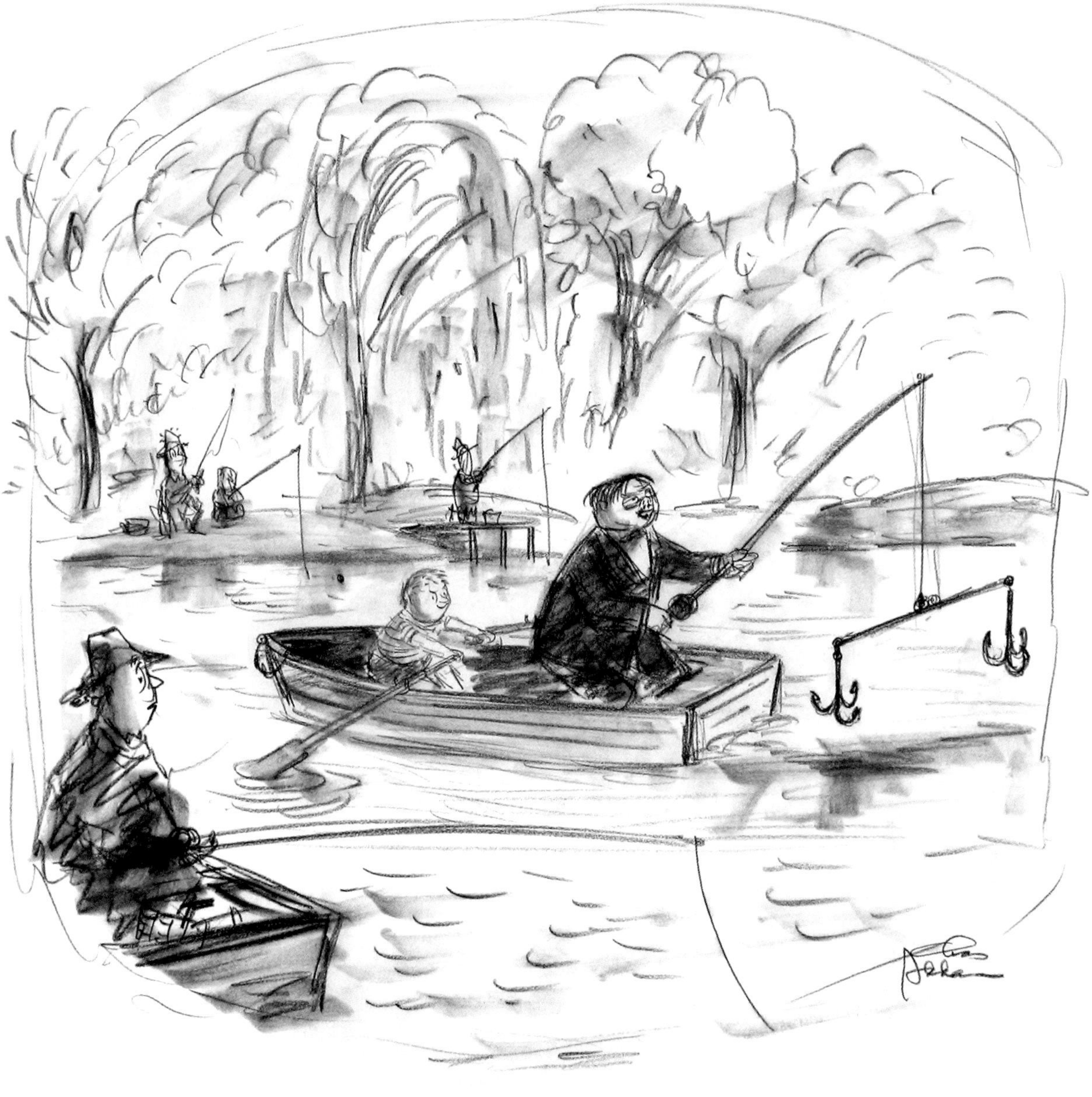

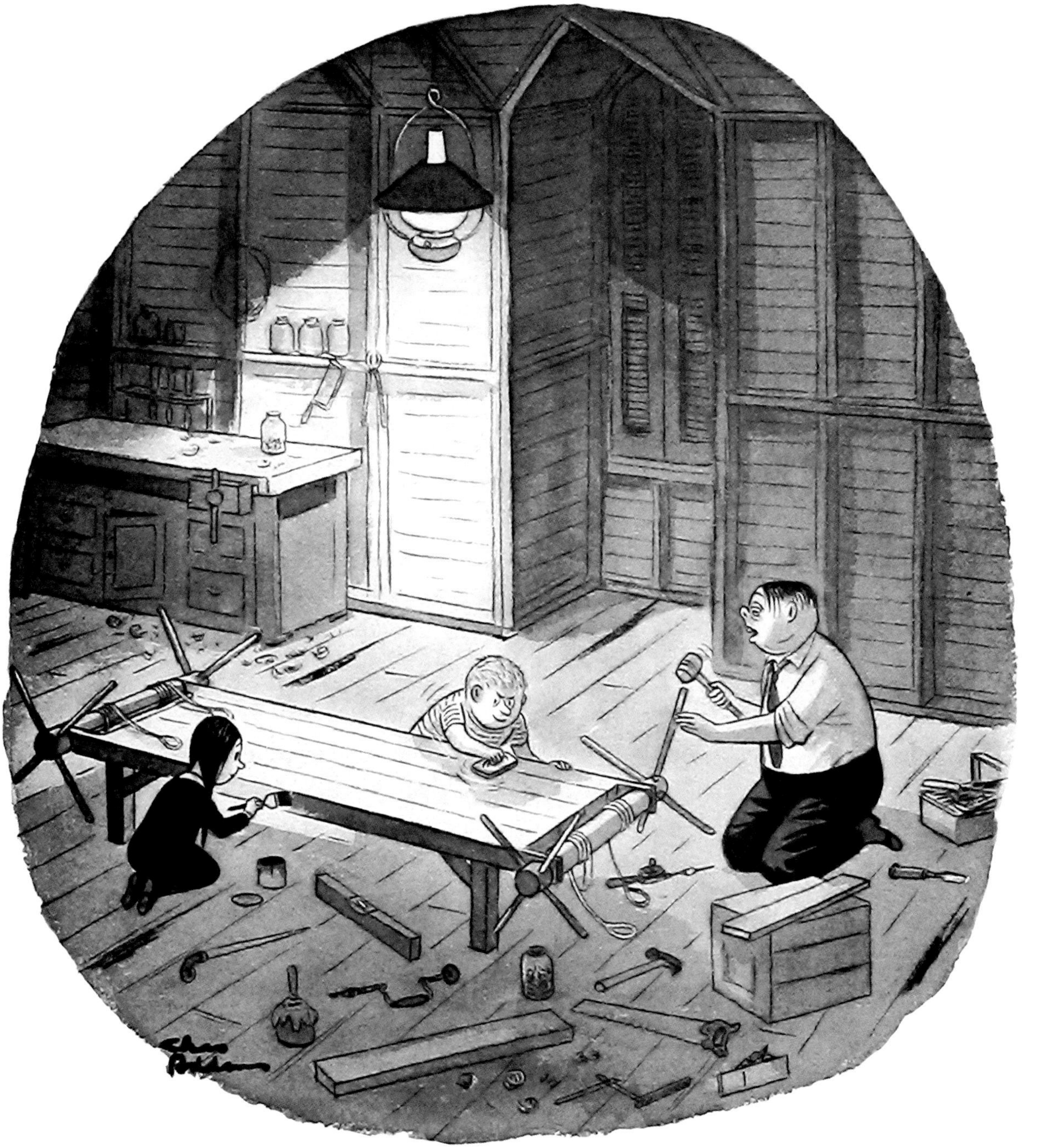

"You'll see, chicks, that half the fun is in making it yourself."

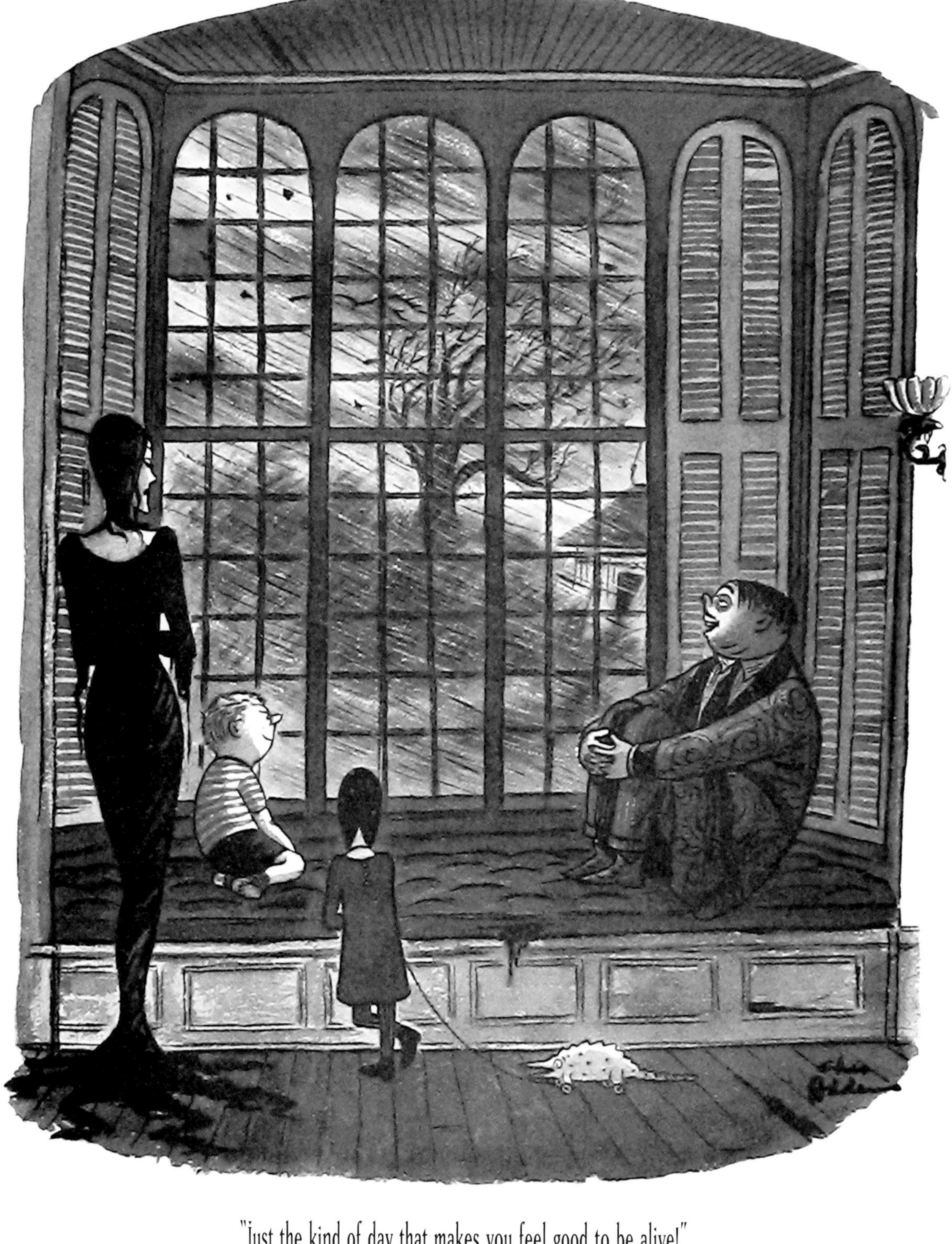

"Just the kind of day that makes you feel good to be alive!"

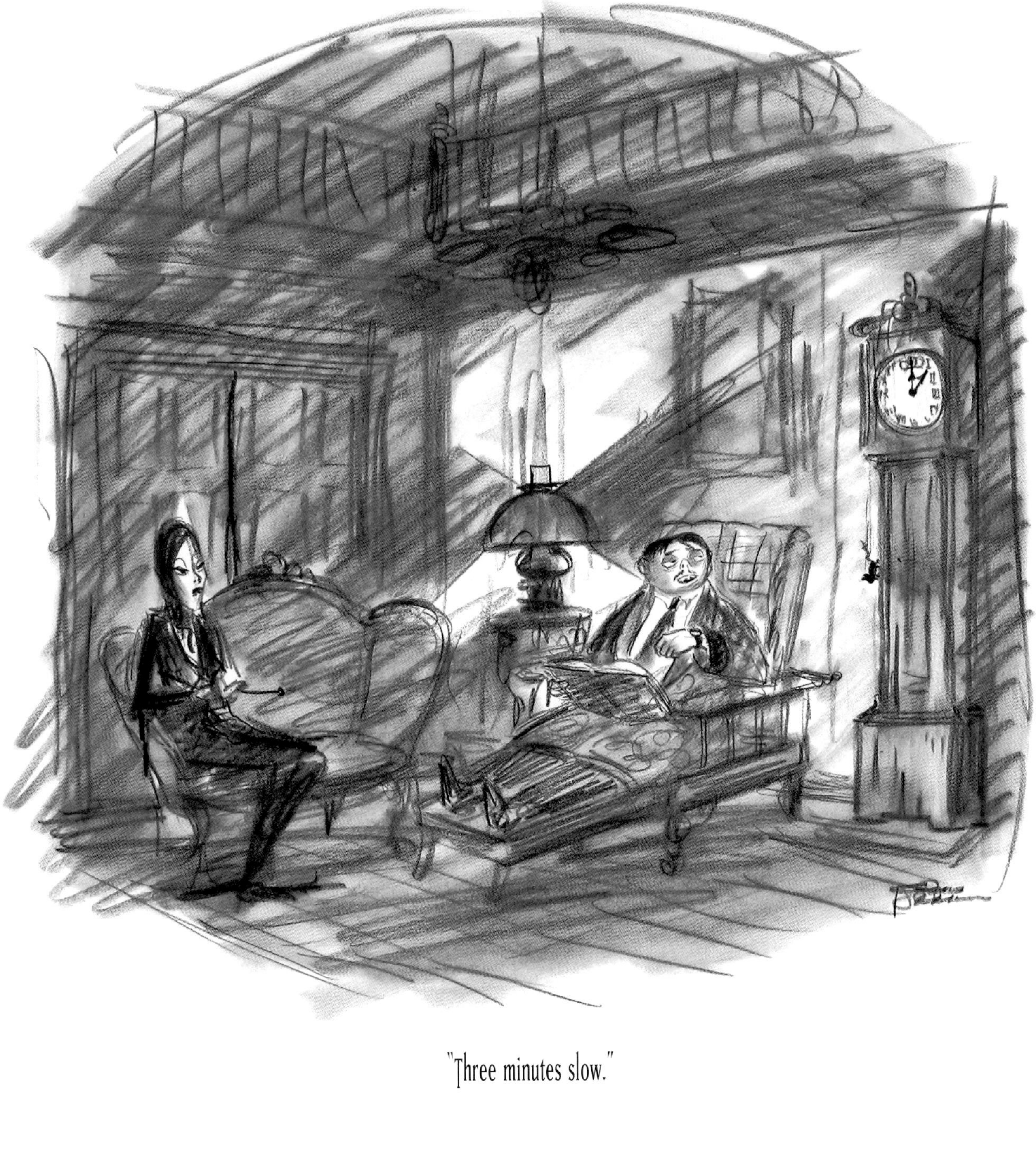

"Three minutes slow."

"... and remember, Love, how upset we were at first, when your Daddy refused us permission?"

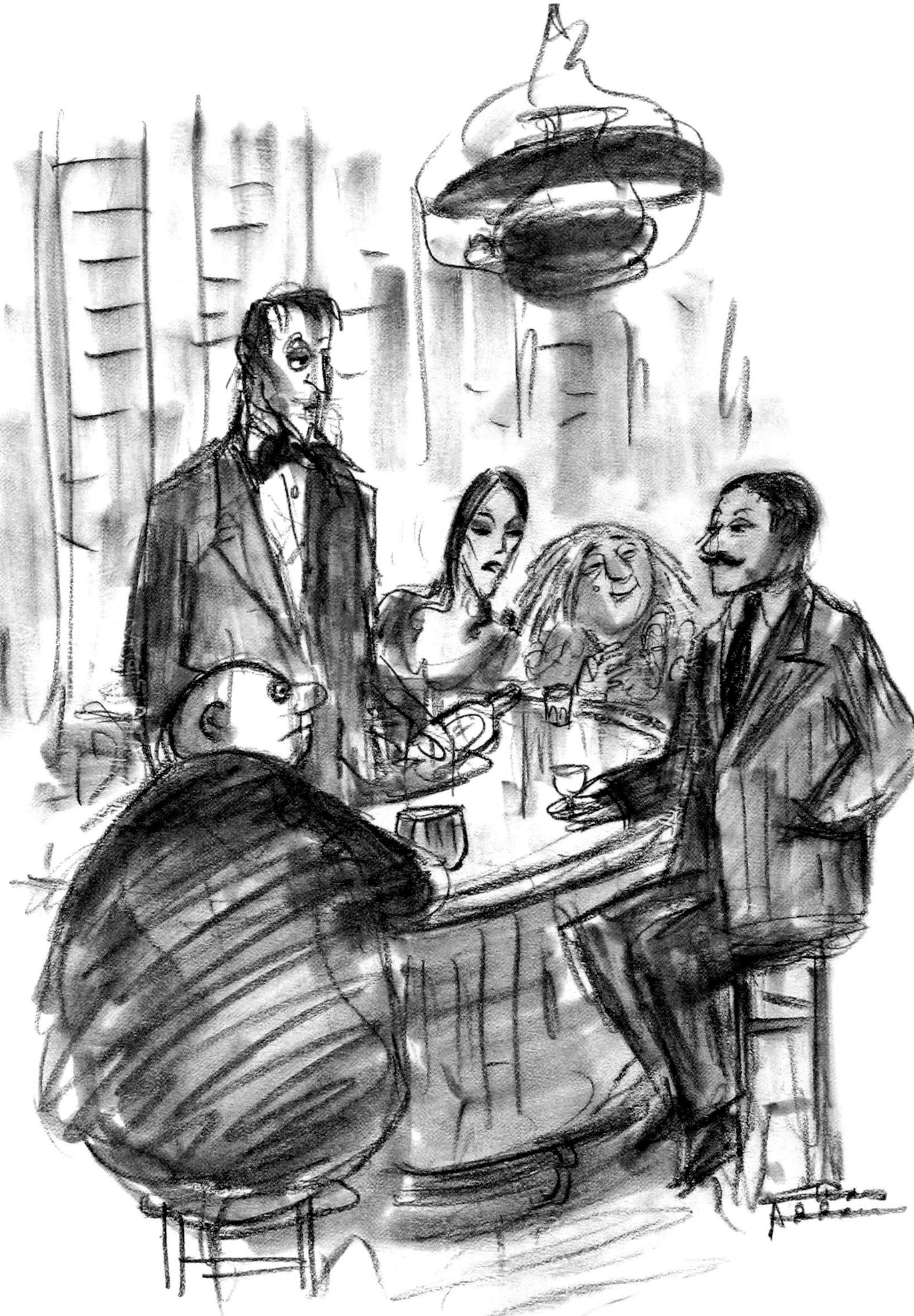

"It must have been Moonglow."

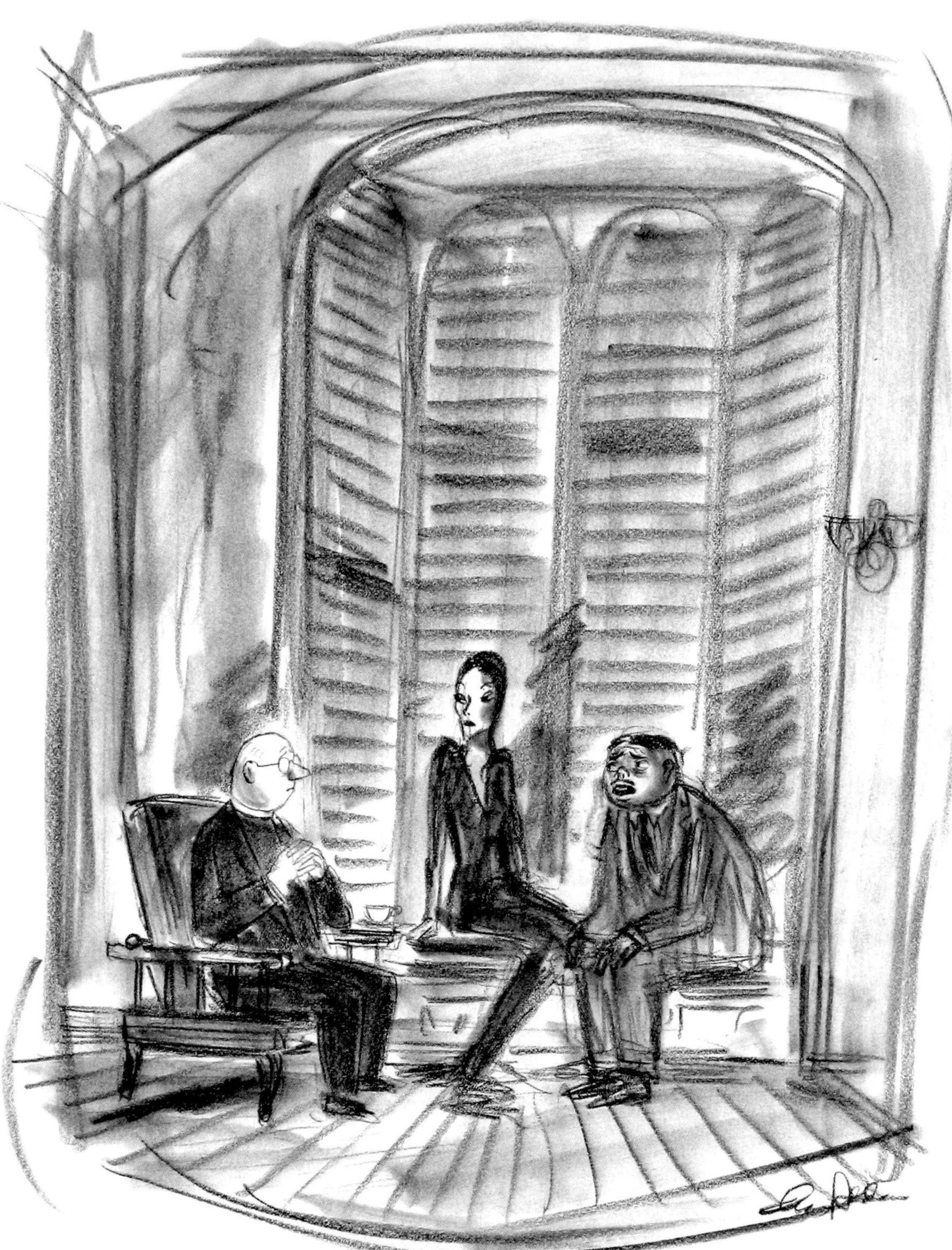

"Please, Dr. Bradford, try to keep your voice down. The children might hear."

"In addition to refusing to cultivate any wholesome interest in group activities, he is perverse, crafty, and wanton in those in which he does engage. These are, I feel compelled to emphasize, far beyond the outcroppings of normal juvenile mischief; in fact, they are the evidences of what may be an extraordinary morbid ingenuity. I have gone to such length in describing the situation because I know you will want to be thoroughly informed of the facts."

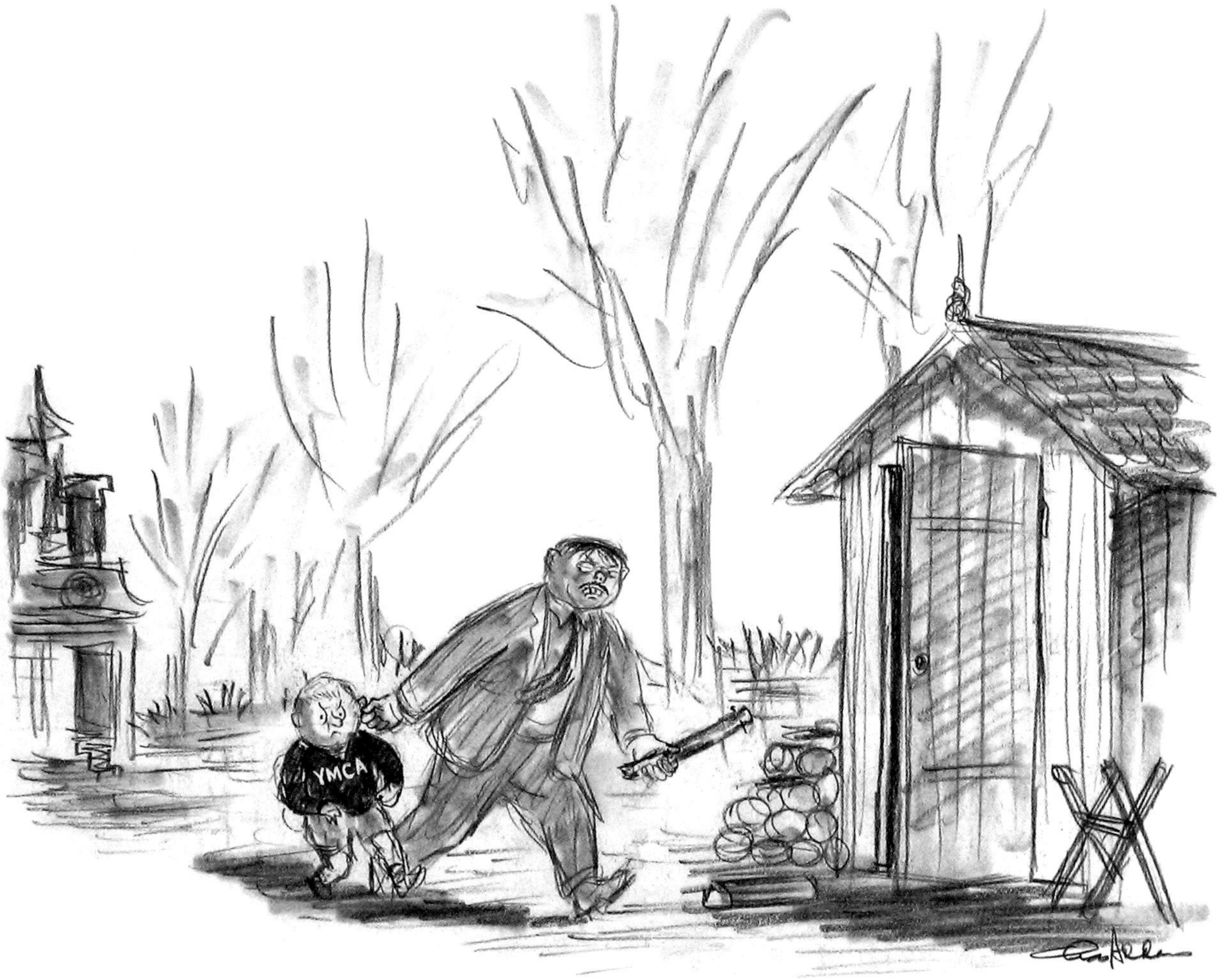
YMCA

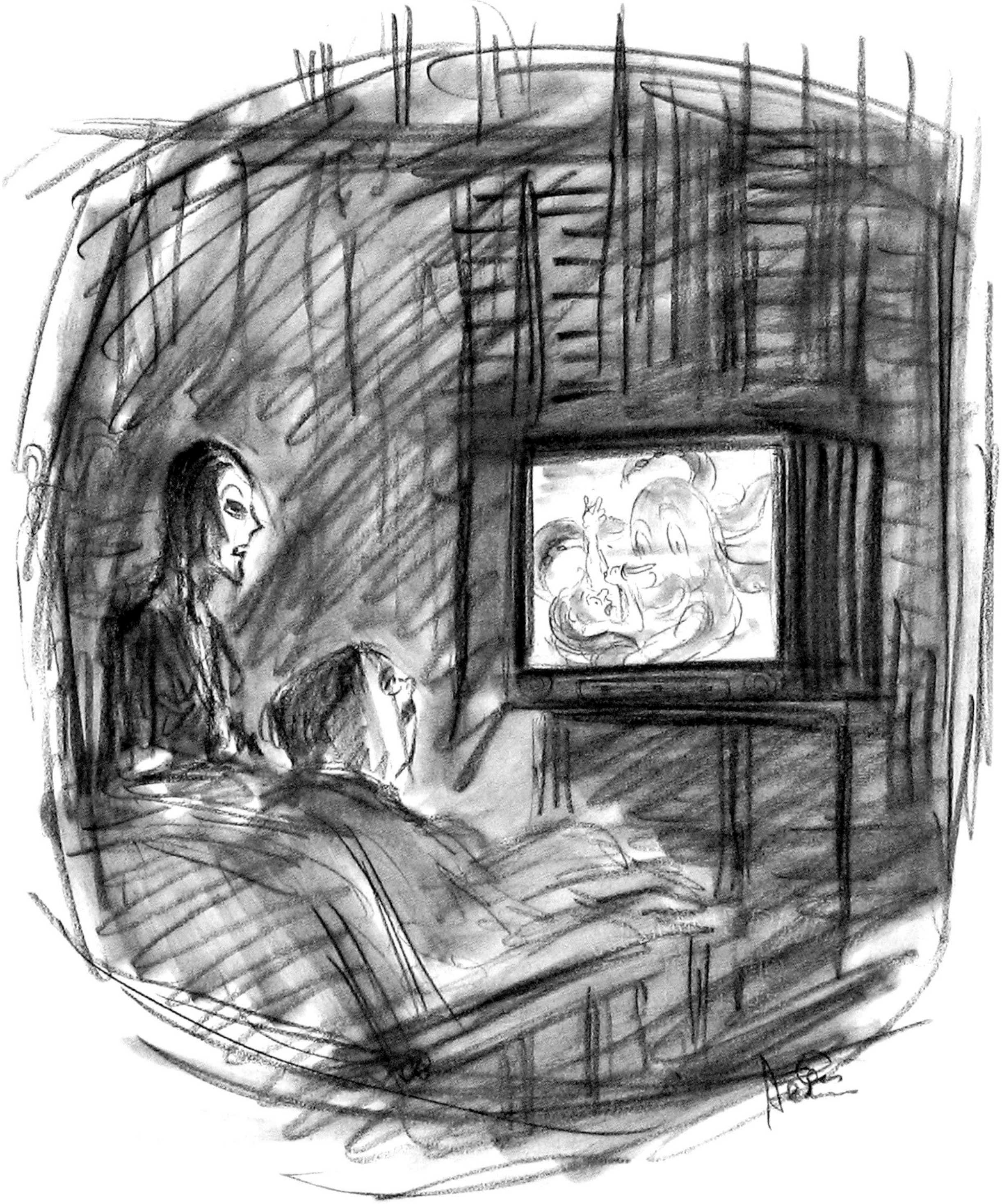

"It's a pity these children's programs are on so late."

"... then good old Scrooge, bless his heart, turned to Bob Cratchit and snarled, 'Let me hear another sound from you and you'll keep Christmas by losing your situation.'"

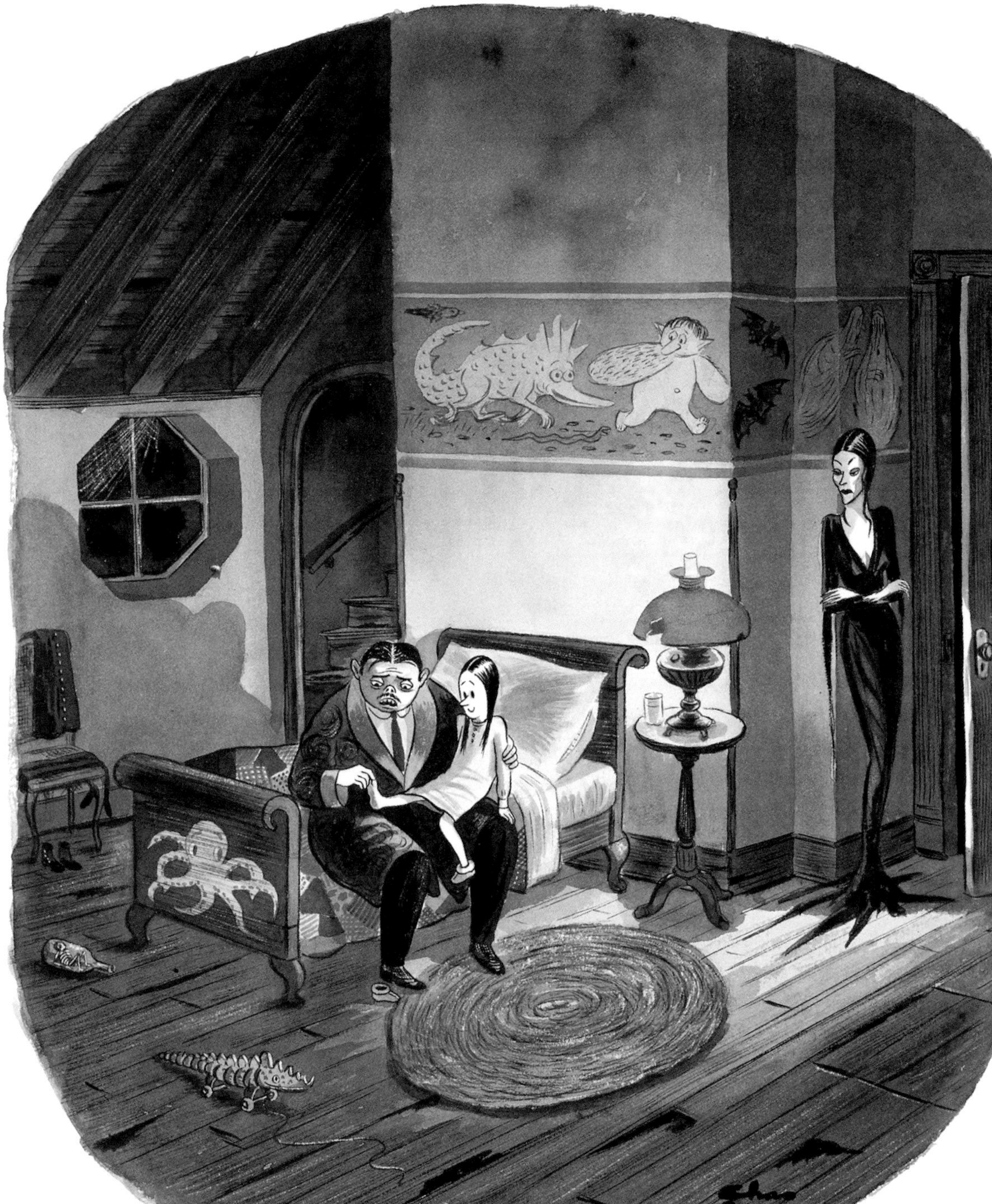

"This little piggy went to market, this little piggy stayed home, this little piggy had roast beef, this little piggy had none, this little piggy went wee wee wee all the way home, and this little piggy . . ."

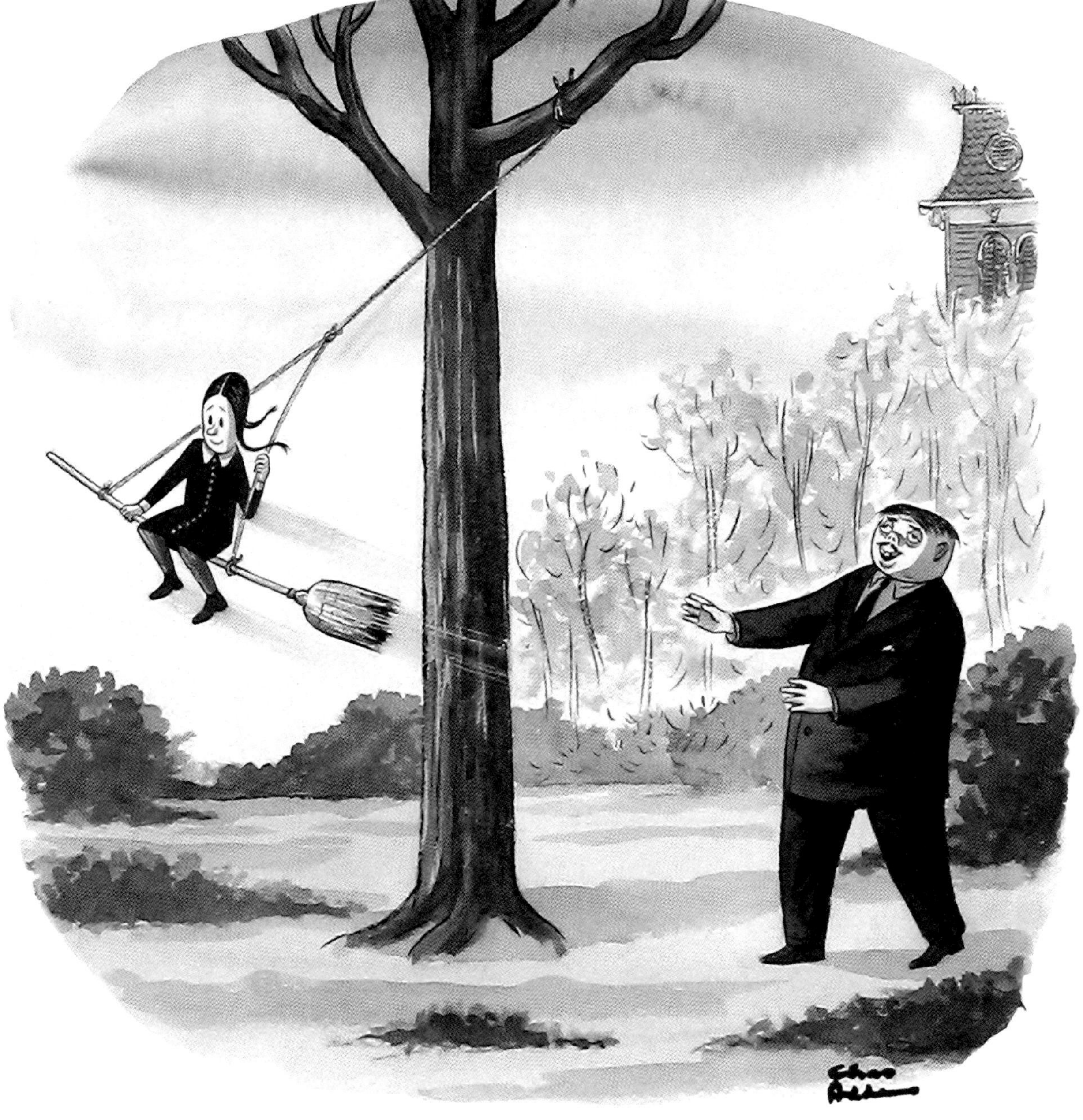
Chas Addams

WEDNESDAY

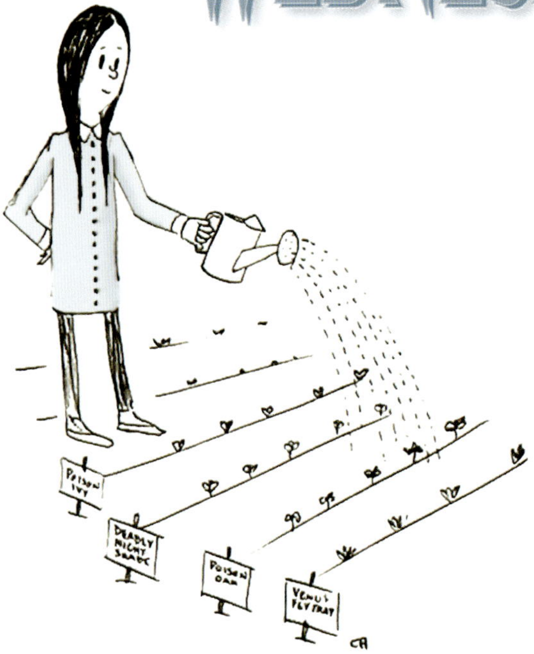
POISON IVY
DEADLY NIGHT SHADE
POISON OAK
VENUS FLY TRAP

Child of woe, is wan and delicate with her mother's dark black hair and white complexion. Sensitive and on the quiet side, she loves the picnics and outings to the underground caverns often planned by Morticia and Gomez. She is a solemn child, prim in dress and, on the whole, pretty lost. Gomez is wild about her. Secretive and imaginative, poetic, seems underprivileged and given to occasional tantrums. Has six toes on one foot.

Chas Addams

THE BOY PUGSLEY

An energetic monster of a boy about nine years old—blondish red hair, popped blue eyes and a dedicated troublemaker—in other words, the kid next door. Genius in his own way, he makes toy guillotines, full-size racks, threatens to poison his sister, can turn himself into a Mr. Hyde with an ordinary chemical set. He is, nevertheless, easily controlled by Morticia, though Lurch and Gomez keep their backs to the wall at all times when he's around. His voice is hoarse.

Chas Addams

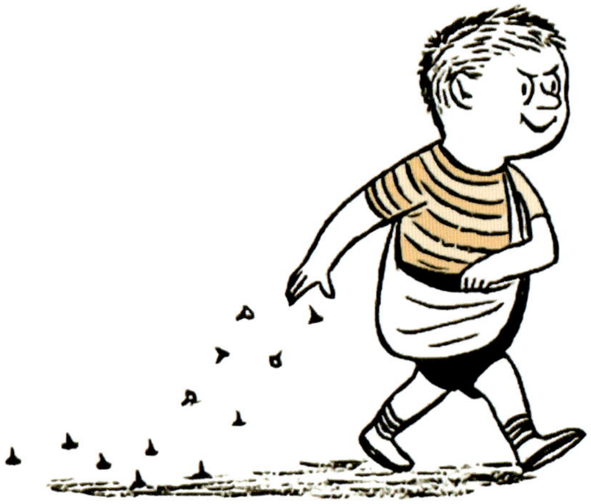

WHEN, in 1963, it came time to name the unfailingly evil little boy for *The Addams Family* television series, the very child who had been the prototype for the buildup to stardom as a pivotal member of The Addams Family from as early as 1941, Charles Addams merely named him Pubert. Short and to the point, the name expressed exactly how Addams felt about the creativity and energy locked up in young boys; he relished every cunning and divisive scheme for which they were responsible. Unfortunately, television at that time was a bit embarrassed by this frankness, so Addams was obliged to find a different name. He chose the name of a small river in the Bronx, Pugsley, because he "just liked the name." That was an acceptable alternative, and so it was approved.

A year earlier, a Manhattan-based company named Aboriginals, Ltd., had opted to manufacture stuffed fabric dolls based on the Addams Family characters. Addams had been thinking about Morticia as the name of the skeletal beauty in black rags, Gomez was already Gomez, and a friend had suggested that the pallid little girl he was drawing certainly suggested Wednesday, the child of woe from the traditional nursery rhyme. Addams liked it. However, the naming of her younger brother was still in limbo, and the company decided to call him Irving. Unfortunately, the lives of the dolls—which also included a Granny Frump doll added several months later—did not last much past 1963, and by then Pugsley had been forever named.

The first inkling of an idea about a sad little girl possibly facing the world on her own came with the cartoon in the June 29, 1940, *New Yorker* showing a concerned working-class couple witnessing a scrawny little waif with long black hair skipping rope at night on a city street, with the caption, "Twenty-three thousand and one, twenty-three thousand and two, twenty-three thousand and three . . ." She looks more exhausted than woeful, but it was surely the beginning of Addams's longtime use of children as leading characters in many of his fifties and sixties works. In fact, Harper & Row's 1967 publication of *The Chas. Addams Mother Goose* resurrected his weary jump-roping girl as Wednesday to illustrate the rhyme "Little Jumping Joan."

In 1941 and 1942, five drawings featuring a cross-purposed little boy as a scout, or as the son of concerned parents, or even as a bystander watching an octopus drag a pedestrian down a manhole on a New York City street, had been published in the *New Yorker*. However, it seems fair to cite the cartoon in the June 19, 1943, issue of the magazine as the first true appearance of the evil one who would become Pugsley, more because of his activity. An industrial arts class of little boys is busy building wooden birdhouses and wastepaper baskets when the instructor happens upon an exceptional lad in a striped T-shirt who is putting the finishing touches on a wooden coffin—no caption necessary.

Regardless of either character's development, both of which were relatively quick, the *New Yorker*'s August 26, 1944, issue introduced Morticia as a mother and Pugsley and Wednesday as her children: the distressed little girl stands before her in an upstairs hallway while Morticia says, "Well, don't come whining to me. Go tell him

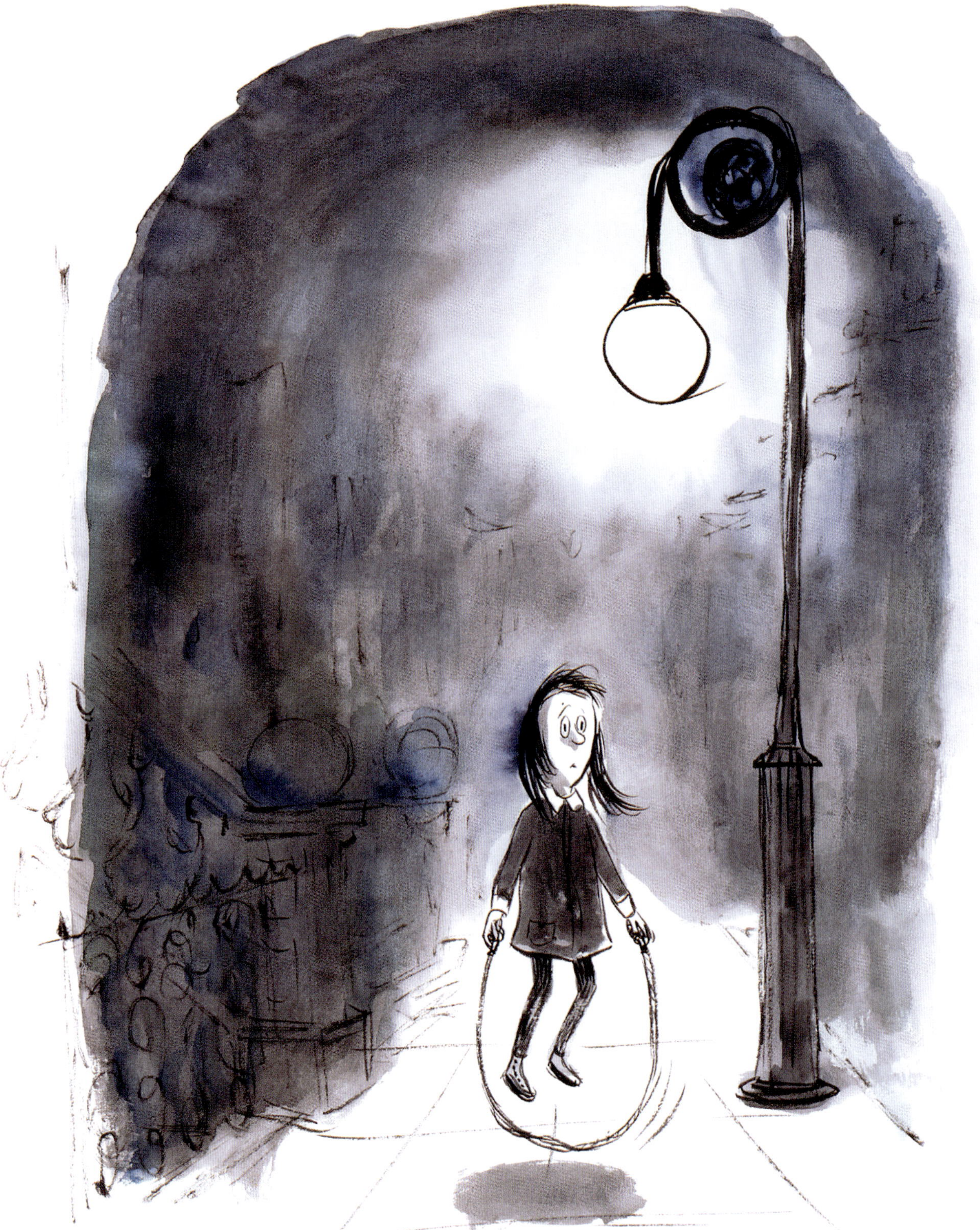

you'll poison him right back." This drawing set the tone for every cartoon of the children's games and interactions for the rest of their published lives.

Individually, the children are more than capable of entertaining themselves. Wednesday decorates her dollhouse with a black wreath of mourning or a skeleton; she marvels at an odd string of paper dolls of her own creation. Pugsley devises miniature disasters in the bathtub and plots real-life sliding board accidents. But they are at their best when they are together, complementary siblings making the most of their deft imaginations.

One image in particular stands out as one of Addams's best, and he admitted it came from a bit of a hangover he had while visiting friends at the tiny resort of Fire Island, across the Great South Bay from Long Island, New York. It was a particularly hot weekend, and the old natural-shingled house smelled of sticky salt air mixed with the prior evening's festivities, while sand and flies drifted in and out of the screen doors as the children

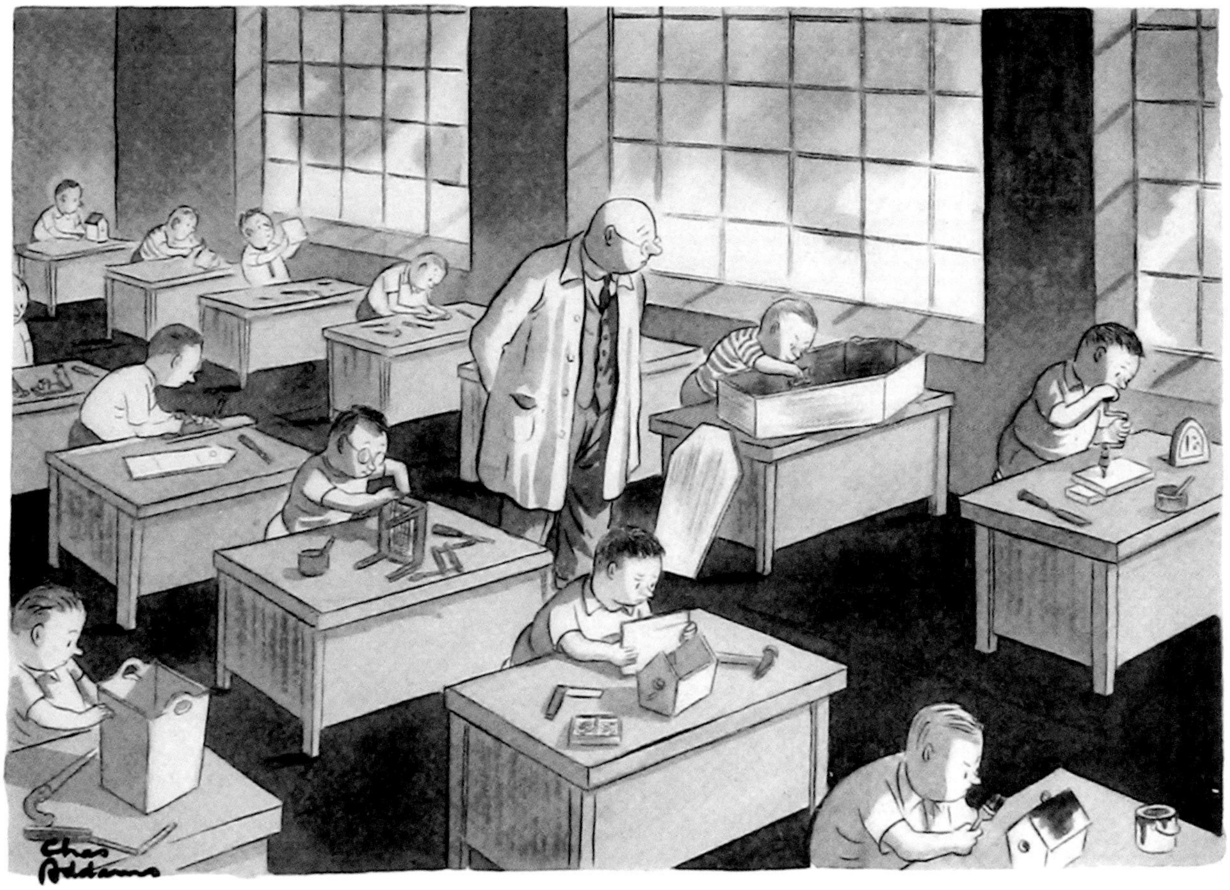
Chas Addams

screamed and hollered and ran around doing children things. In the midst of this, the hostess reminded everyone that the two older children would be coming back from camp the next day, which caused Addams to imagine two cages. Hence his August 30, 1947, drawing of the Railway Express deliveryman standing at The Addams Family's front door holding two pet carriers as Morticia addresses Gomez with "It's the children, darling, back from camp."

Charles Addams was forever accused of hating children, yet most of his work adores them and praises their foul deeds. He appreciated their ingenuity and fearlessness. He drew Wednesday and Pugsley behaving in the same way he witnessed "normal" children interacting, except that the Addams children loved each other while sharing a mutual joy in private torture. Similarly, his characterizations of "normal" adults reveal their ruthlessness, whereas his Addams Family adults simply adored one another and life from their viewpoint. The December 10, 1949, issue of the *New Yorker* says it all. Morticia, standing at the top of the cellar stairs, calls, "Come along, children—time for your nap." Downstairs, a candle burns in the neck of a wine bottle and Pugsley is alone, having just finished a mortar-and-brick job on a basement wall. Another Addams act of sweet-hearted sibling rivalry has been successfully executed, and we know that both children enjoyed the process. There is no sign of struggle, and they both got what they wanted. We also know it will never be the end of Wednesday, the child of woe.

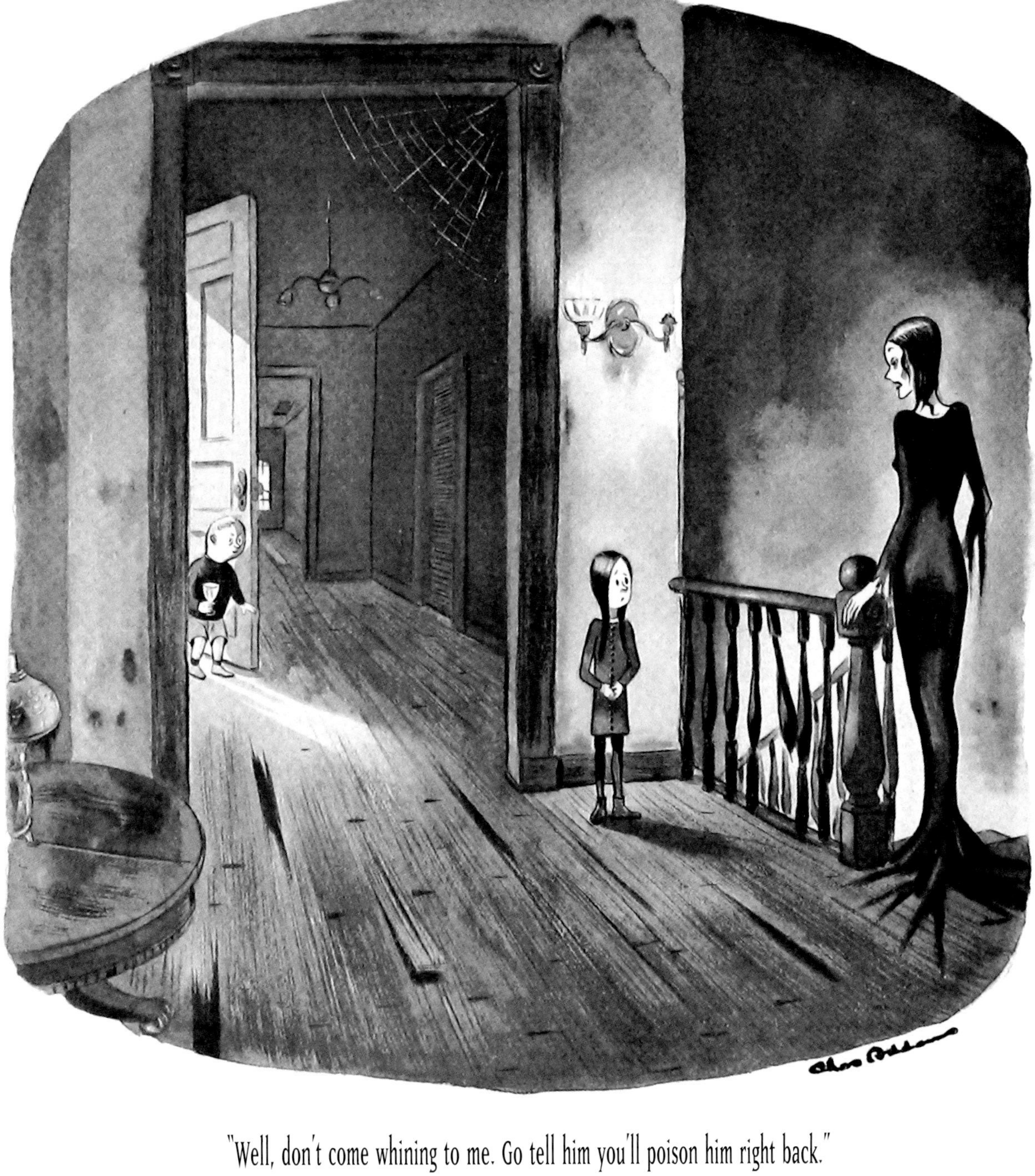

"Well, don't come whining to me. Go tell him you'll poison him right back."

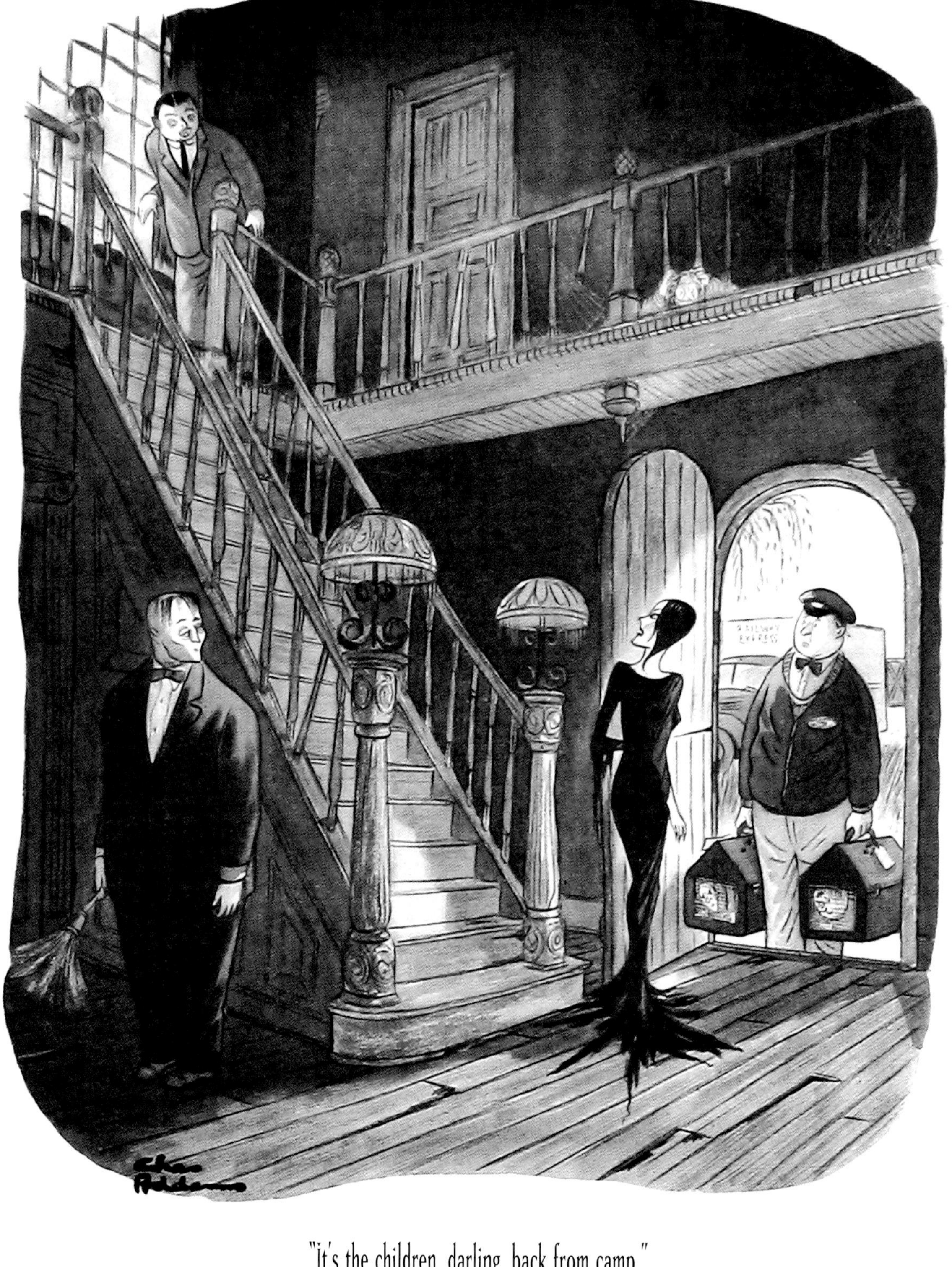
Chas Addams

"It's the children, darling, back from camp."

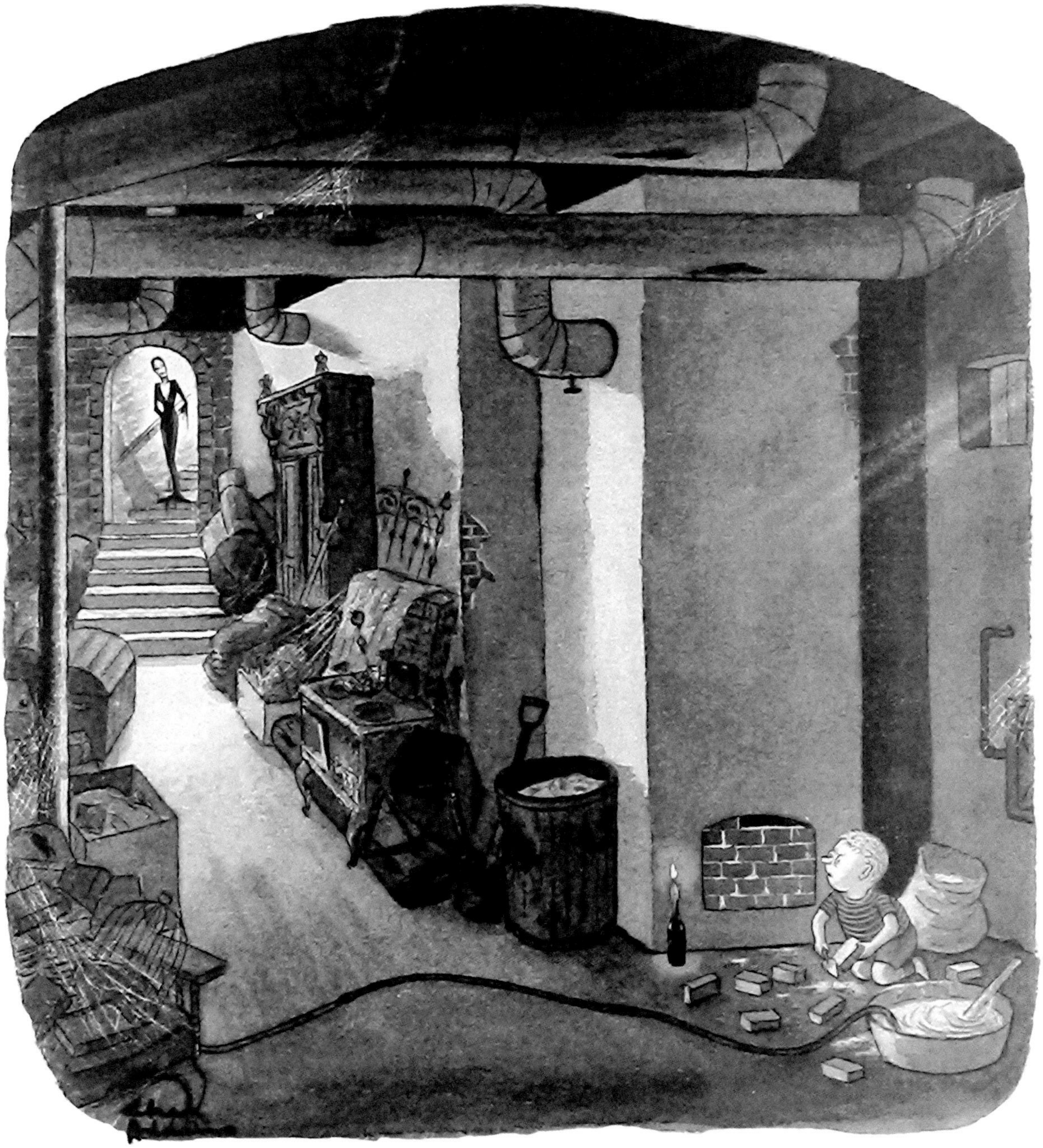

"Come along, children—time for your nap."

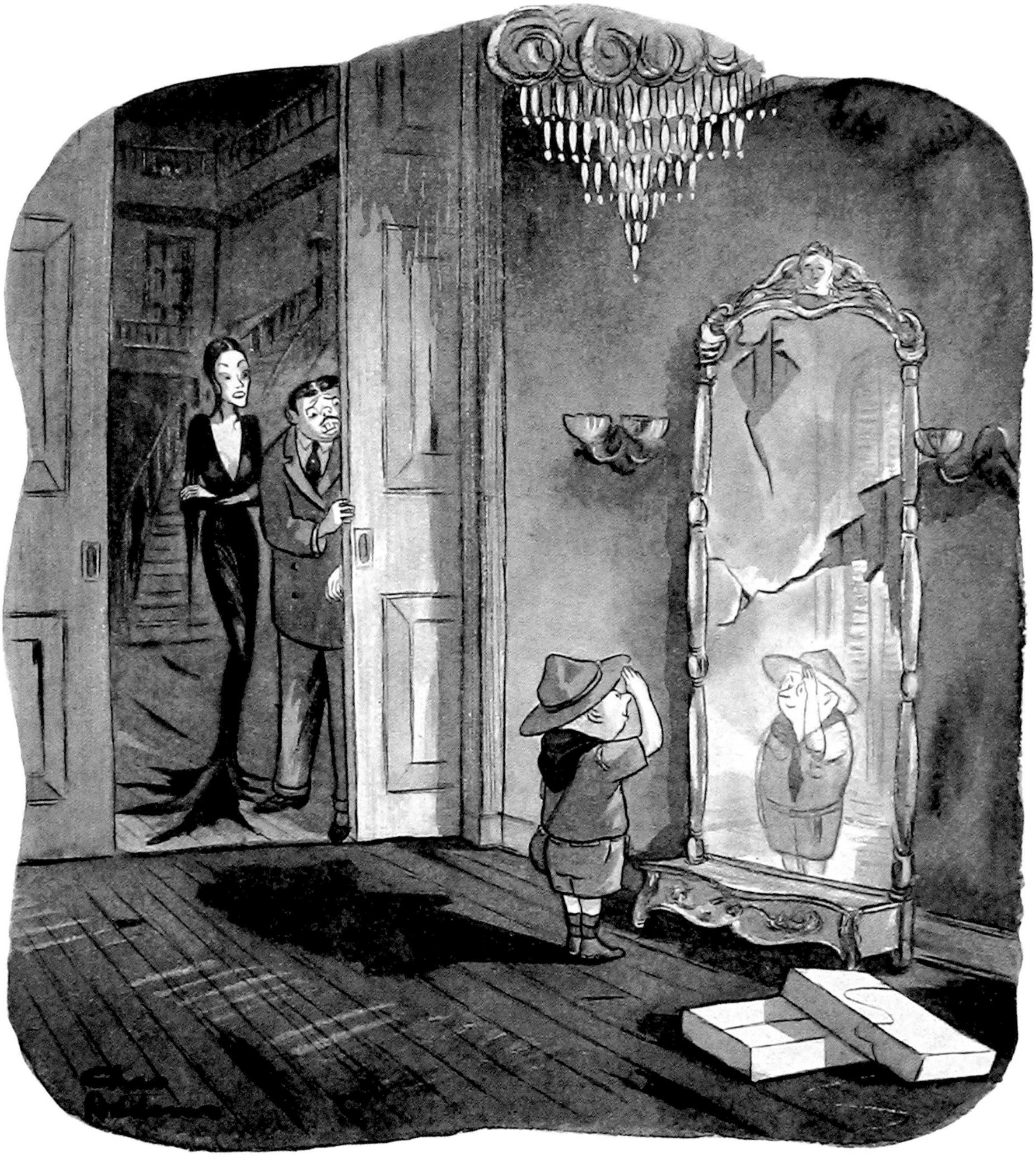

"Well, he certainly doesn't take after my side of the family."

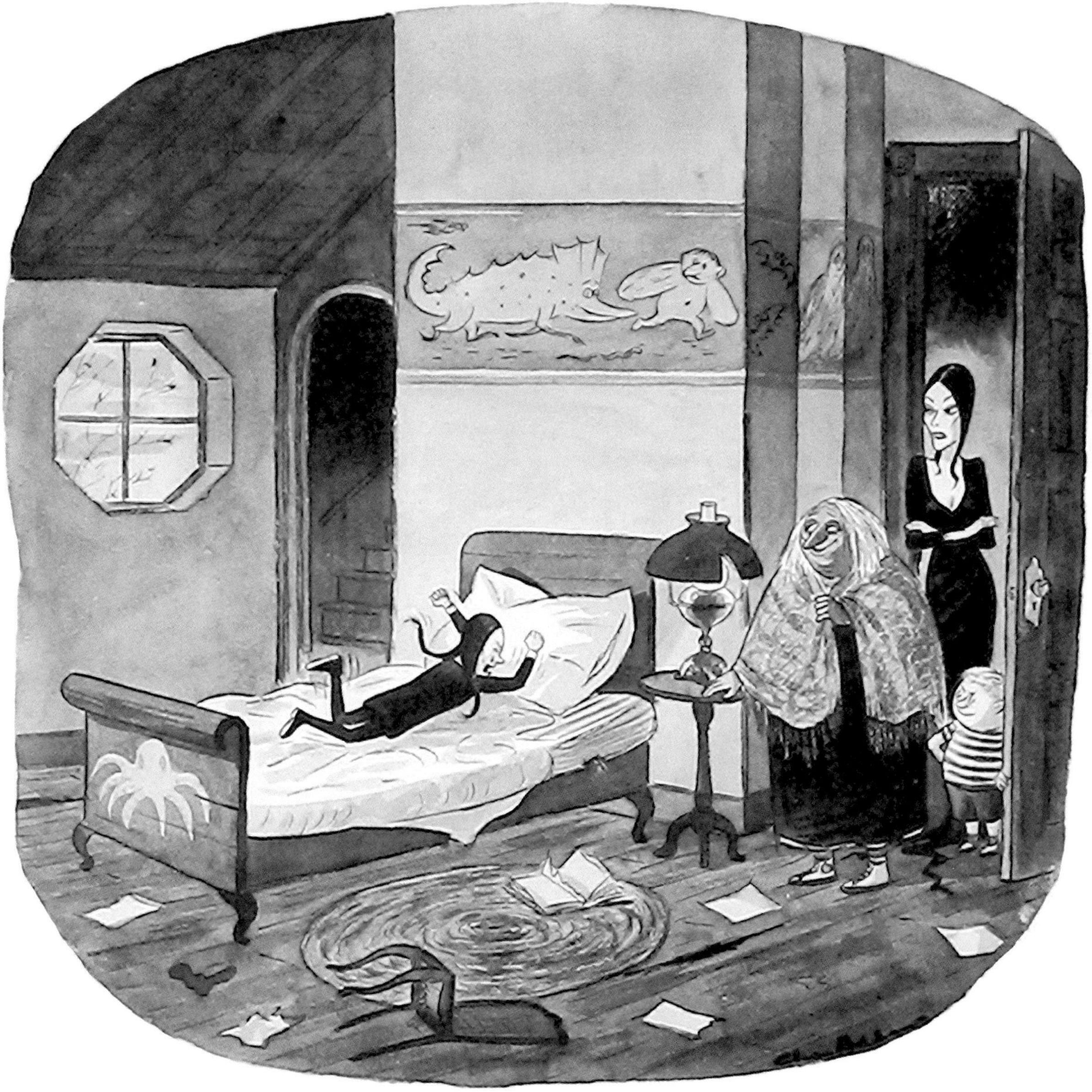

"Oh, she's furious because they put her on the honor roll at school."

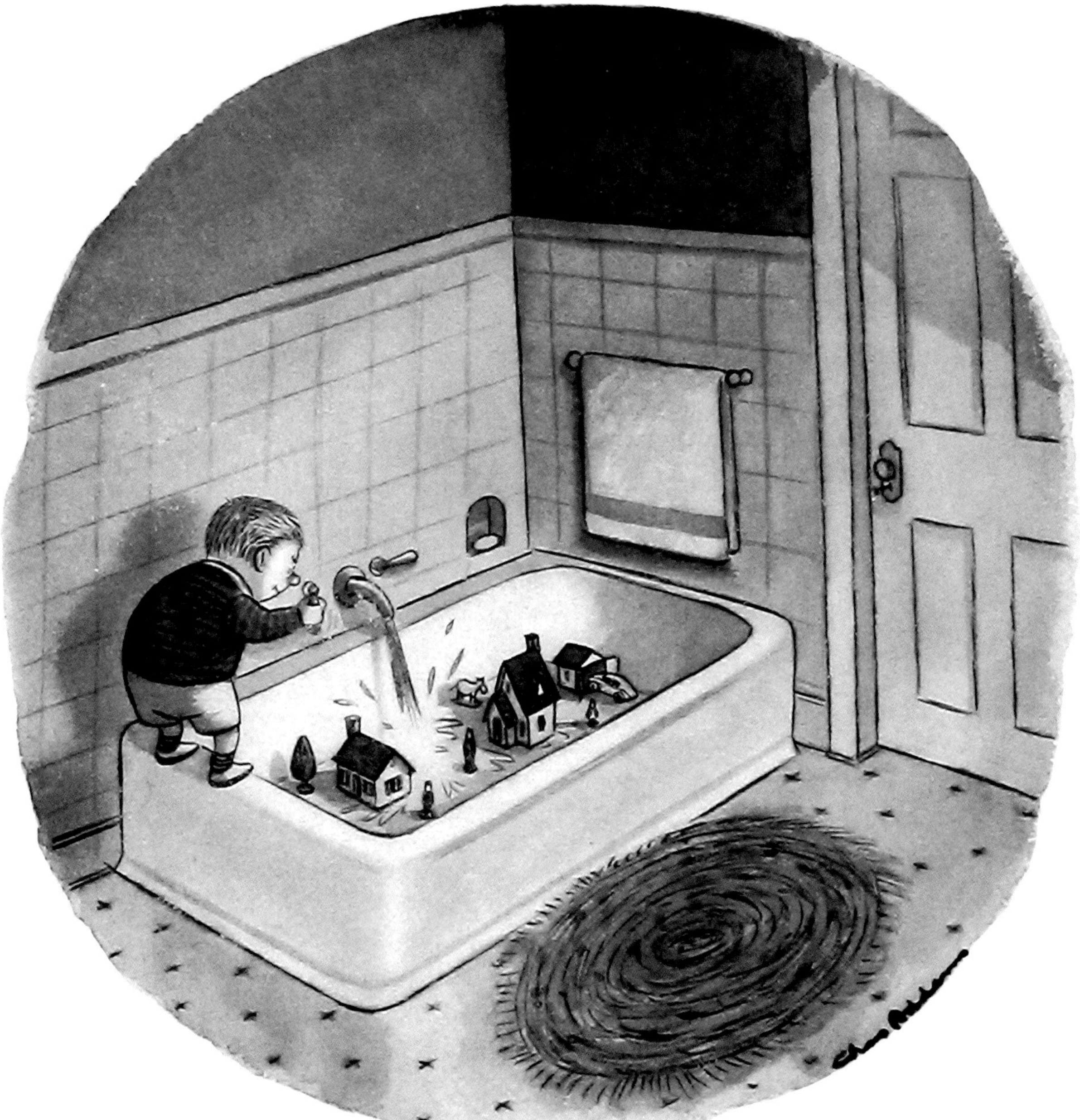

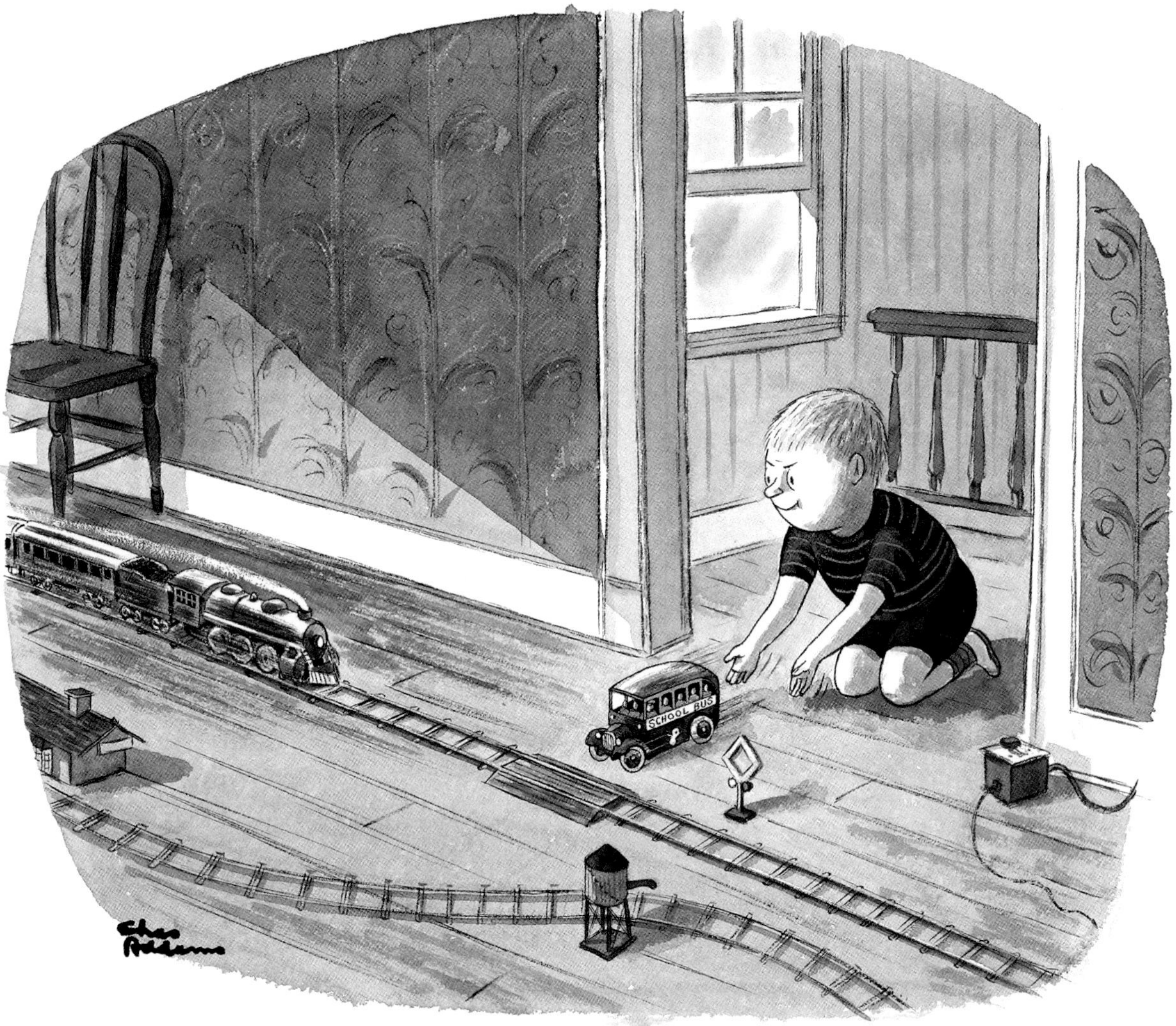
SCHOOL BUS
Chas Addams

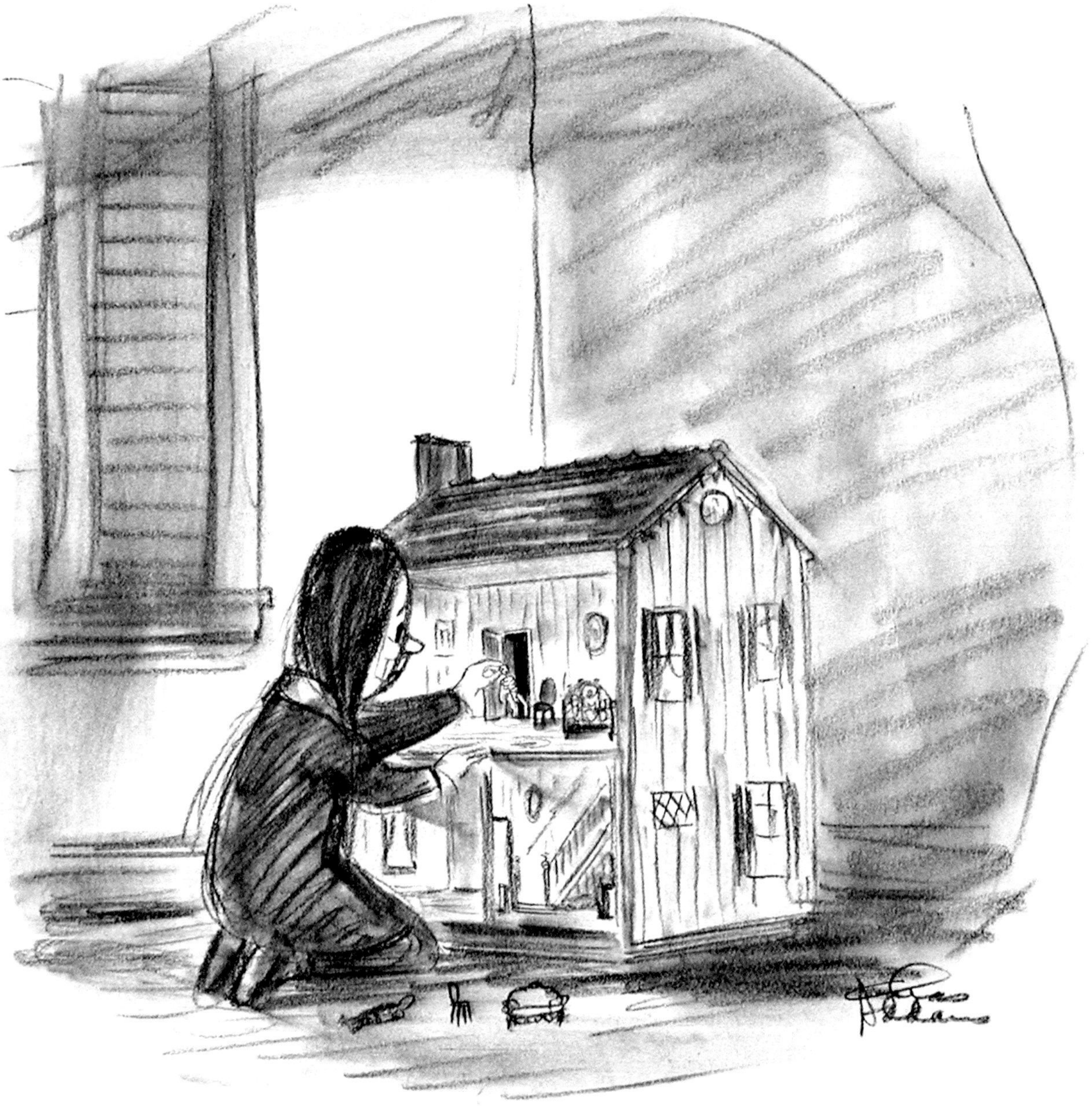

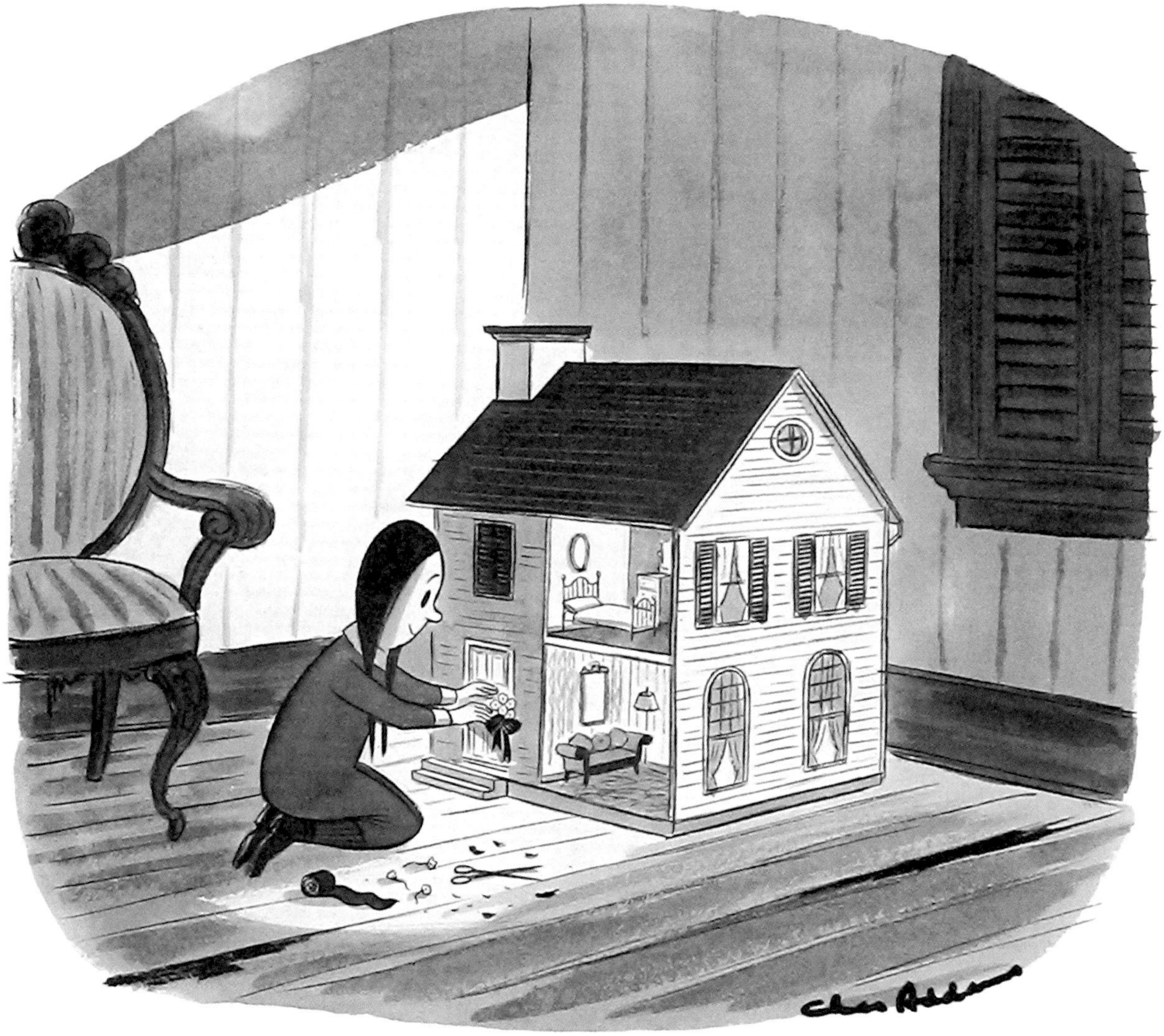
Chas Addams

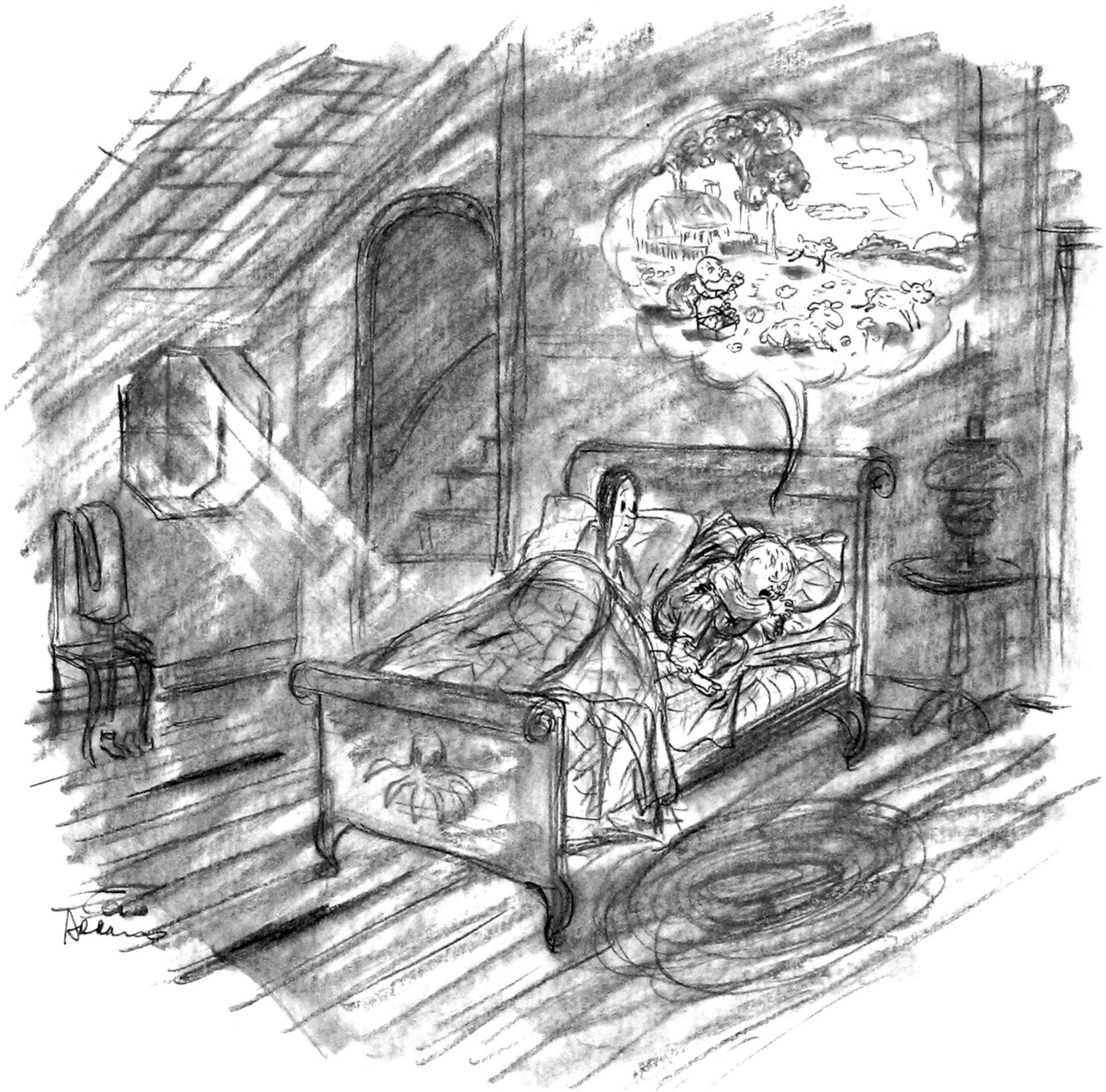

"Isn't it wonderful to think we'll always have this record of their golden childhood days?"

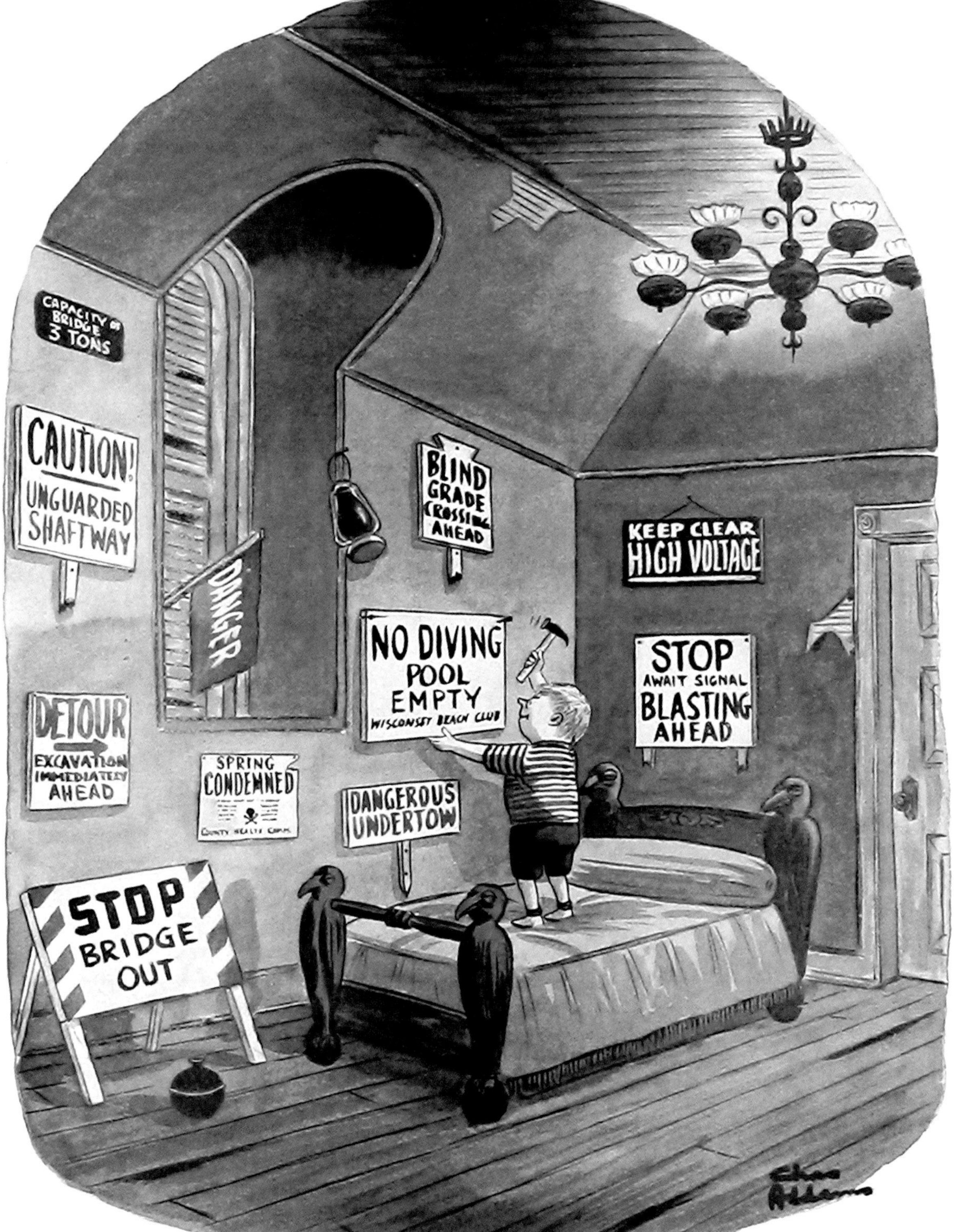
CAPACITY OF BRIDGE 3 TONS
CAUTION! UNGUARDED SHAFTWAY
DANGER
BLIND GRADE CROSSING AHEAD
KEEP CLEAR HIGH VOLTAGE
NO DIVING POOL EMPTY
WISCONSET BEACH CLUB
STOP AWAIT SIGNAL BLASTING AHEAD
DETOUR
EXCAVATION IMMEDIATELY AHEAD
SPRING CONDEMNED
DANGEROUS UNDERTOW
STOP BRIDGE OUT
Chas Addams

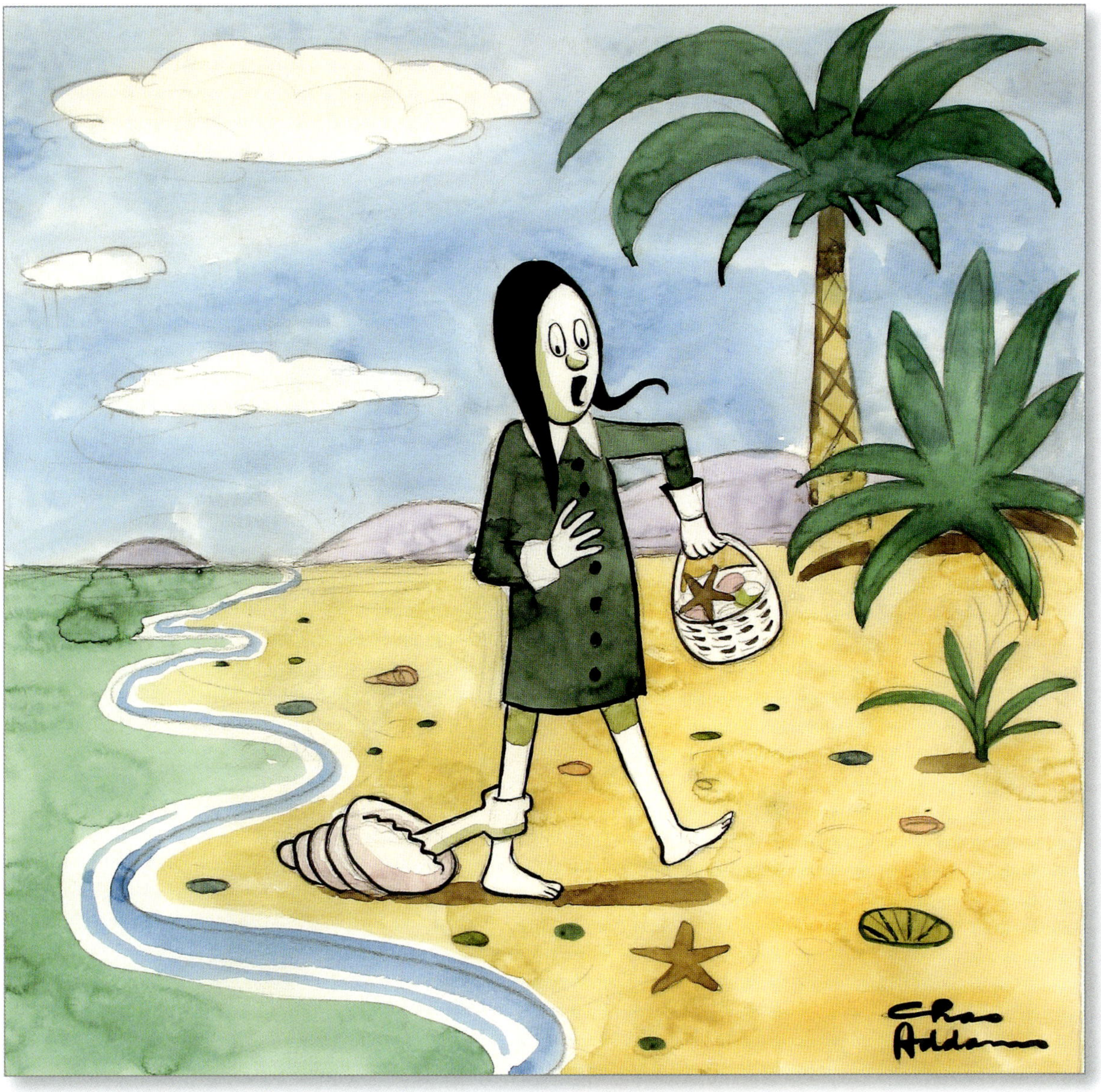
Chas Addams

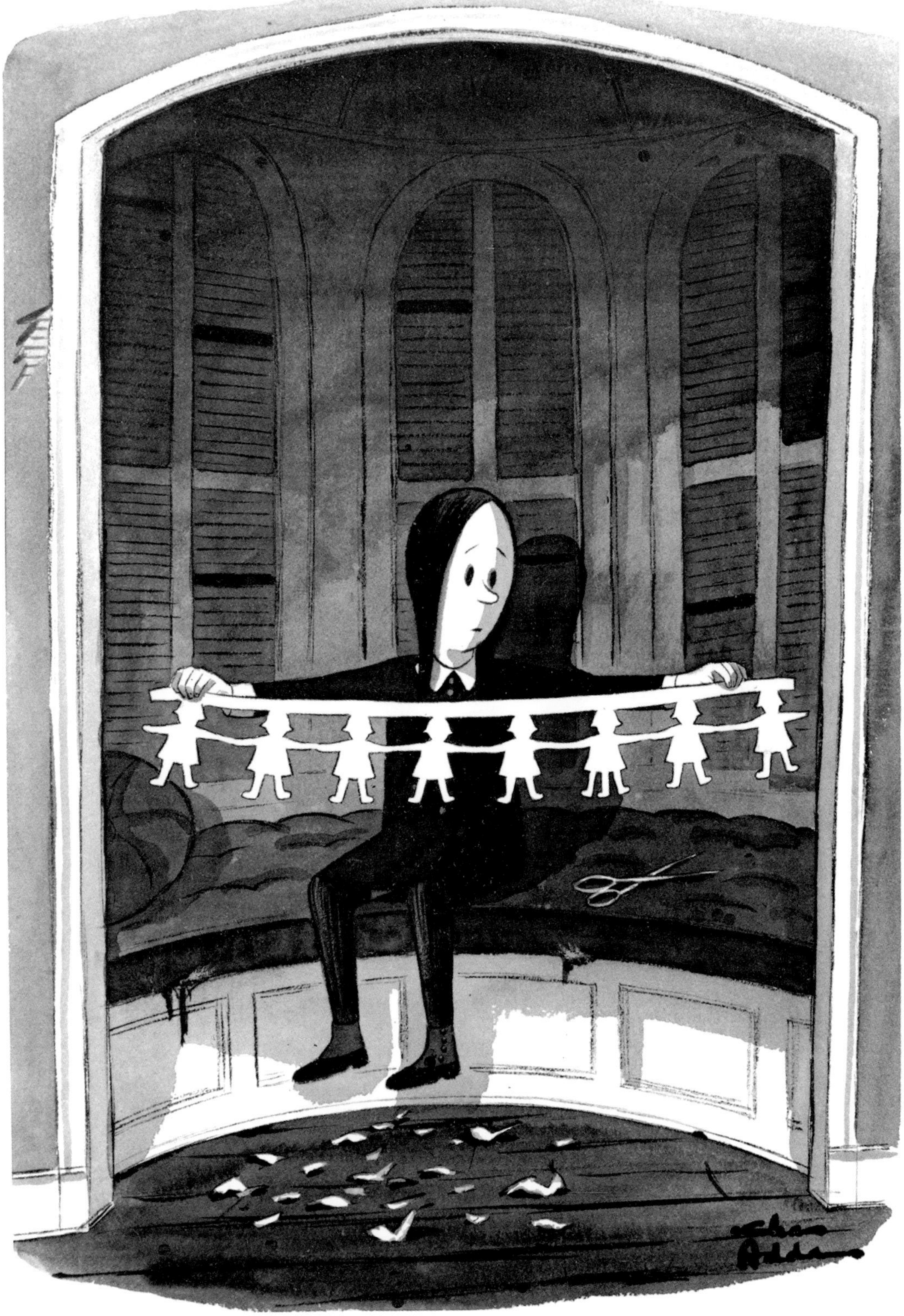

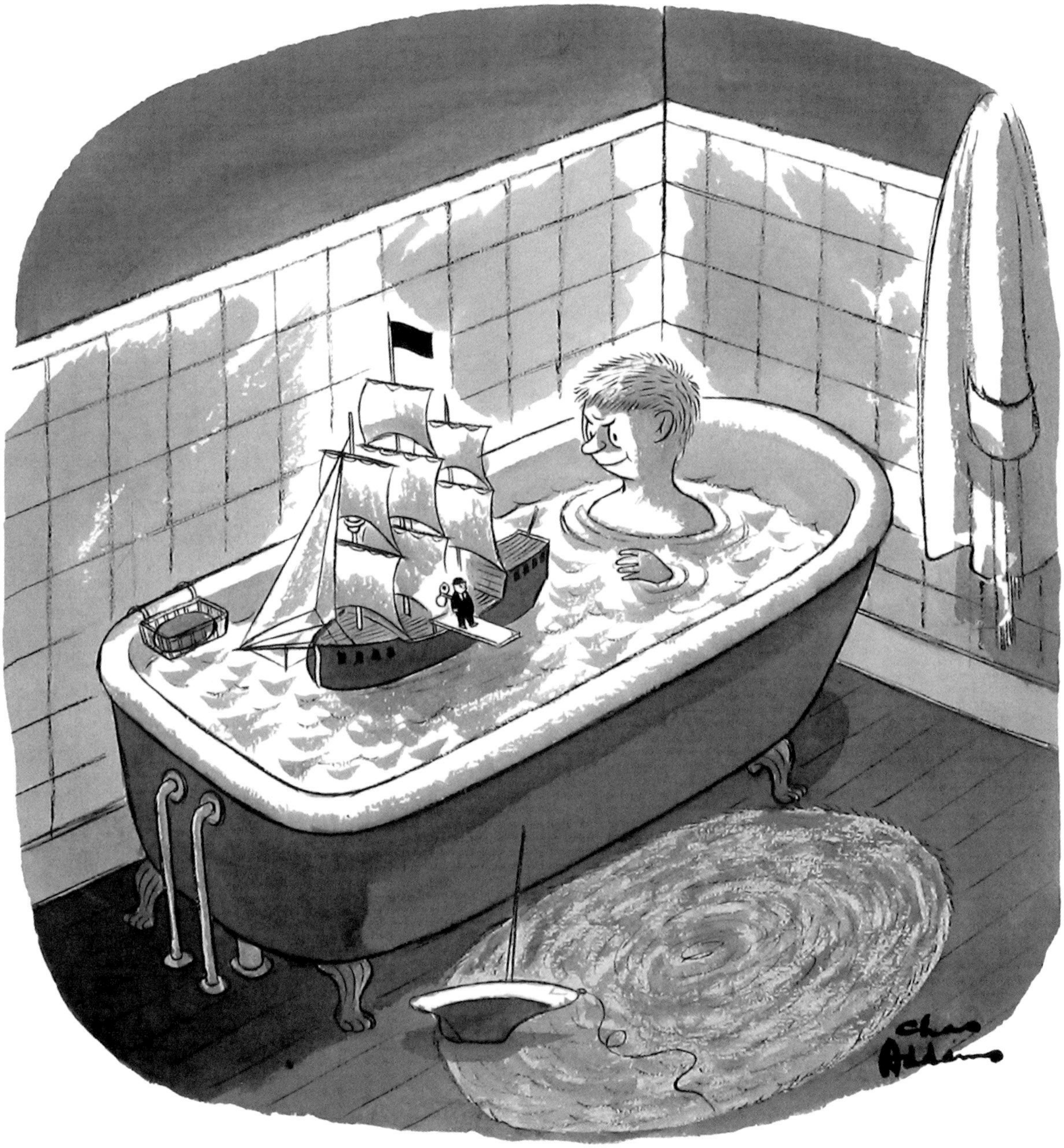
Chas Addams

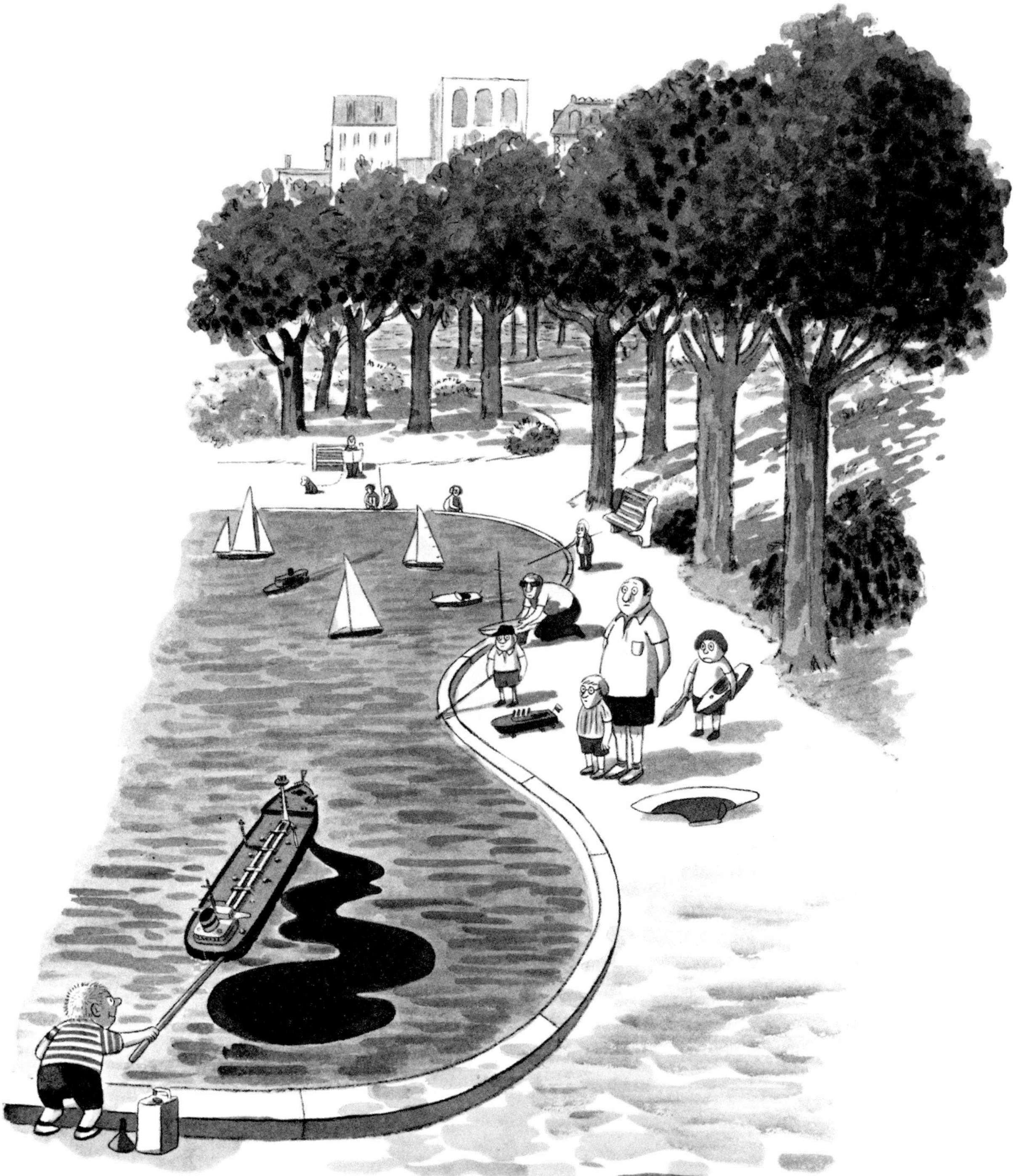
Chas Addams

"All right, children, a nice big sneer now."

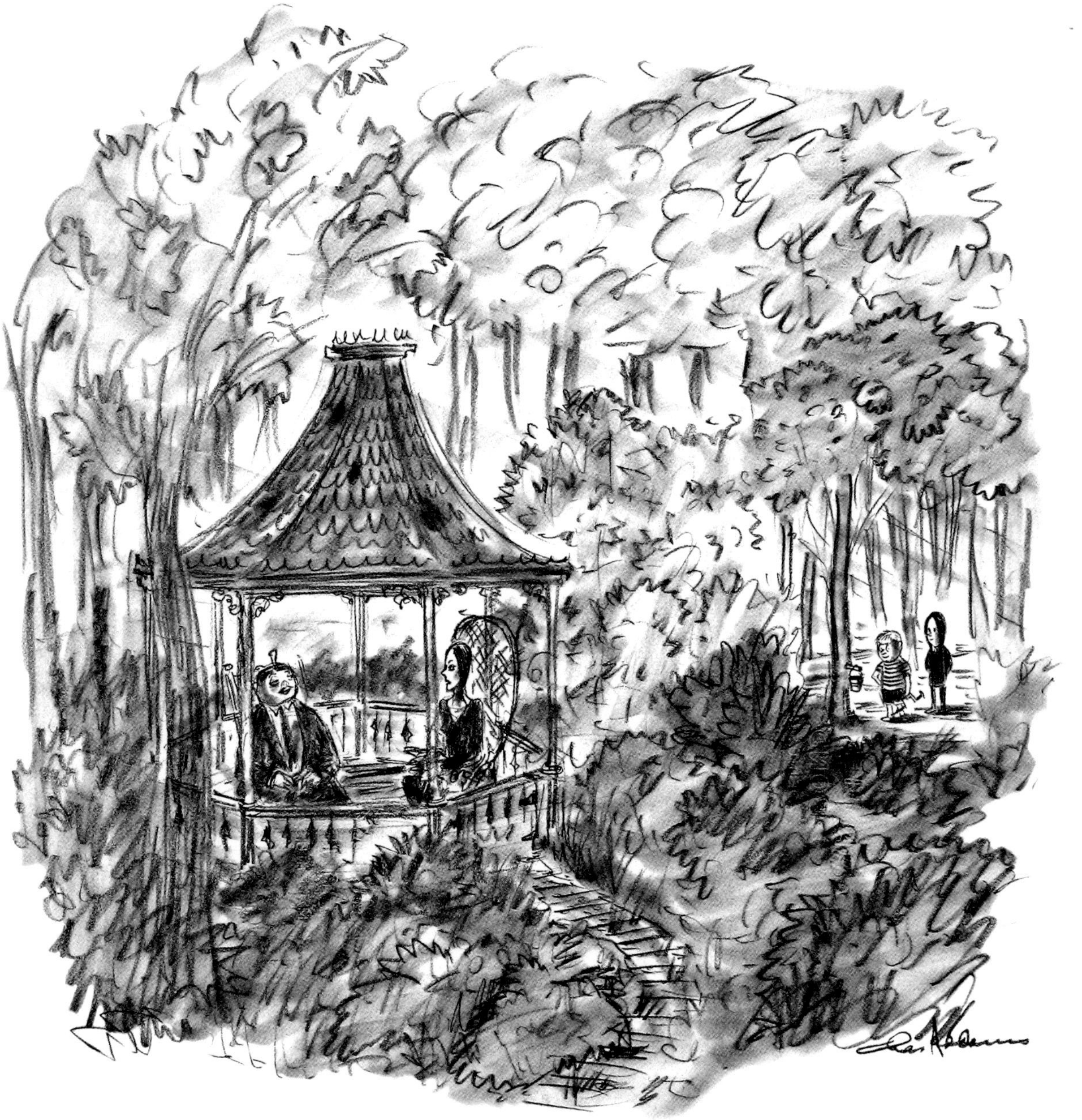

"The children? I think they're playing in the hemlock grove."

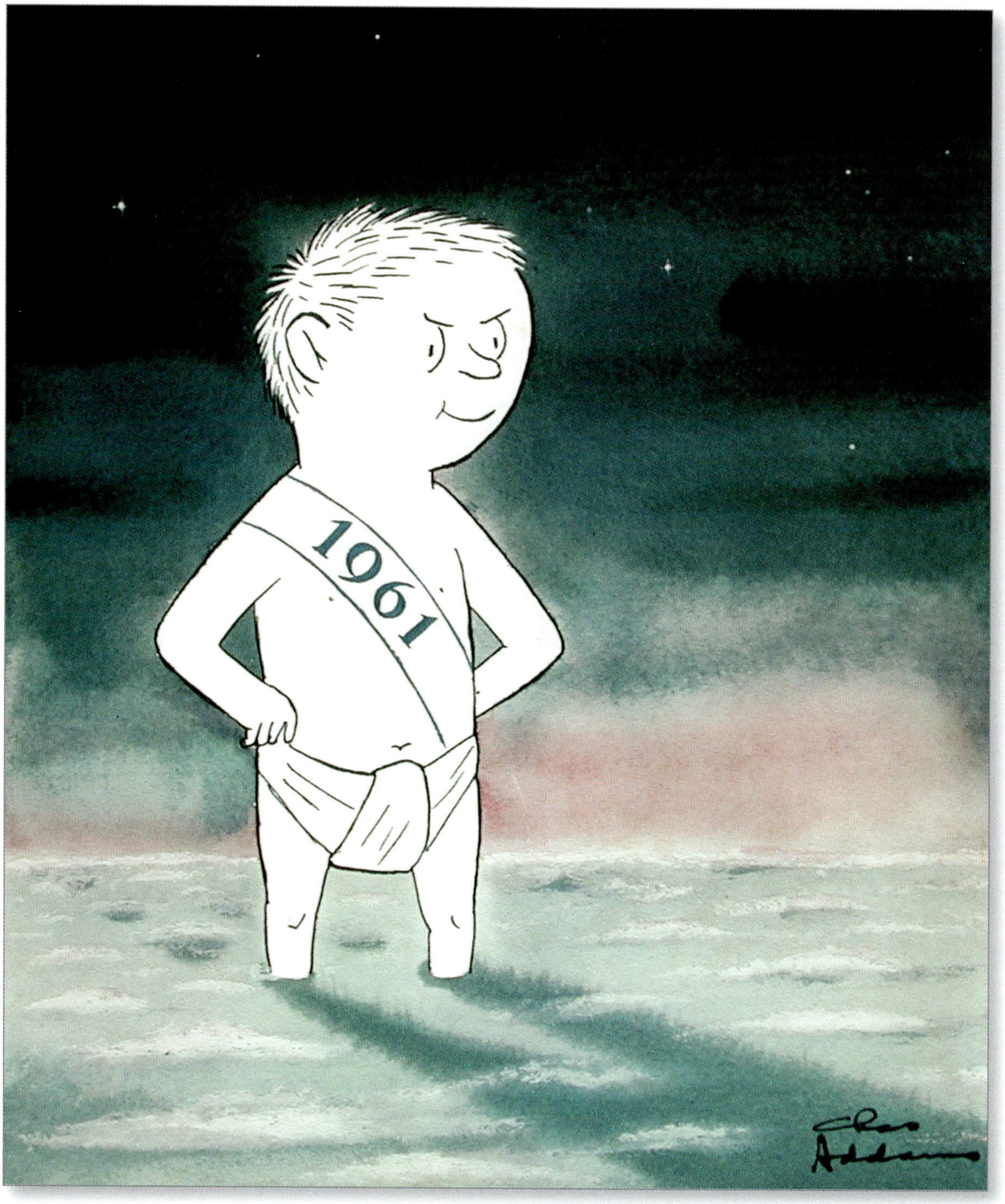
1961

"Ma . . . Ma."

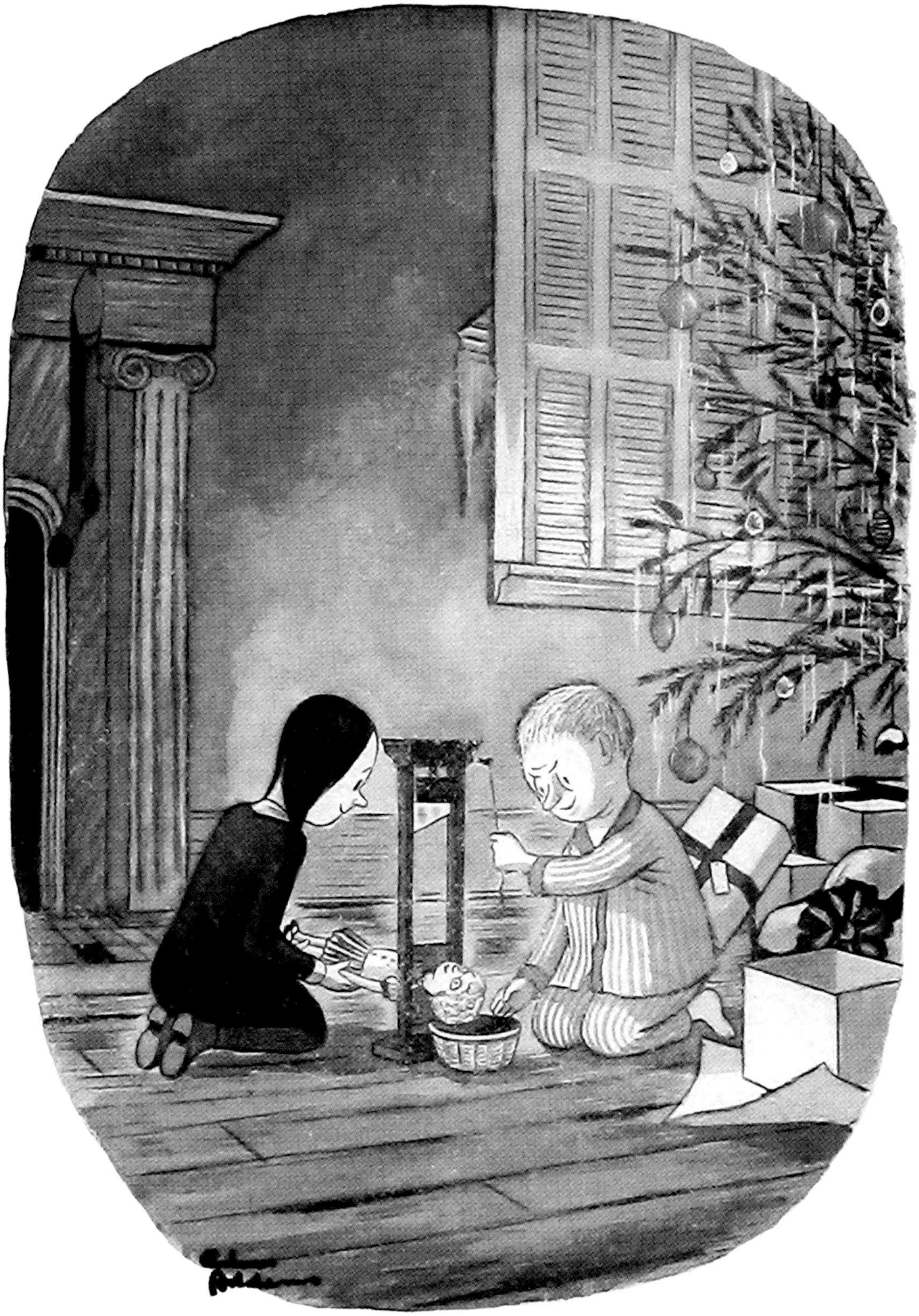

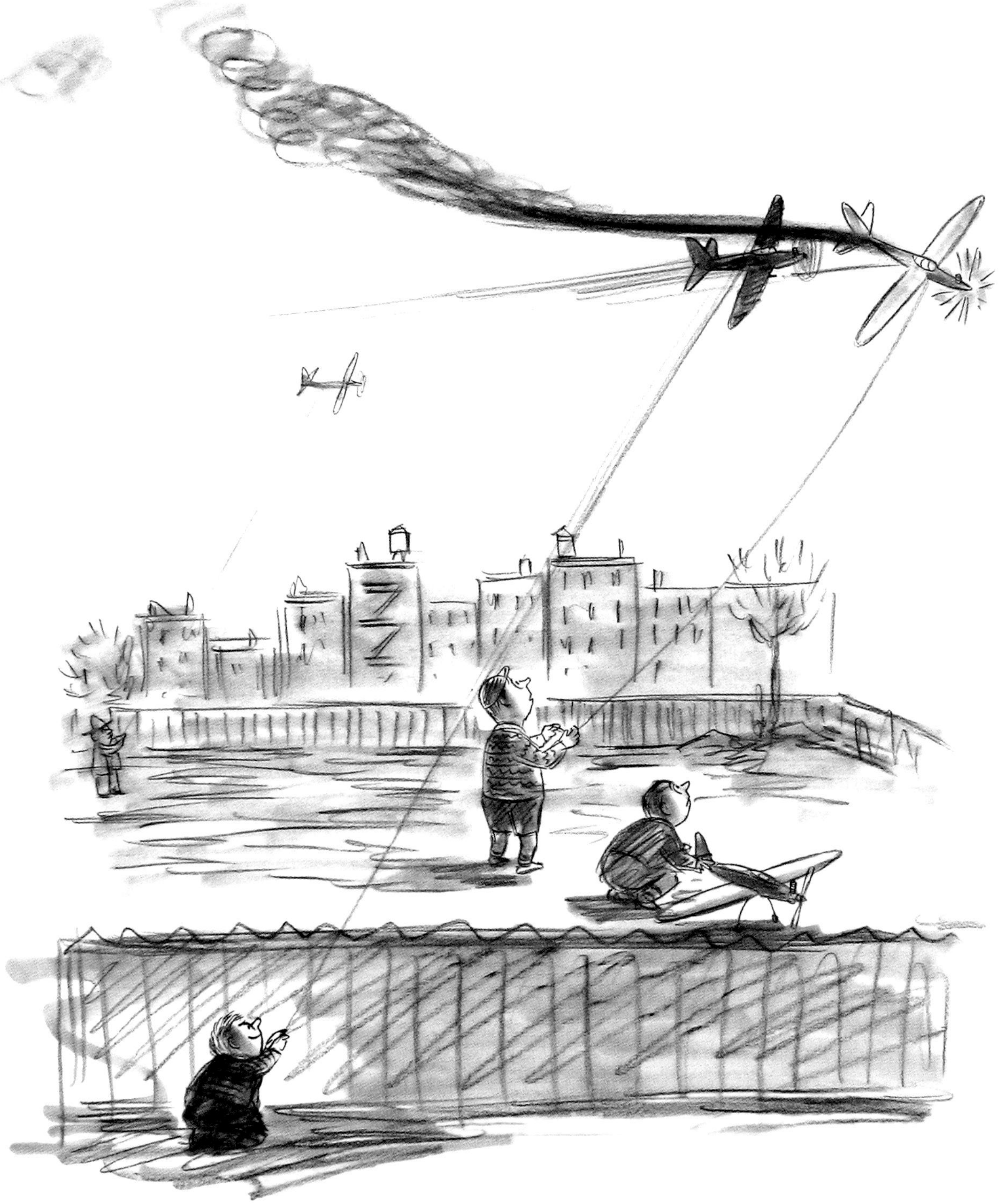

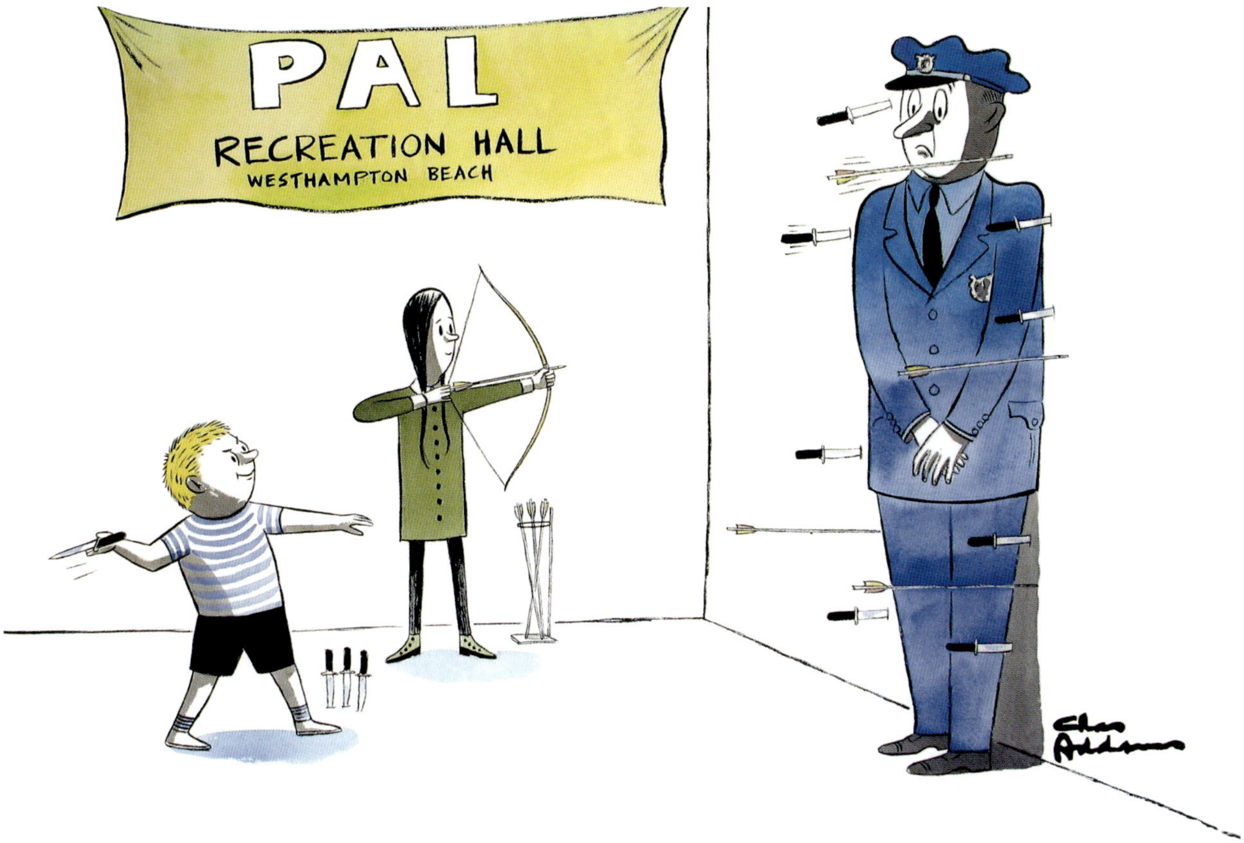
PAL
RECREATION HALL
WESTHAMPTON BEACH
Chas Addams

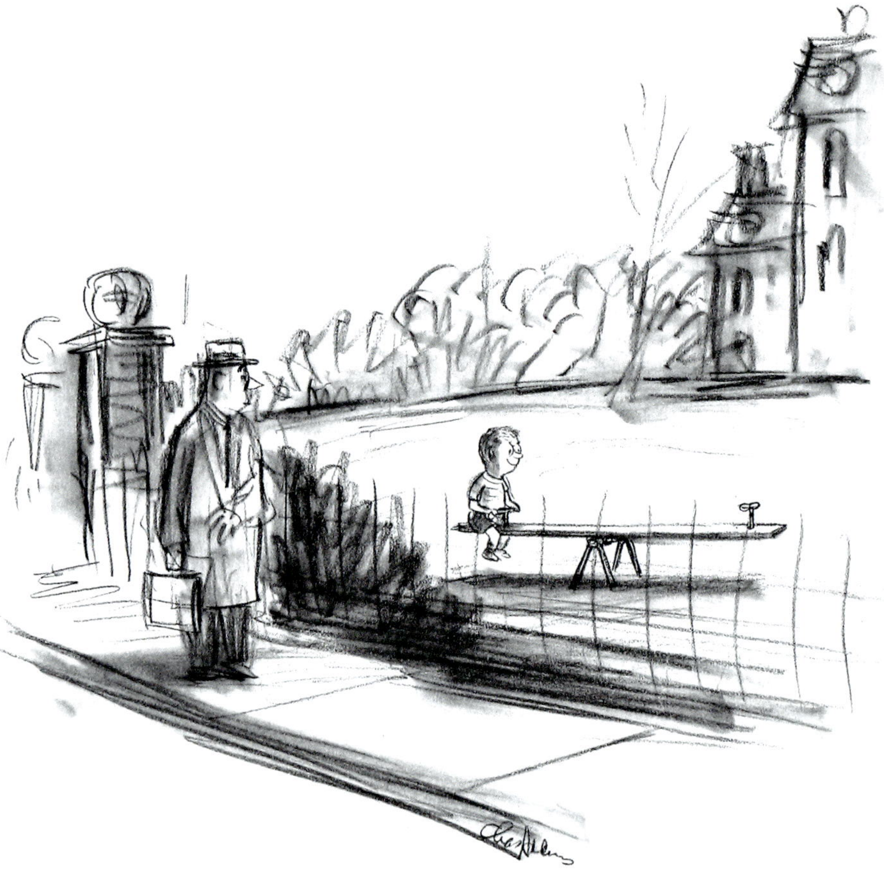

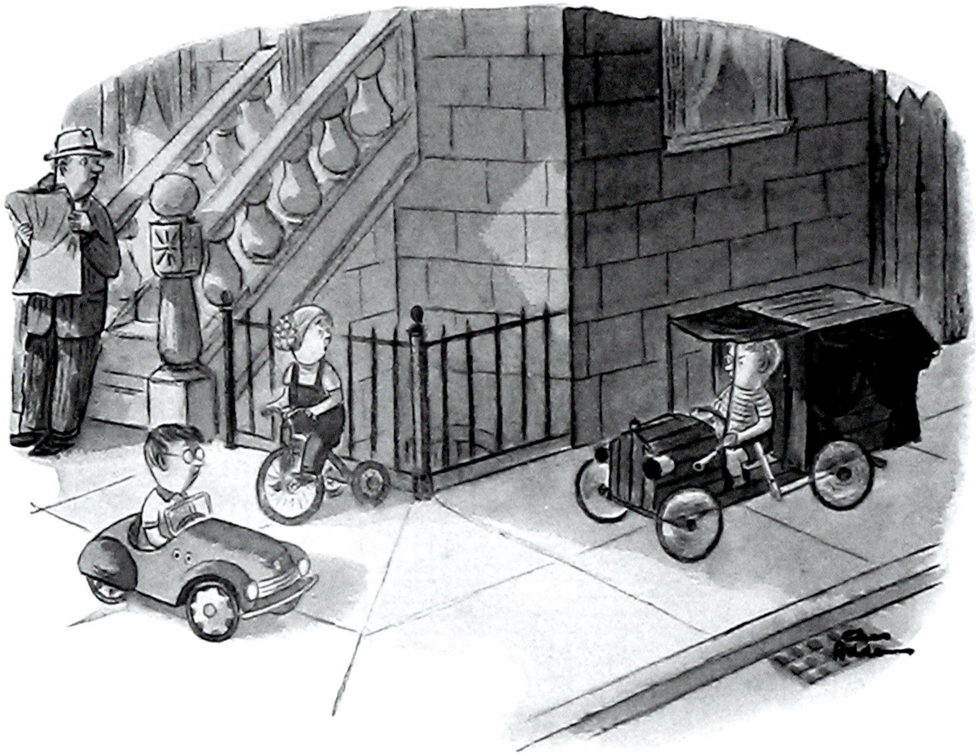

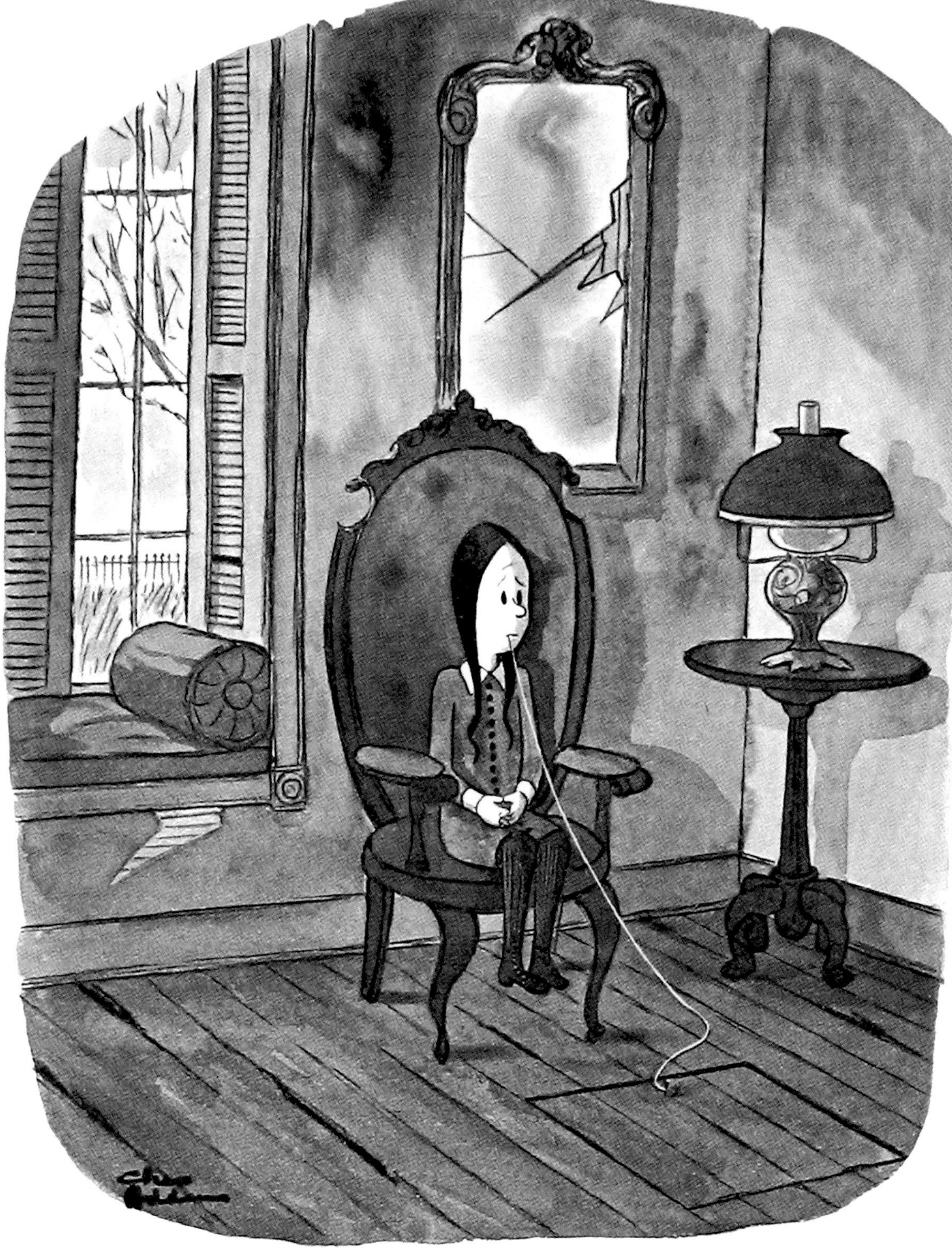
Chas Addams

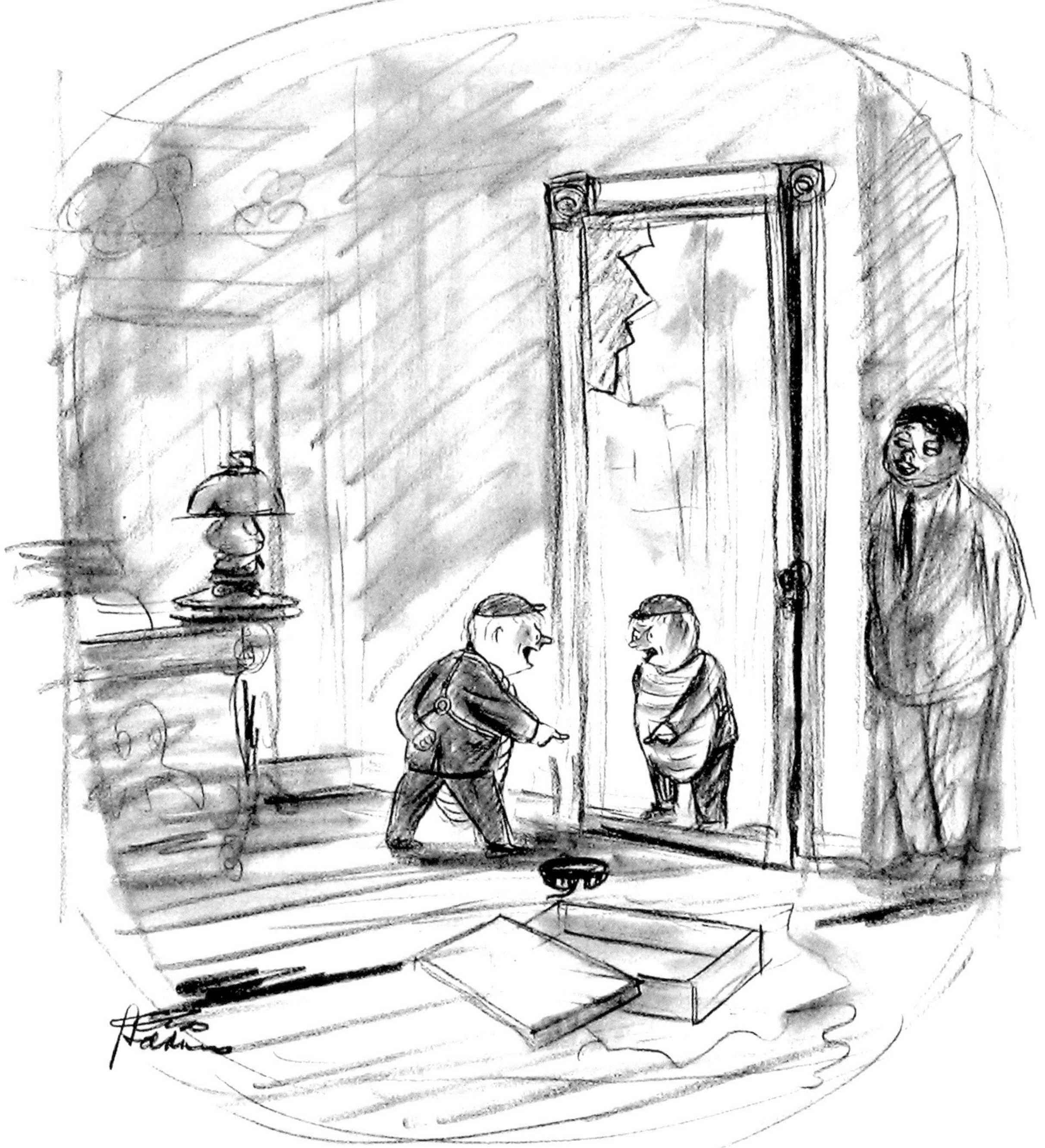

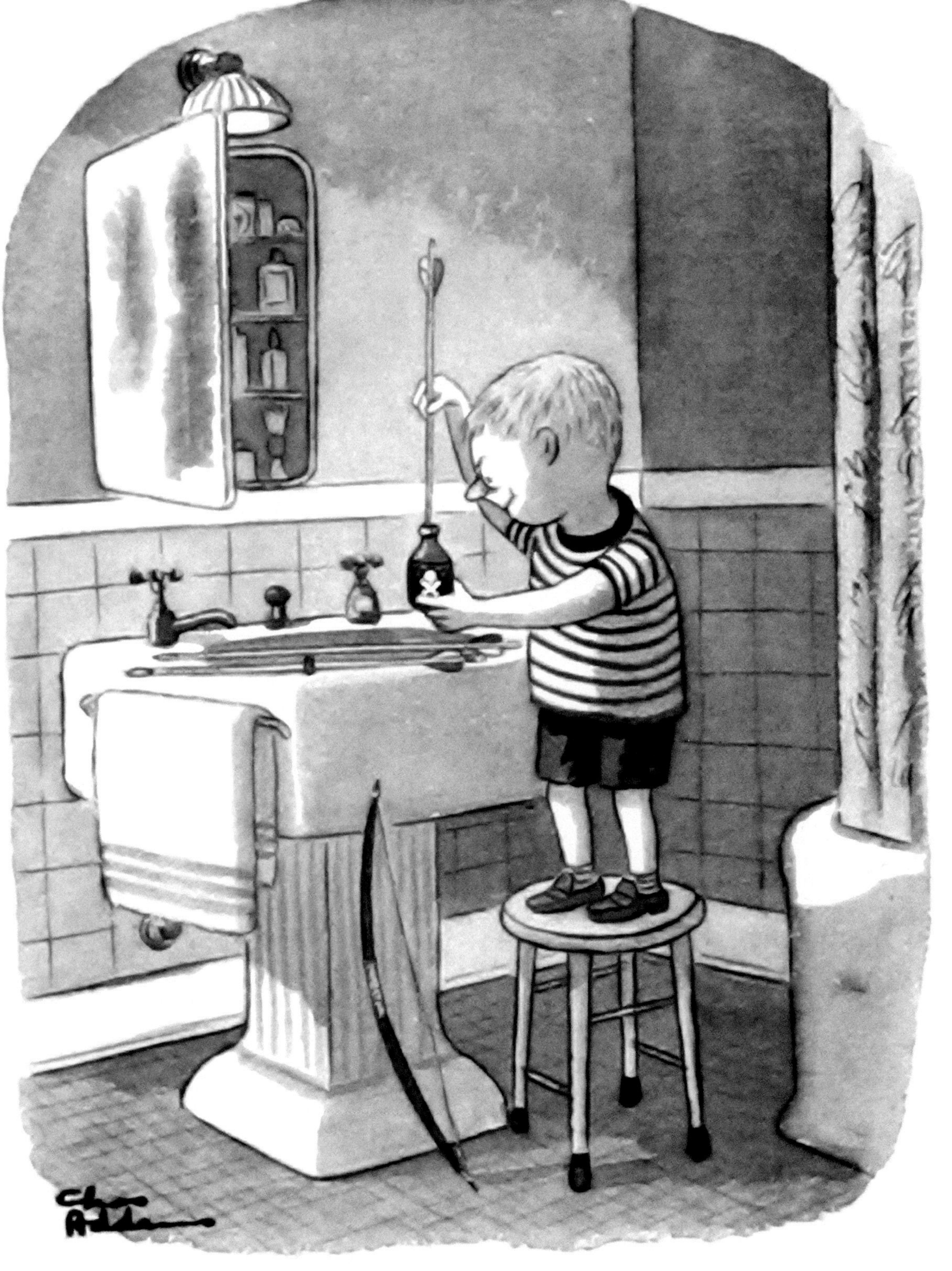

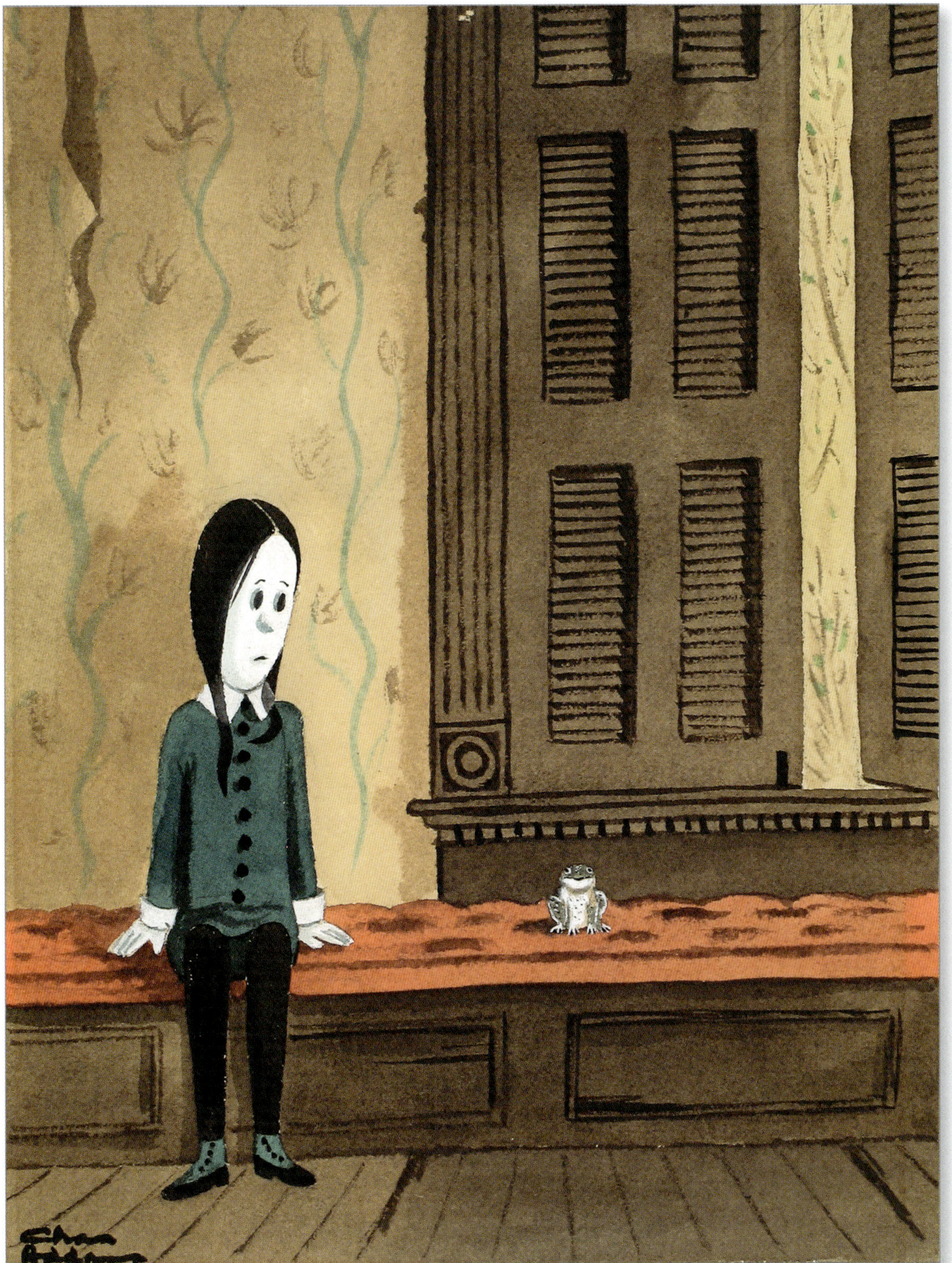
Chas Addams

LURCH THE BUTLER

This towering mute has been shambling around the house forever. He is not a very good butler, but a faithful one. He is often sent on local errands to pick the awful herbs from the garden, for instance, but will often forget the most important ingredient of all, say Eye of Newt. He is shame-faced about his oversight and the object of good-natured ridicule from the family. The children are his favorites and [he] guards them against good influences at all times. One eye is opaque; the scanty hair is damply clinging to his narrow, flat head. He will gladly undertake to dump the boiling oil on the carol singers, but, generally, the family regards him as something of a joke.

— Chas Addams

WHAT haunted household consisting of innumerable species of the crawling, walking, and slithering varieties could possibly be worthy of notice without the assistance of a big, hulking, silent butler? The Addams Family homestead certainly benefits from the presence of its majordomo in the person of the handsome creature named Lurch.

Lurch made his debut in the *New Yorker* on August 6, 1938, with Morticia and The Thing. He was a bulbous-nosed, scruffy-haired, bearded stiff with huge hands, and we knew immediately that he said little, if anything at all. In retrospect, this version had little distinction from Charles Addams's depictions of cavemen, save the three-piece suit. By the end of 1939, in Lurch's only second appearance, Addams had made him more to his liking and in keeping with his 1963 description as having one opaque eye and scant hair atop a flat head. He is the perfect servant in a household of disrepair. Lurch comes with the house and appears nowhere else in the Addams oeuvre but within the Family setting, whether at home or on an outing. They rely upon him and are grateful for whatever he can do, and he is an accepted and trusted member of the Family, the bonus given to

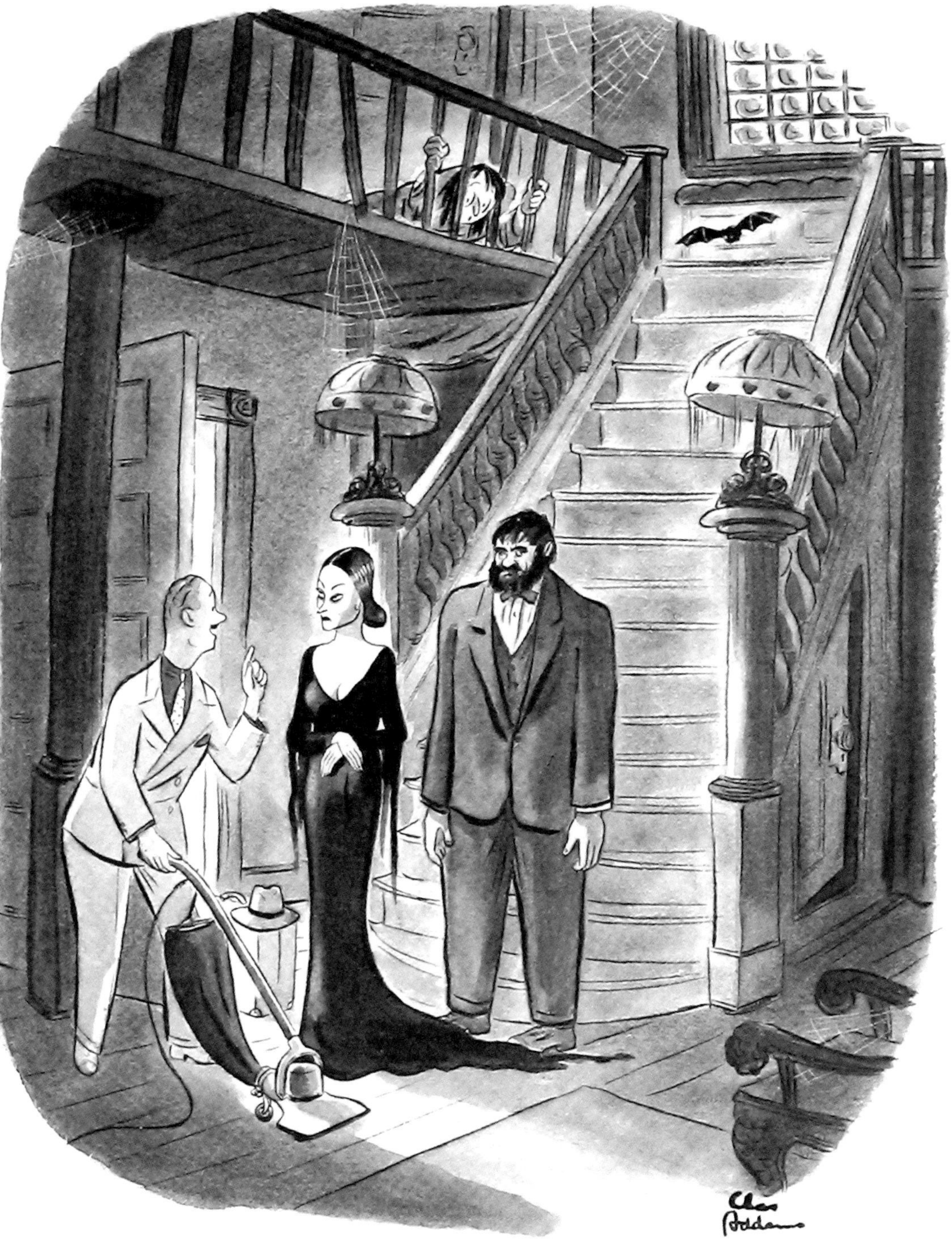
Chas Addams

"Vibrationless, noiseless, and a great time and back saver. No well-appointed home should be without it."

all faithful servants. The Addamses and Lurch have much in common with filmdom's Irene Bullock, her eccentric family, and their savior, Godfrey; with Scarlett O'Hara and her beloved Mammy; and with Bertie Wooster and his irreplaceable Reginald Jeeves.

Of course, Lurch's comparison to Mary Shelley's monster as portrayed by Boris Karloff in the 1931 film *Frankenstein* was inevitable. This was further encouraged by Random House publisher Bennett Cerf's decision to invite Karloff, who was his backyard neighbor in Manhattan, to write the foreword to the first Addams compilation, *Drawn and Quartered* (1942). Karloff thanked Addams for immortalizing him as "the witch's butler." Addams, however, may have honored the actor's appearance but not necessarily "the monster." When pushed by any number of interviewers, Addams agreed with the supposition that his butler was a bit Frankensteinian. But if it is truly necessary to explain Lurch's source rather than simply credit his creator, he more closely resembles a later Karloff character, in the 1932 Universal Studios film *The Old Dark House*. Here Karloff portrayed a great, lumbering mute and alcoholic family butler named Morgan. It must also be noted that two years after Lurch's 1939 appearance, Karloff played Jonathan Brewster, the psychopathic killer in Joseph Kesselring's play *Arsenic and Old Lace,* on the New York stage, a role later reprised by Raymond Massey in the Frank Capra film version, and both actors resembled Lurch.

Like Jonathan Brewster and Morgan, Lurch was not composed of body parts from formerly living persons; he did not have neck bolts to make him animated, and he was born with his own brain. Unlike the Frankenstein monster or Jonathan Brewster or Morgan, Lurch was slow-witted but truly kind. He scared no one until the television adaptation suggested that his appearance should be frightening to the general public. He was so kindly that the drawing of Lurch tethered to the vegetable garden, waving his arms to scare away the crows, was never published. Maybe Charles Addams just did not believe it himself.

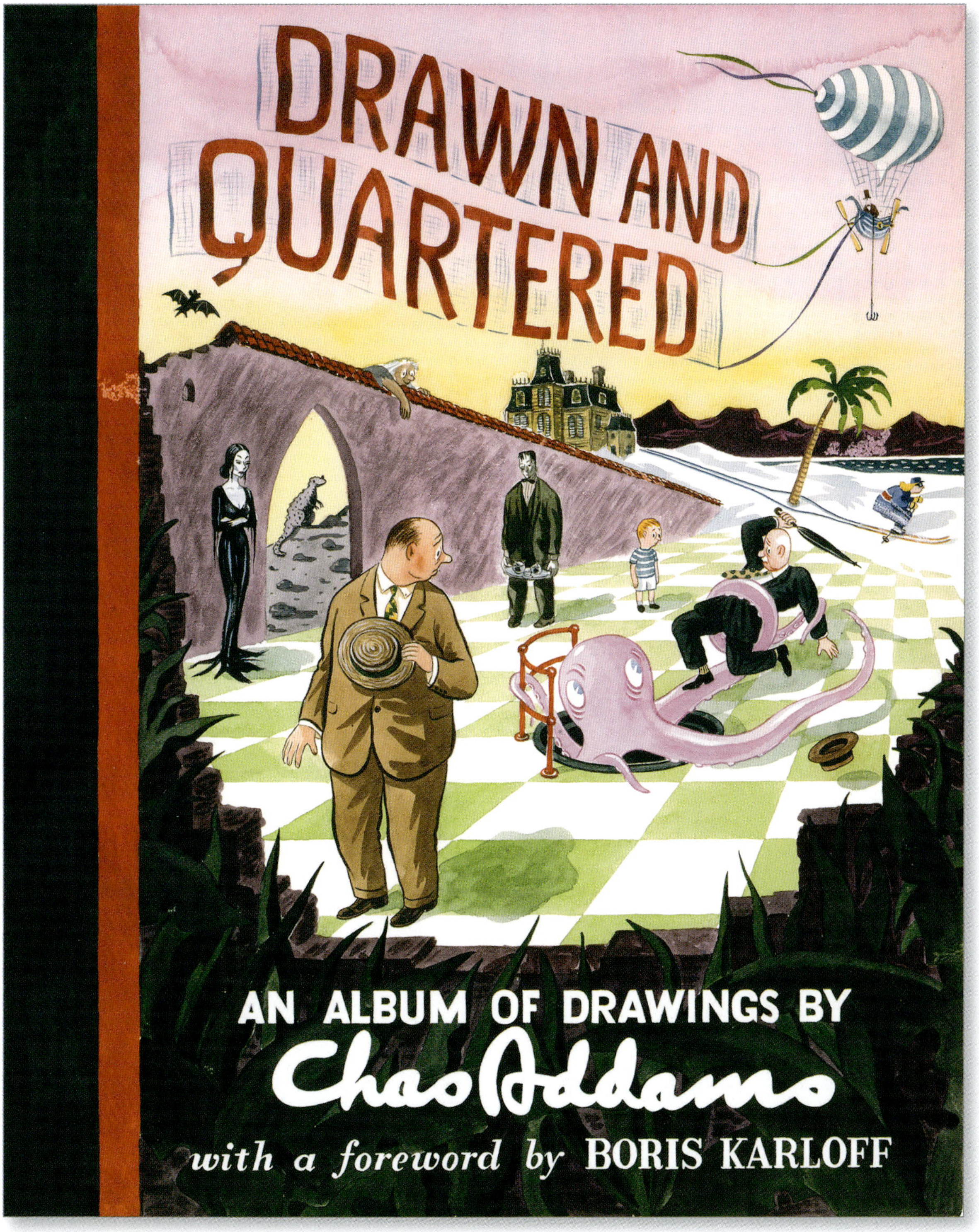
DRAWN AND QUARTERED
AN ALBUM OF DRAWINGS BY
Chas Addams
with a foreword by BORIS KARLOFF

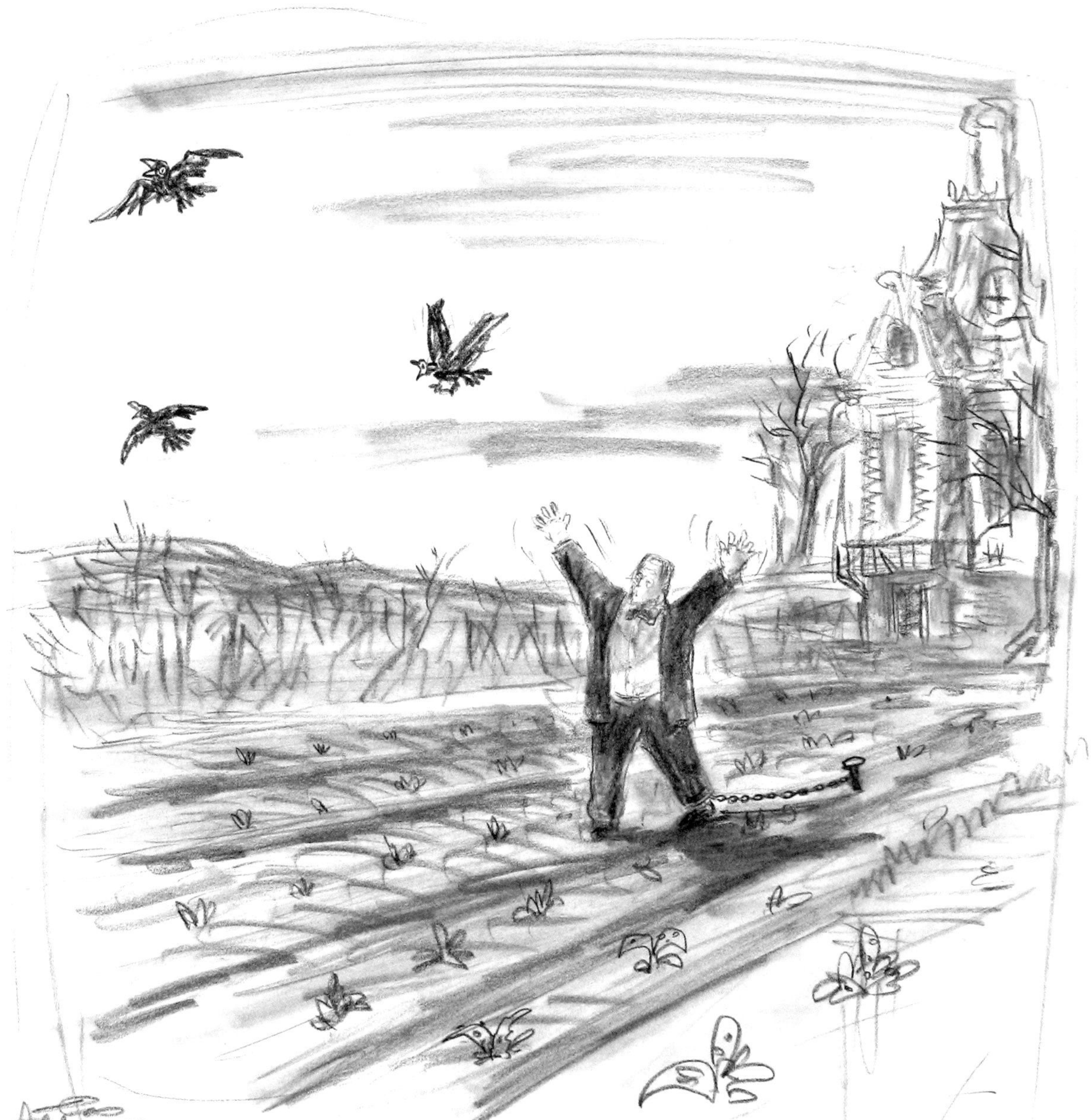

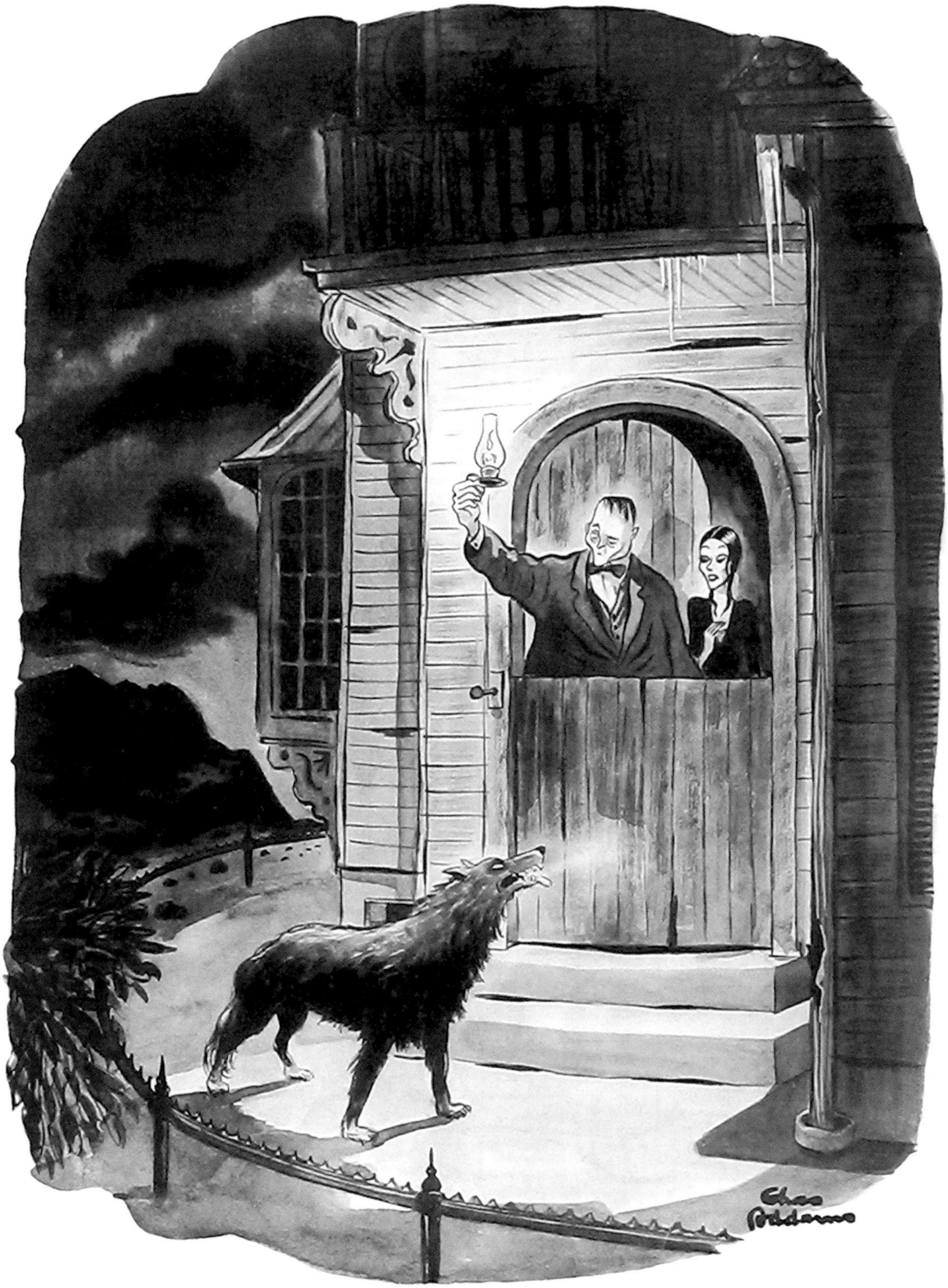
Chas Addams

"Is it anyone we know?"

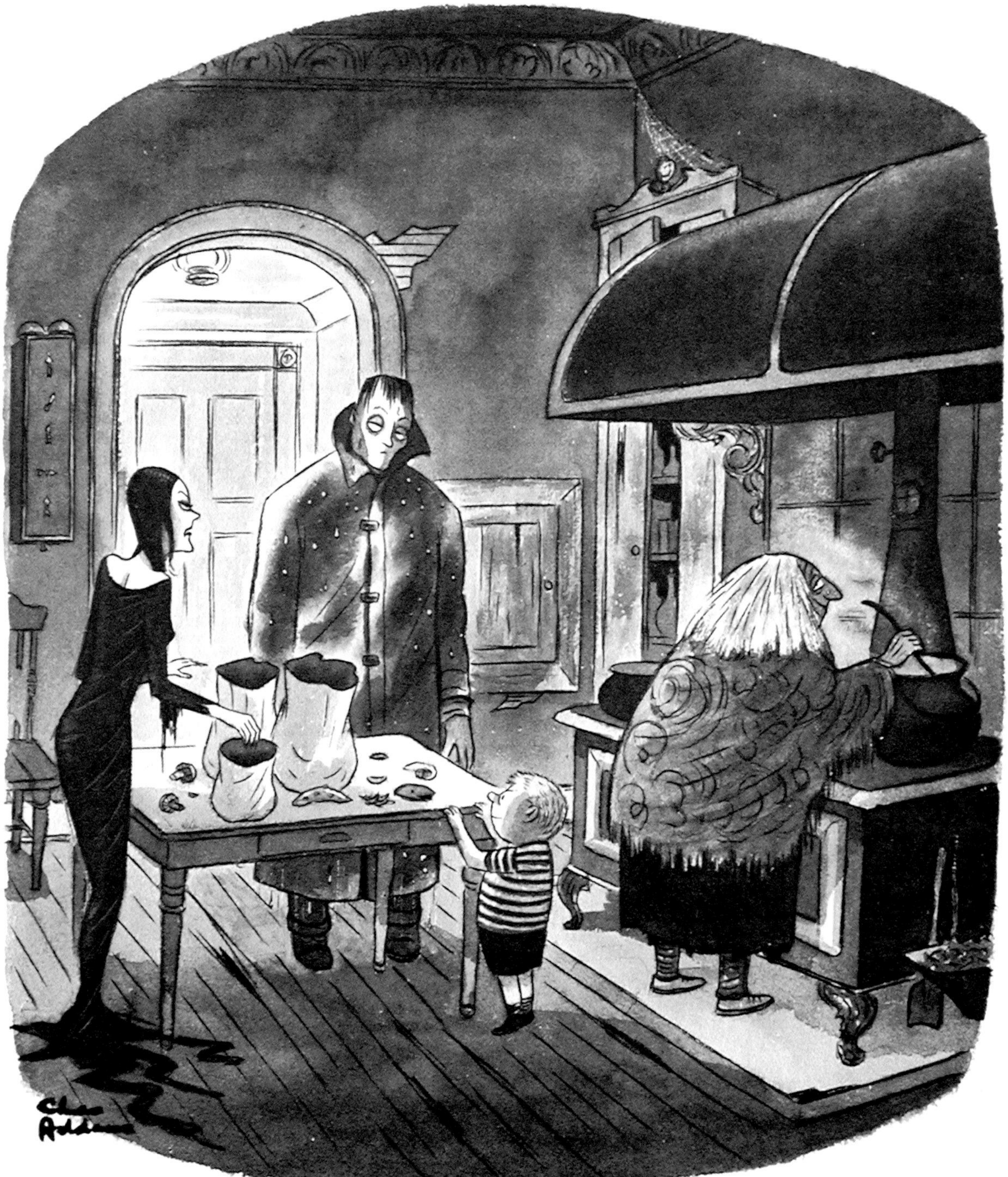

"You forgot the eye of newt."

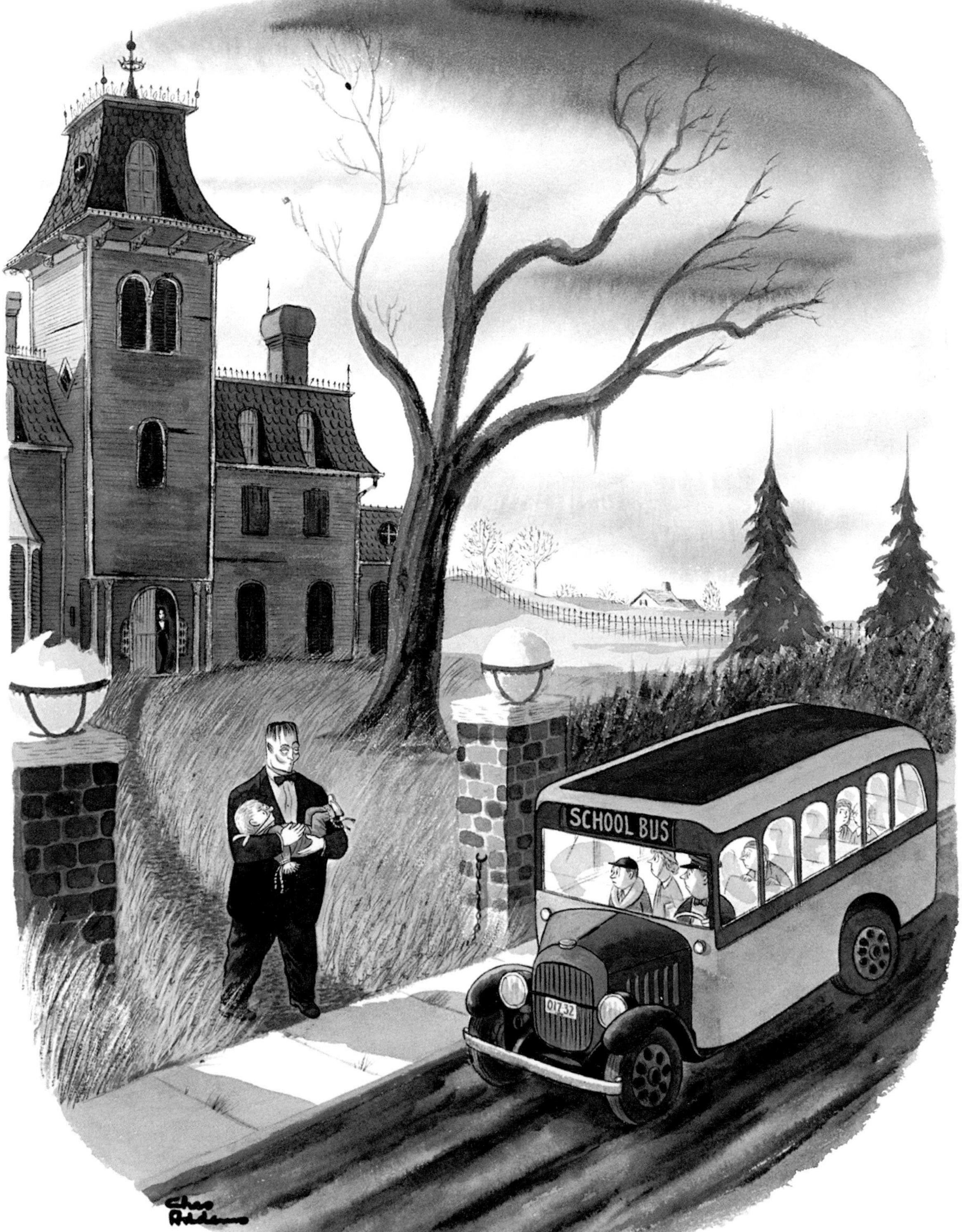
SCHOOL BUS
017.32
Chas Addams

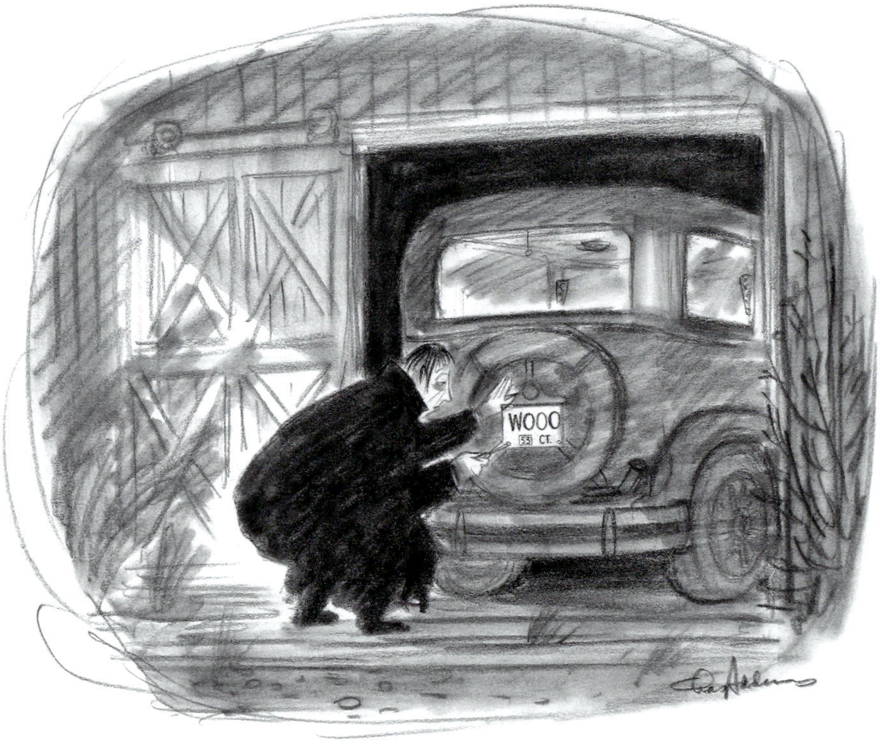
WOOO

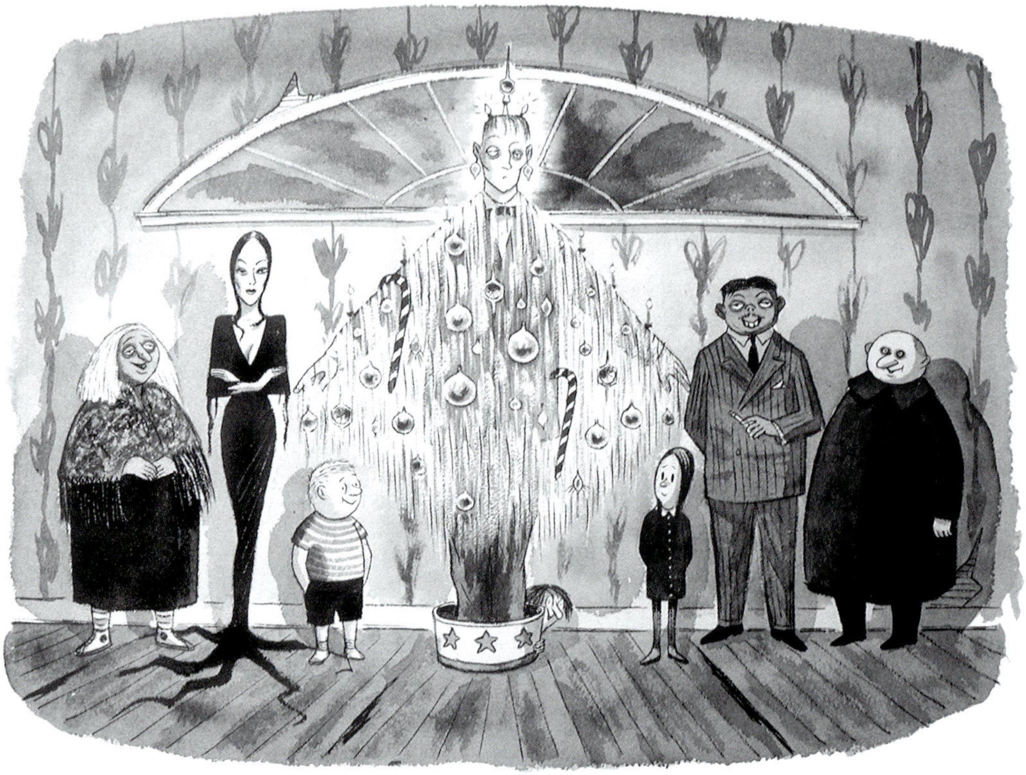

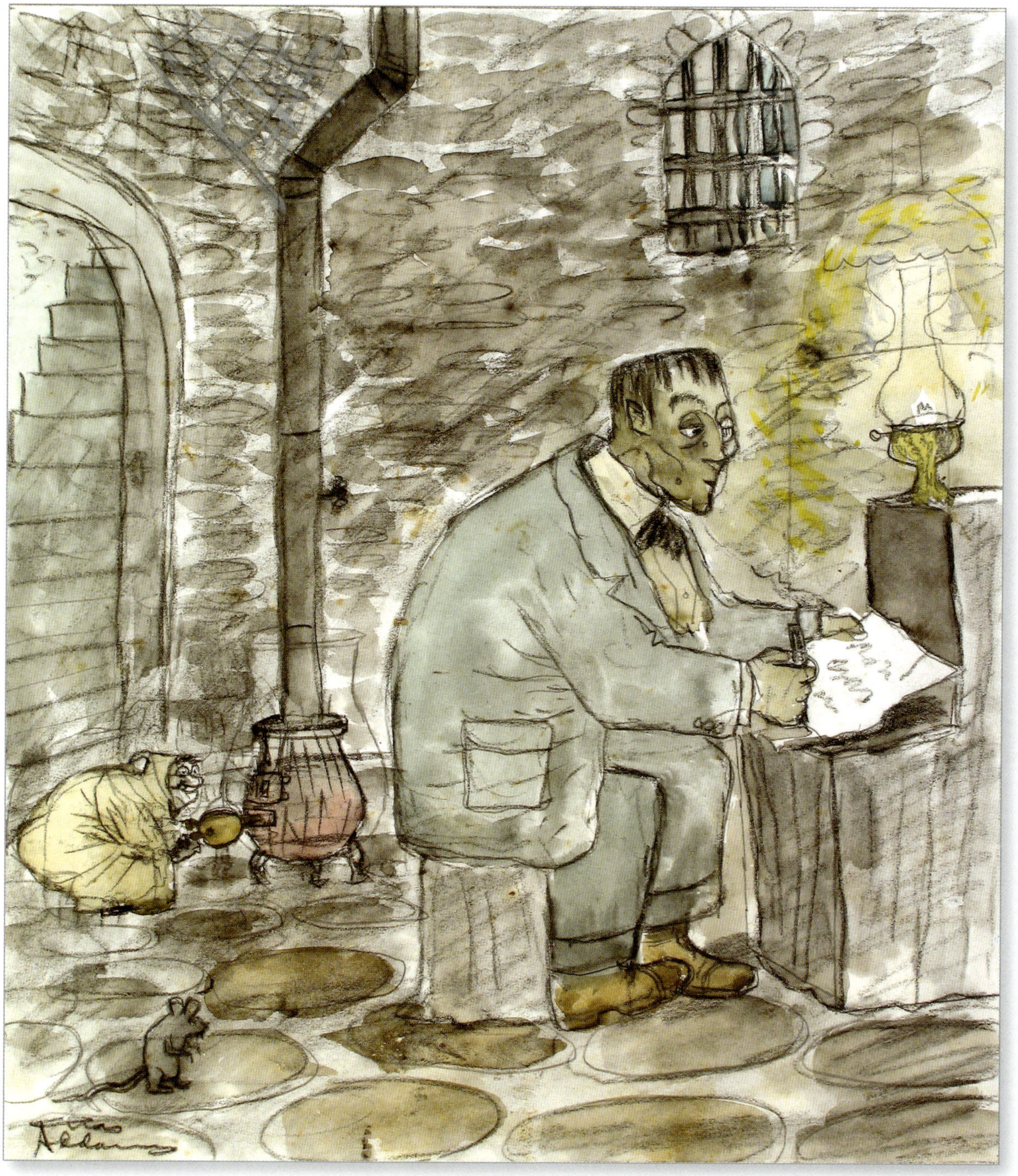

GRANNY FRUMP (A.K.A. GRANDMA FRUMP)

This disrespectful old hag is the mother of Gomez (husband of Morticia). She willingly helps with the dishes, cheats at solitaire and is thoroughly dishonest. She, too, is a favorite with the children and will make them cookies in the shape of bats, skulls and bones. Good humored about all and can be garrulous. The complexion is dark, the hair is white and frizzy and uncombed. She has a light beard and a large mole. She wears a shawl on all occasions, thick socks and fleece slippers under a bombazine skirt.

Chas Addams

THE hag at the Dutch door of an imposing mansion in true Addams dereliction, from whom Morticia requests a cup of cyanide in 1941, is the character who becomes Granny Frump. She technically joined the Family with her second appearance, on the cover of Charles Addams's *Monster Rally* (Simon & Schuster) in 1950. But the unpublished drawing, circa 1950—captioned "Oh, good! They're home" and showing the characters who would become Uncle Fester and Granny Frump entering the driveway to the Addams house while vultures circle above—suggests that Addams had not yet decided that either character was to live within the mansion walls. Granny Frump was confirmed as an in-house member by the cartoon in the October 16, 1954, issue of the *New Yorker*. In it she, Pugsley, and Morticia witness Wednesday throwing a tantrum in her bedroom; the caption reads, "Oh, she's furious because they put her on the honor roll at school" (page 89). We do not see Granny again until the summer of 1958, when she again wears the official costume she is never without from that point onward, the paisley shawl over the bombazine skirt. Addams often claimed that she slightly resembled his "Grandma Spear in the early morning—just before breakfast," but any possible physical resemblance is where the similarity stops, as he adored his maternal grandmother.

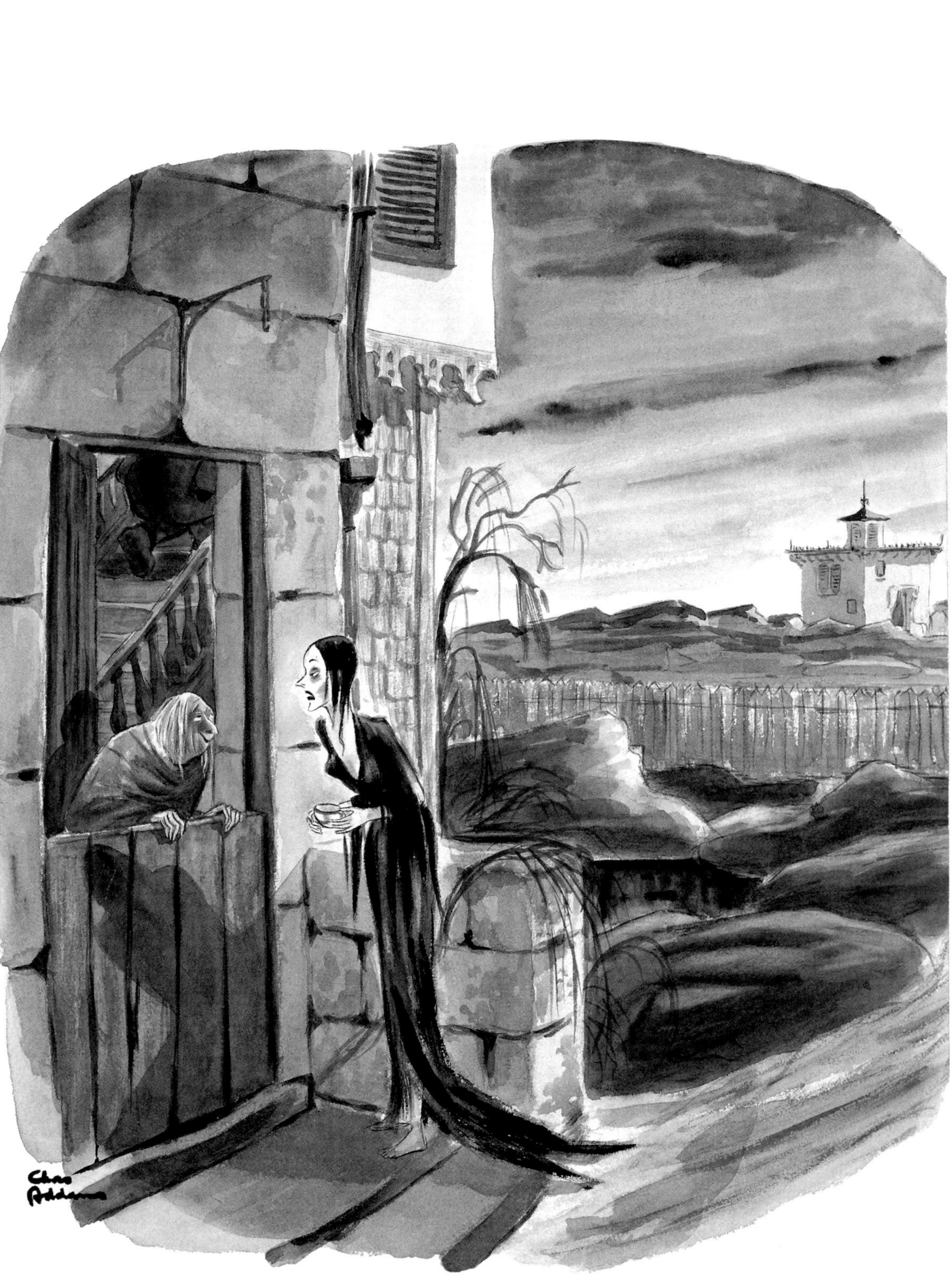
Chas Addams

"May I borrow a cup of cyanide?"

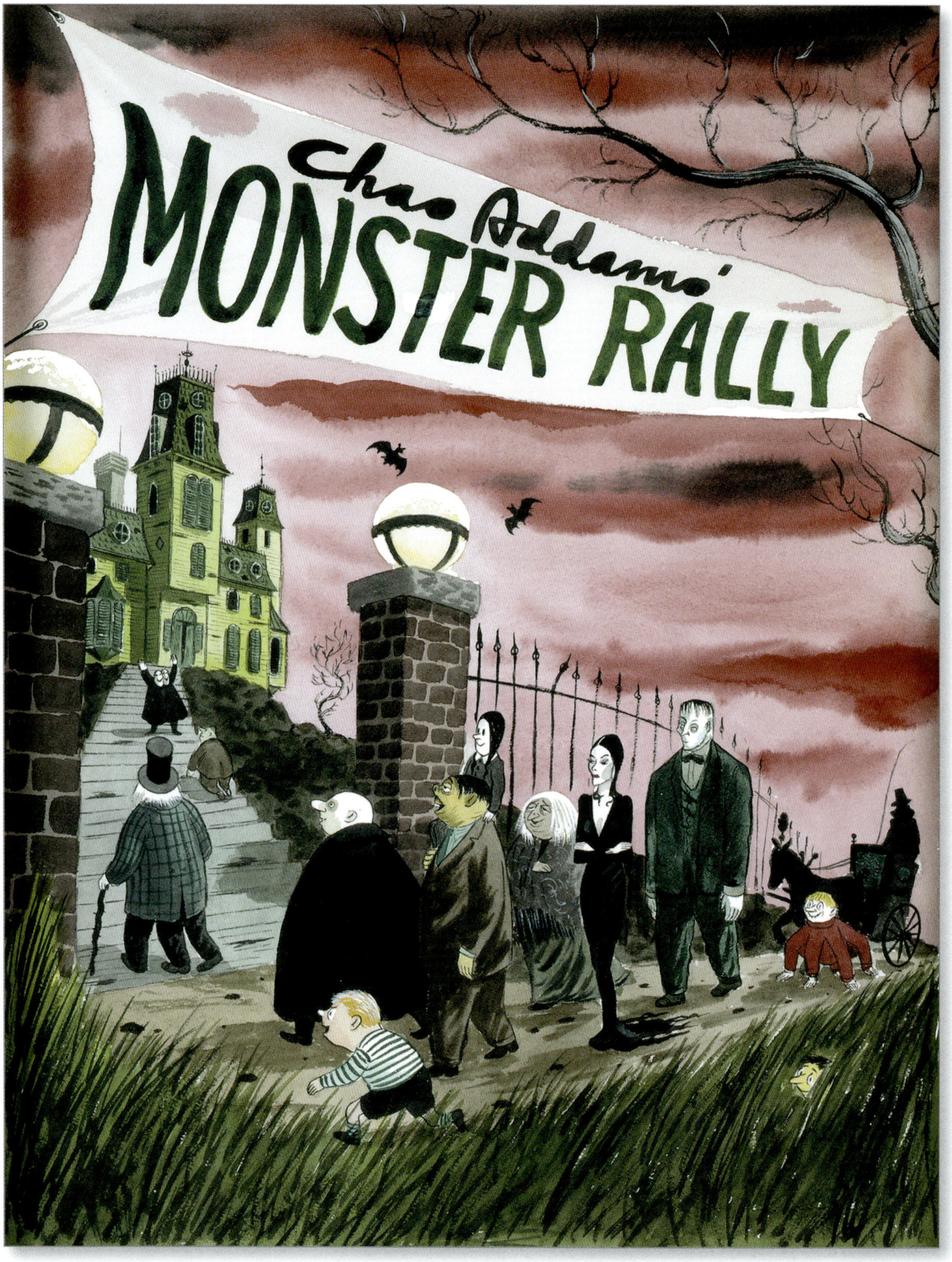
Chas Addams'
MONSTER RALLY

Charles Addams drew many, many witches, both sweet and wicked, but he drew only one Granny Frump, and she possessed both traits. As had been the case with Addams's remembrances of his own grandmother when she lived with his family, Granny's duties to the Family mainly consisted of cooking, not as a job but as her way of feeling included. Though no beauty, Grandma was the family's embodiment of the fifteenth century's Lucrezia Borgia, in her expertise with sweet poisons, and of the nineteenth century's "Typhoid Mary" Mallon, surely capable of spreading disease and causing a quarantine. In a 1948 drawing it is even suggested that Granny is ageless: we witness her sewing in the Addams Family attic, using as a dress form the medieval torture device known as the iron maiden—which is in her likeness. We also see her spending time with the children, telling stories and baking cookies—in the shapes of bats, snakes, and skulls and crossbones—two perfectly innocent grandmotherly delights. And the children respond to her well.

The "f" in Frump was capitalized by Charles Addams in his 1963 character description, so one would assume he intended that to be her last name rather than an adjective to suggest her demeanor. This would lead one to think of her son as Gomez Frump, but when the 1964 television program was to be named, *The Addams Family* was the chosen title. So, once again, creative license is responsible for changing the intentions of the artist and establishing the production team's interpretation of the material as fact. The producers rewrote Morticia as Morticia Addams, née Frump, and created characters for her mother, Hester Frump, and her grandmother, Grandma Frump, also referred to as Grandmama within the series. In the Addams drawings, Granny Frump was positioned as Morticia's mother-in-law, with a dark complexion not unlike her son's and a short, squat frame, again not unlike her son's. This does not really change Addams's characterization of the grandmother figure, but when reviewing Addams's cartoons it is useful to note that the relationship between Granny Frump and Morticia was one of marriage, not blood.

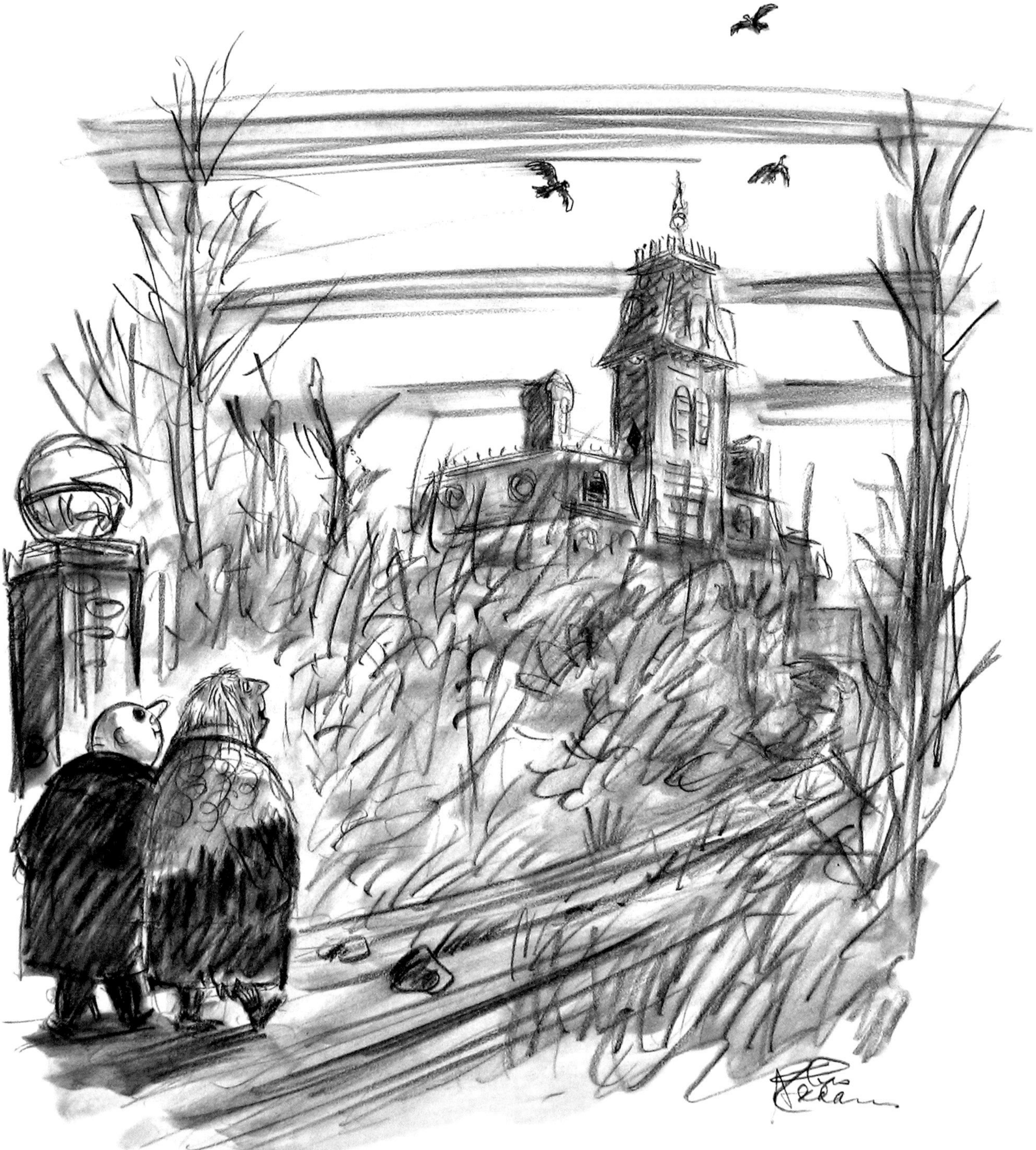

"Oh, good! They're home."

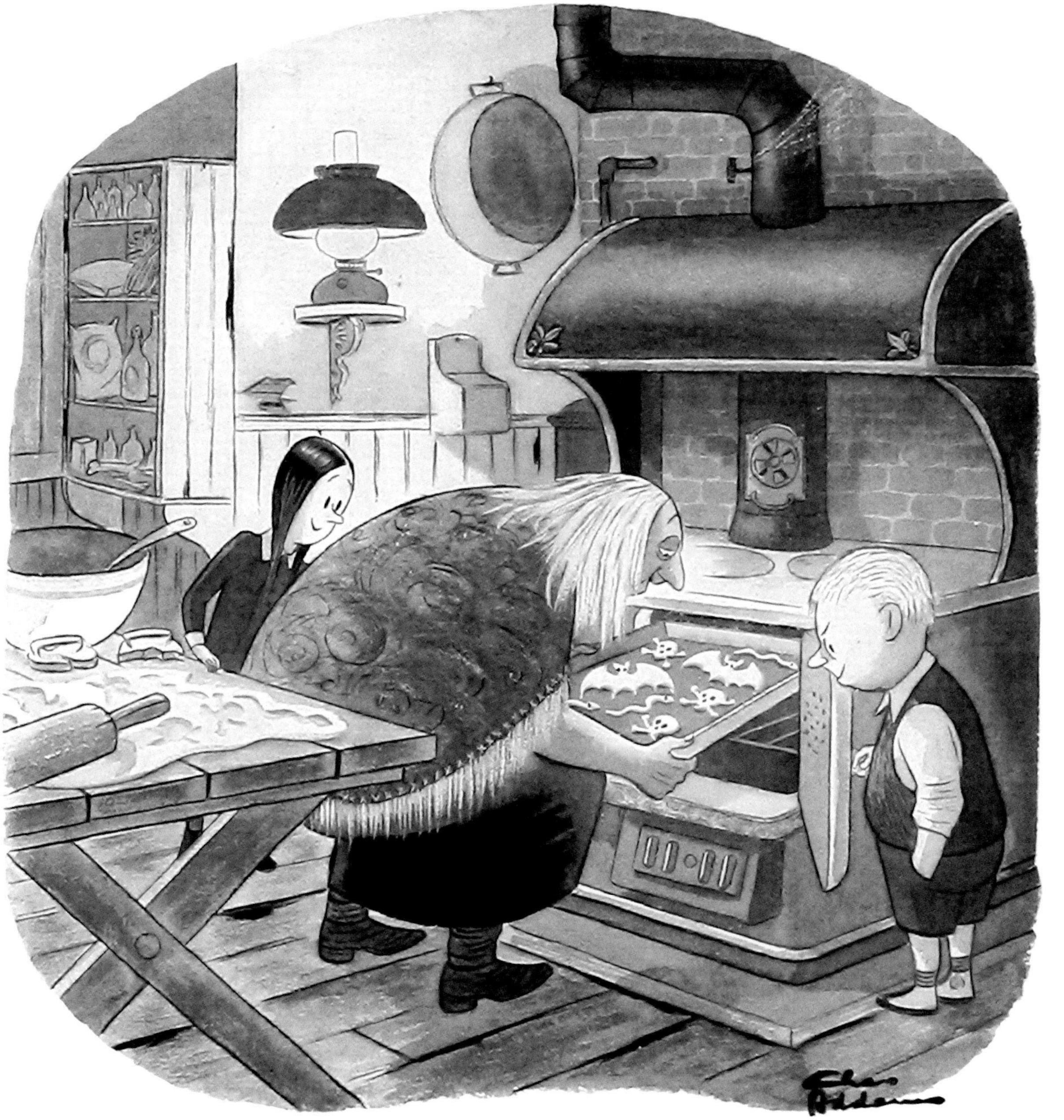

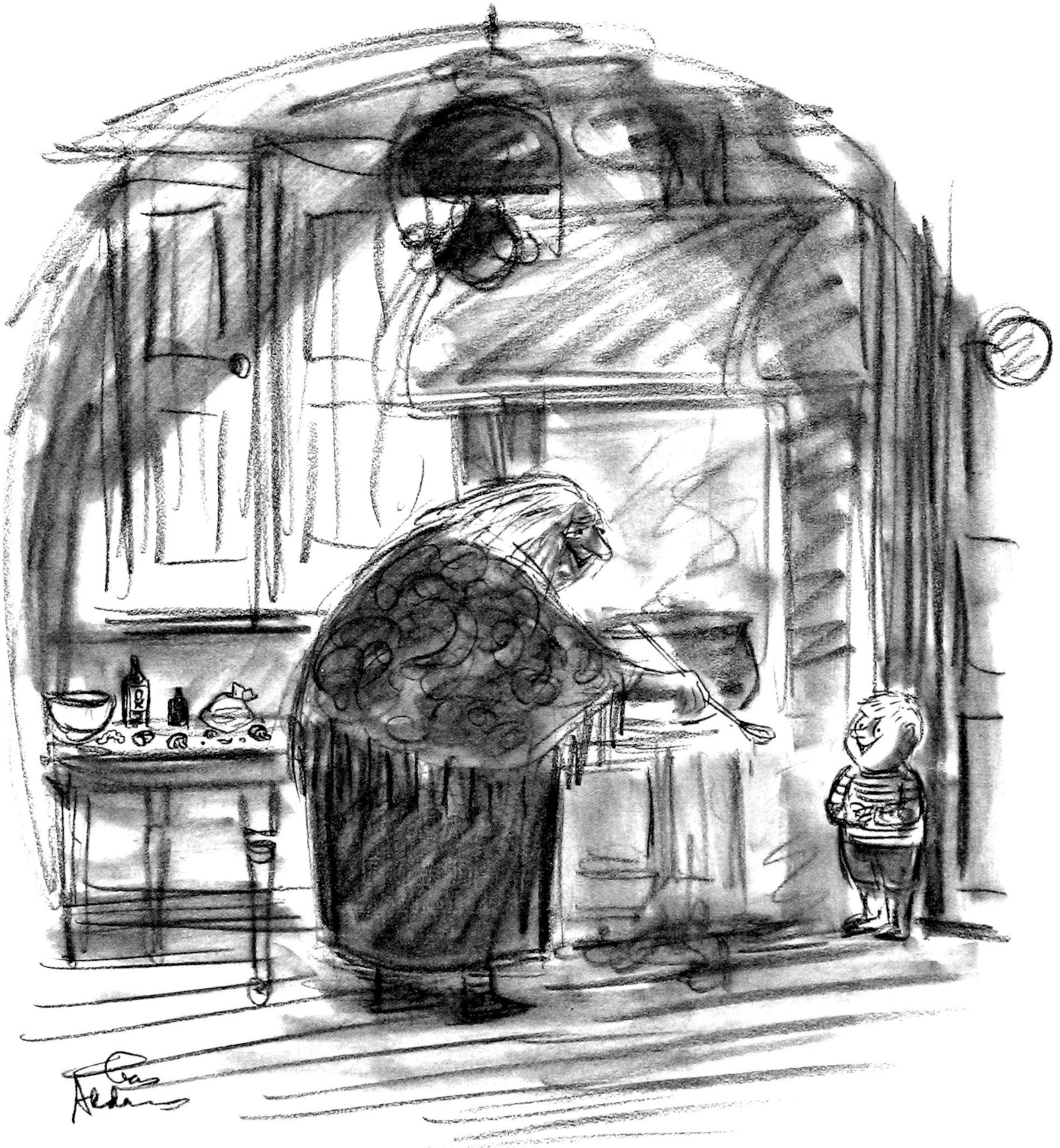

"All right, all right. Now you can lick the spoon."

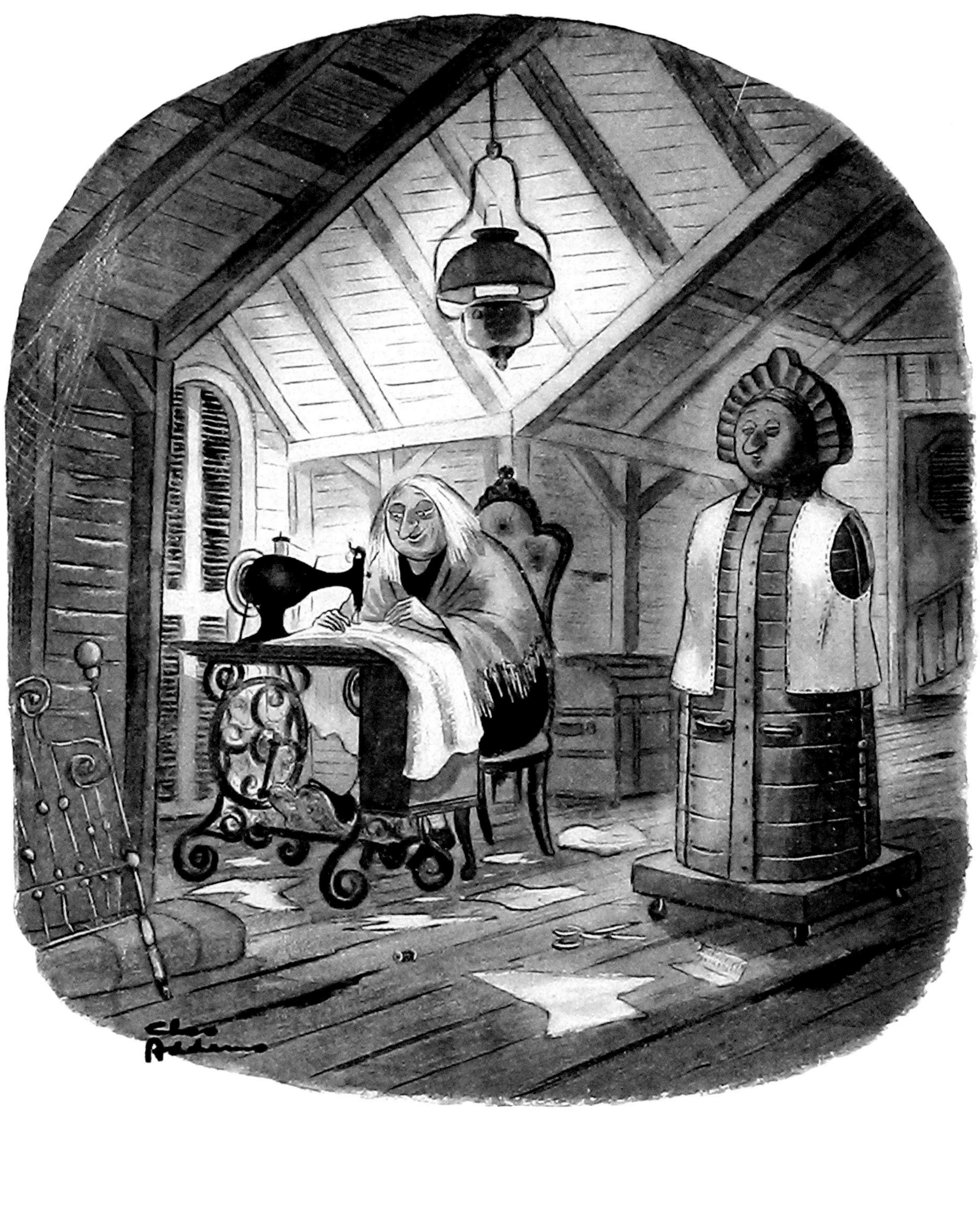
Chas Addams

OIL OF NEWT
Scruples. III
TOAD VENOM
drops XI
POWDER. SKINK
TOMB DUST

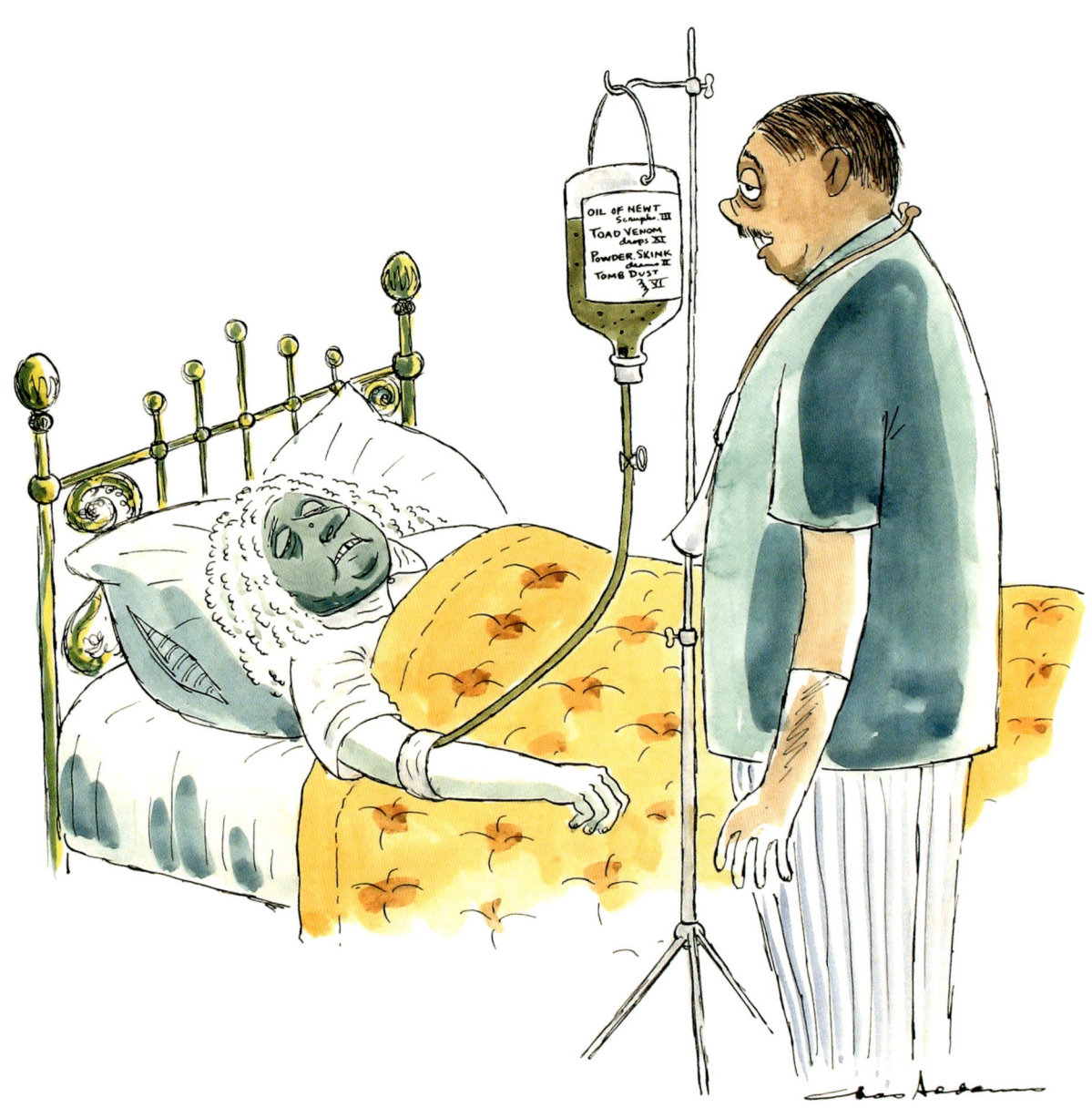

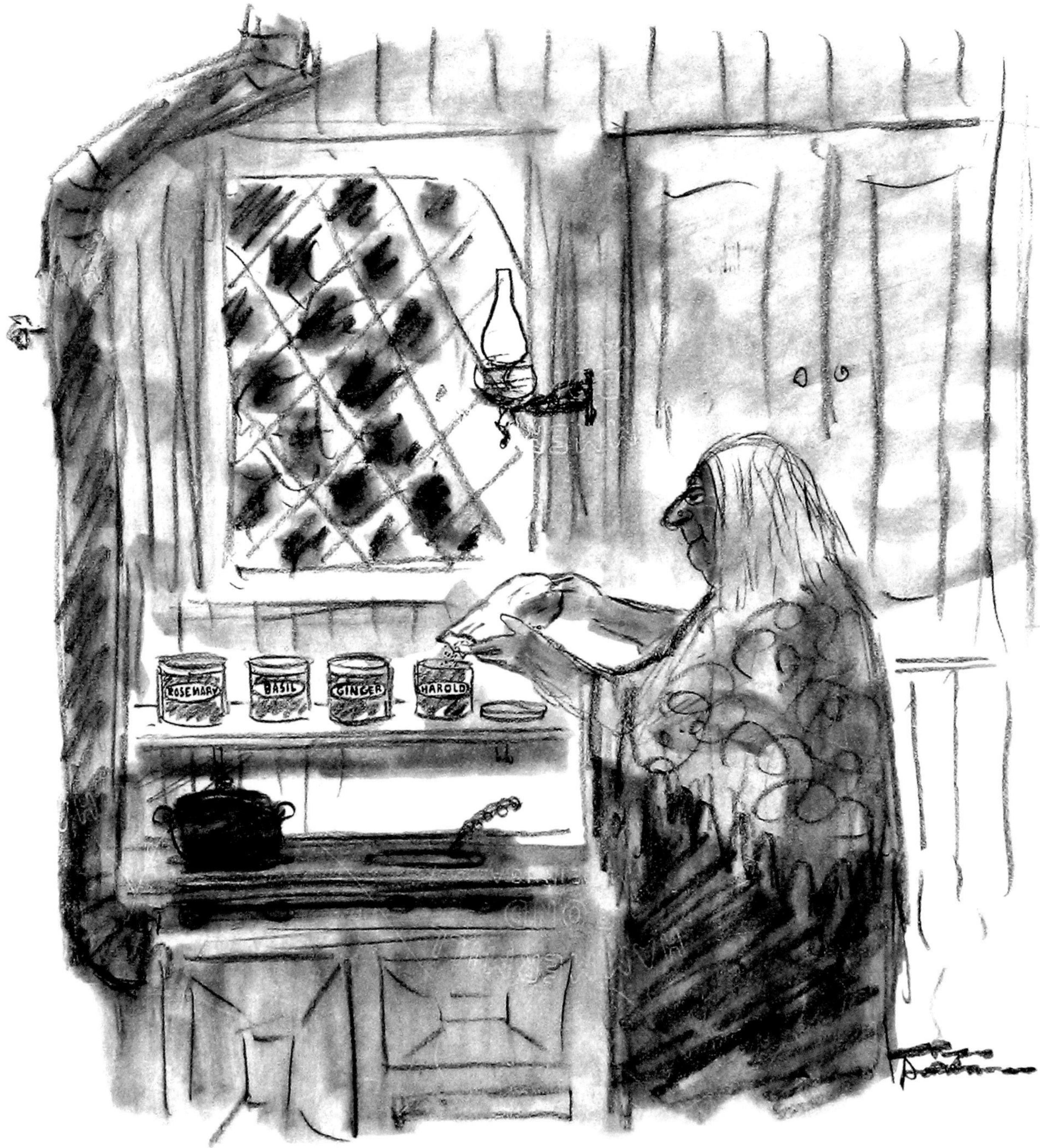
ROSEMARY
BASIL
GINGER
HAROLD

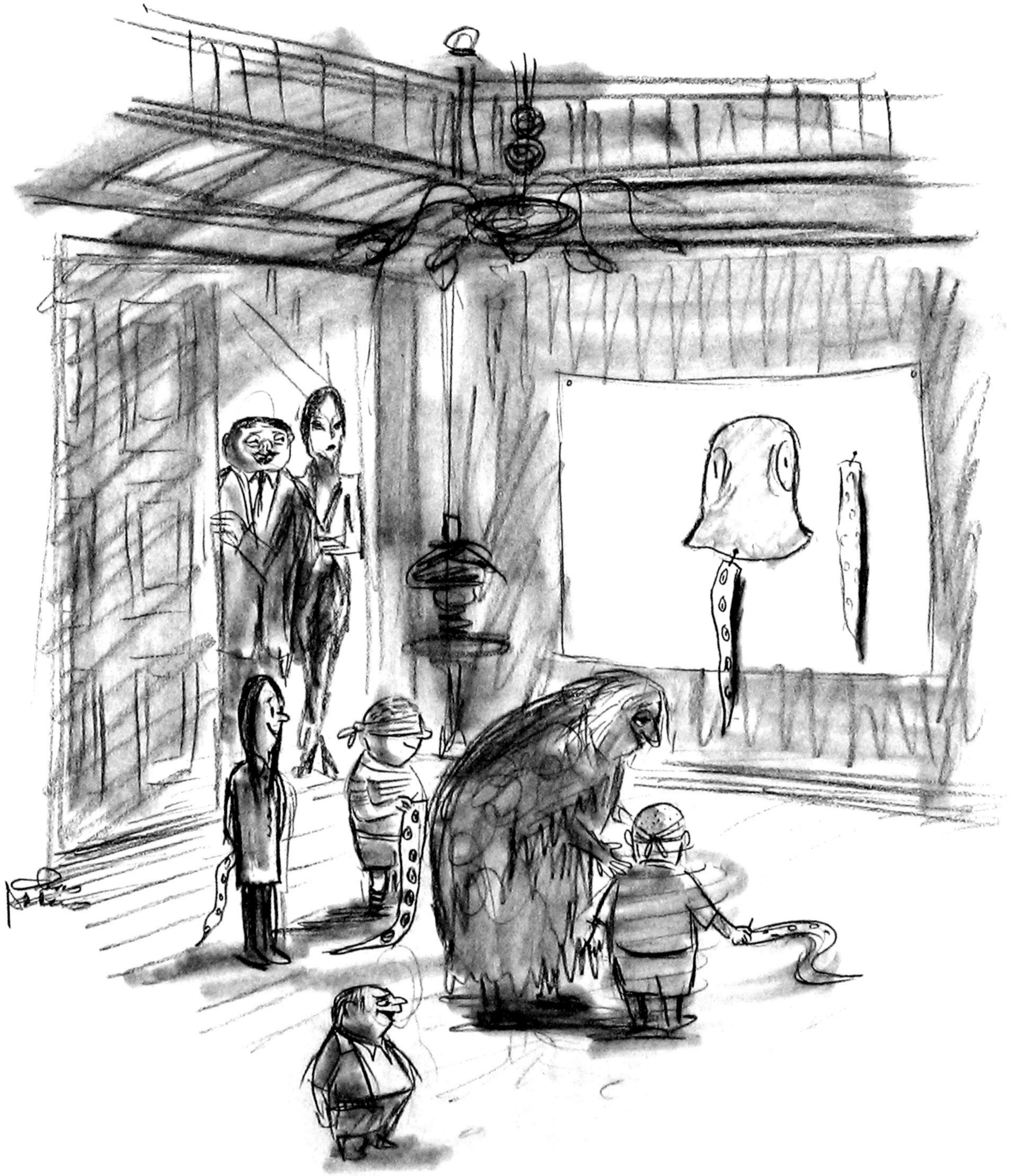

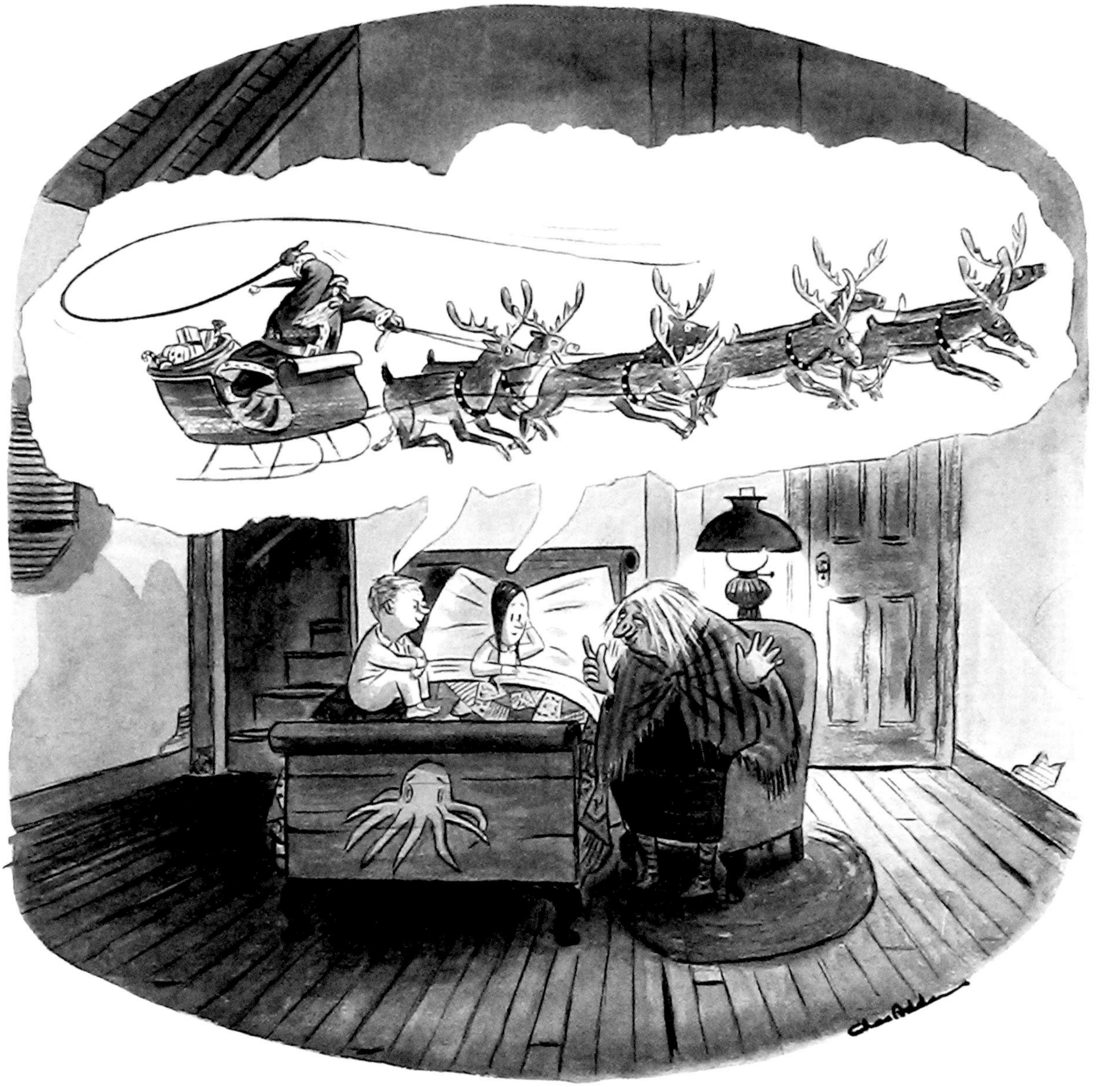

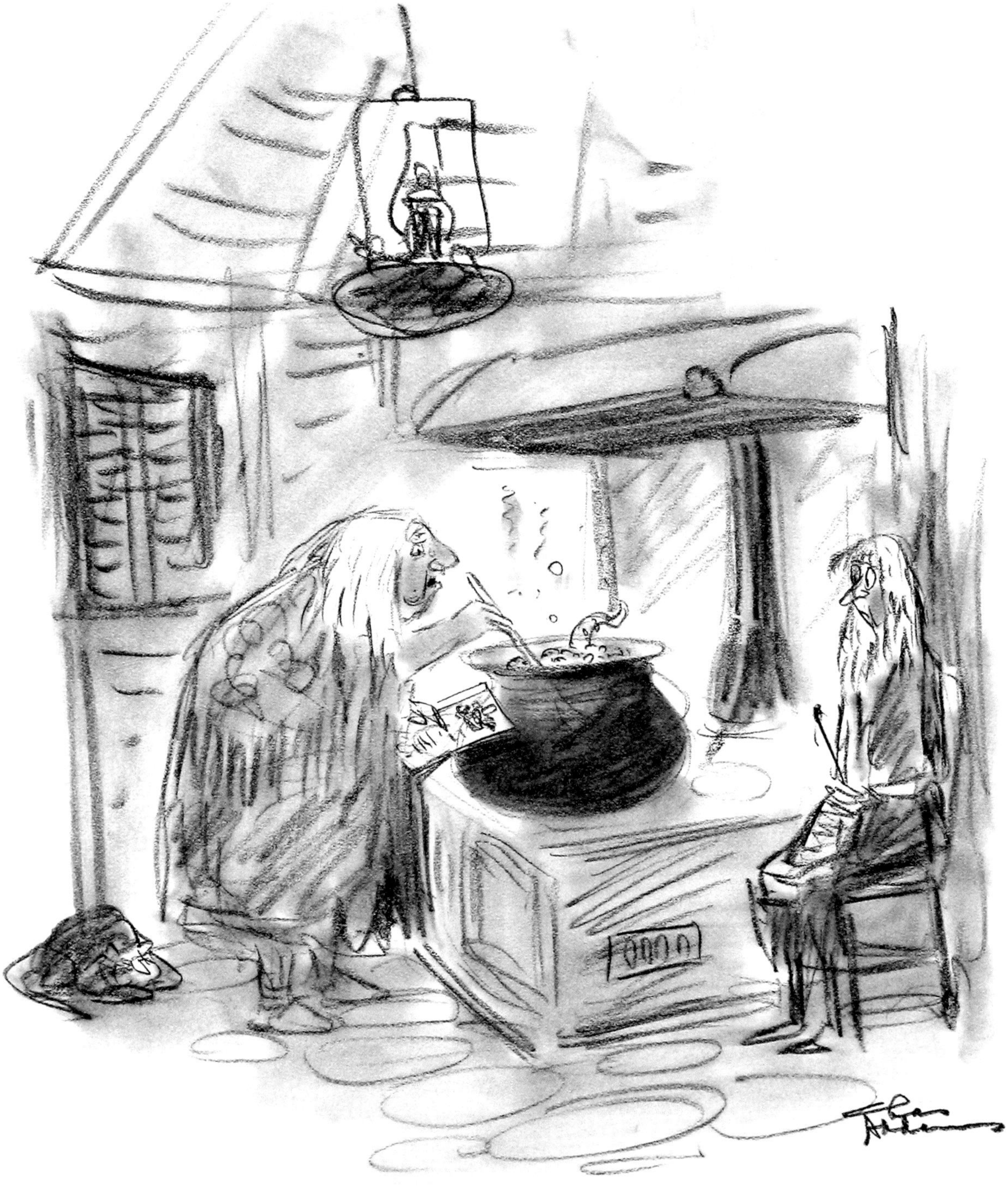

"The recipes never come out the way they look in pictures."

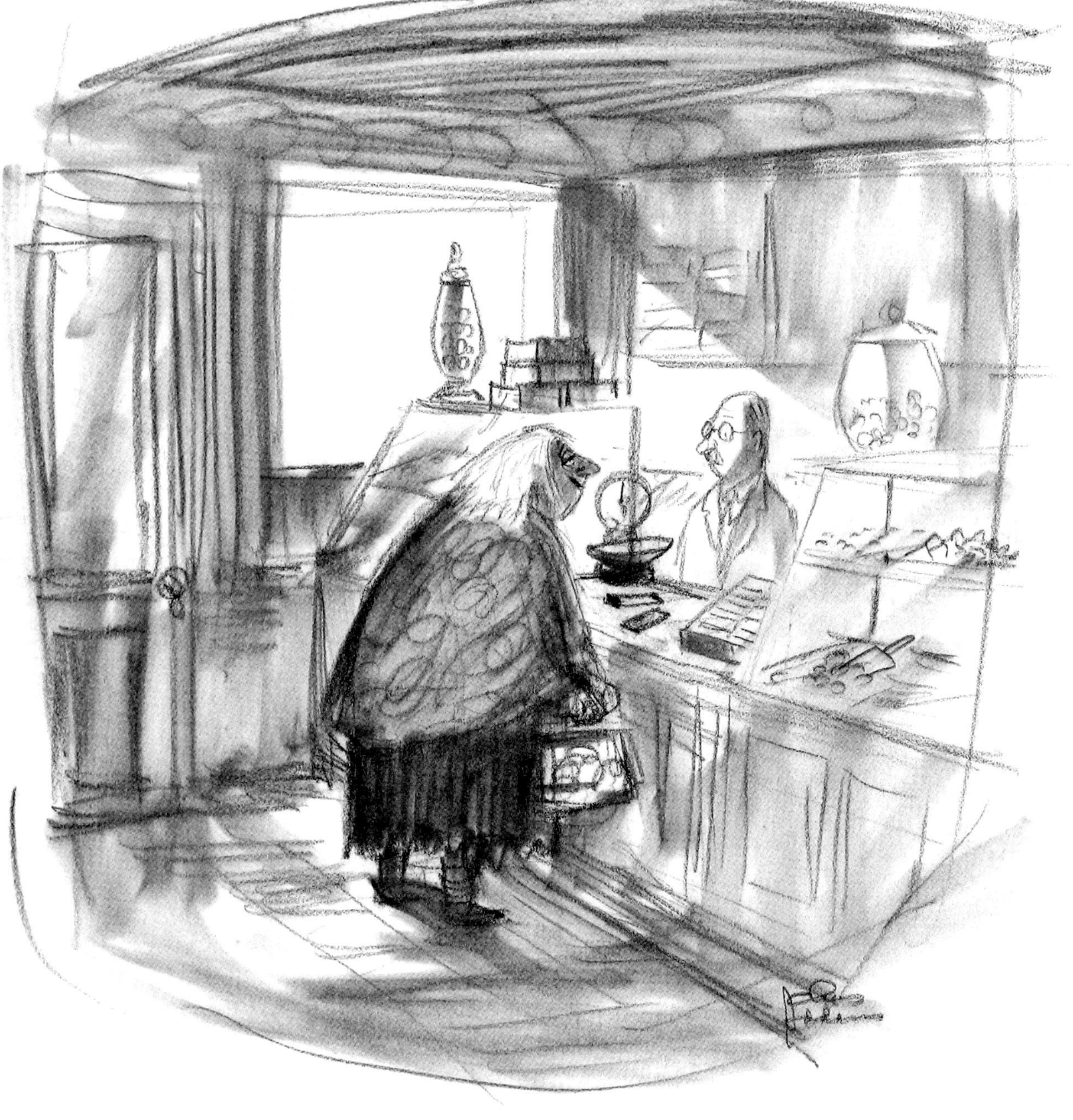

"Don't you have the chocolate bars with the bitter almonds?"

"Then, the dragon gobbled up the handsome young prince
and his lovely bride and lived happily ever after."

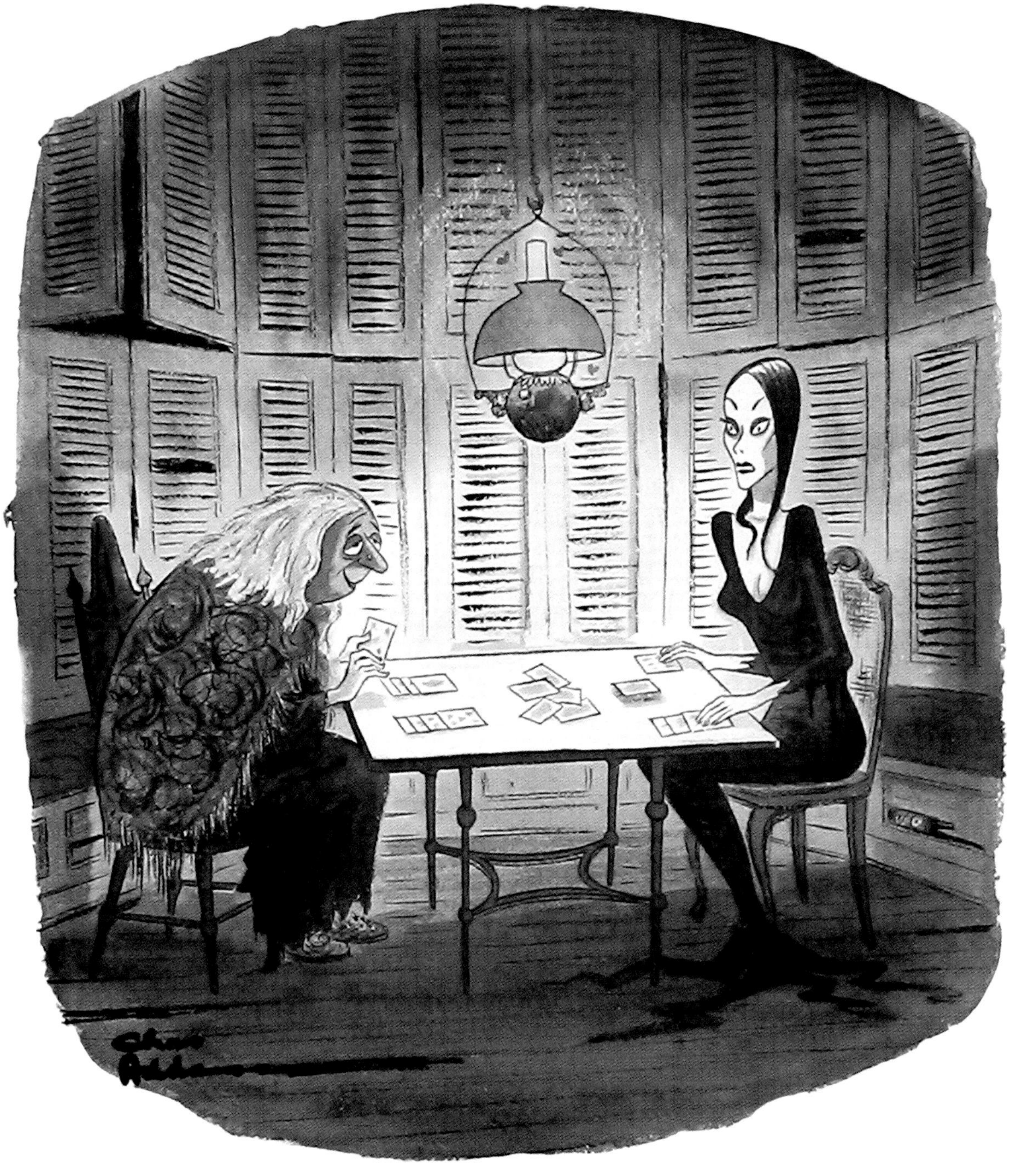

"Grandmother! You're not cheating!"

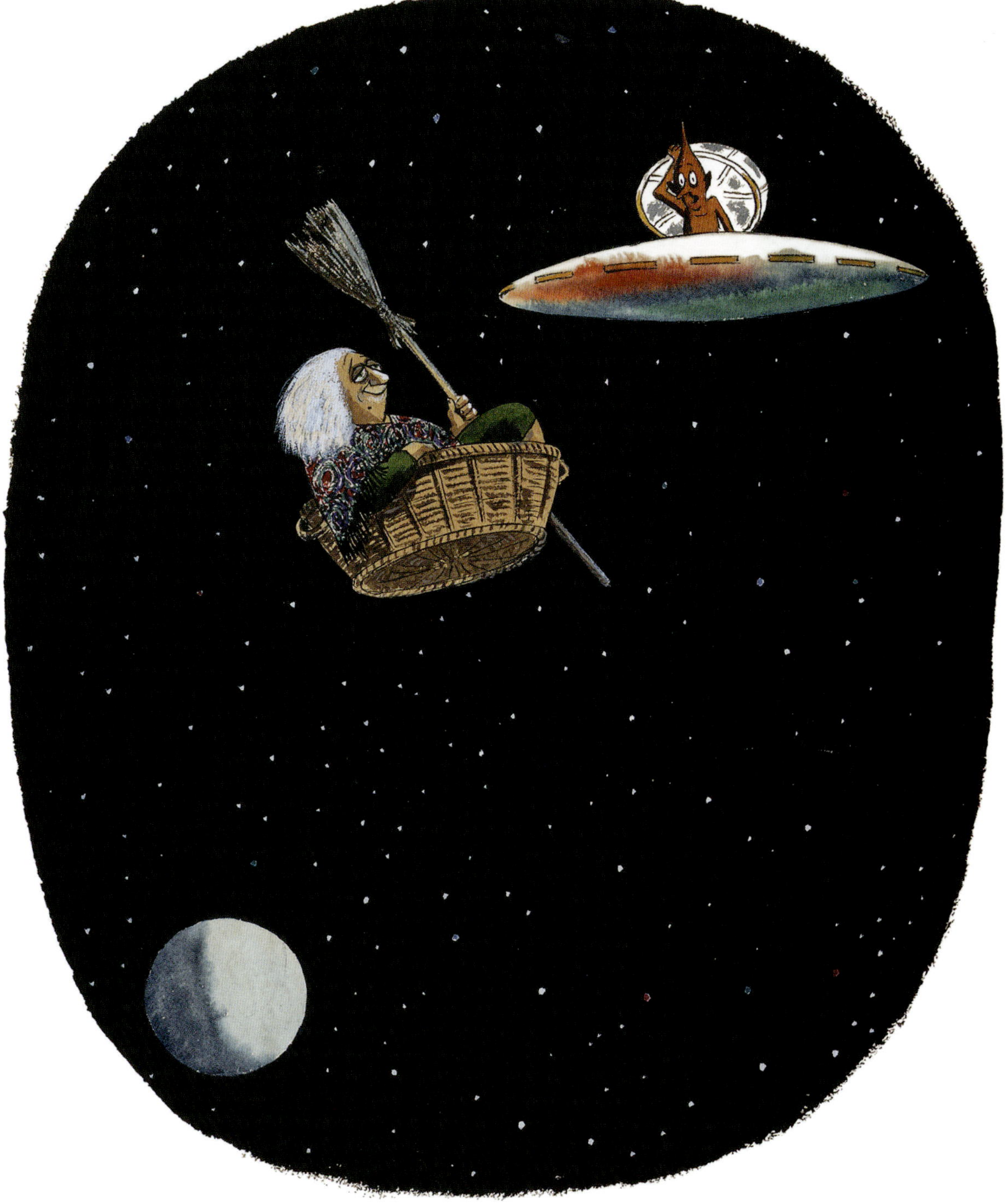

Uncle Fester

. . . is incorrigible and, except for the good nature of the family and the ignorance of the police, would ordinarily be under lock and key. The complexion, like [that of] Morticia, is dead white, the eyes are pig-like and deeply imbedded, circled unhealthily in black—no teeth and absolutely hairless. He likes to fish but usually employs dynamite or any other unfair means. He keeps falcons on the roof which he uses for hunting. His one costume is a black greatcoat with an enormous collar— summer and winter. He is fat with pudgy little hands and feet.

—Chas Addams

BASED on the work centered on this character's development alone, Uncle Fester—and the diversified specimens he was before being named as a member of the Family—has the most prevalent position within the Addams oeuvre. The character, who joined The Addams Family long after the seven other integral members, had his first incarnation in the January 18, 1941, issue of the *New Yorker* as the desperate husband of a simple, dowdy wife. He stands at the New York Central Railroad ticket office in Grand Central Station and quietly requests from the dismayed clerk "A round trip and a one-way to Ausable Chasm." With the exception of the dark circles around his eyes and the off-putting sideward glance, the drawing appears almost sweet, but the caption confirms the uneasiness in the pits of our stomachs. This was long before Charles Addams's first marriage, so no biographical inference is necessary—it was simply a wickedly funny thought.

Although he claimed that he named Uncle Fester as was befitting "a rotten guy," Addams drew him as quite likable, even within the context of his dastardly activities. He was never as bumbling as the television series or films made him out to be. If Addams intended for Fester to be related to anyone, it seems as though he was leaning a bit toward Morticia, if only in their similar complexions. But Fester may not have been related to the Family at all. It was, and perhaps still is, very common practice for upper-class parents to refer to, and to

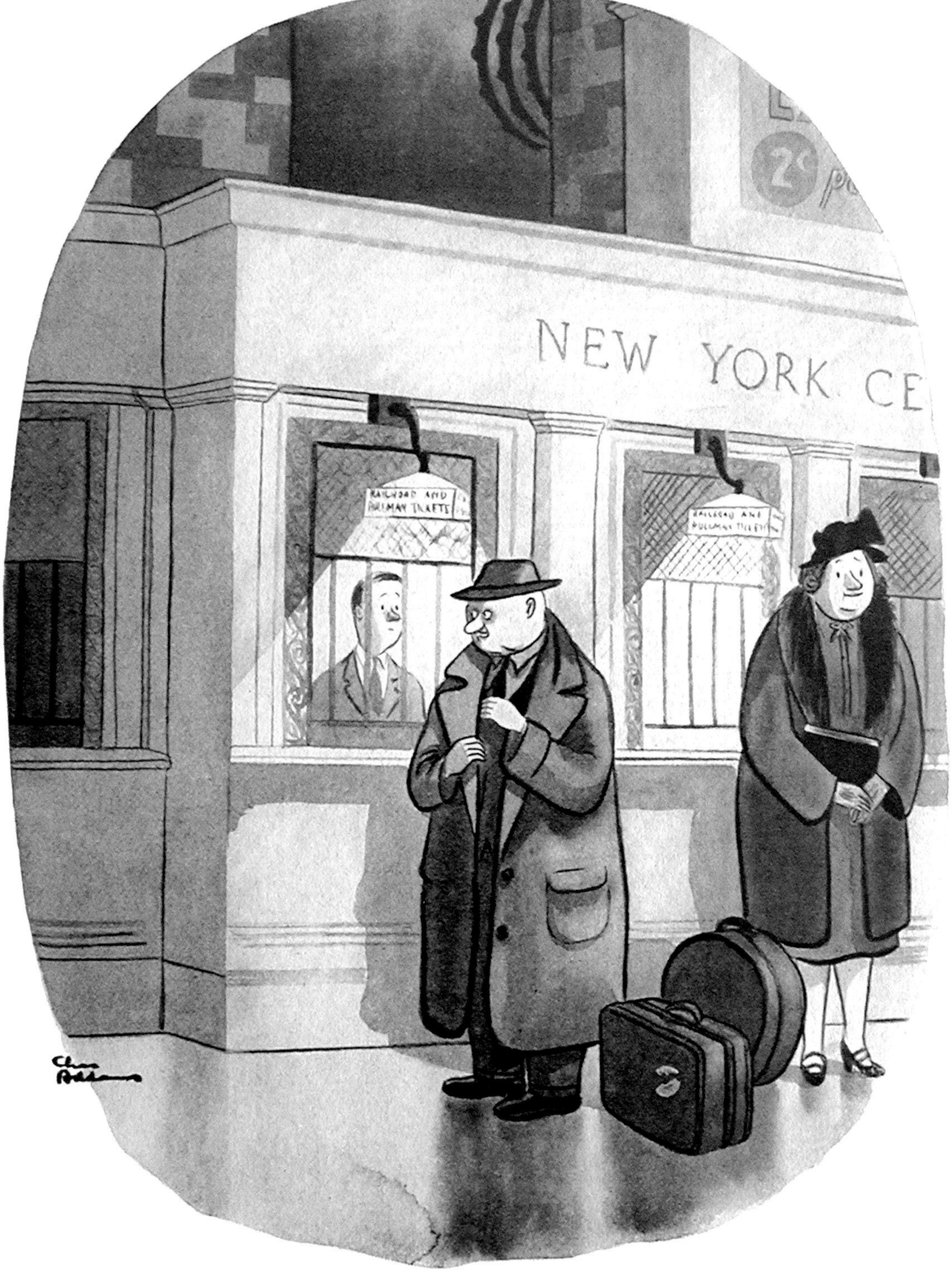
NEW YORK CE

"A round trip and a one-way to Ausable Chasm."

nickname, for their children's sakes, their best friends as "Uncle" and "Aunt" or "Oncle" and "Tante," and this practice could have alleviated the need to explain any lineage for Fester whatsoever. For all we know, he could have been Granny Frump's brother or brother-in-law, thus making him a great-uncle.

On a number of occasions, Addams stated that Fester was "like me—or how I feel I look—with a bit more hair." In fact, Charles Addams was Uncle Fester's alter ego. He was the smart one, the one who created him, the one who put thoughts and ideas in his large head, but it was really all the "Uncle Festers" who ran the Addams show. Addams gave them the presence to carry out his own ingenious mischievousness. Charles Addams was a man of few words, and Uncle Fester—the name hereinafter referring not only to the individual who *was* Uncle Fester but also to all the characters who eventually became him and those who appeared outside the Family— speaks through his actions, not words. Uncle Fester has ears and a nose similar to those of Charles Addams. Fester is round and has darkly circled eyes, whereas Addams had a virile build and sparkling, happily squinted eyes. And, in contrast to Fester's pudgy little hands and feet, Charles Addams had great hands, strong enough to pull back a crossbow cable yet gentle enough to escort a date onto the dance floor.

Uncle Fester appears as the only laughing man in an audience of weeping viewers in the March 23, 1946, issue of the *New Yorker,* wearing what Charles Addams refers to as his "greatcoat." Eight months later, in the Uncle Fester–like persona's second and final speaking line, he appears in a liquor store in a near-ankle-length overcoat and a hat pulled down to his eyes, carrying a bag of cement, and requests from the blank-faced proprietor, who clearly knows his Edgar Allan Poe, "A cask of Amontillado, please." He returns in 1949 as a fiend releasing his falcon from a city rooftop in hopes of retrieving a few birds from an unsuspecting rooftop pigeon keeper. In 1950 Uncle Fester makes his real debut as one of the Family on the cover of the Simon & Schuster publication of Addams's third compilation book, *Monster Rally*. All through Addams's fifty-five years of being published, Uncle Fester continued to appear as a Family member while moonlighting as a counterculture figure in the form of an electronics fiend, a subway train driver for the very scary "Z" line, a diner at an automat in New York City, owner of a one-man armed submarine, a dungeon jailer, a toxicology enthusiast, both a garden cultivator and killer, the devil, and even a proud father peering in at his evil child in a hospital nursery.

Charles Addams was a charming man-boy. The Addams drawing table was his and Uncle Fester's meeting place where they could indulge their mutual love of boyhood delight, tempered with, or more likely fueled by, a good measure of Addams's off-center, dry humor. They had a long and enduring relationship.

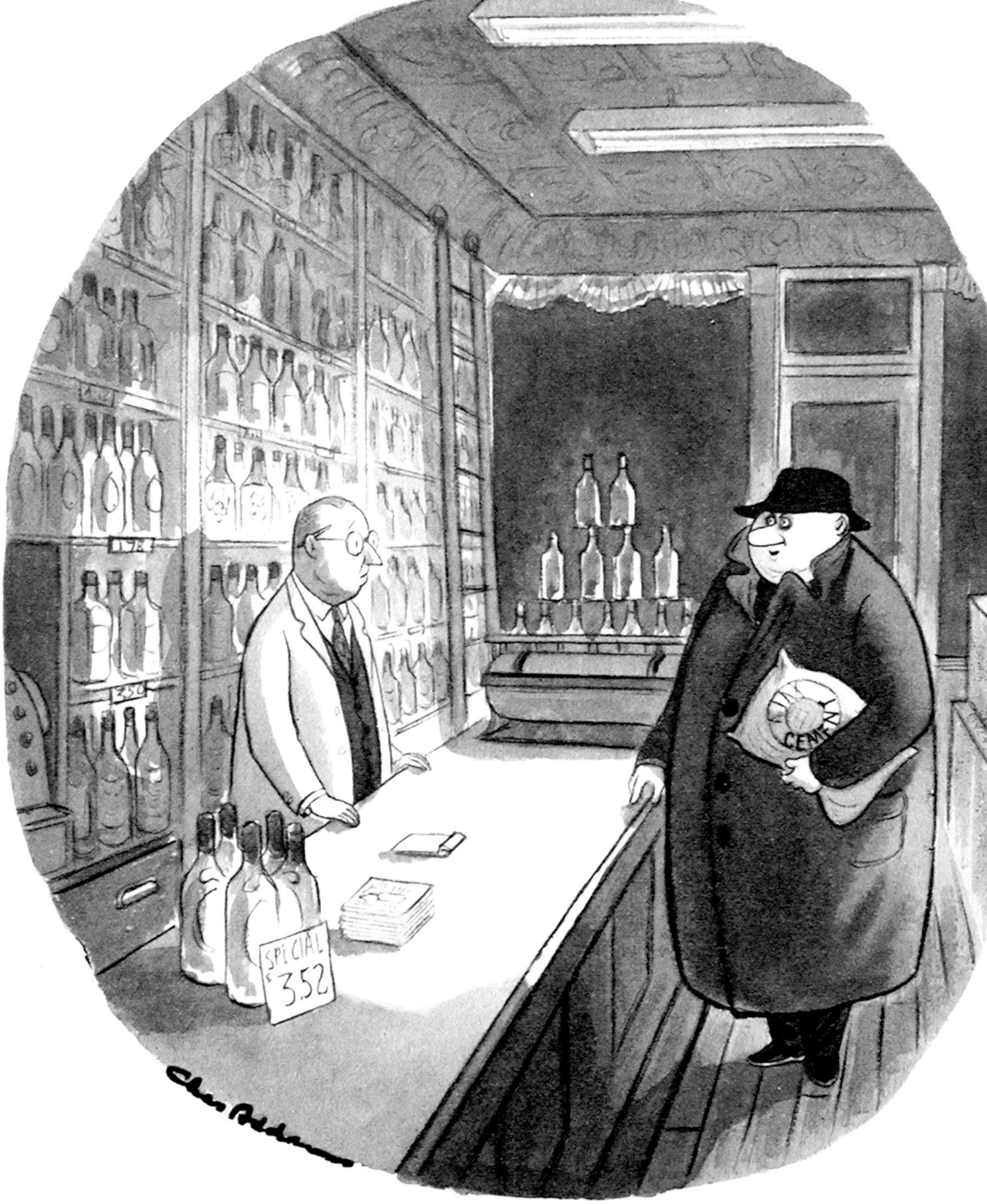
SPECIAL
$3.52

"A cask of Amontillado, please."

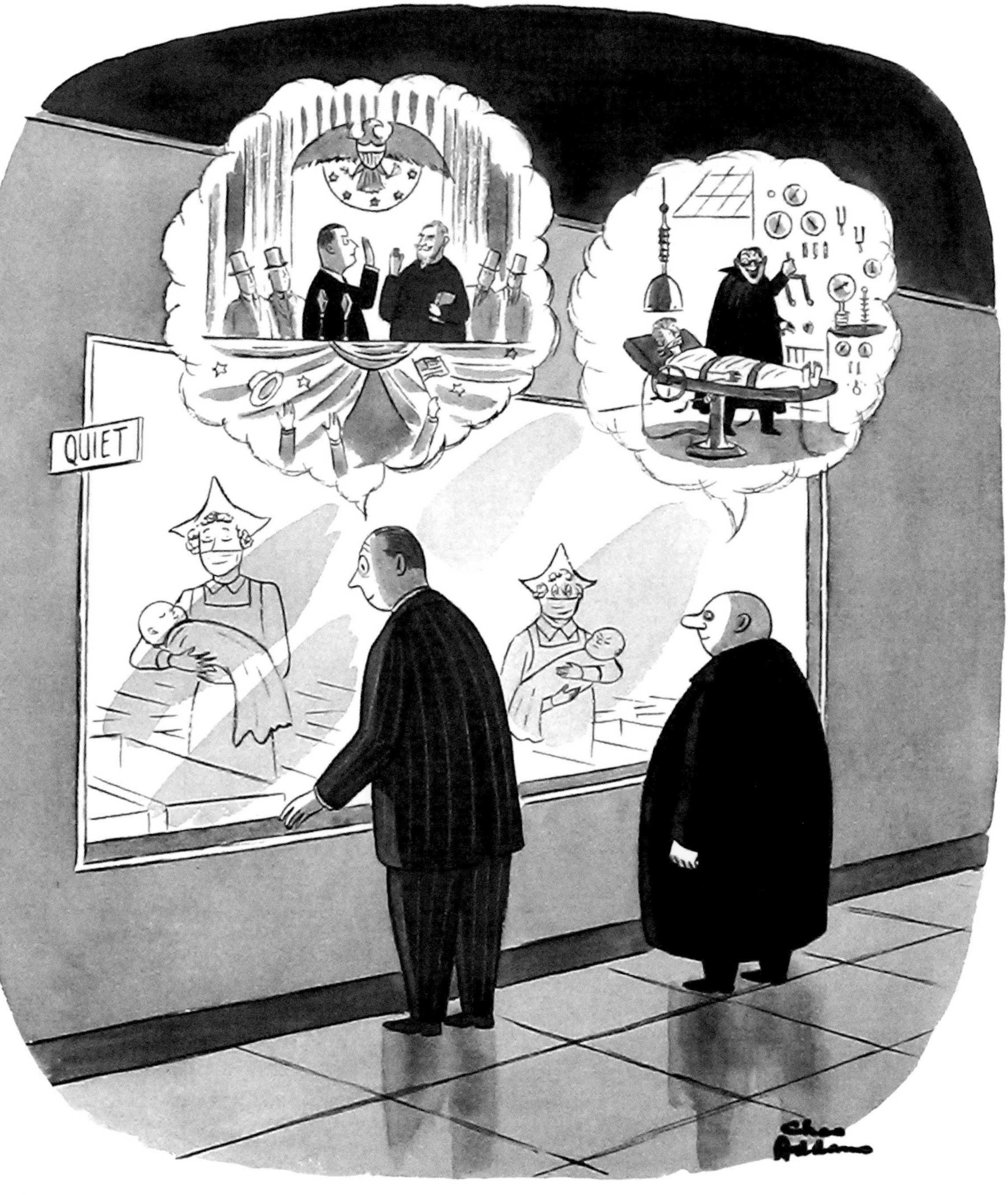
QUIET
Chas Addams

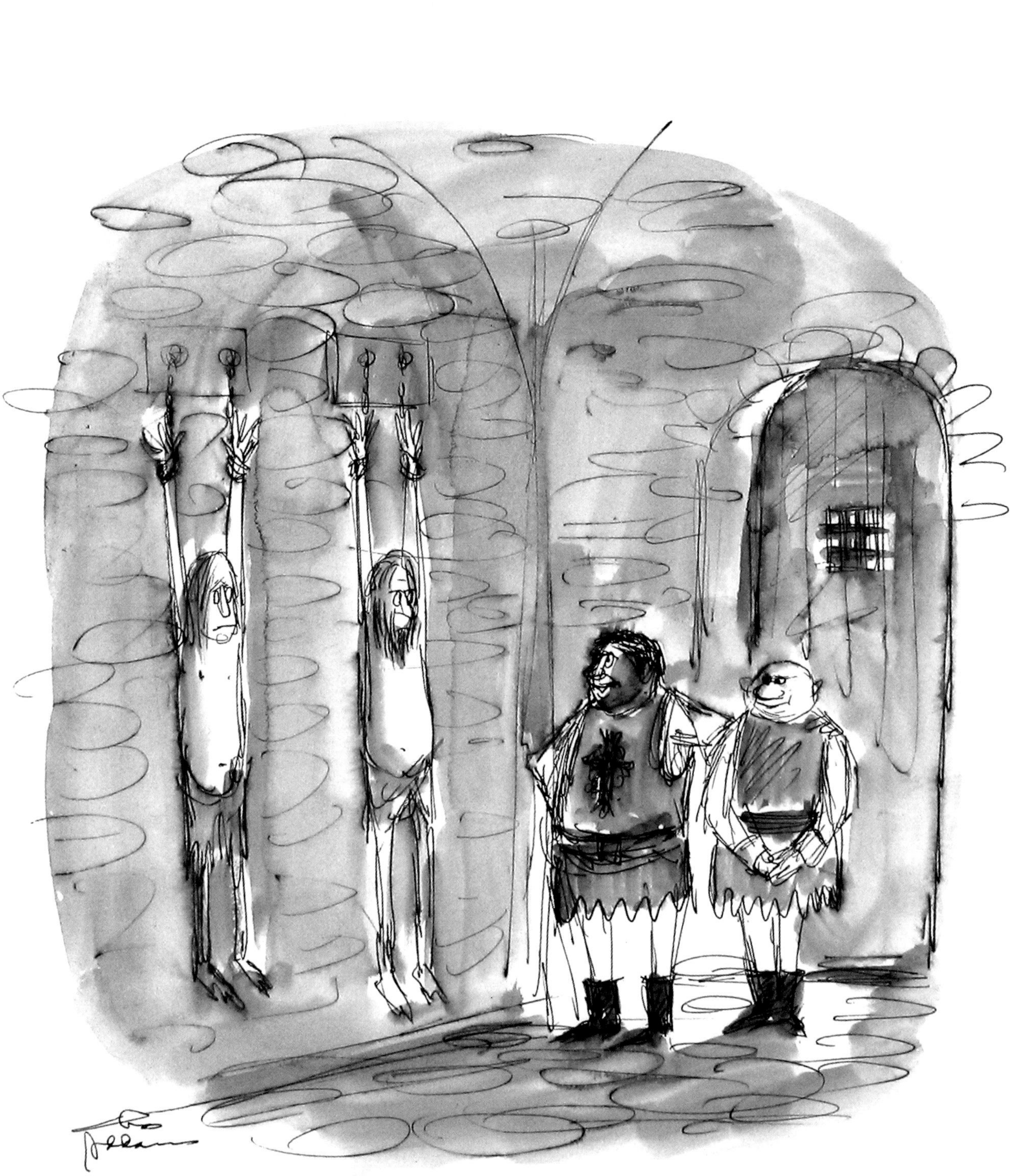

"Fellows, I'd like you to meet the gentleman who will be in charge while I'm on vacation."

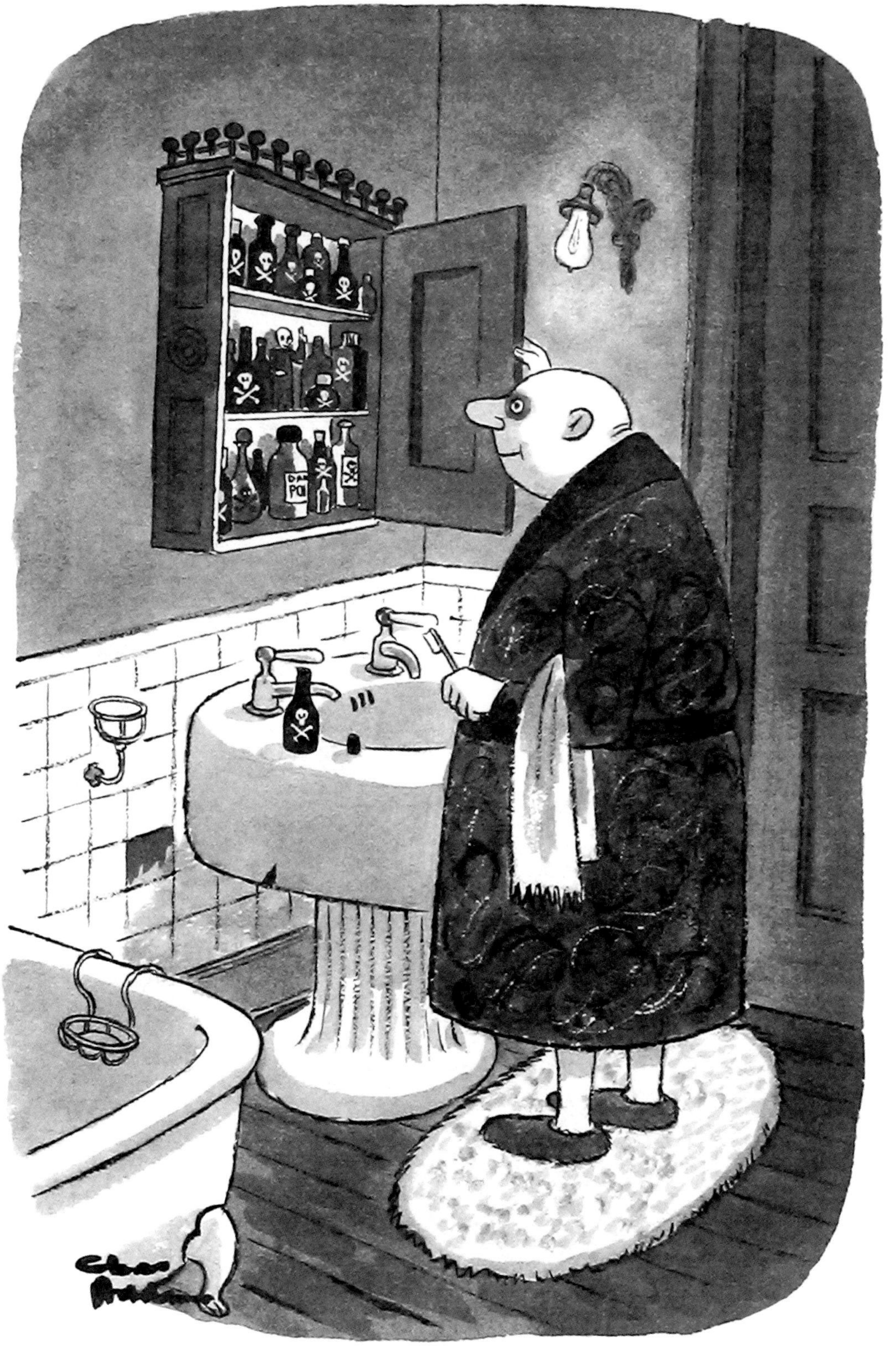

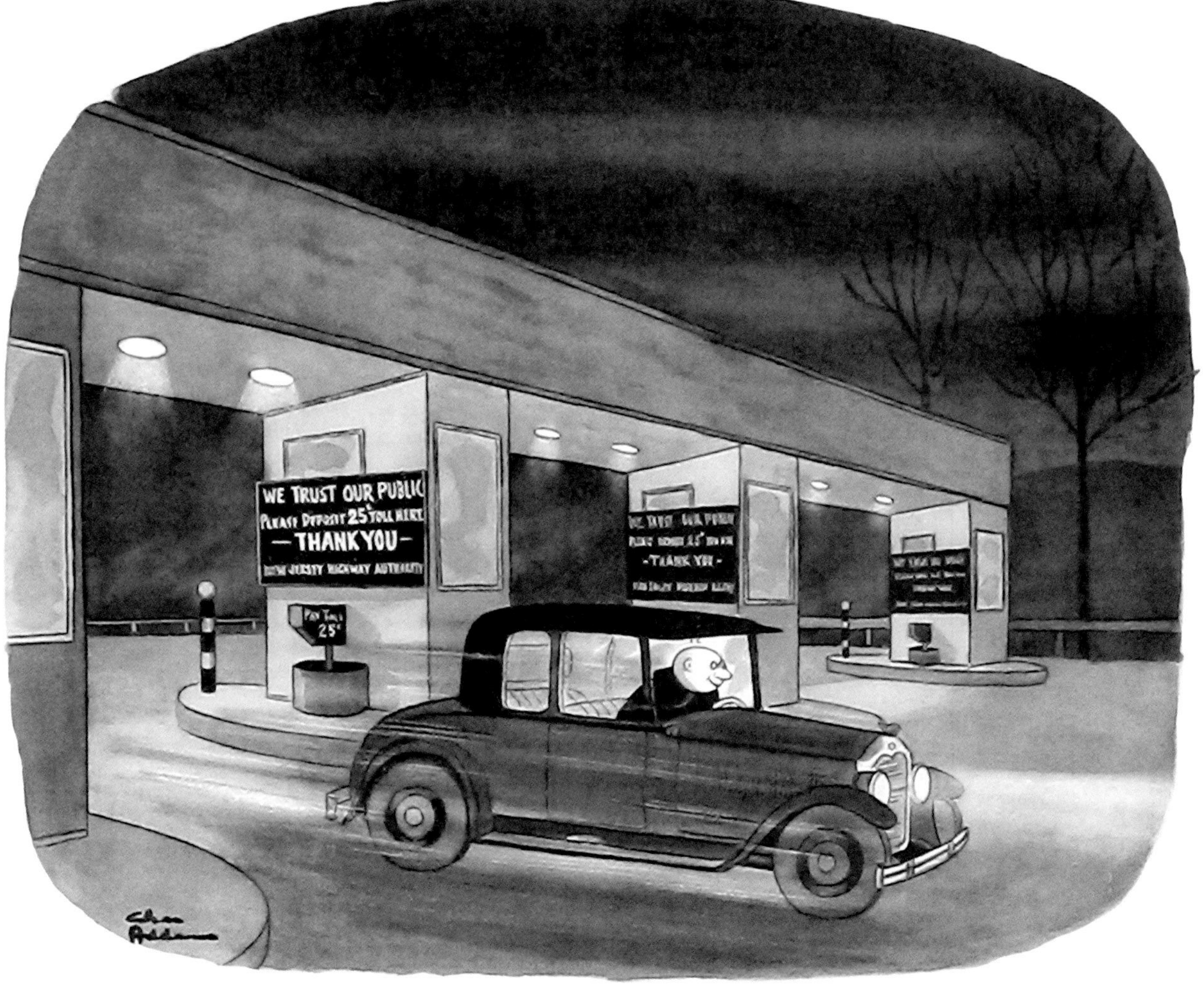
WE TRUST OUR PUBLIC
PLEASE DEPOSIT 25¢ TOLL HERE
— THANK YOU —
PAY TOLL
25¢

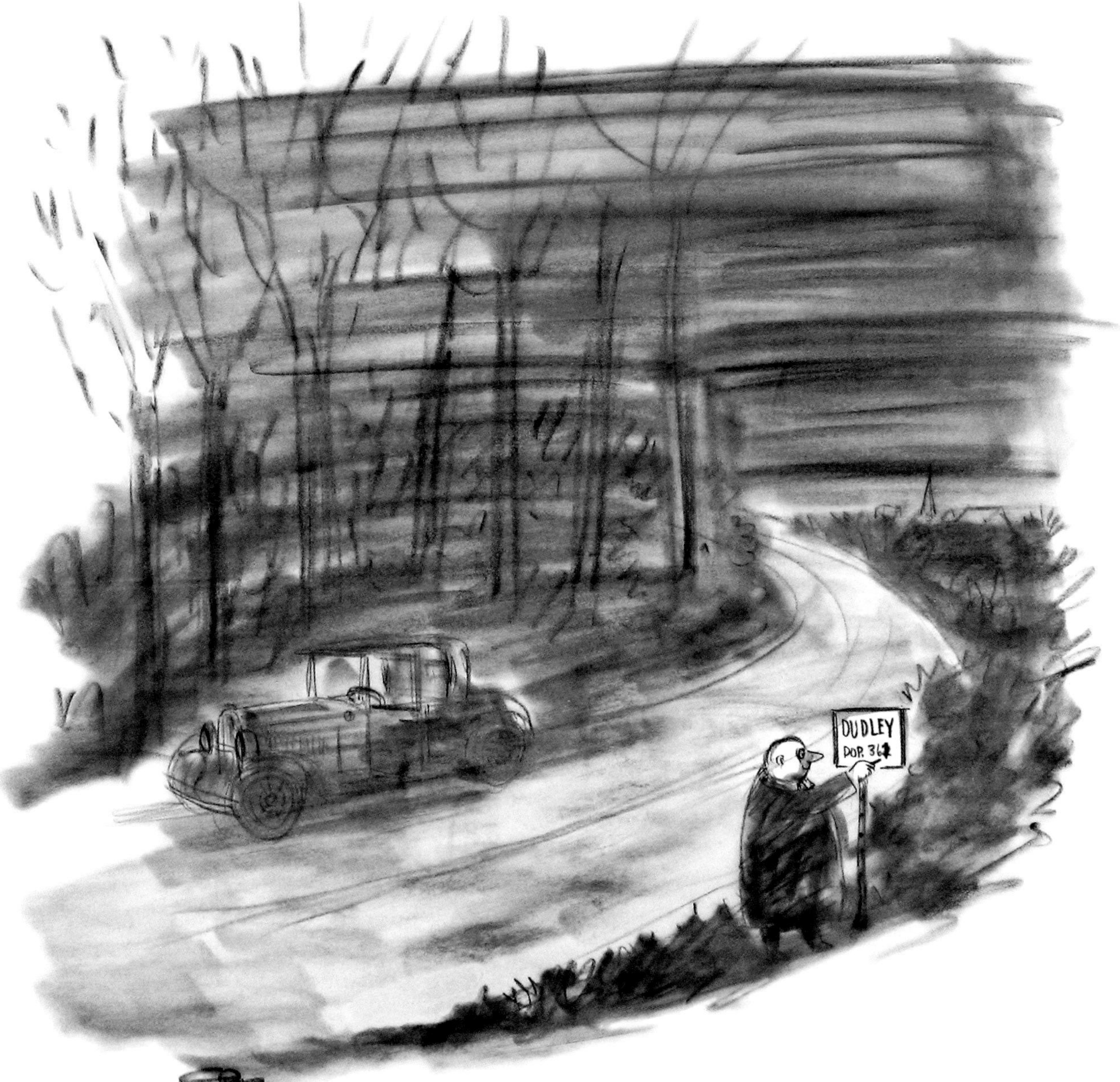
DUDLEY
POP. 36

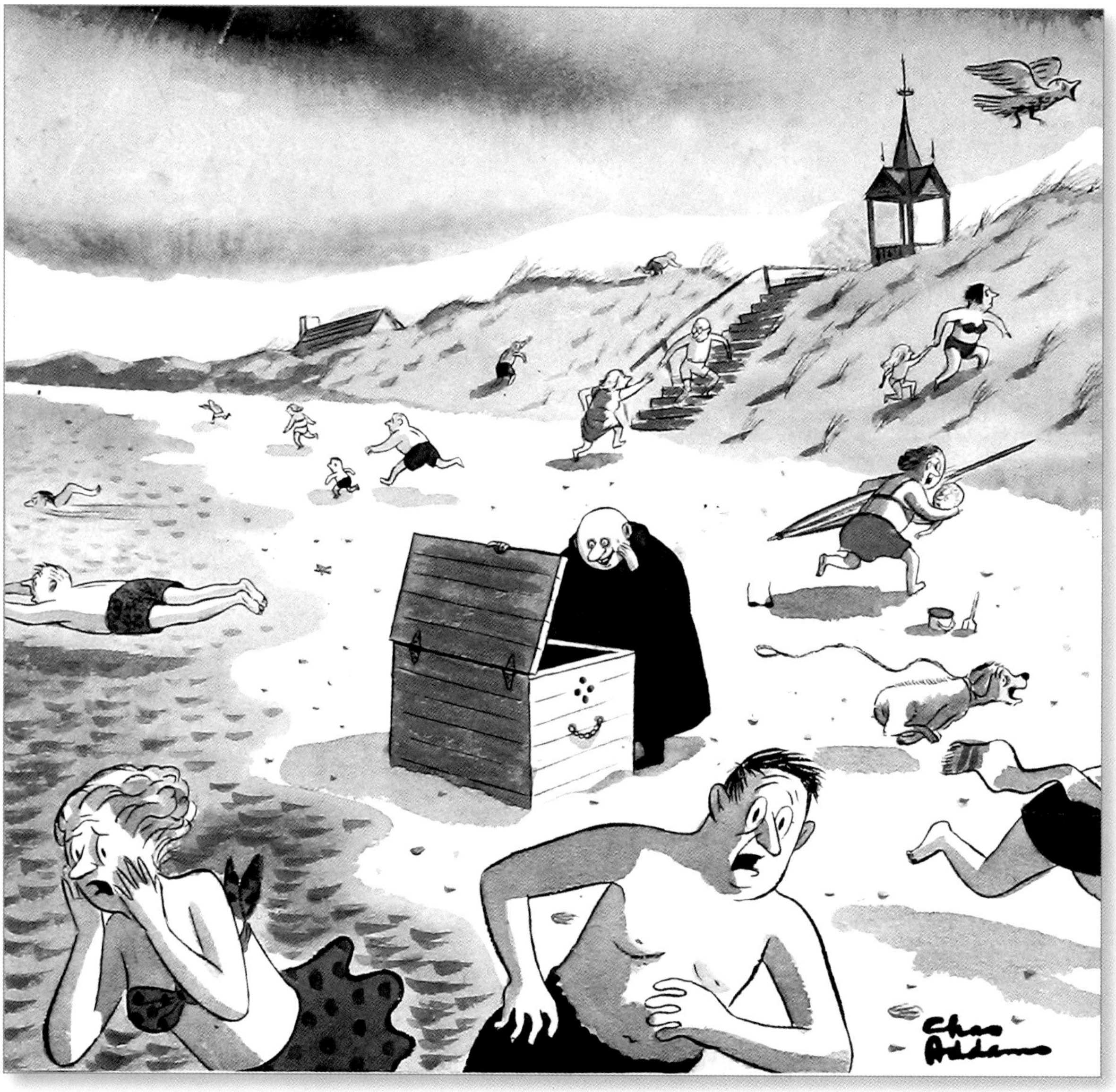
Chas Addams

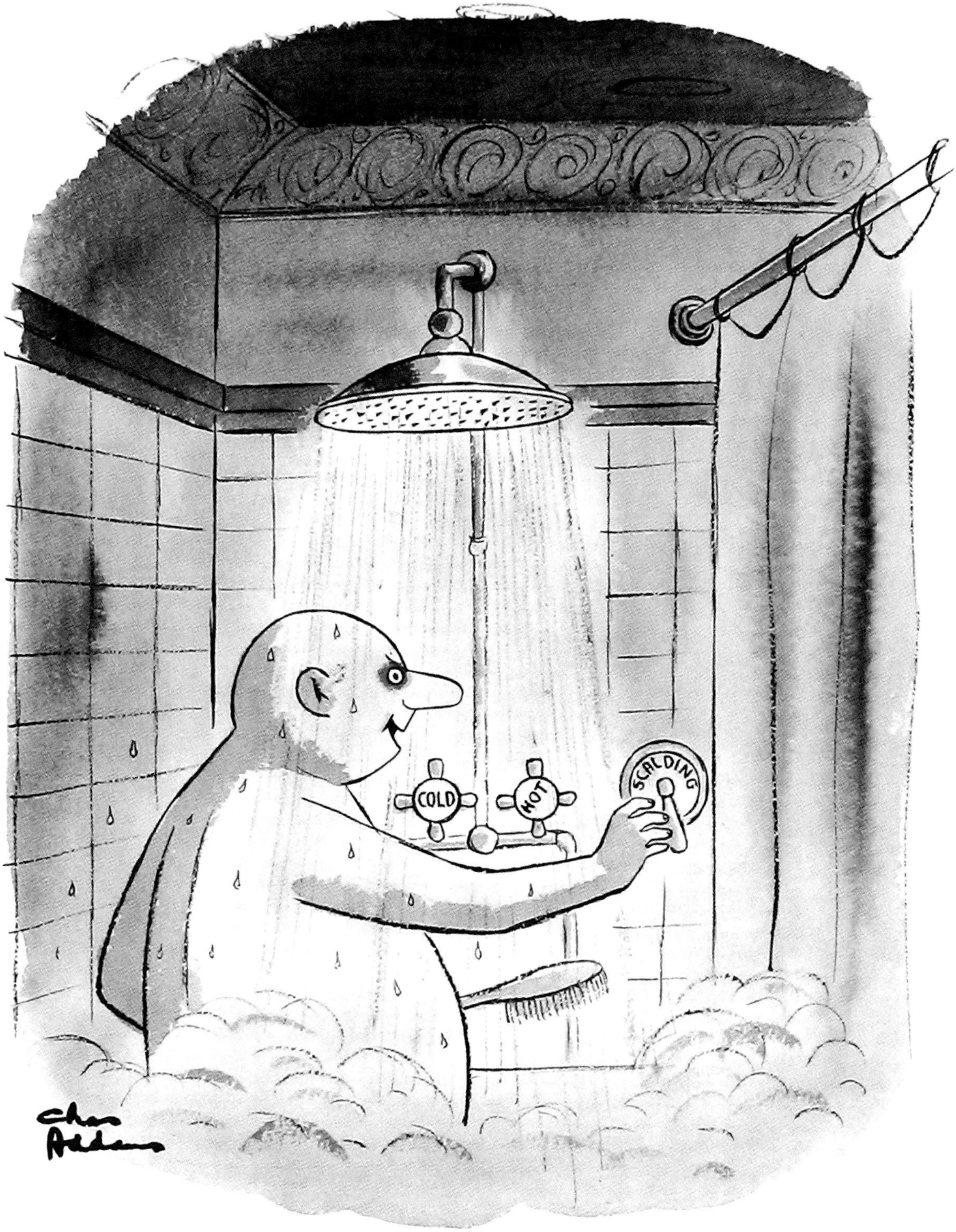
COLD
HOT
SCALDING
Chas Addams

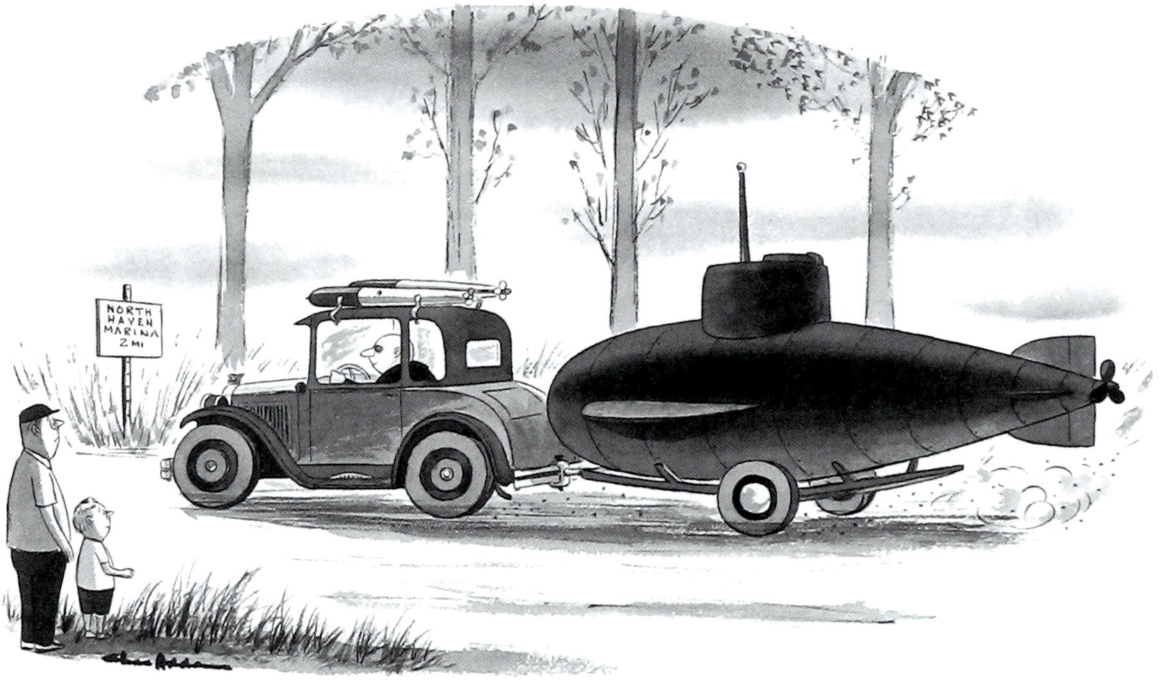
NORTH HAVEN MARINA 2 MI

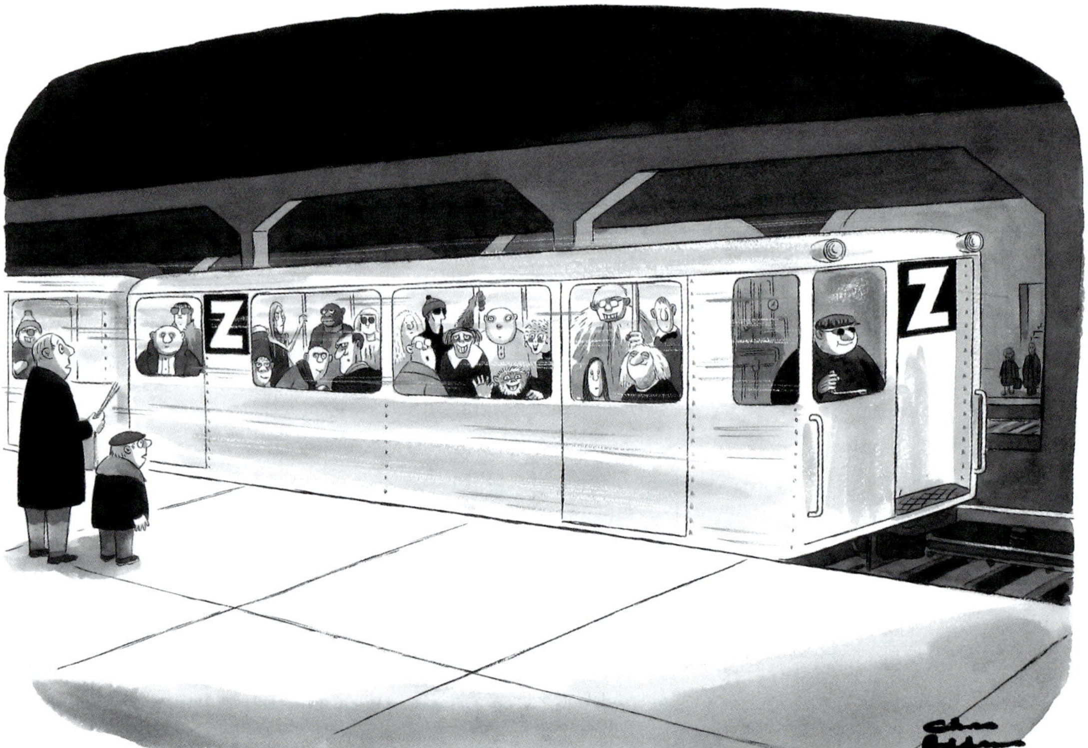
Z
Z

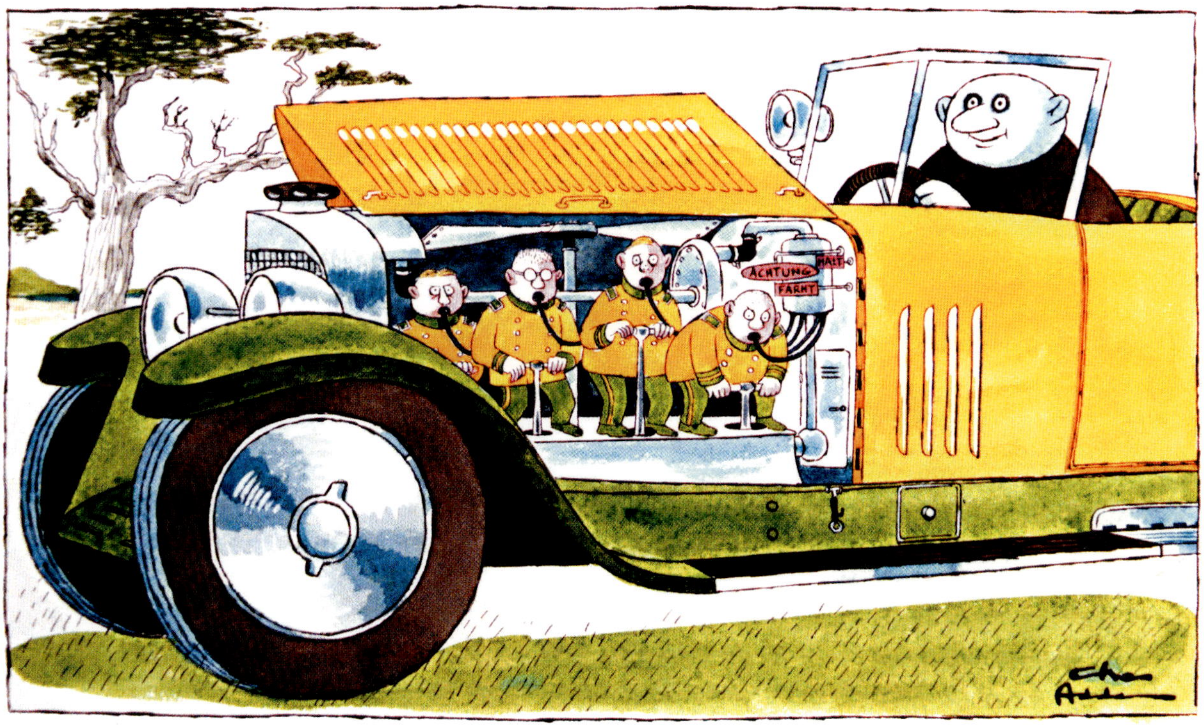
ACHTUNG
HALT
FARHT

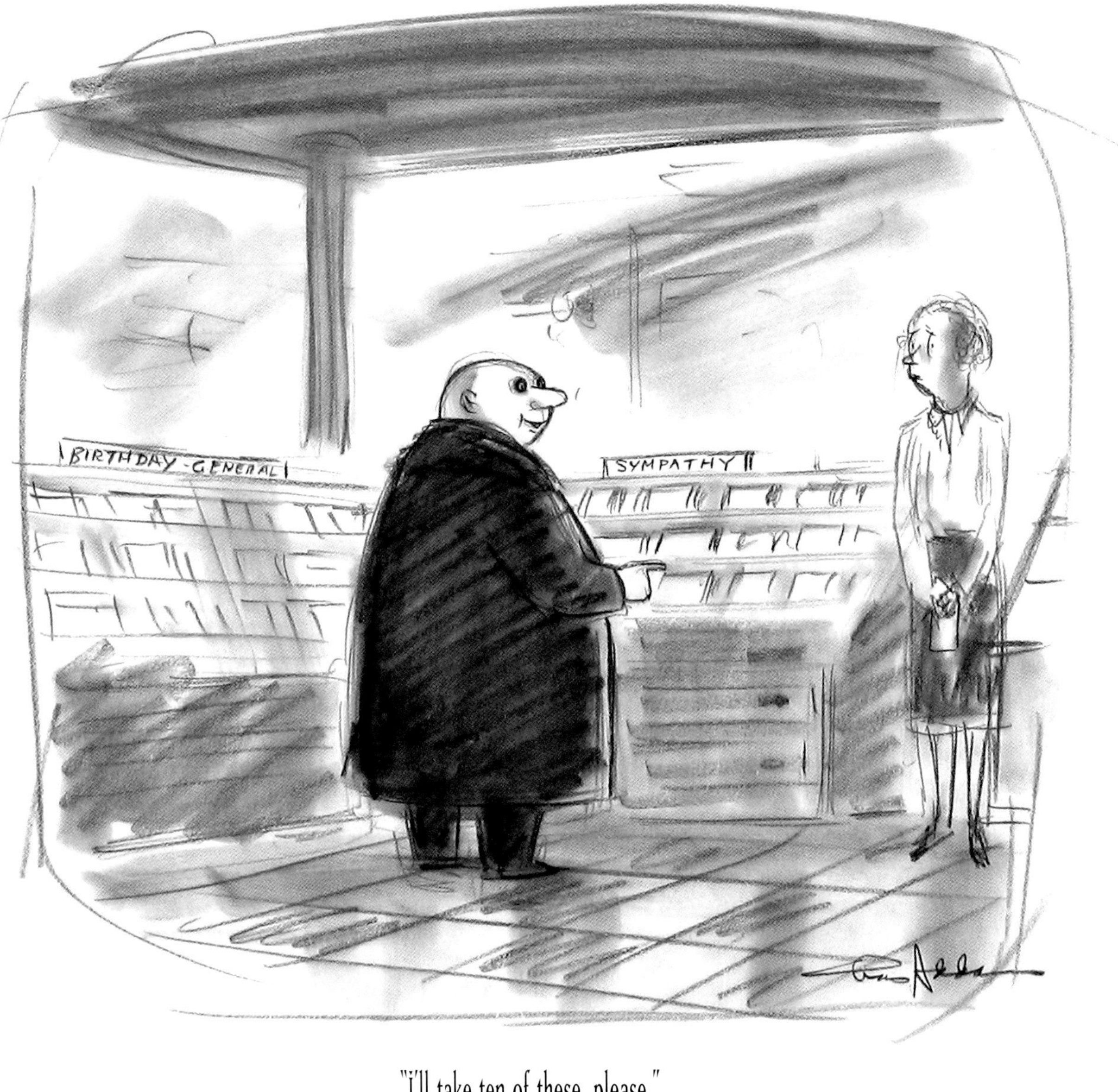
BIRTHDAY - GENERAL
SYMPATHY

"I'll take ten of these, please."

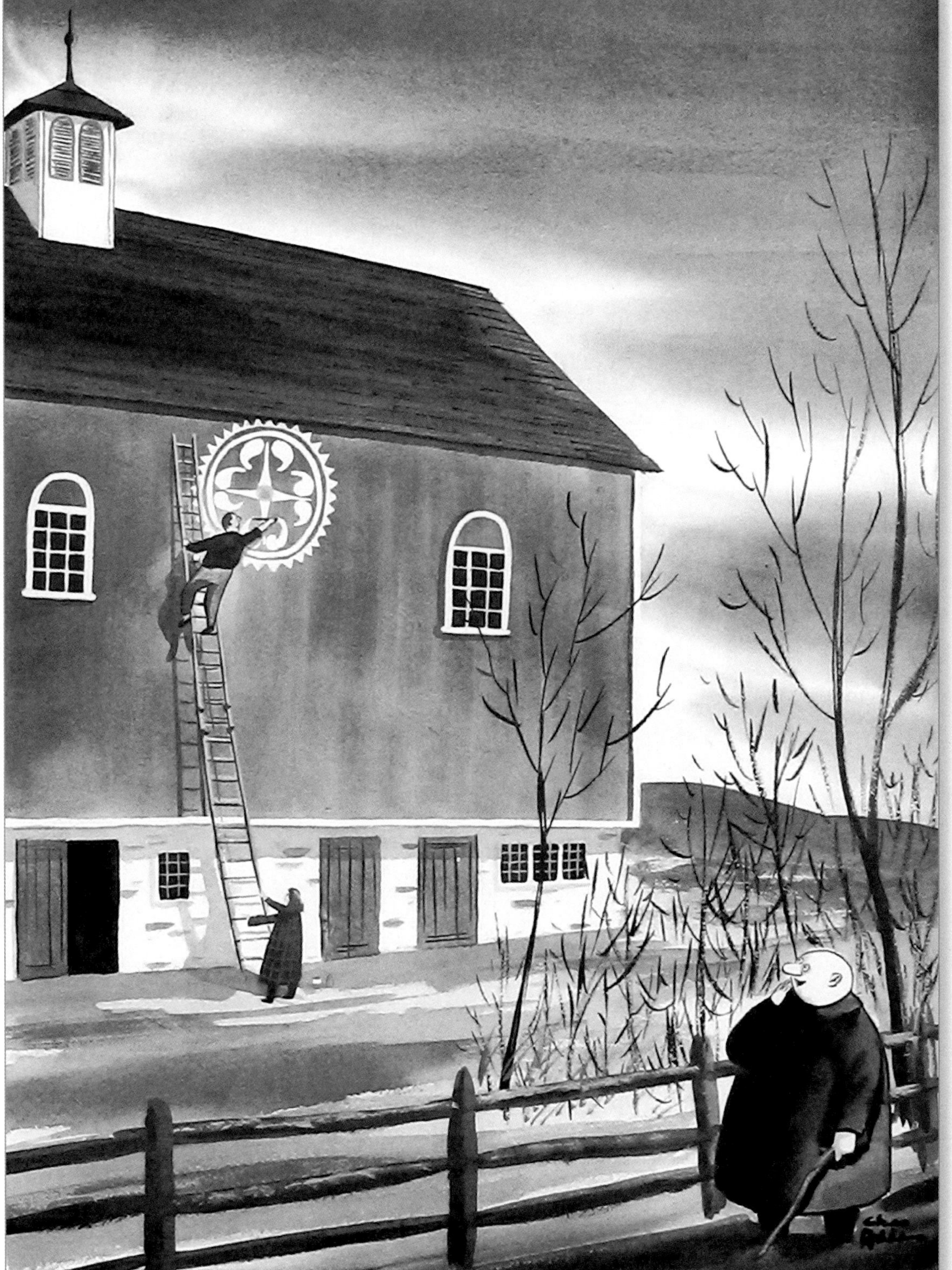

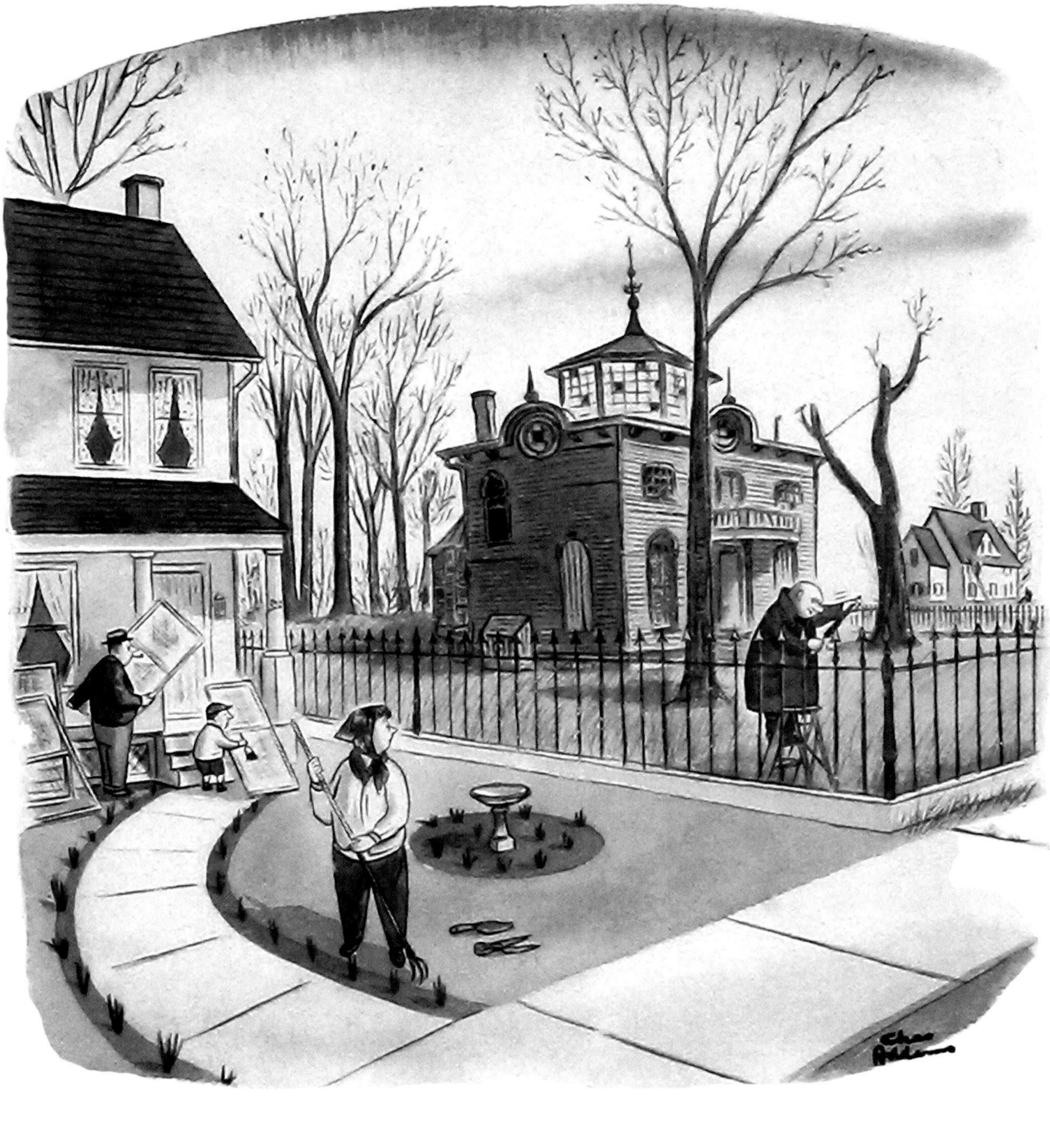
Chas Addams

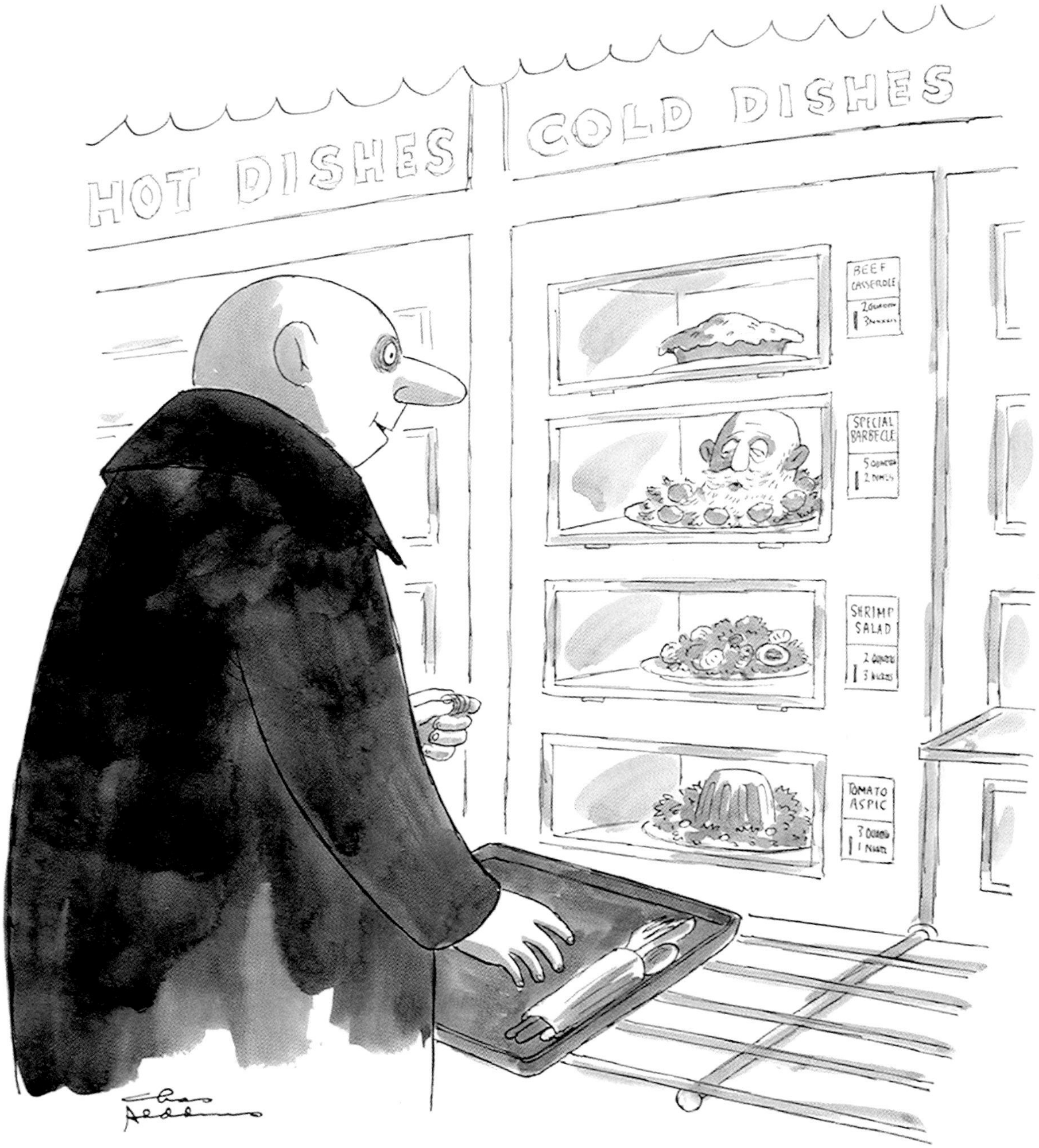
HOT DISHES
COLD DISHES
BEEF CASSEROLE
SPECIAL BARBECUE
SHRIMP SALAD
TOMATO ASPIC

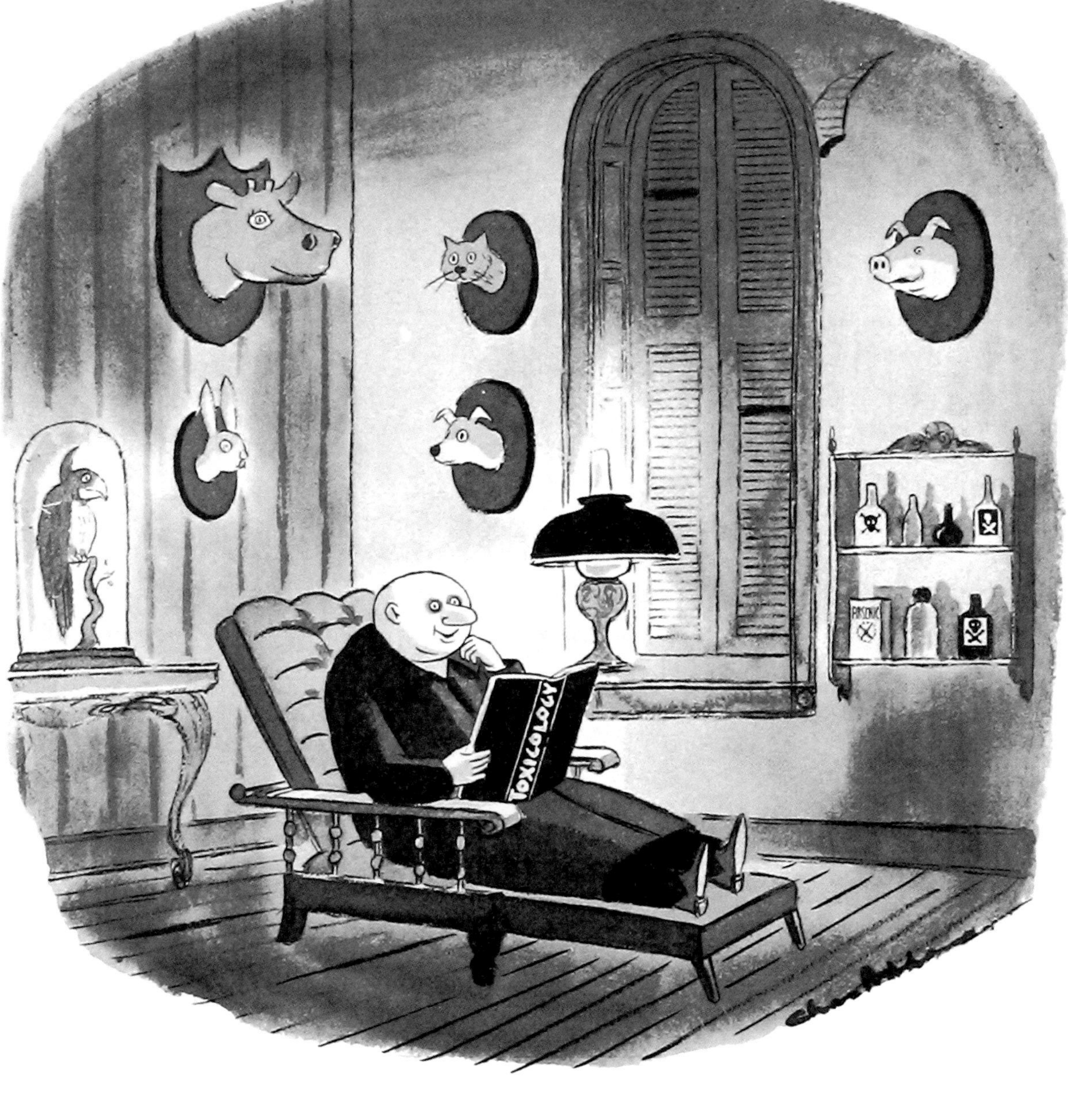
TOXICOLOGY
ARSENIC

"Don't forget to lead him a little."

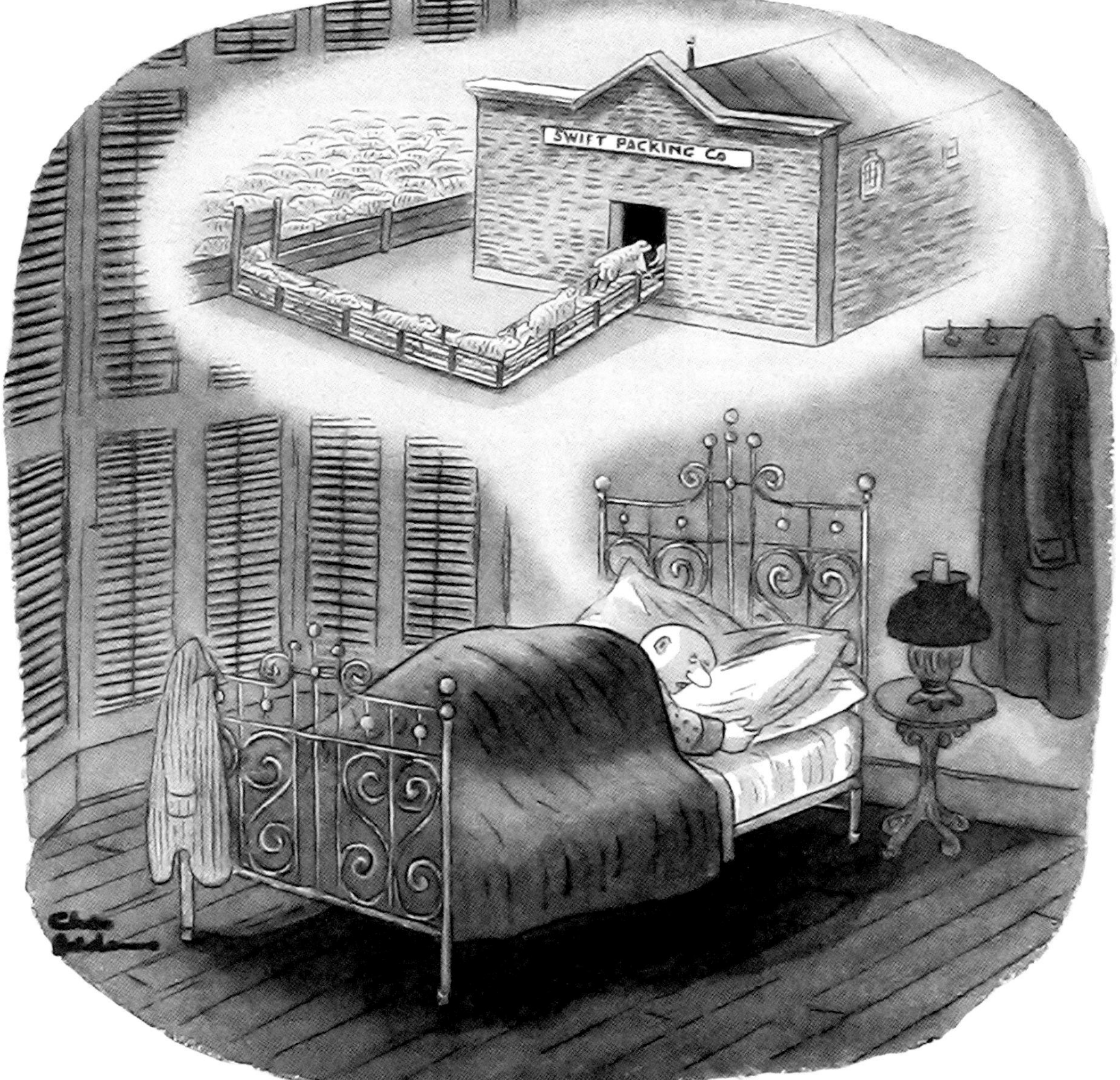
SWIFT PACKING CO

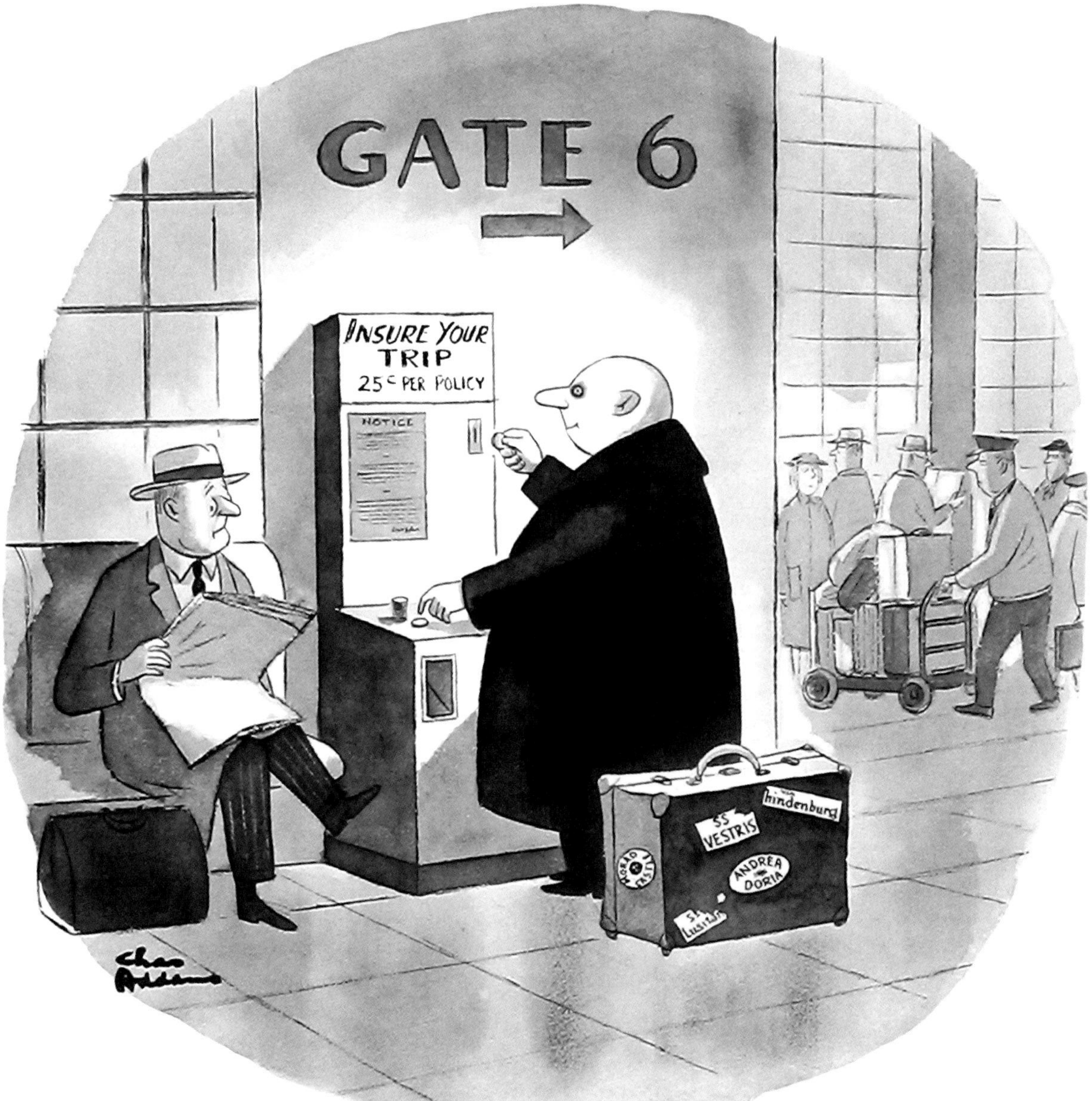

GATE 6
INSURE YOUR TRIP
25c PER POLICY
NOTICE
hindenburg
SS VESTRIS
ANDREA DORIA
Chas Addams

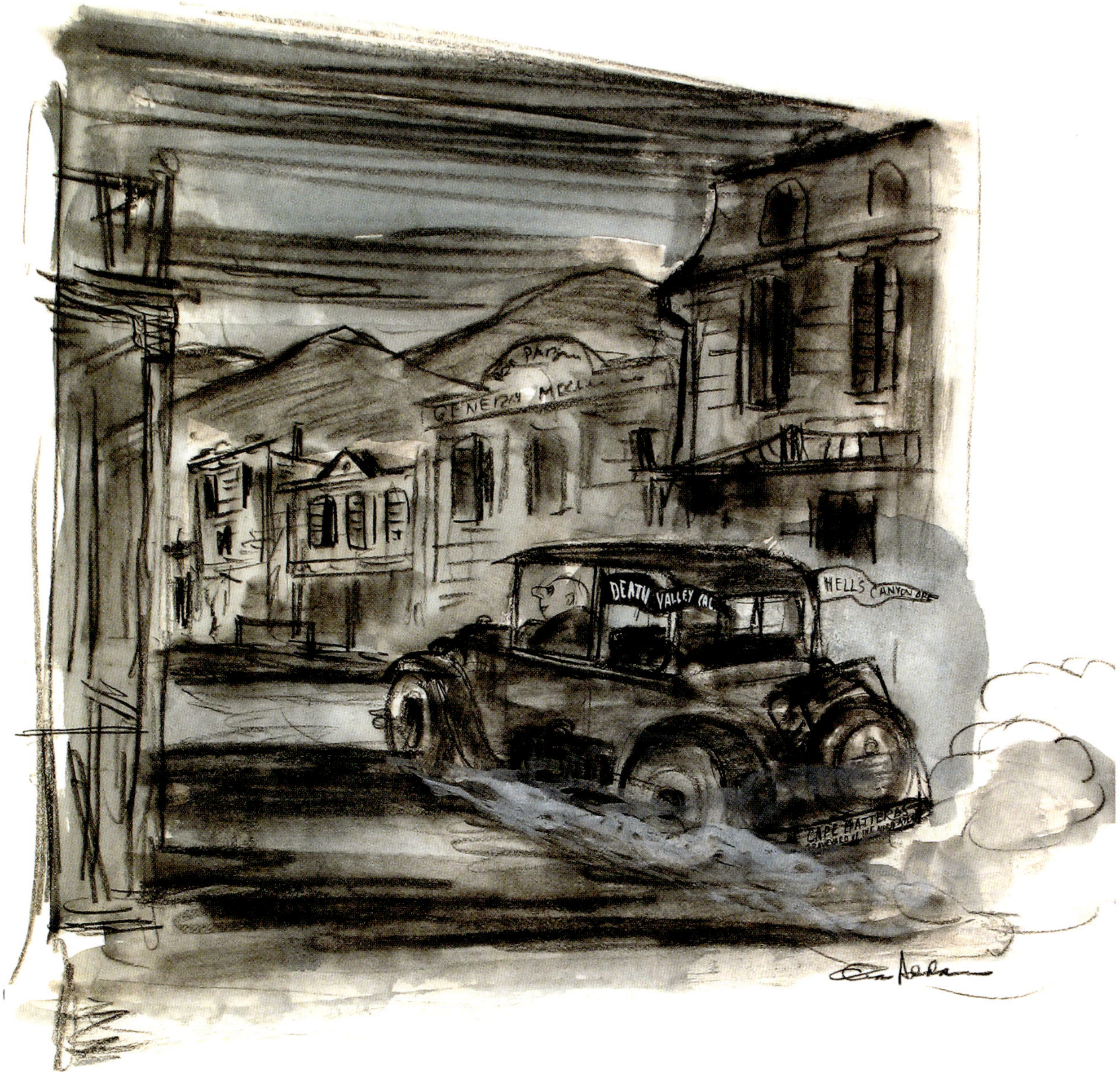
DEATH VALLEY CAL
HELL'S CANYON
CAPE HATTERAS

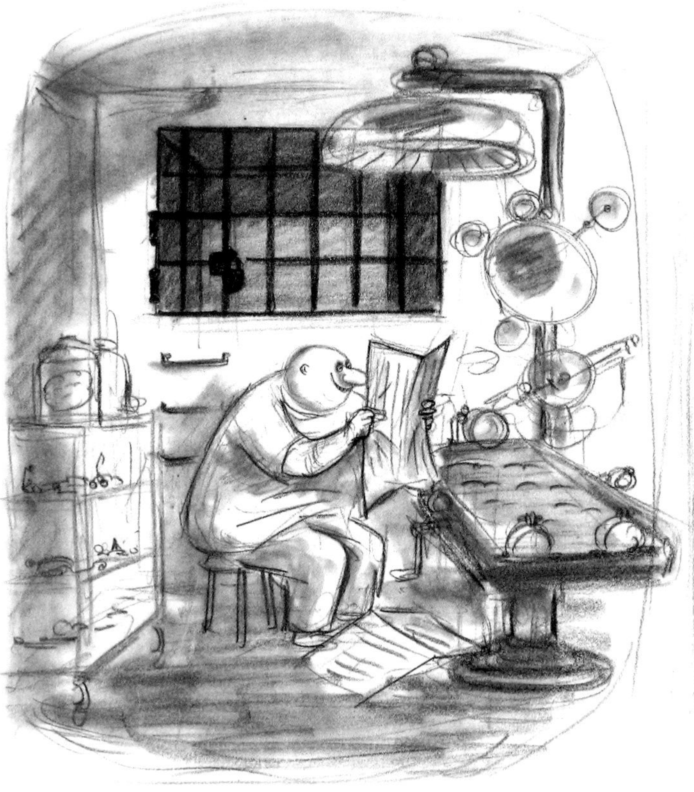

"Retired executive, Christian, single, regular habits, scientific turn of mind, seeks change. Would like room in remote section L.I. Box 178 Times."

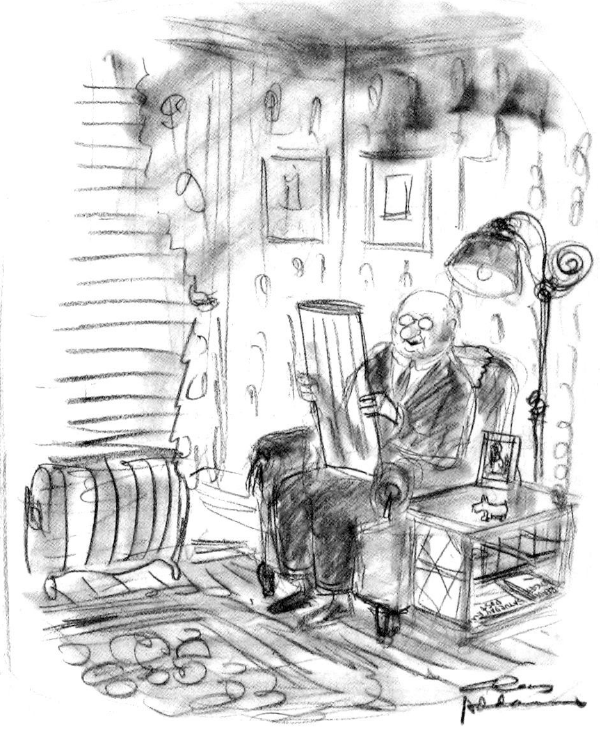

"L.I. country home, channel island will rent room to single gentleman. Private, soundproof, separate entrance, scientific atmosphere. Box 131 Times."

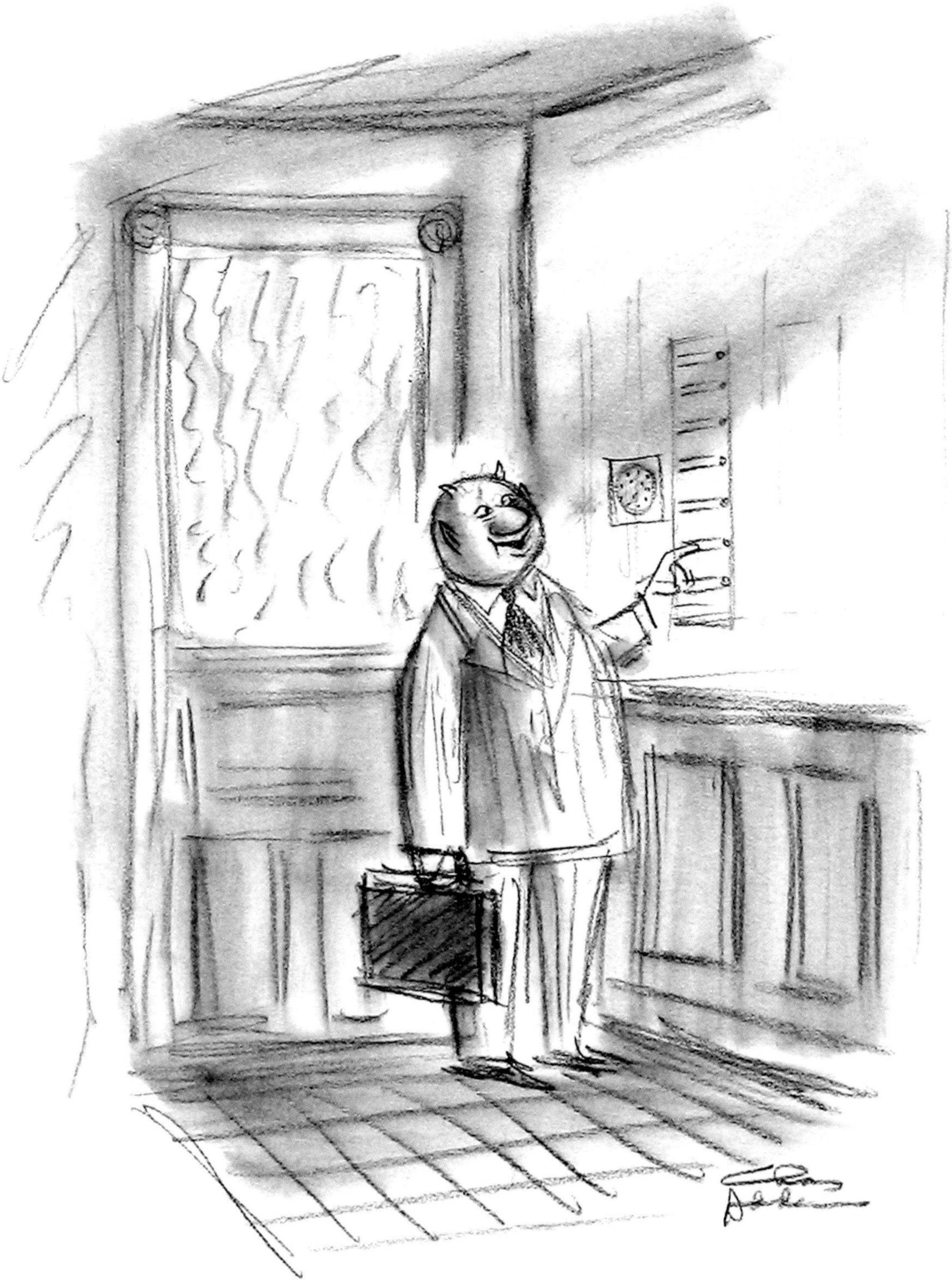

"It's not just another salesman. I have an attractive offer for you."

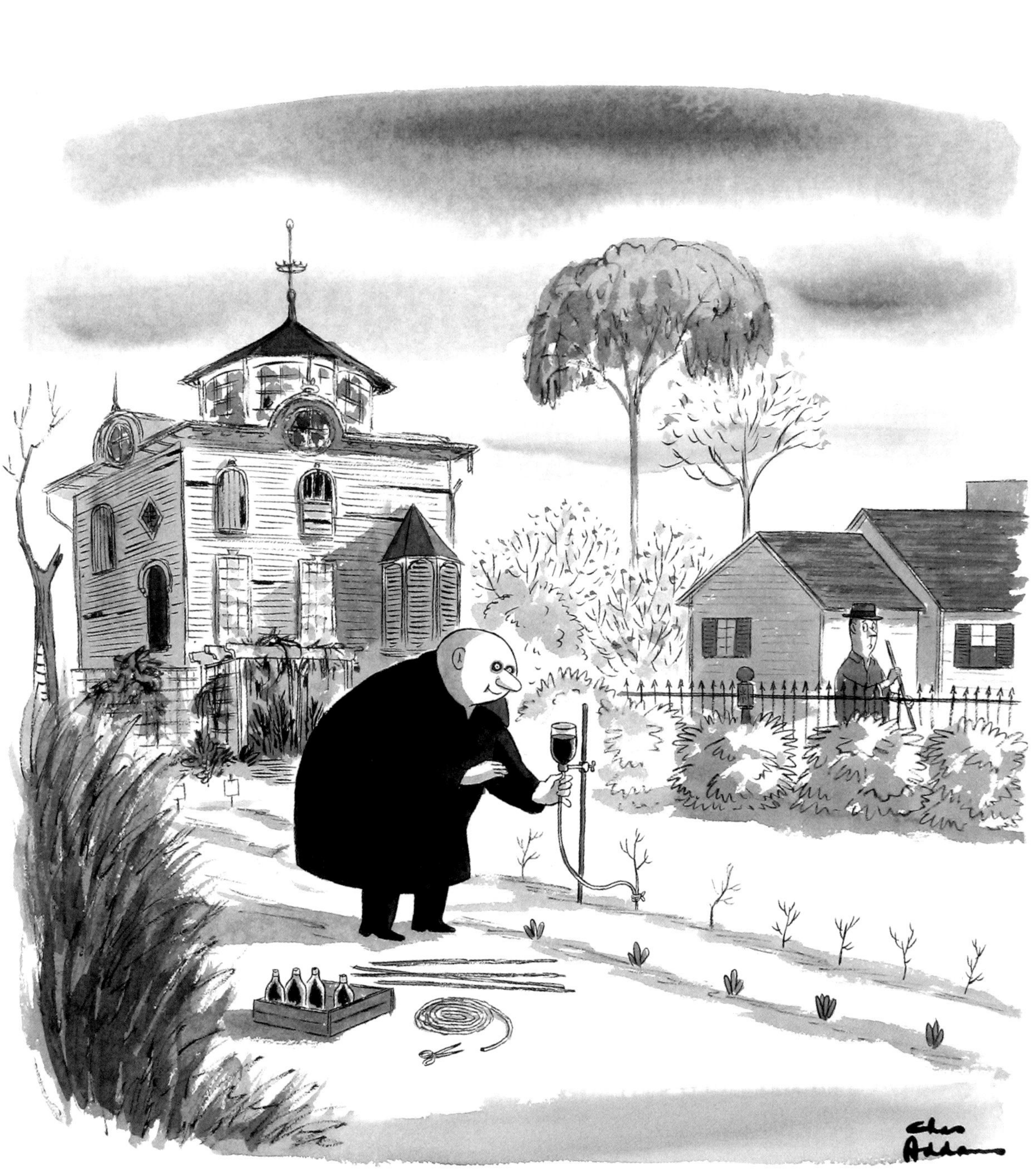
Chas Addams

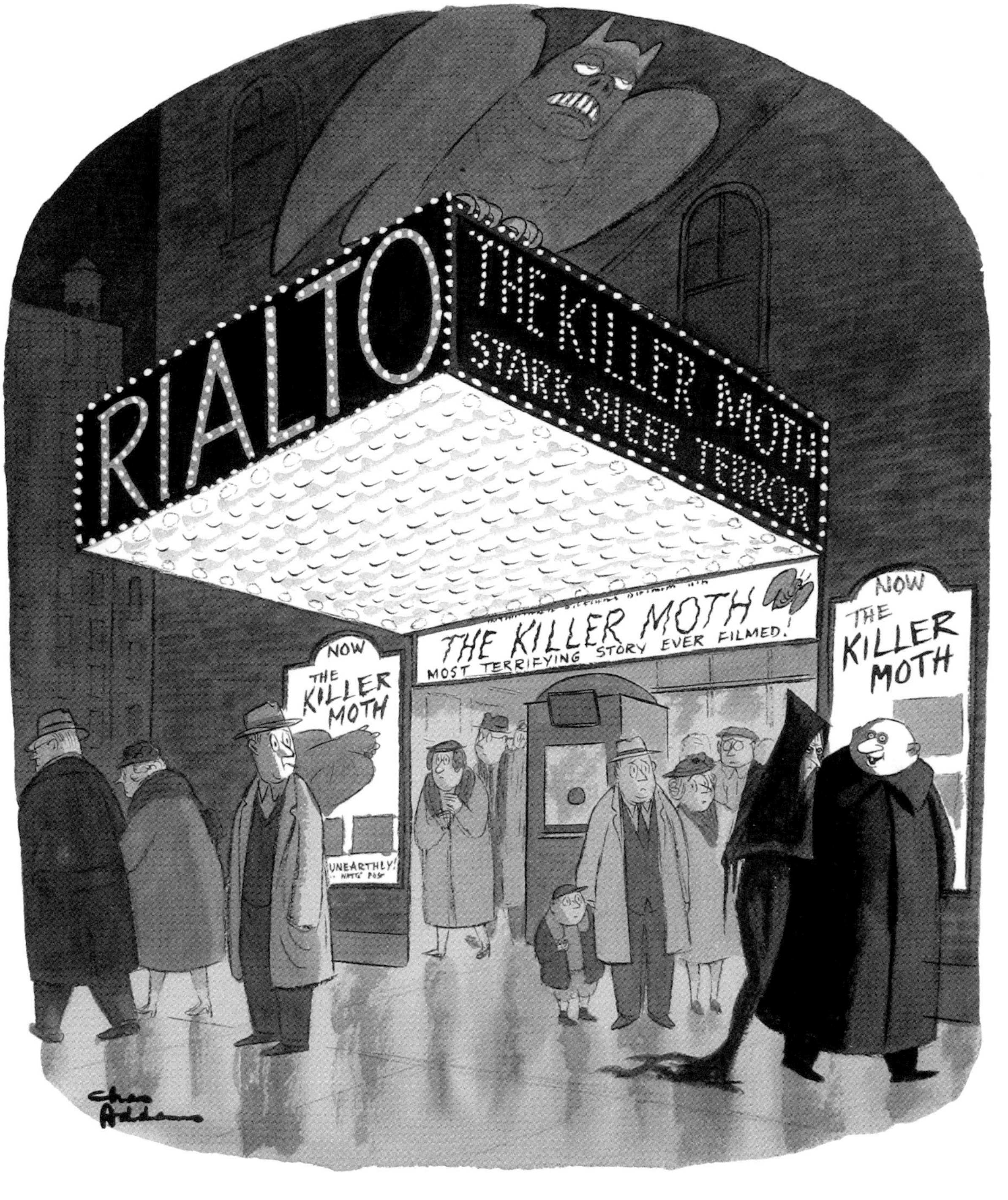
RIALTO
THE KILLER MOTH
STARK SHEER TERROR
NOW
THE KILLER MOTH
THE KILLER MOTH
MOST TERRIFYING STORY EVER FILMED!
NOW
THE KILLER MOTH
UNEARTHLY!
Chas Addams

"Well, at least it was true to life."

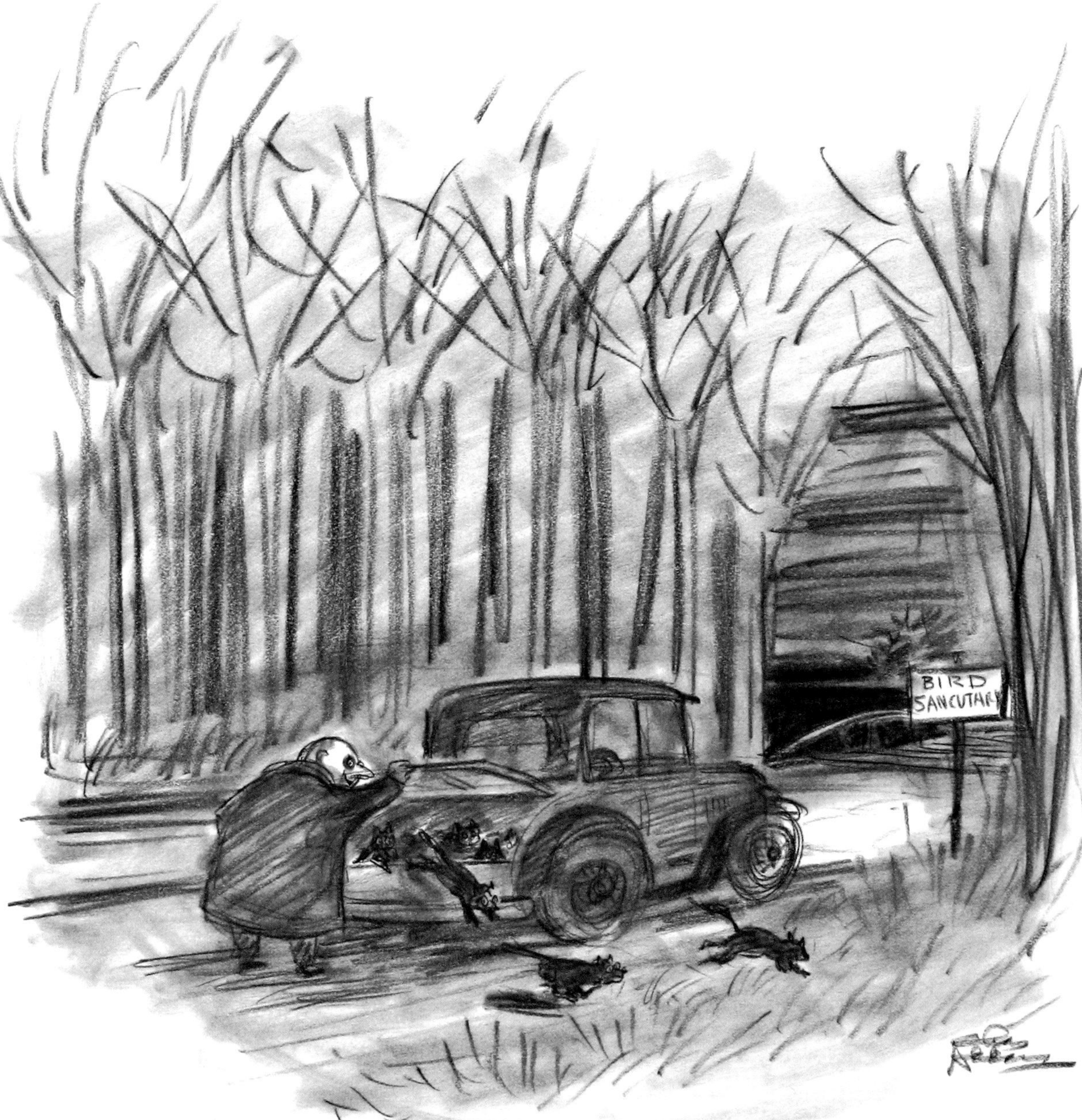
BIRD
SANCUTARY

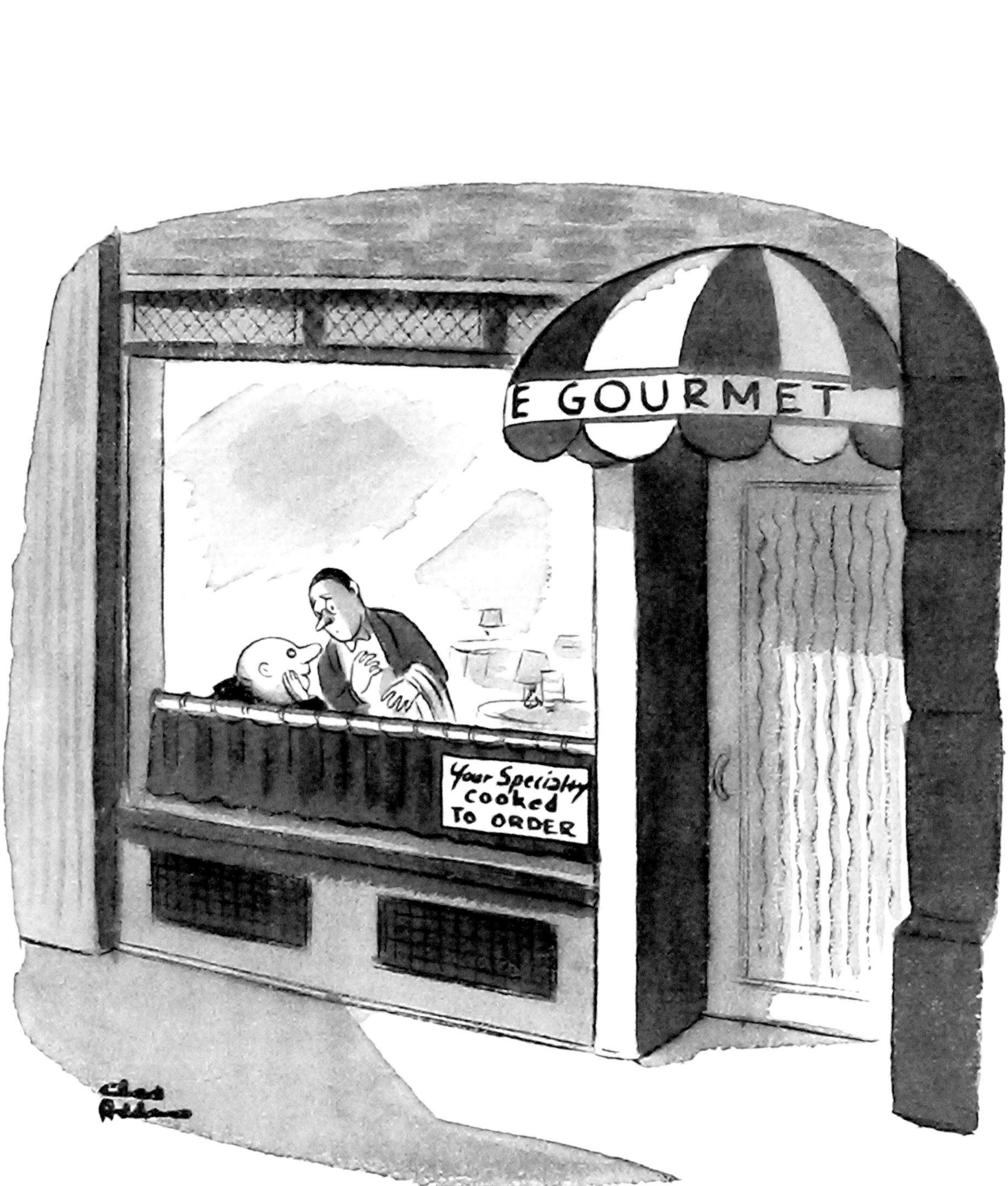
E GOURMET
Your Specialty cooked TO ORDER

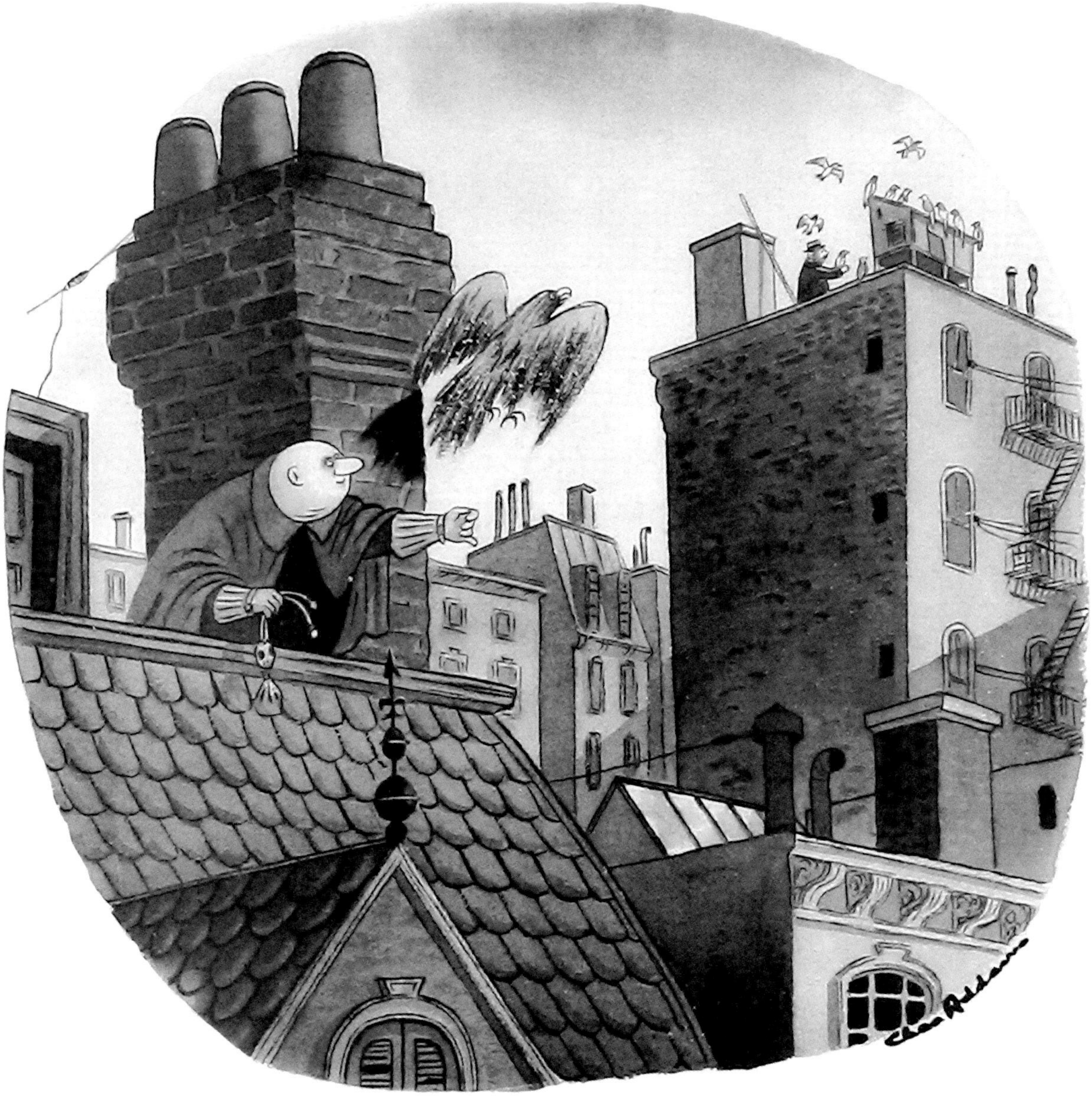
Chas Addams

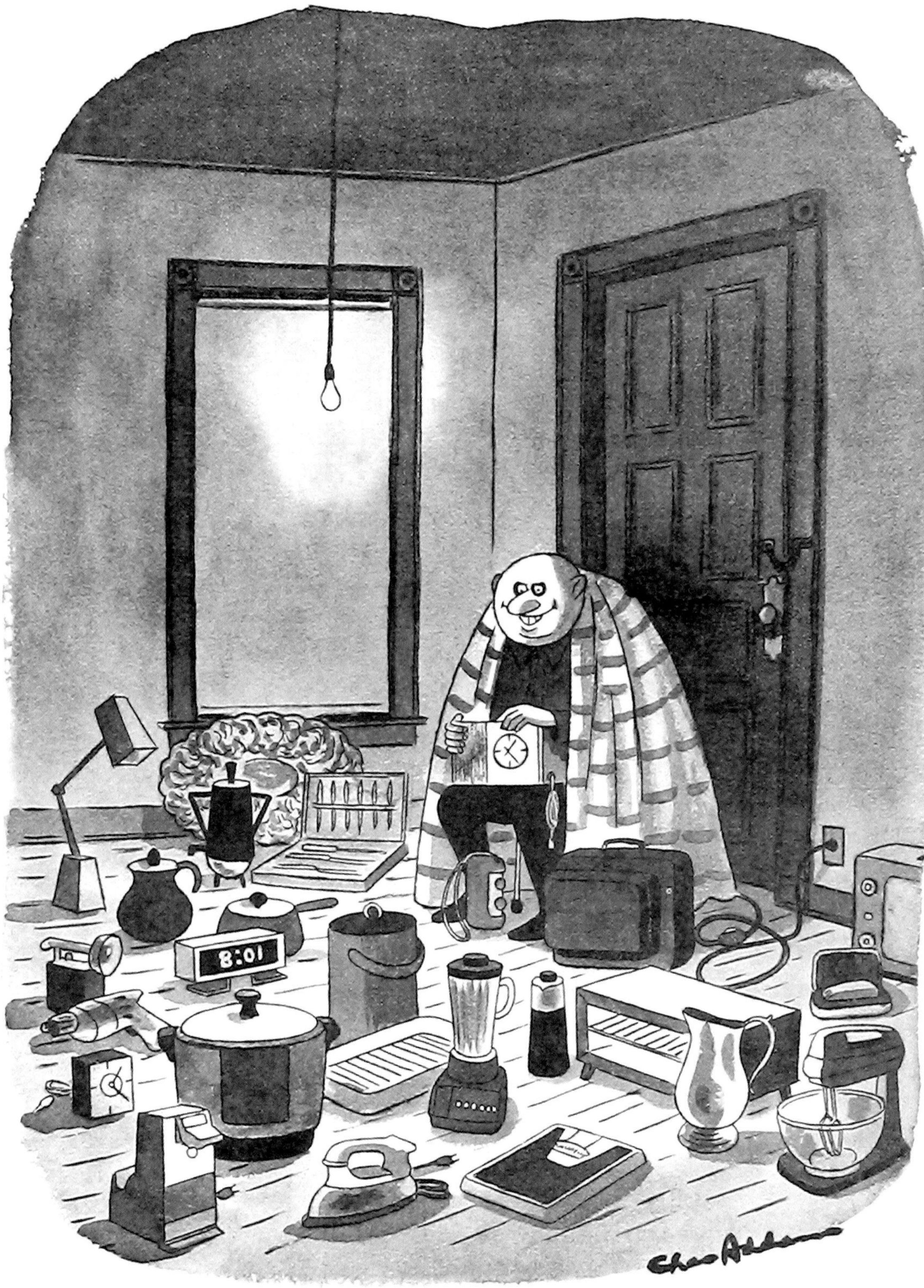
8:01
Chas Addams

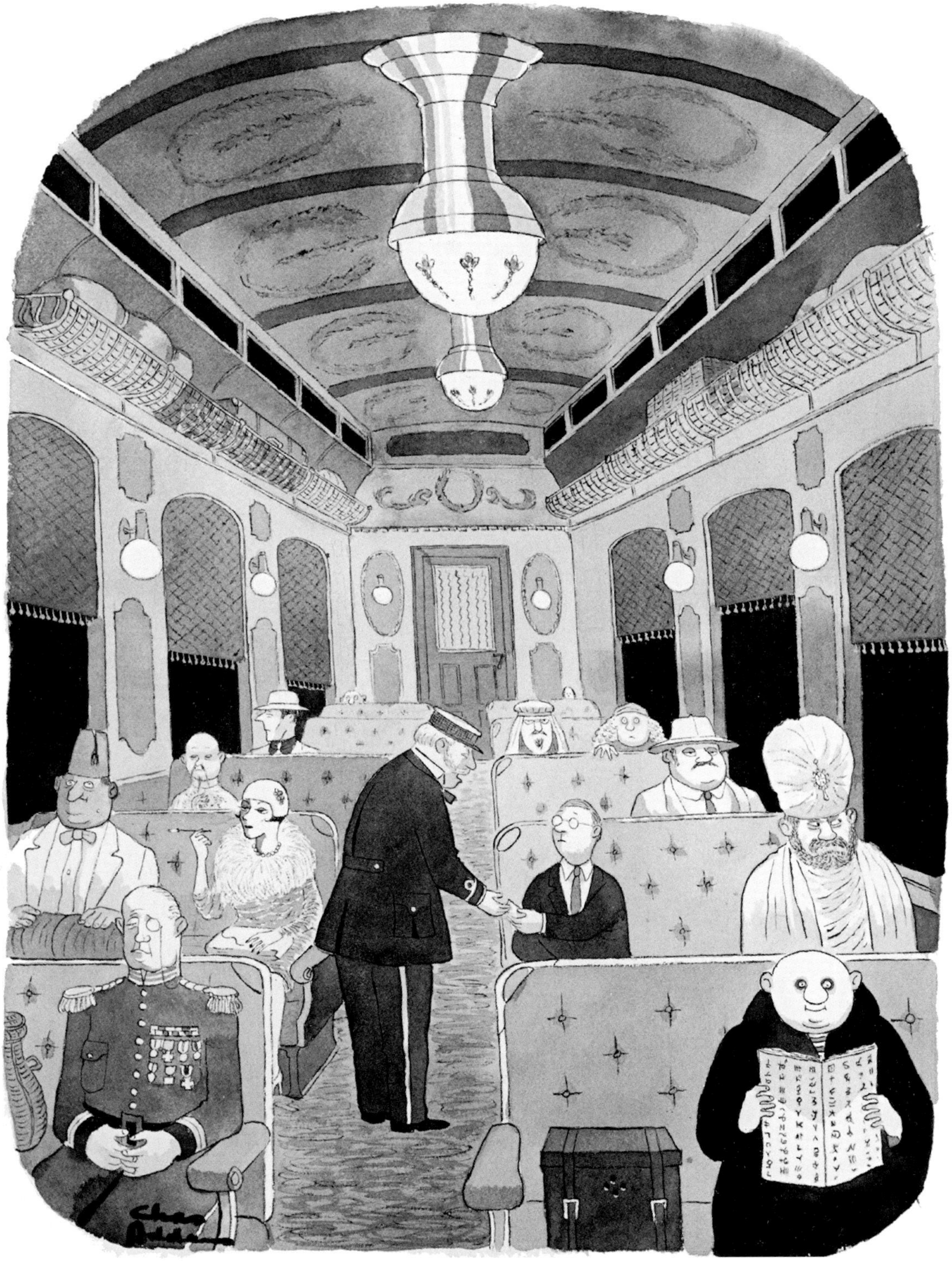

"No, this is not the 12:38 to Bridgeport."

THE THING

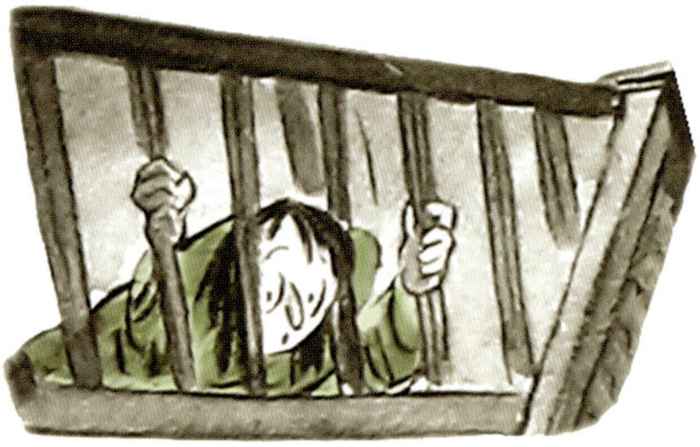

. . . is often observed watching the family through the balustrades of the balcony over the living room. We don't know quite who or what he is, but, whatever, he's the soul of good nature—at least, he grins perpetually and may occasionally whimper.

Chas Addams

"THING" became known as such when the producers of *The Addams Family* altered his appearance to suit their needs and abilities in mid-sixties television production. As the character never appeared in his entirety in any of Charles Addams's drawings—he was most often seen only from the shoulders up—and never spoke a word, Filmways stretched the premise a bit further by having Thing be seen only as a hand, and usually, if not always, a right hand.

Perhaps this notion was realized by referring to the Addams cartoon that was published in the March 20, 1954, issue of the *New Yorker*. Gomez, Morticia, Pugsley, and Wednesday are busy unto themselves while collected in the den listening to records on an old upright phonograph. The records are being changed by two arms reaching out from within the phonograph cabinet.

From the sign BEWARE OF THE THING at the chained end of the Addams driveway leading up to the cold and foreboding house, pictured in the November 10, 1945, *New Yorker,* one might imagine a horrible creature to be within such a house. Yet every rendering of the character who would be named The Thing is of a meek, timid, shy creature with a grin that suggests incompetence but not harm. Given that the characters were not named until 1963, it would seem that the 1945 reference to "The Thing" had little or no connection with the character who had been appearing in Addams Family cartoons since 1938. Then again, Addams's work has always

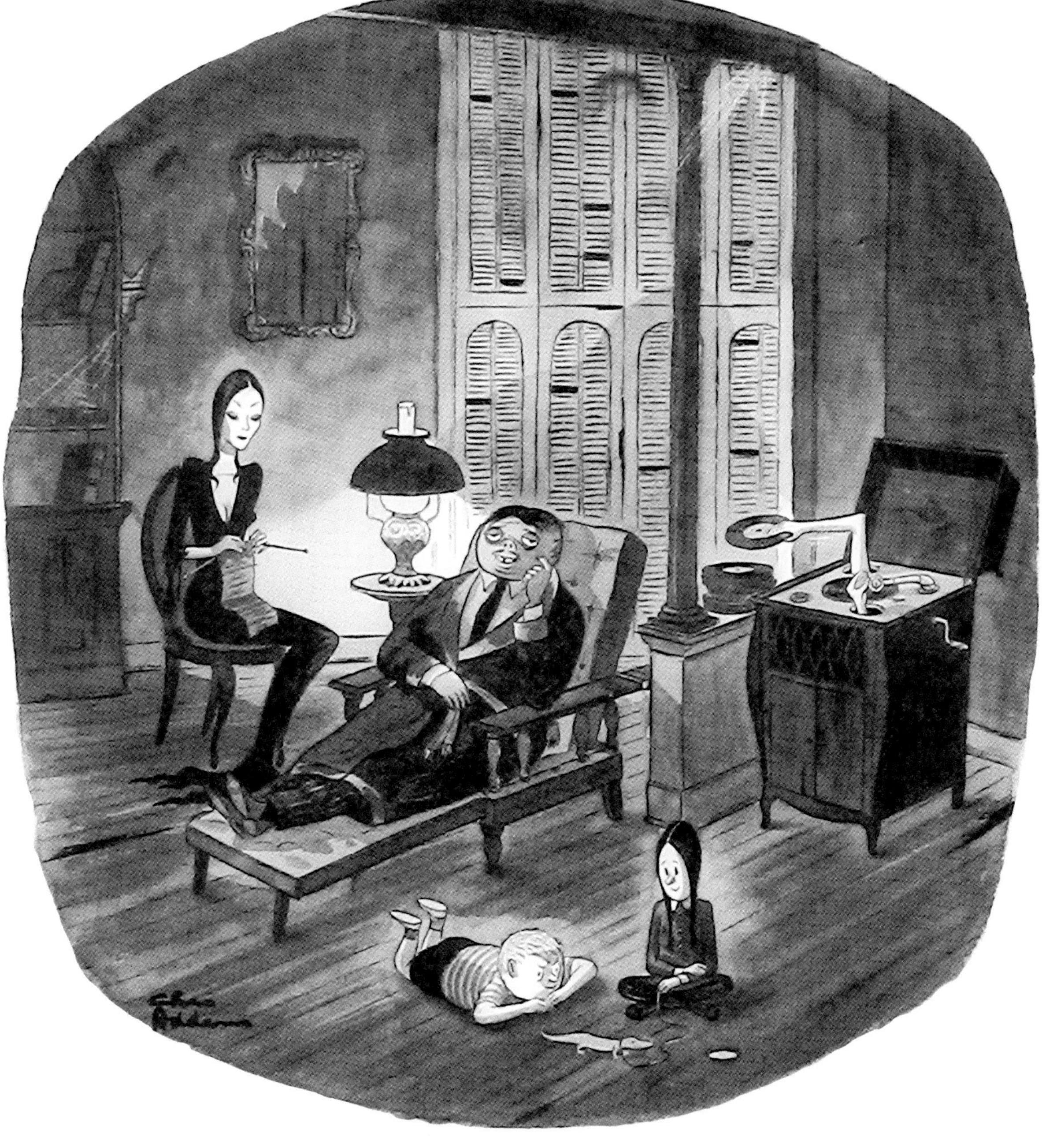

reflected the possibility of terror inflicted by the mildest of soft-spoken men and genteel women, any of whom might have just caused the demise of a spouse.

Appearing in nearly thirty Addams Family drawings and book covers, The Thing most often looks down from between the gallery balustrades within the Family home. However, on close scrutiny, we can find him crawling from beneath the snow on the cover of the book *Dear Dead Days: A Family Album* (Putnam, 1959), at the Family's feet in the back of the paddy wagon on the cover of the compilation *Black Maria* (Simon & Schuster, 1960), and peeking through the parlor pocket doors in the 1948 drawing captioned "Now kick Daddy good night and run along to bed."

And, though television decided to make Thing the first truly helping hand, the Addams drawings have never suggested that the character does anything to assist in the functions of the house other than record changing. He is in attendance as a witness and seems unnoticed by the Family while clearly enjoying all Family activities. Equally clear by the drawings, The Thing is not part of the household staff, a position enjoyed by Lurch alone.

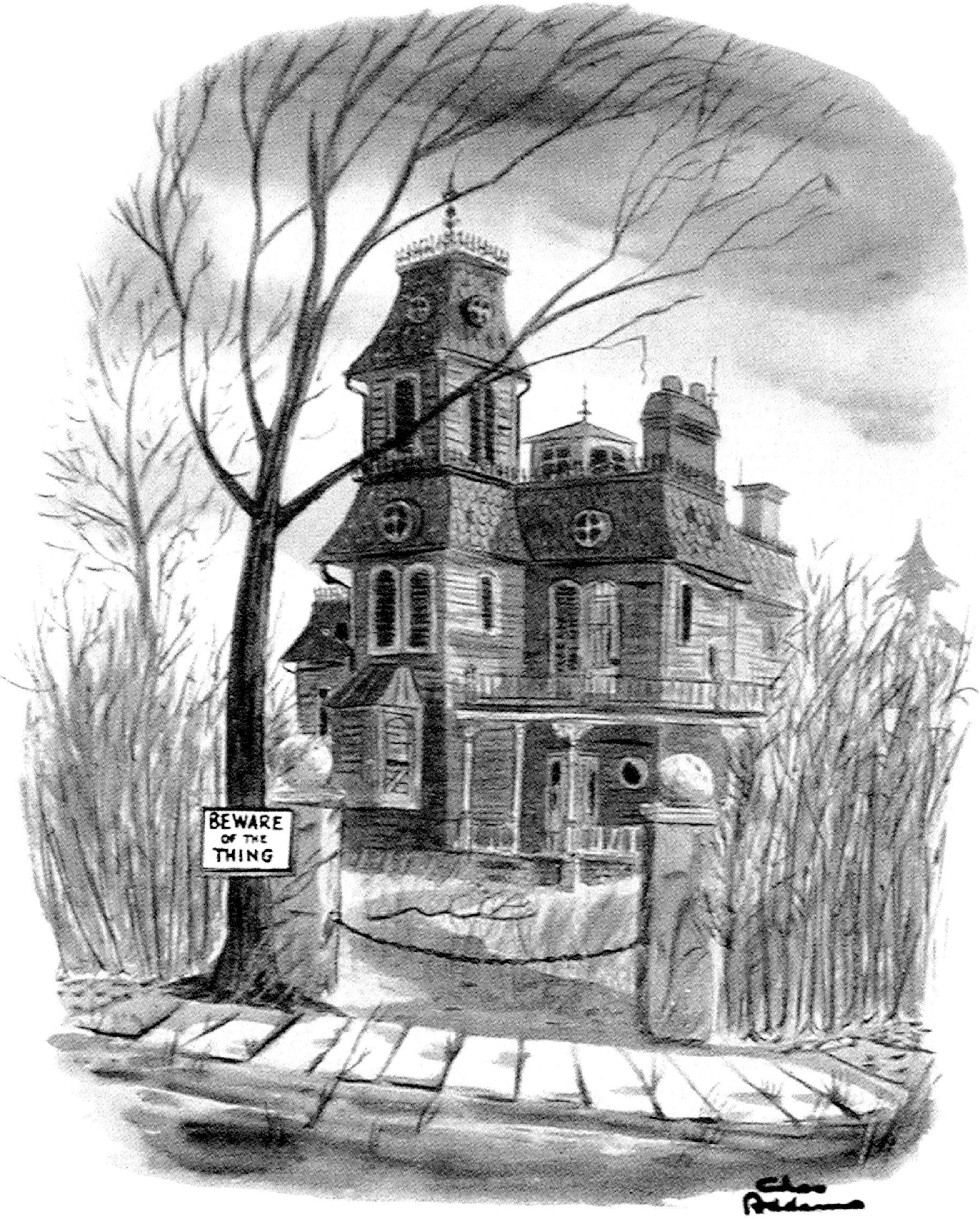
BEWARE
OF THE
THING

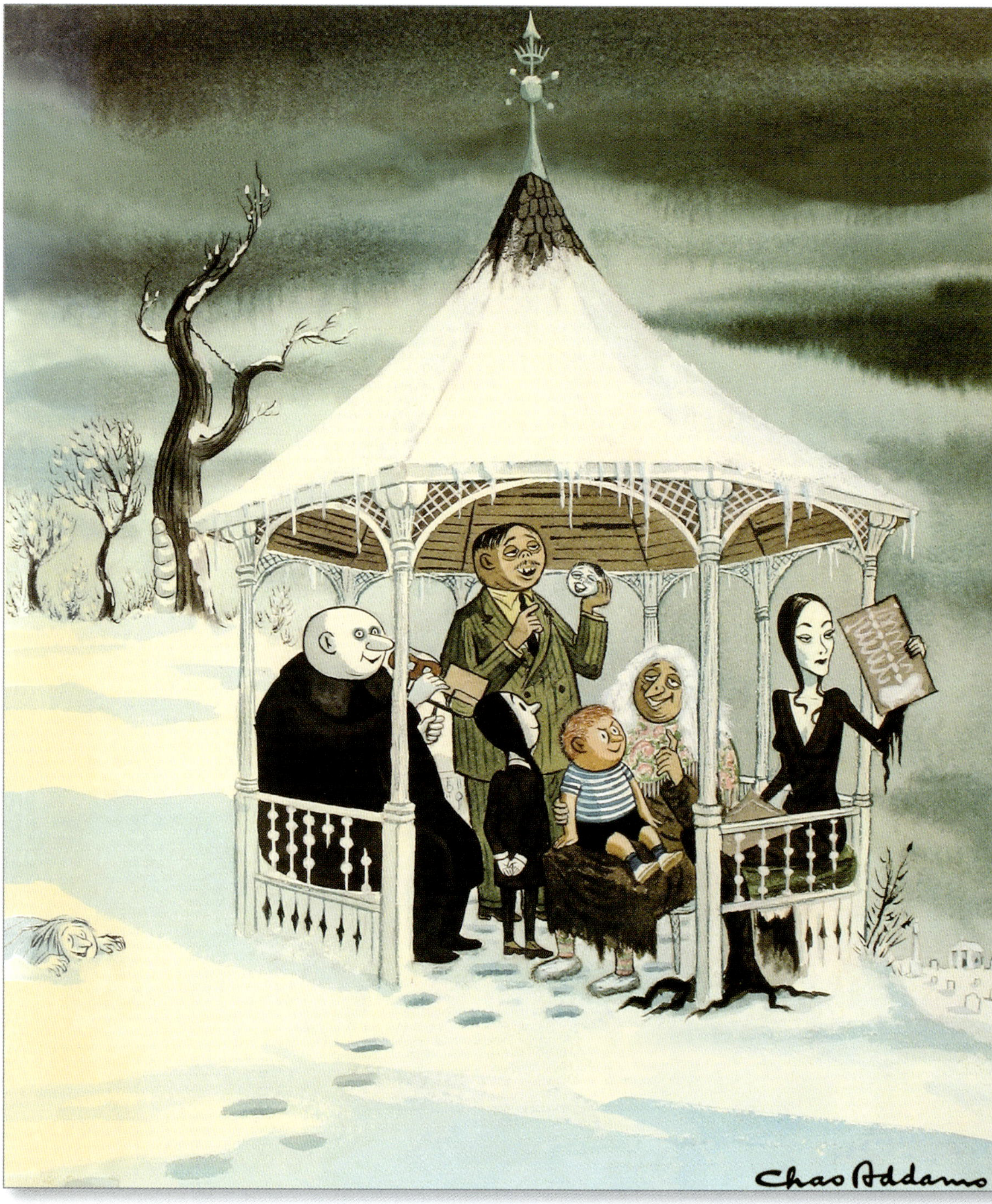
Chas Addams

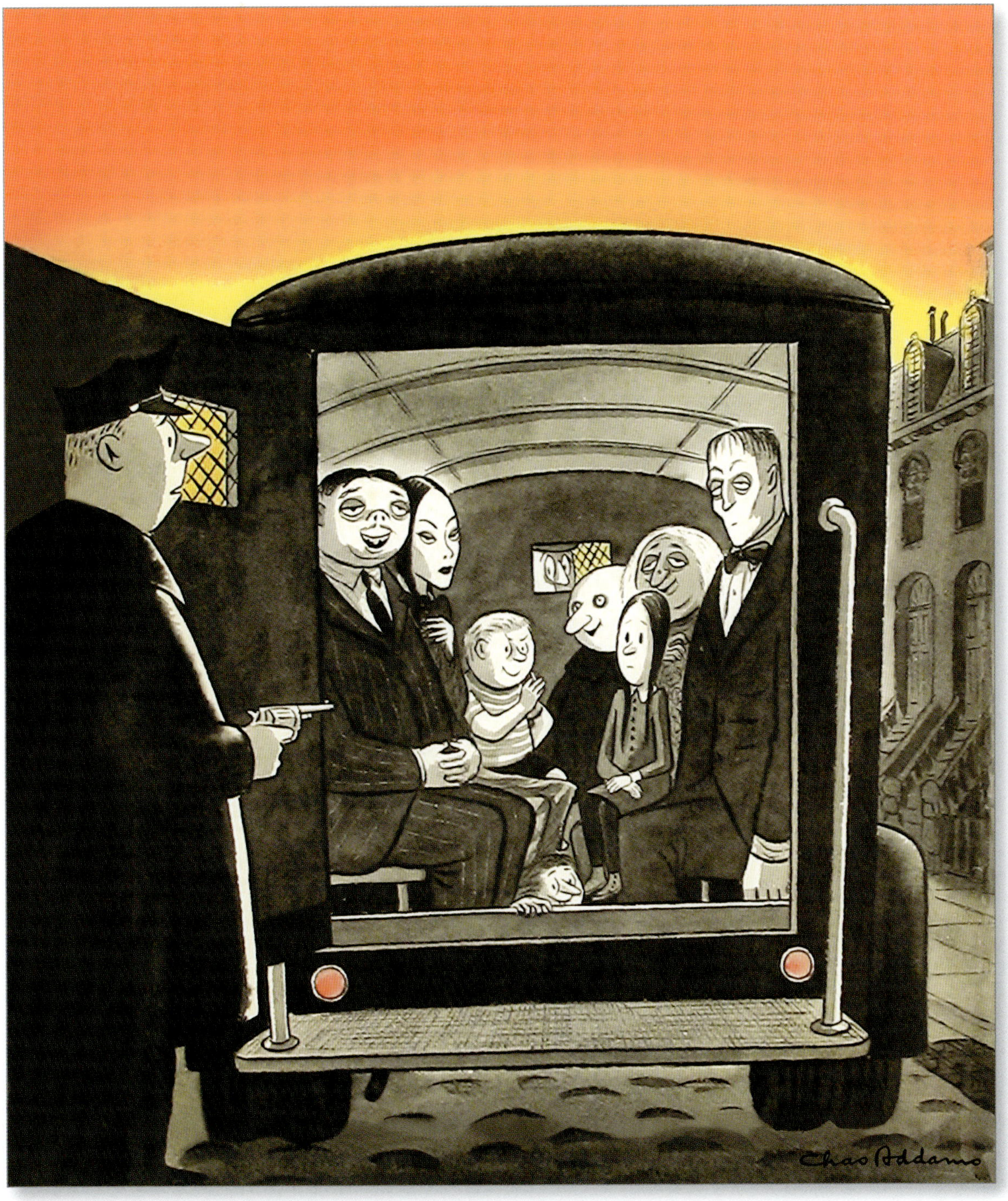
Chas Addams

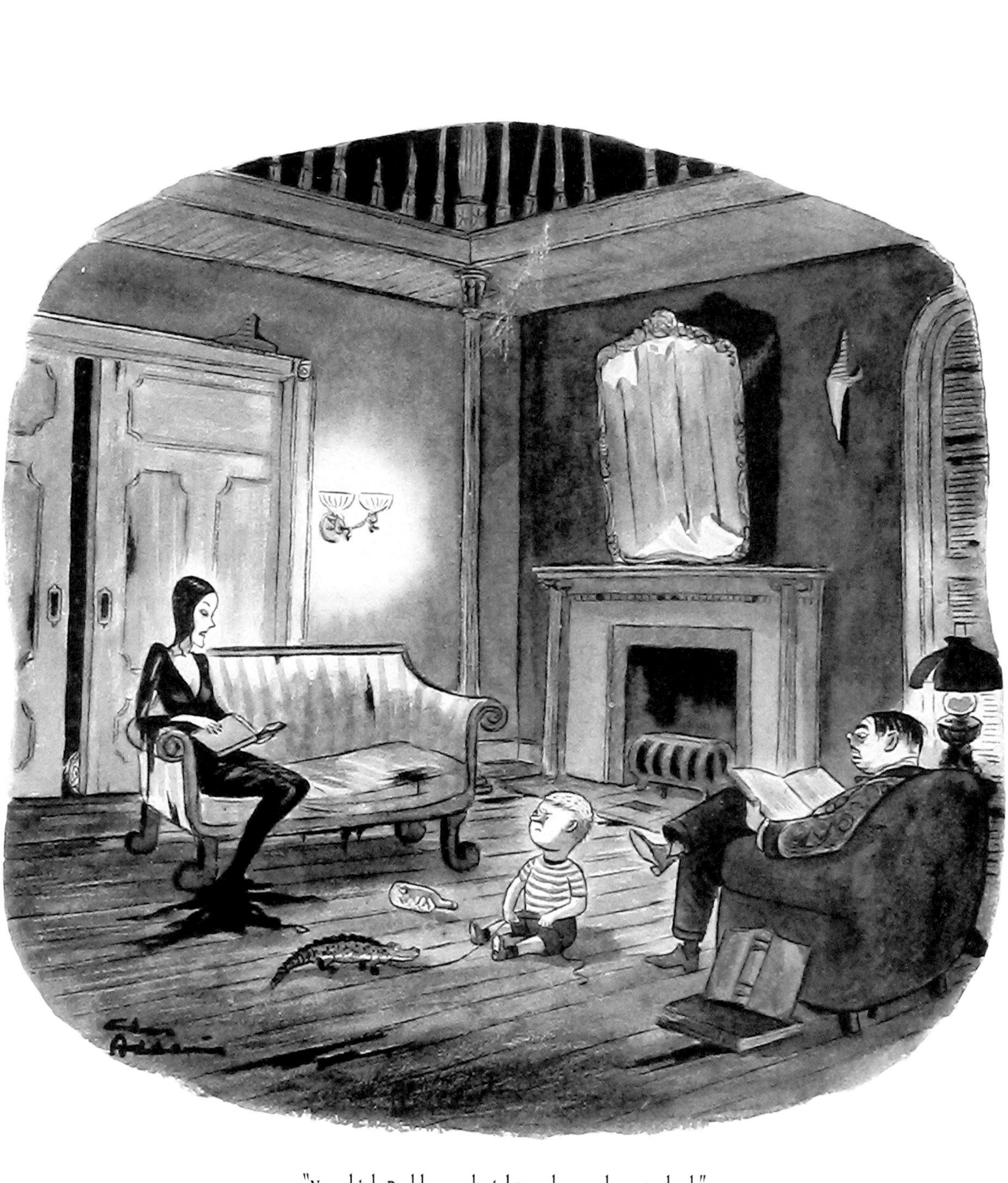

"Now kick Daddy good night and run along to bed."

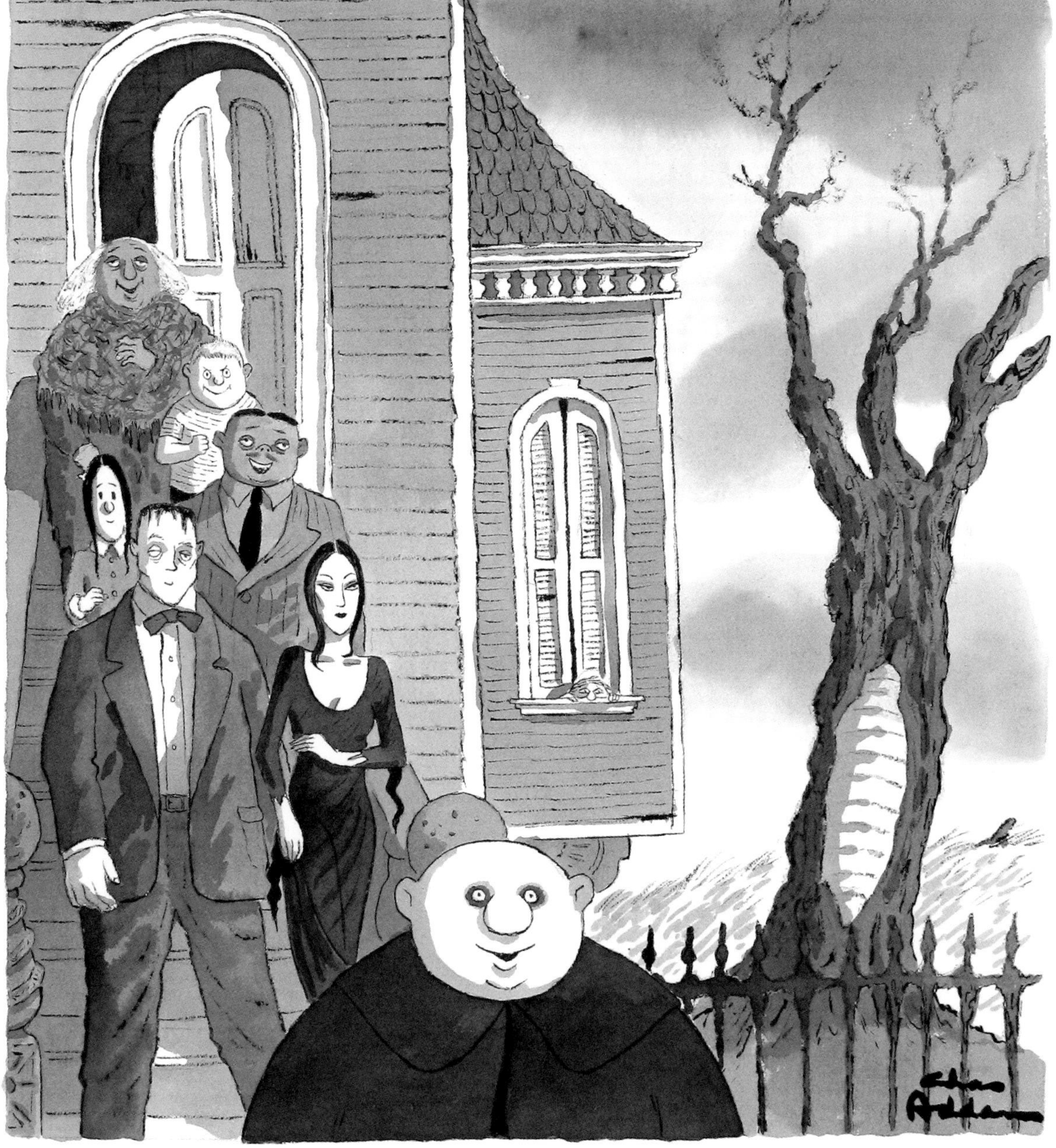

"We're on our way to The New Yorker Art Show."

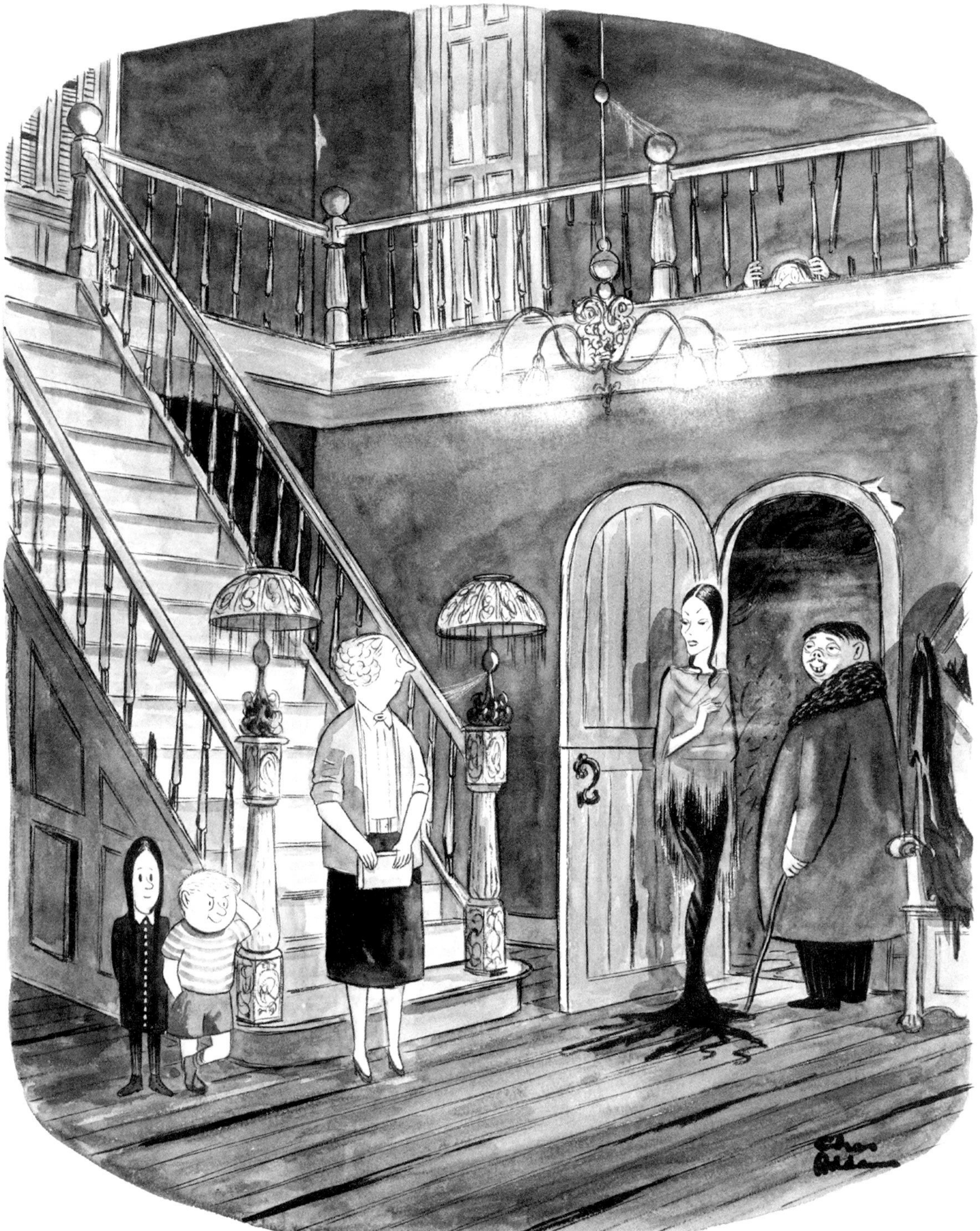

"We won't be late, Miss Weems. Get the children to bed around eight, and keep your back to the wall at all times."

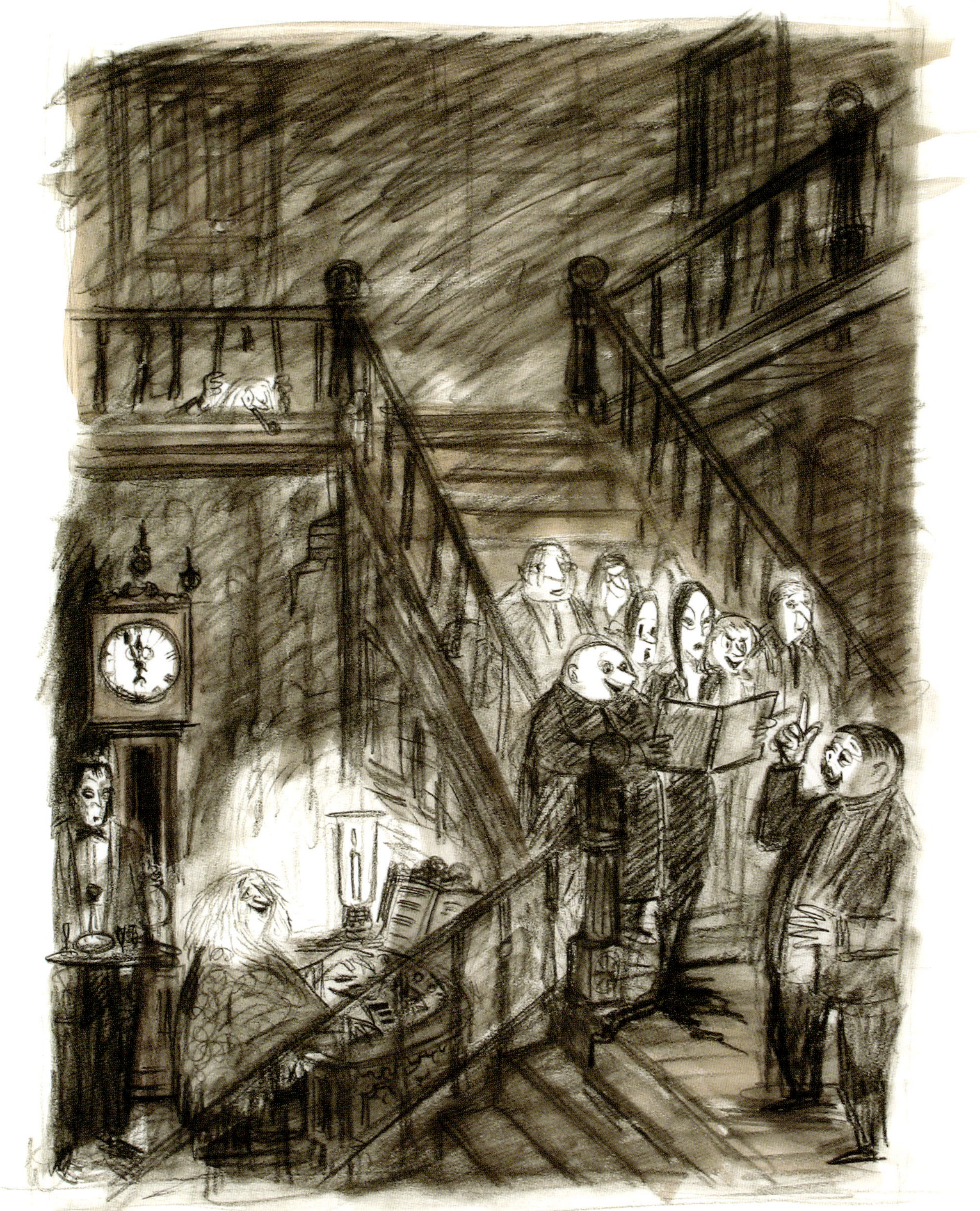

RELATIVES & FAMILY FRIENDS

IN most families there are in-laws and out-laws who seldom partake, and there are close friends who are like family because they join in frequently. The Addams Family is no exception. Any of Charles Addams's unpublished works in this section could have been sketched earlier, but it is more likely that his April 12, 1947, *New Yorker* cartoon—depicting a steel door in the attic that locks from the outside—holds the first extraneous Family member to appear, though we see only Uncle Eimar's hand at the barred window. Addams added an uncle each decade, in the form of a portrait or a story told to the children, and he once considered a strange woman named Cousin Rion, whose forte was nooses. She did not last.

During the fifties and sixties Addams was devoted to the original odd couple he called the "wall-eyed couple," referring to the husband; the wife was childlike, with a flat head and chopped hair. In 1964 Addams went so far as to give them a two-headed toddler, regarding whom Granny Frump naturally observed, "I think he looks a little like both of you."

And, finally, there is It. Charles Addams published only two drawings of the fabled hairball creature. The first work, captioned simply "This is it speaking," was not published until the second month of the television series, the Filmways producers having renamed It as Cousin Itt. It never appeared again until December 21, 1987, when the *New Yorker* either did cult history a favor or discovered a long-lost drawing in "the vault," a bastion of works held for more suitable publication dates. For a subject about which Charles Addams took little note, It created an Addams Family sensation topped only by that surrounding The Thing, thanks to both the television program and feature film character adaptations.

"One for the road?"

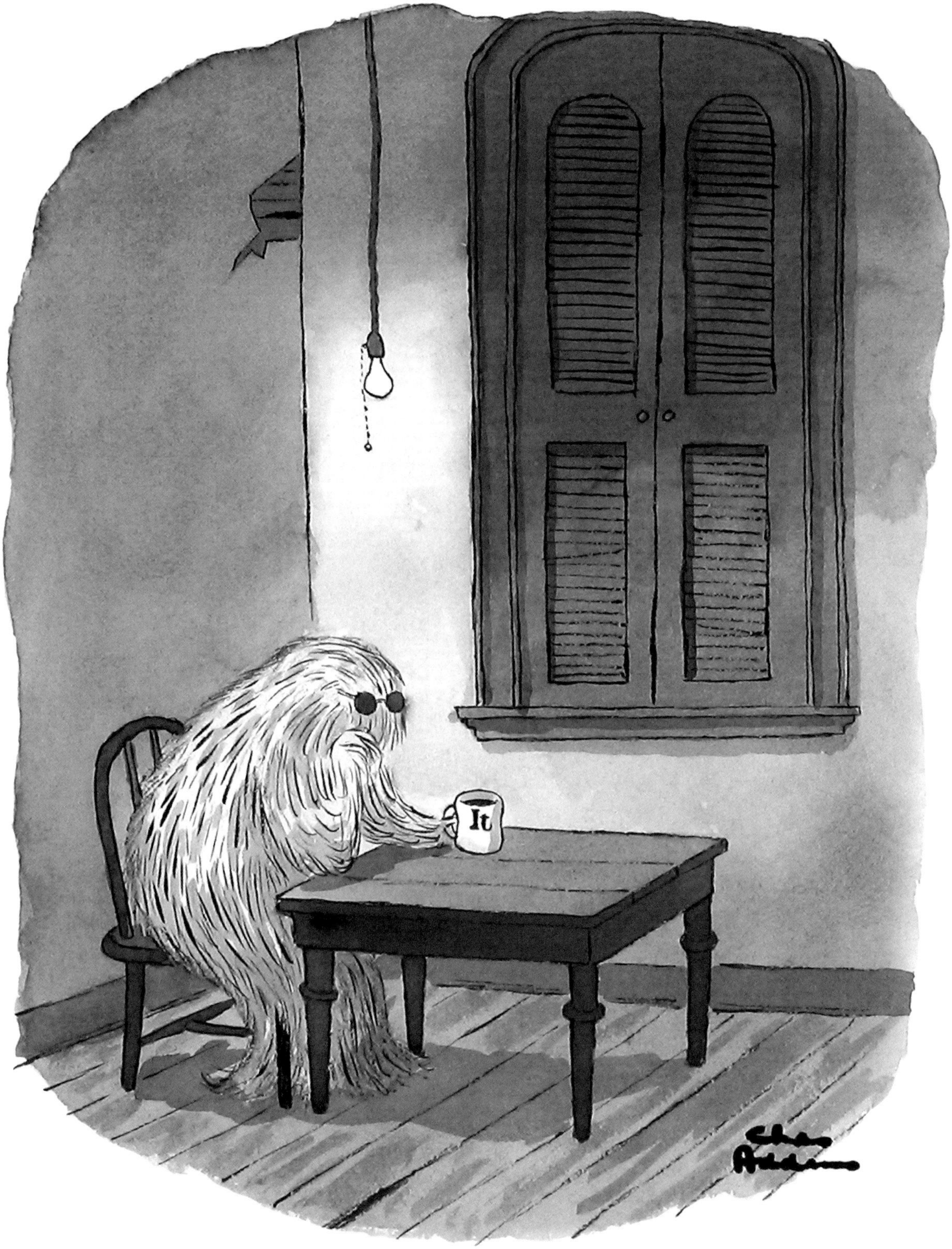
It

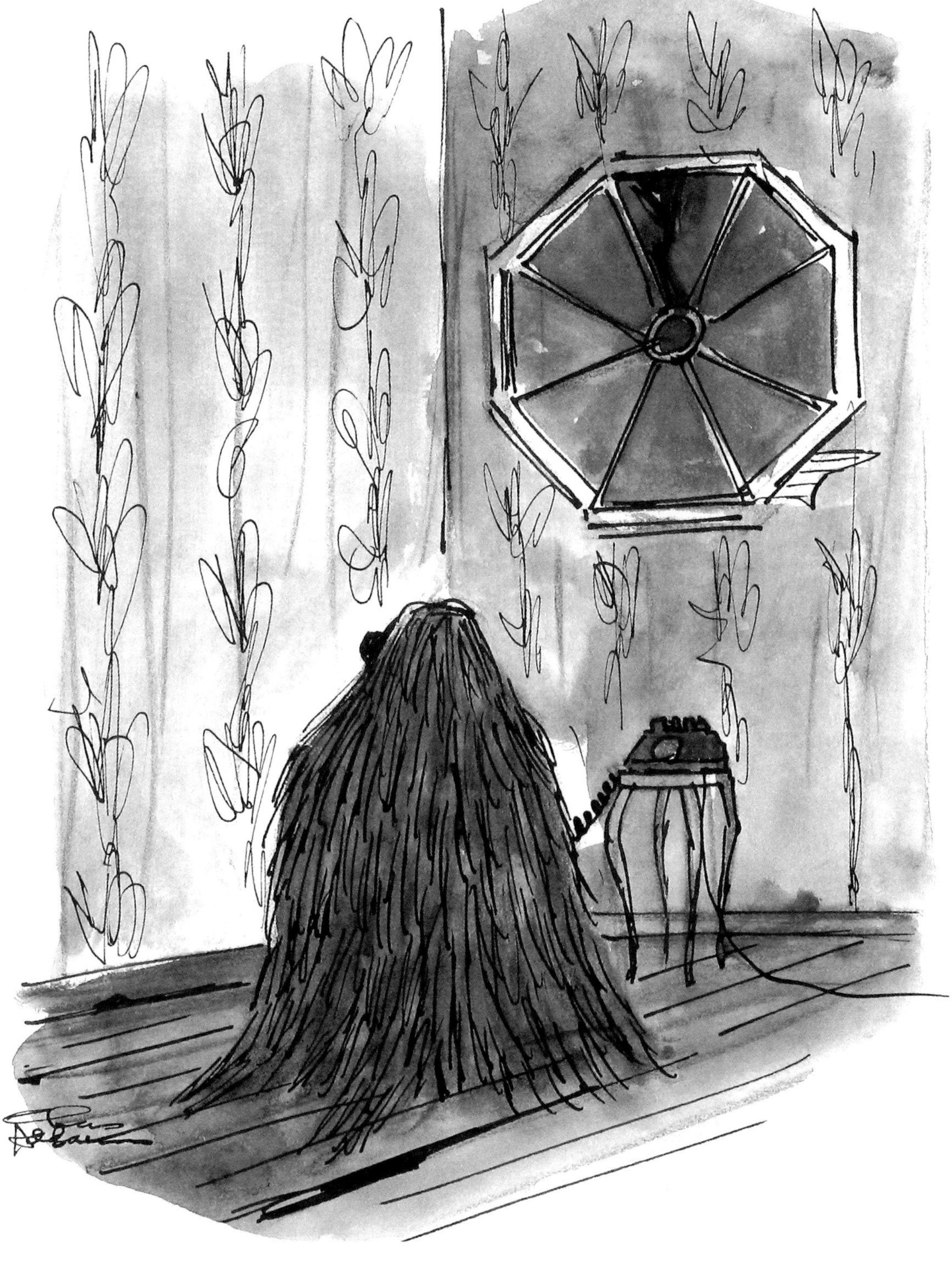

"This is it speaking."

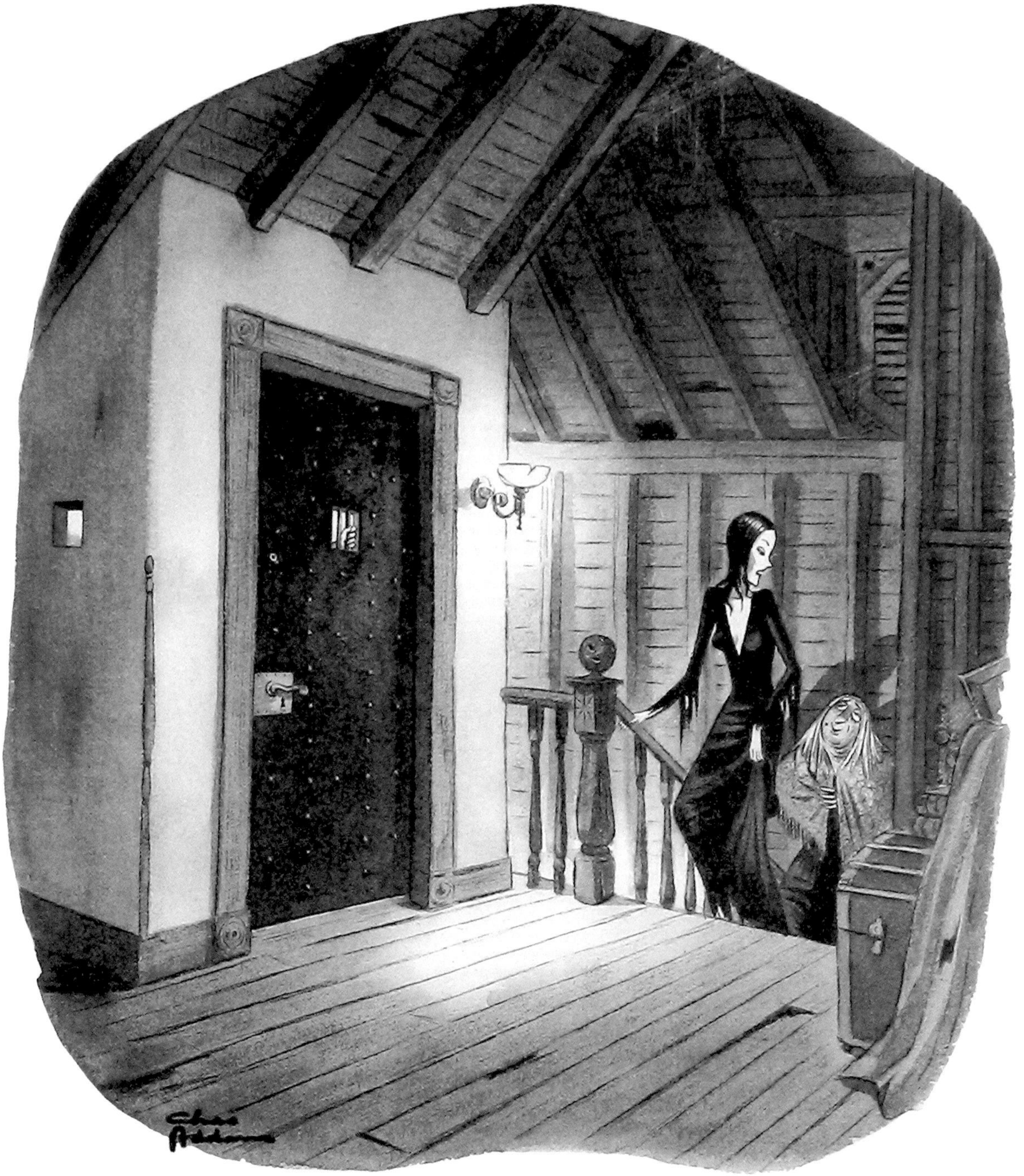

"We've had part of this floor finished off for Uncle Eimar."

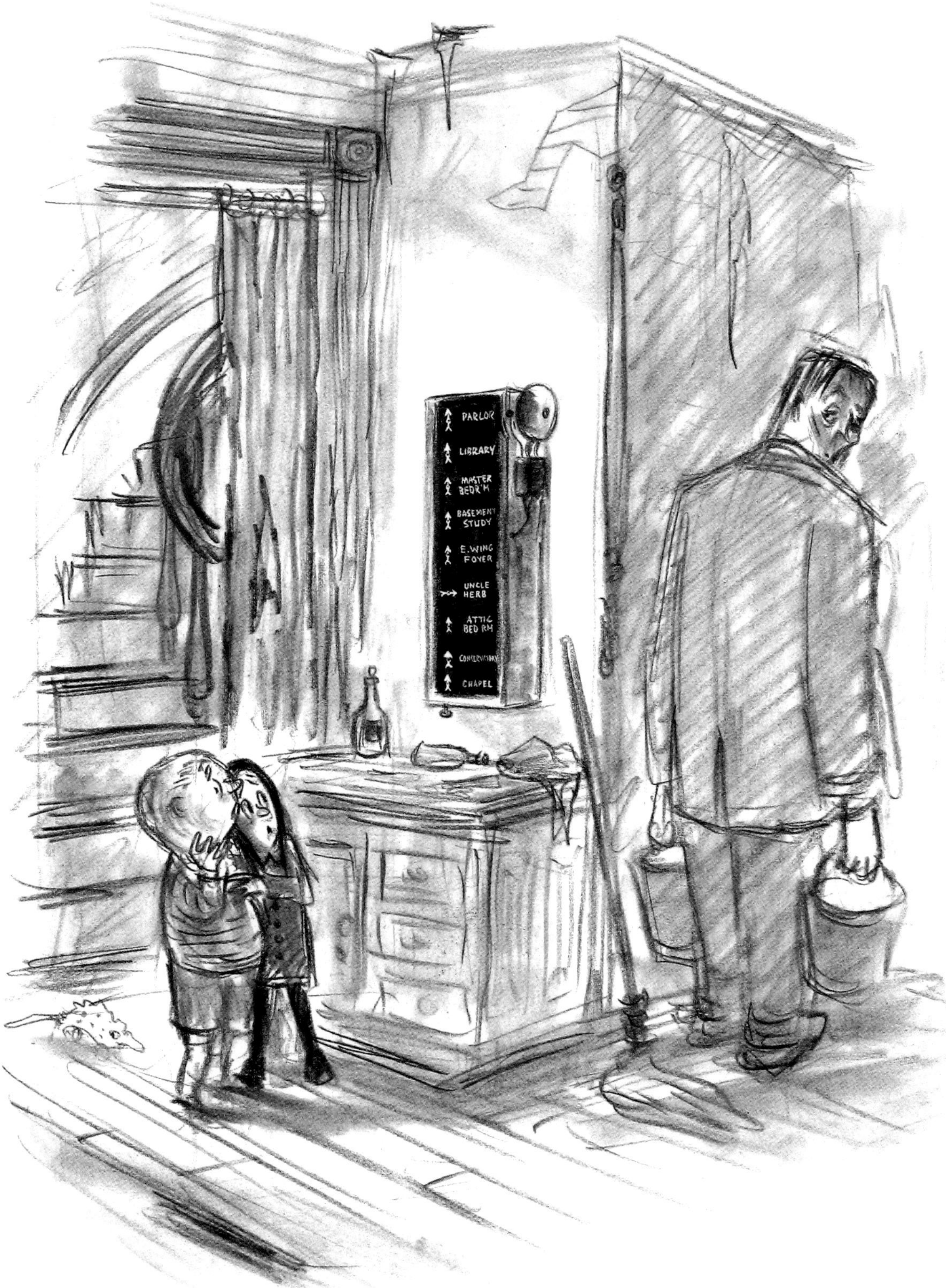
PARLOR
LIBRARY
MASTER BEDR'M
BASEMENT STUDY
E. WING FOYER
UNCLE HERB
ATTIC BED RM
CONSERVATORY
CHAPEL

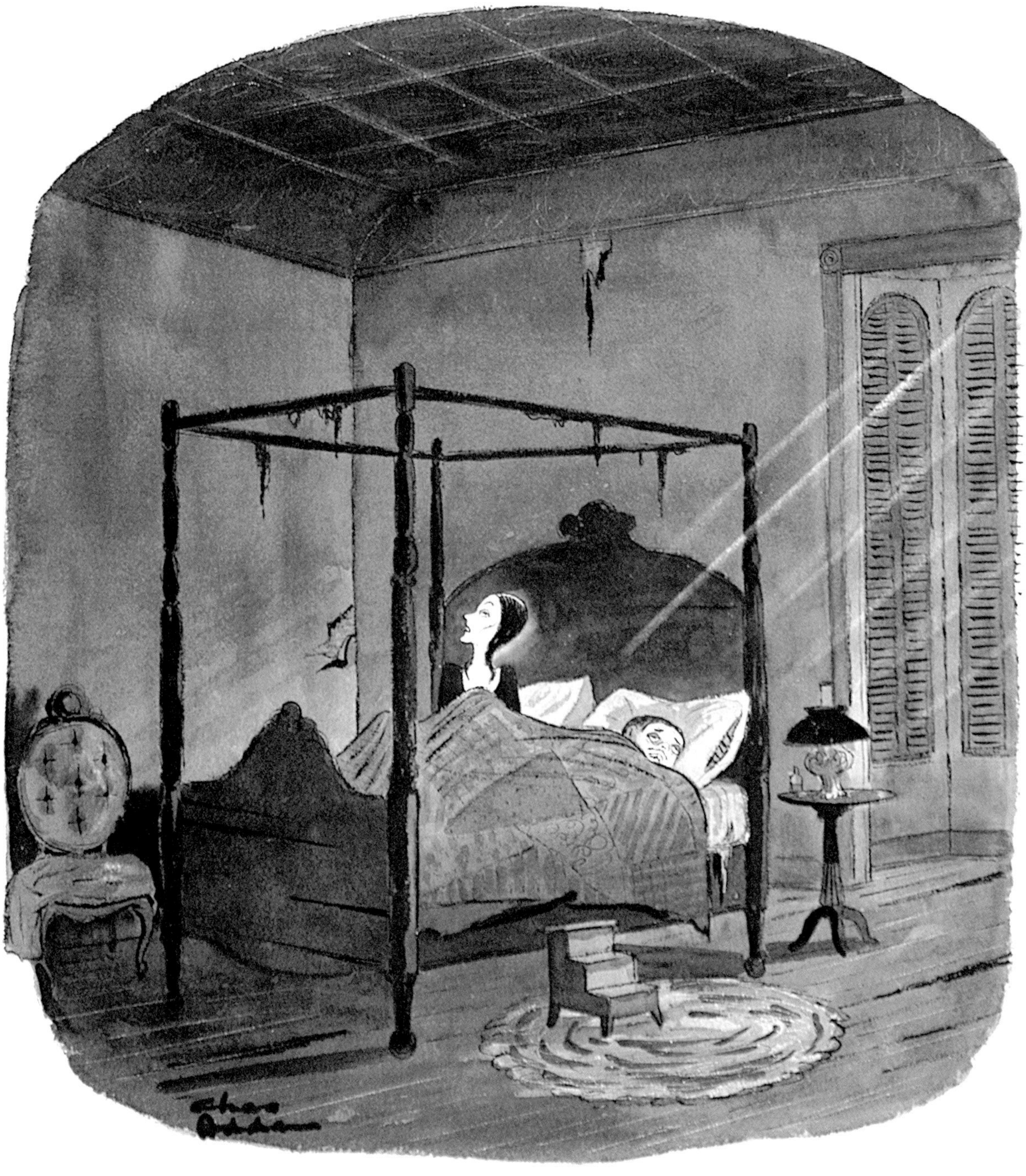

"That's two. Oh, dear, I'll never sleep until he drops the other one."

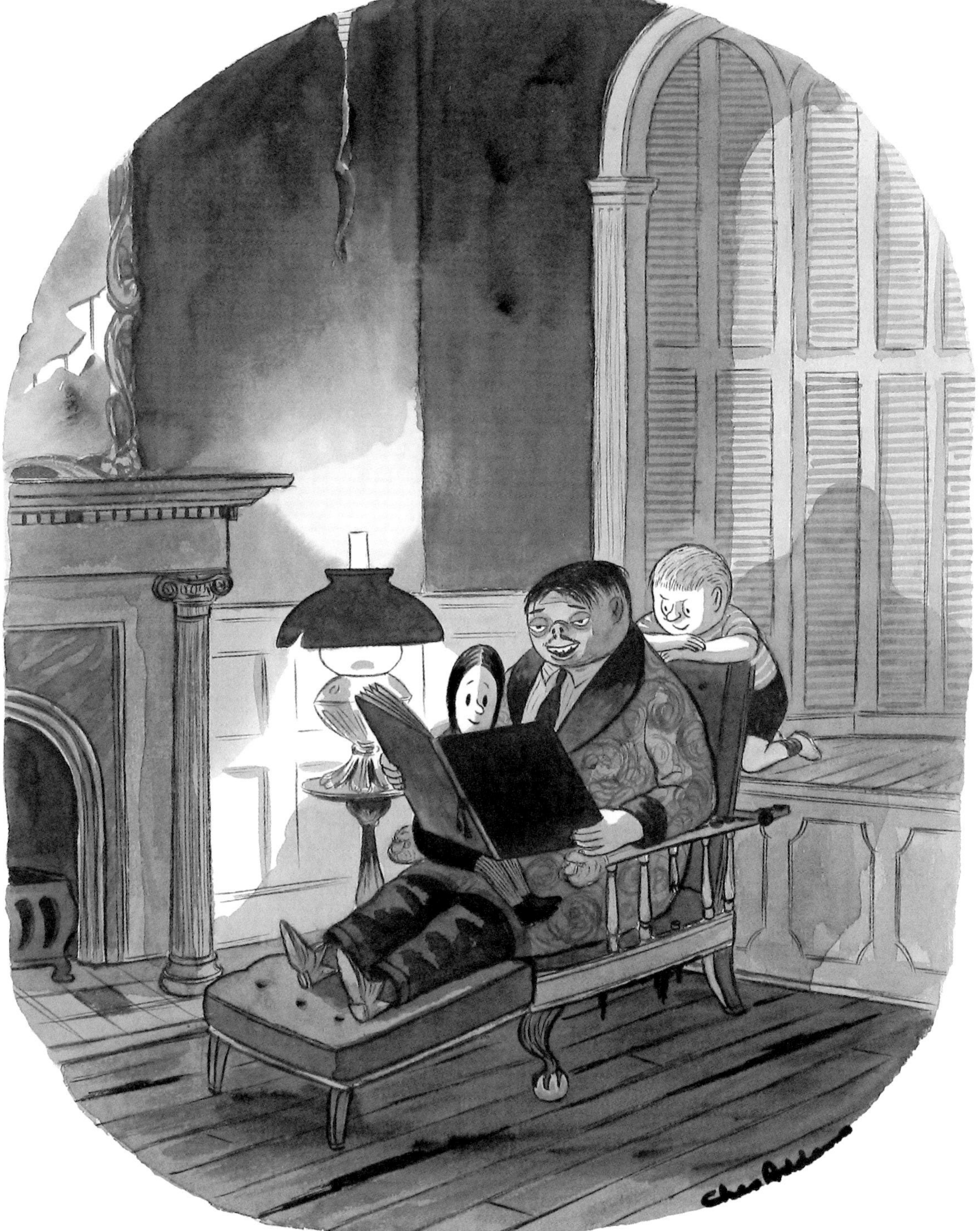

"And this is your Uncle Cosimo, a man of whom it may be truly said
he left the world a little worse for his having lived in it."

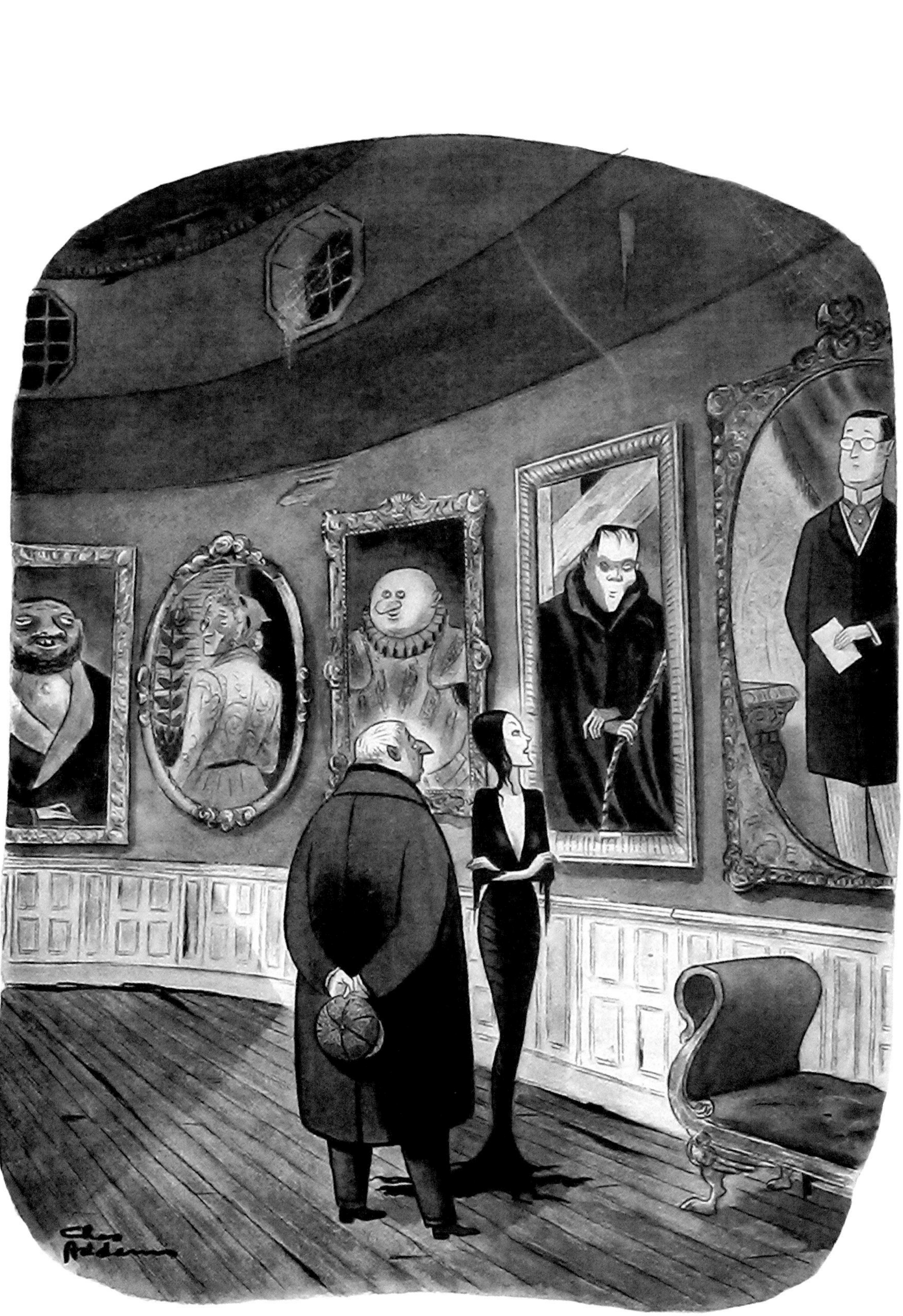
Chas Addams

"This is Uncle Zander. Grandfather always called him the black sheep."

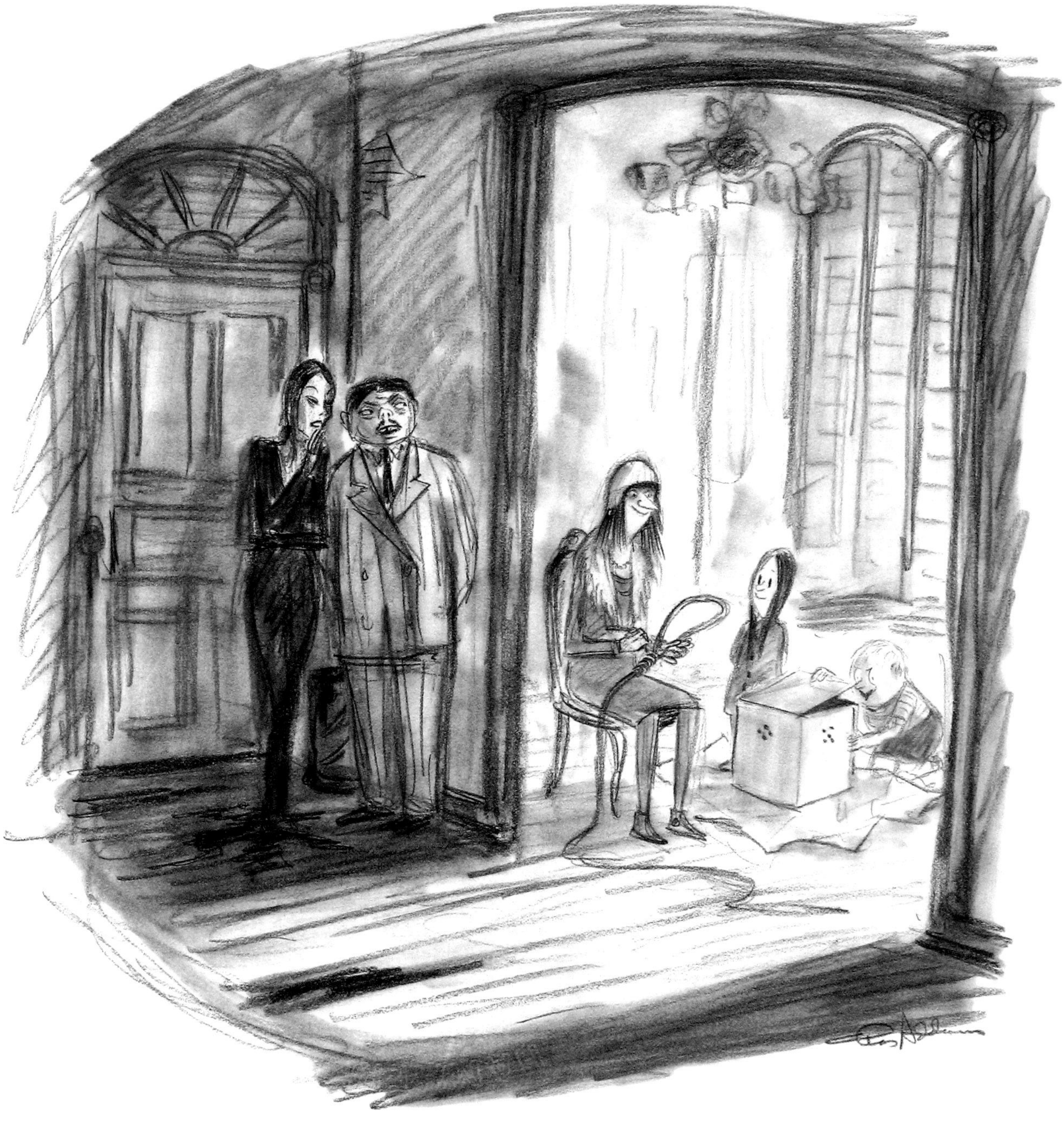

"One of us has to speak to Cousin Rion. She's spoiling the children horribly."

"I like them. They wear well."

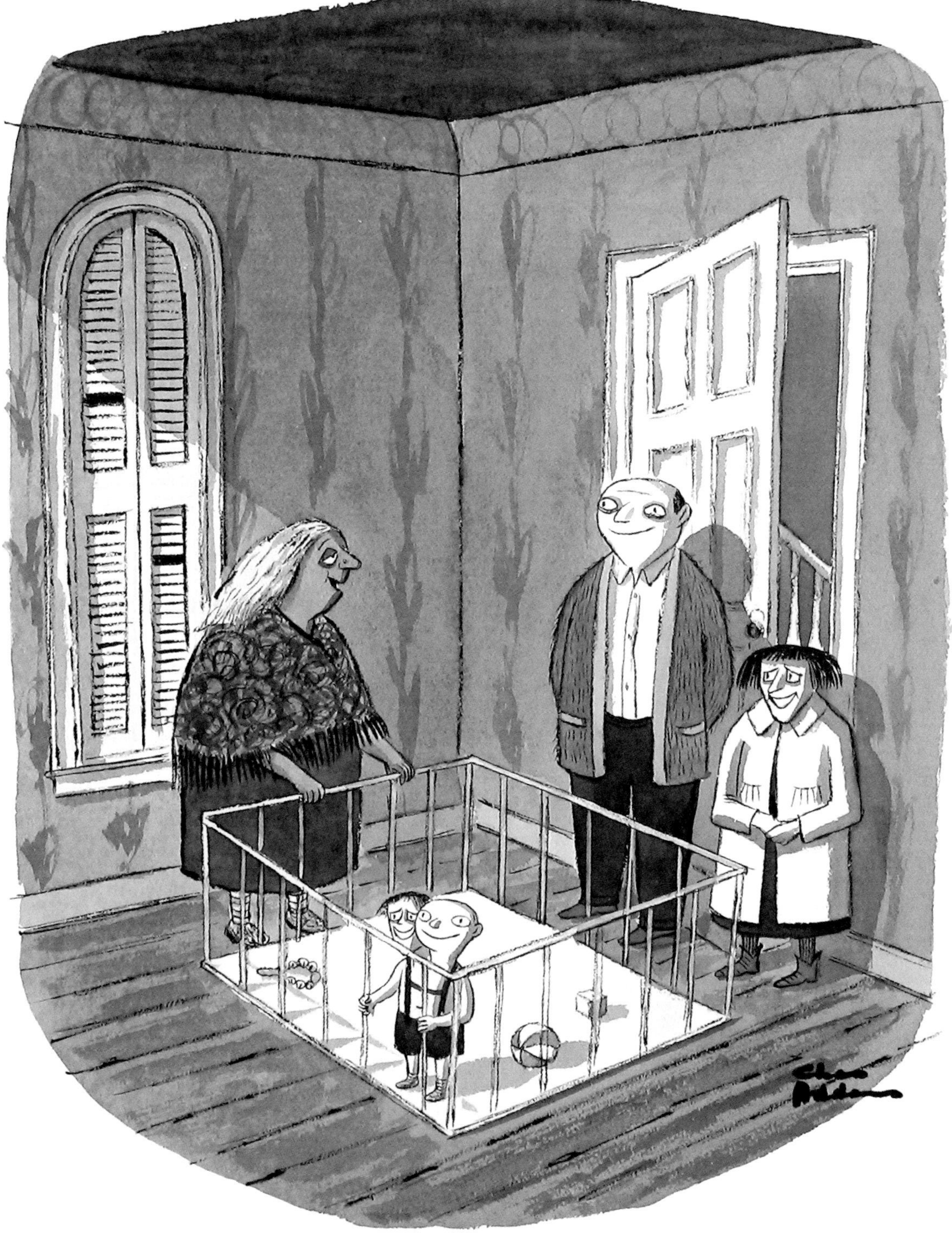

"I think he looks a little like both of you."

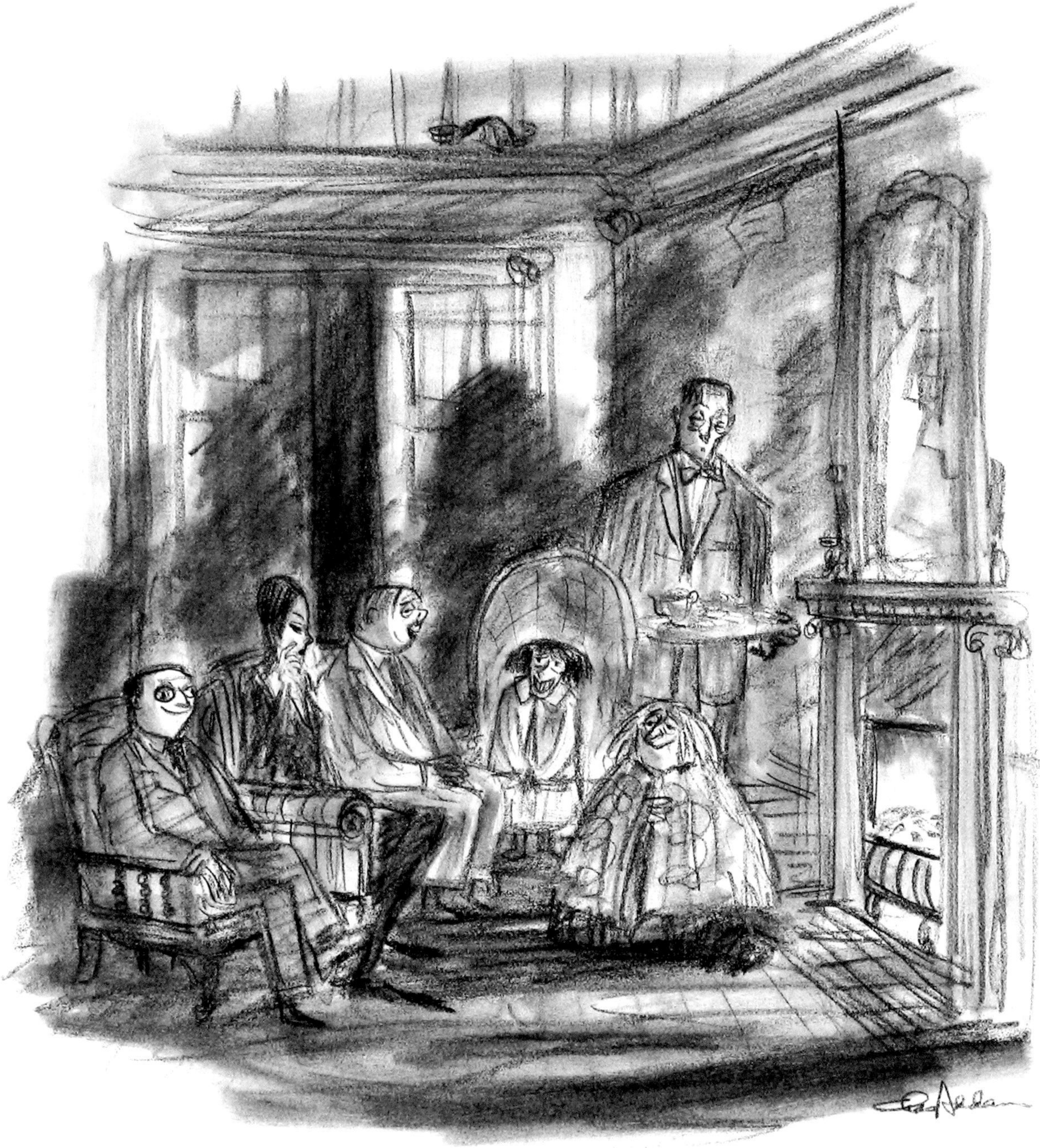

"I've heard it said that there isn't one of us who doesn't have a novel in him somewhere."

"We'd love you to stay, if you don't mind pot luck."

"We think it's a girl."

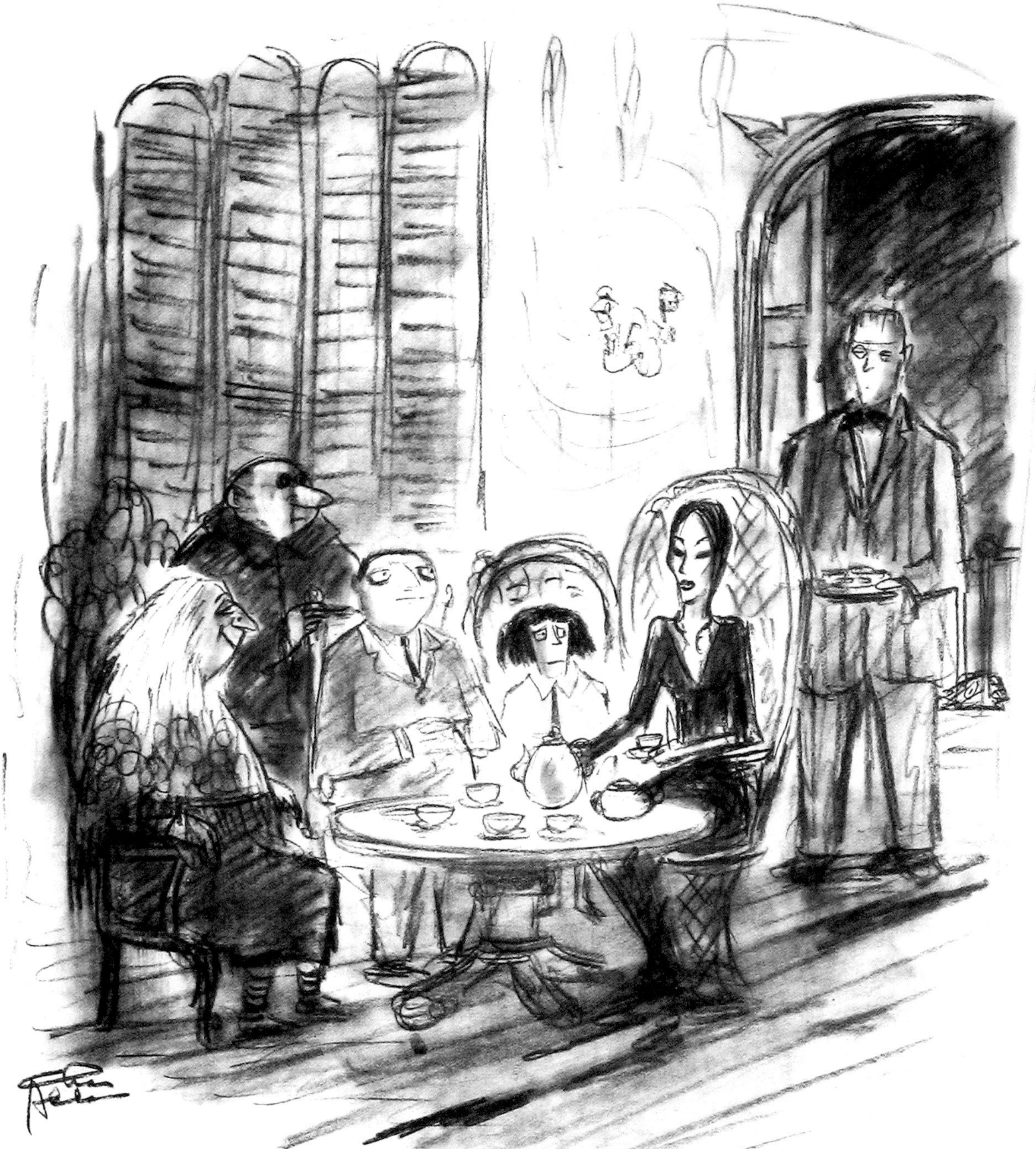

"What worries me most about radiation is the thought of mutations in coming generations."

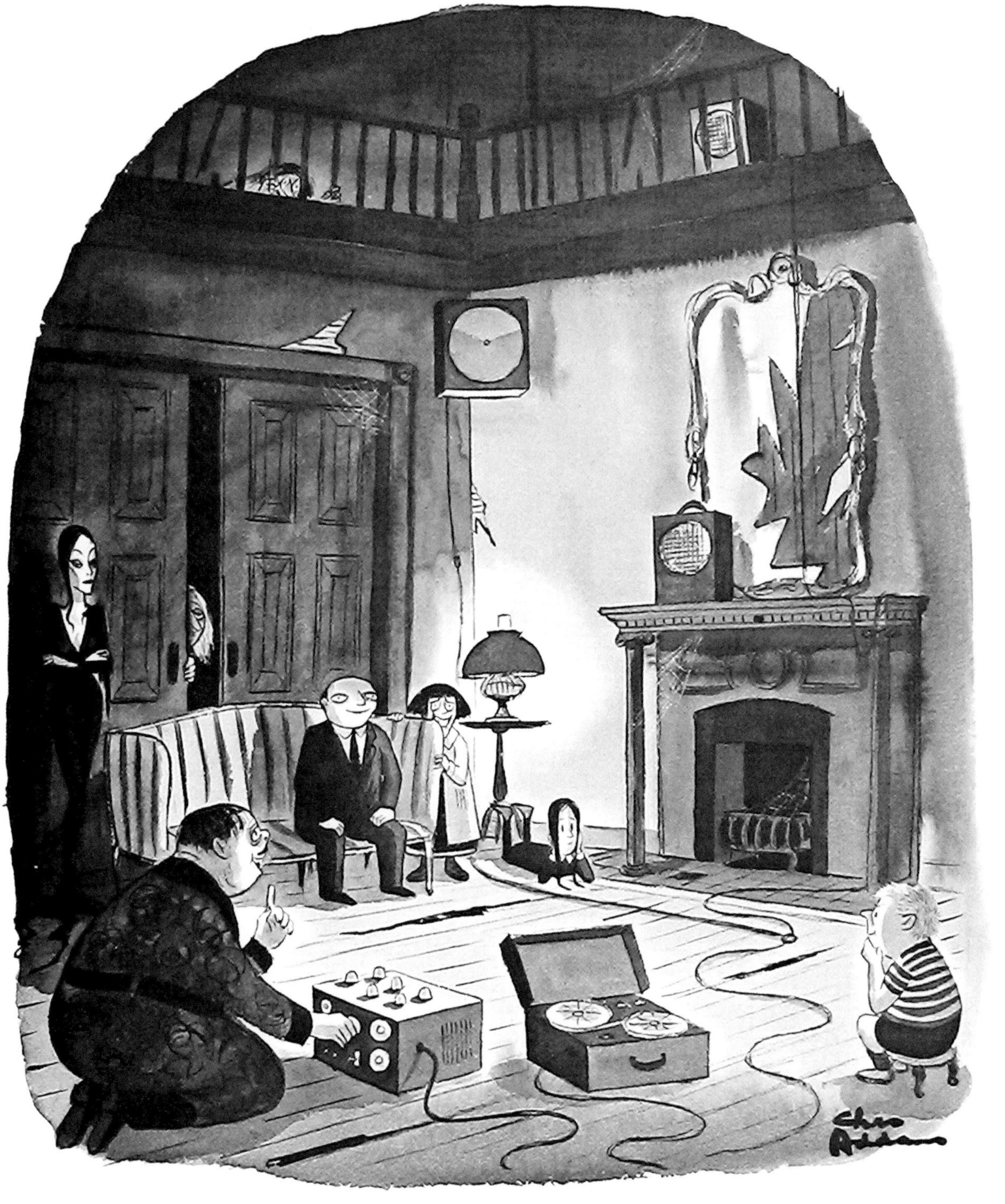

"Now . . . listen to the shriek run through its entire range without peaking."

A House to Die For

PERHAPS the most instantly recognizable work by Charles Addams to have signified The Addams Family as unique in the cartoon world is the December 21, 1946, *New Yorker* publication of what shall be forever known as "Boiling Oil." It is a beautiful painting, a masterpiece of composition, premise, and technique. The substance in the cauldron Lurch is about to pour off the rooftop of the Addams house, under Gomez's supervision and with the approval of Morticia and The Thing, has been speculated to be boiling water, molten lead, or any liquid one wishes to imagine. The Addams Family followed the customs of their ancestors by pouring boiling oil on foes who intended to invade their fortress and interrupt their peaceful existence. Addams lets us know how his Family feels about the suggestion that carolers at Christmastime should make one appreciate strangers sharing "the holiday," regardless of religious or celebratory preferences. It is an out-and-out invasion and must be dealt with accordingly.

The implied threat—a device used in nearly all Addams drawings when the suggestion of harm or death was imminent—of dowsing the sweet interlopers is far more effective than showing them covered in and writhing under boiling oil. What is distinctive about this particular scene is that we cannot help but be drawn into it by the presence of the house. The viewer's perspective is brilliantly engineered to be as one with the Family on the roof, and regardless of how we feel about the well-meaning carolers, we shall help Lurch take care of the perpetration. The warm light cascading through shutters and arched windows onto the snow-covered ground, bathing the carolers with the added help of a child holding a lantern, takes us off our guard by its coziness. Then the reality of the scene comes into focus with Addams's extraordinary use of moonlight as it casts the shadow of a great, leafless tree stretching across the yard, reaching onto the house, striving to grasp the innocent ones at the front door. We notice the icicles and gutter downspouts all frozen in the menacing cold and, finally, the rooftop dormer topped by a widow's walk bordered with a grille of wrought iron arrows framing the deserved response to such unwelcome naïveté. Warm and delicious, freezing and foreboding, daring and menacing, all at the same time.

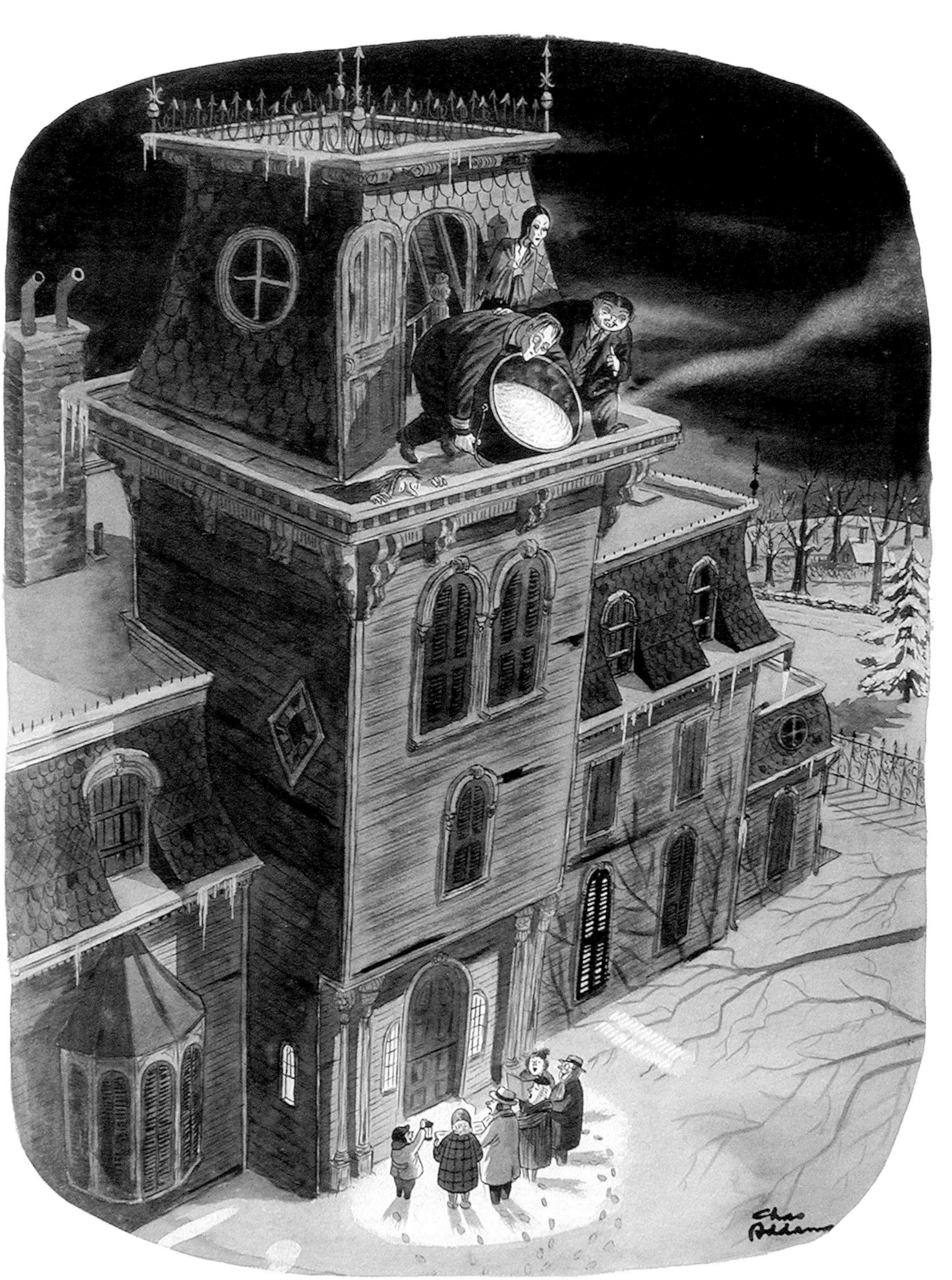
Chas Addams

This is the house of all Addams houses. Every town or village or city in America has at least one. The numerous fans claiming to have the original Addams house within their sights constituted, and still does, a cult unto itself, from Key West to Spokane and back to Rhinebeck, and everywhere in between. Charles Addams loved architecture and loved to construct his own, employing details from a variety of styles and periods. His very dear friend Dona Guimaraes, who eventually became editor of the Home Design and Entertaining sections of the *New York Times*, and with whom he antiqued as long as they both lived, had access to enormous amounts of reference material and supplied Addams with pages and pages of furniture, turrets, windows, grillwork, roofs—everything they both adored about Victoriana and beyond. Thus his interiors of the great, decaying mausoleum are just as fanciful as the exteriors, exhibiting his keen attention to all details.

The most interesting twist to the ongoing speculations about "the Addams house" is that the artist's residence was a "regular" home, albeit filled with bizarre and unique treasures and hundreds of one-of-a-kind gifts from friends and fans. Charles Addams was a consummate artist who designed from fantasy as well as from the familiar.

"You're just in time. We just finished the new wing."

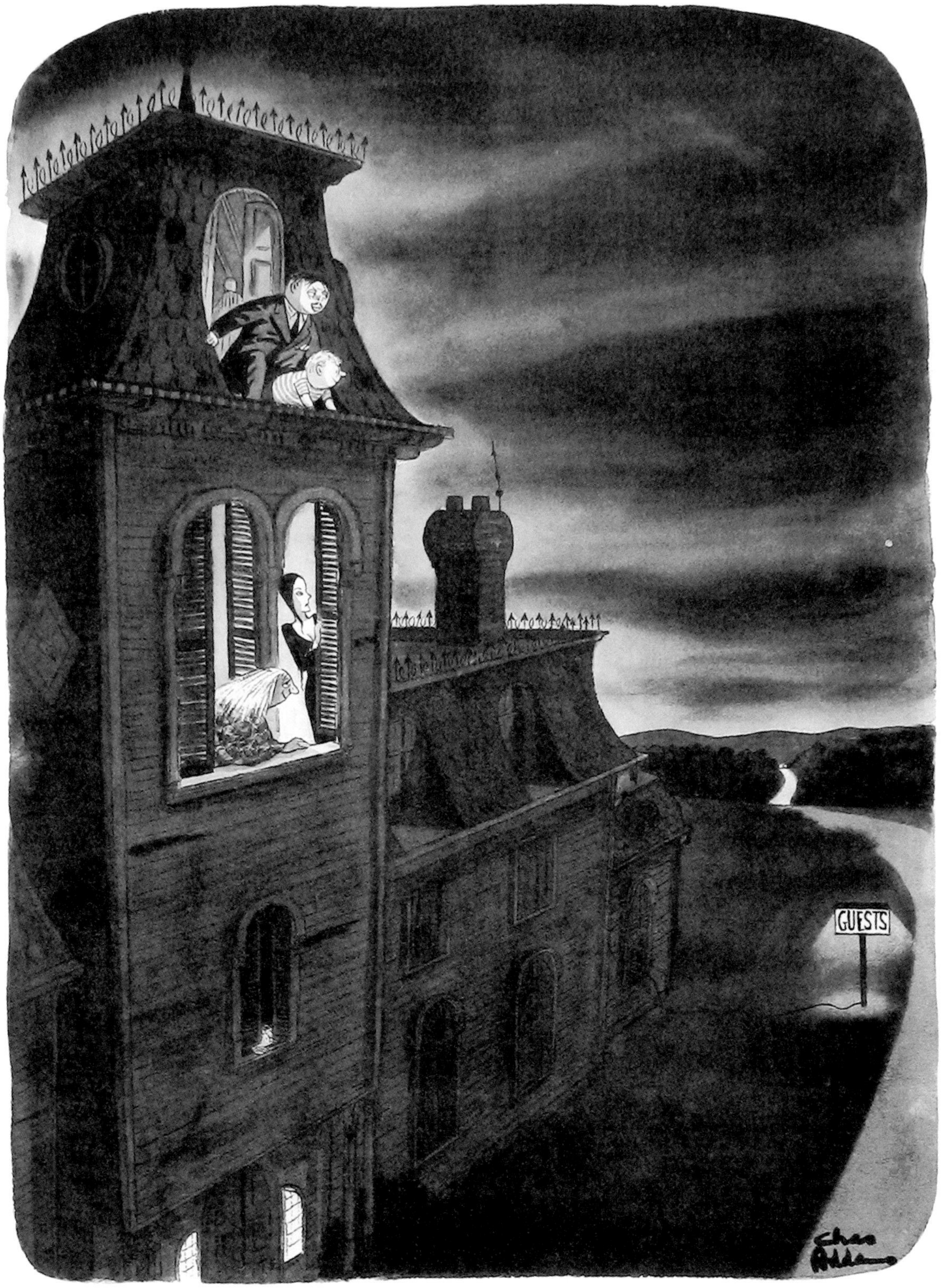
GUESTS
Chas Addams

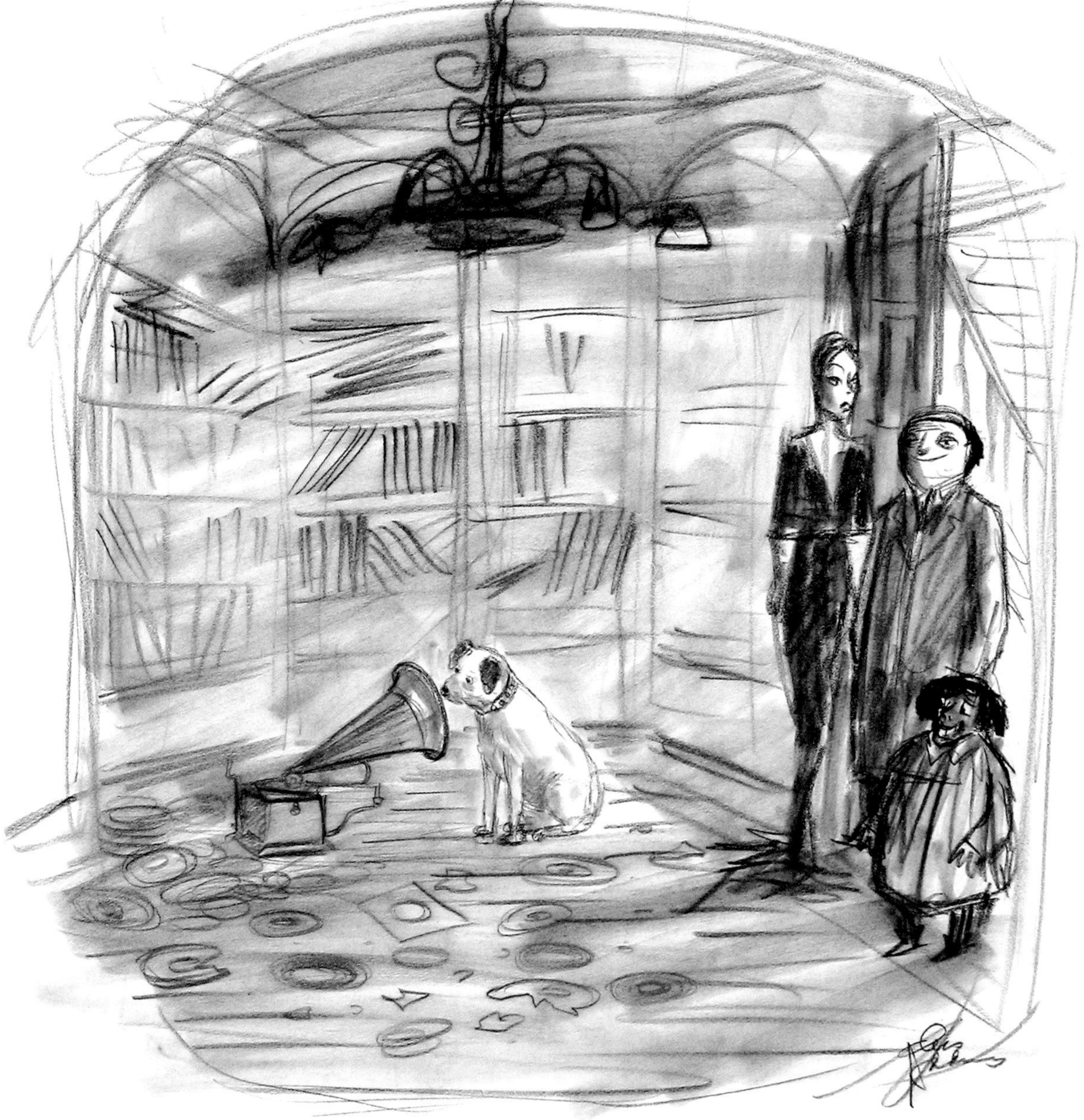

". . . and this is the music room."

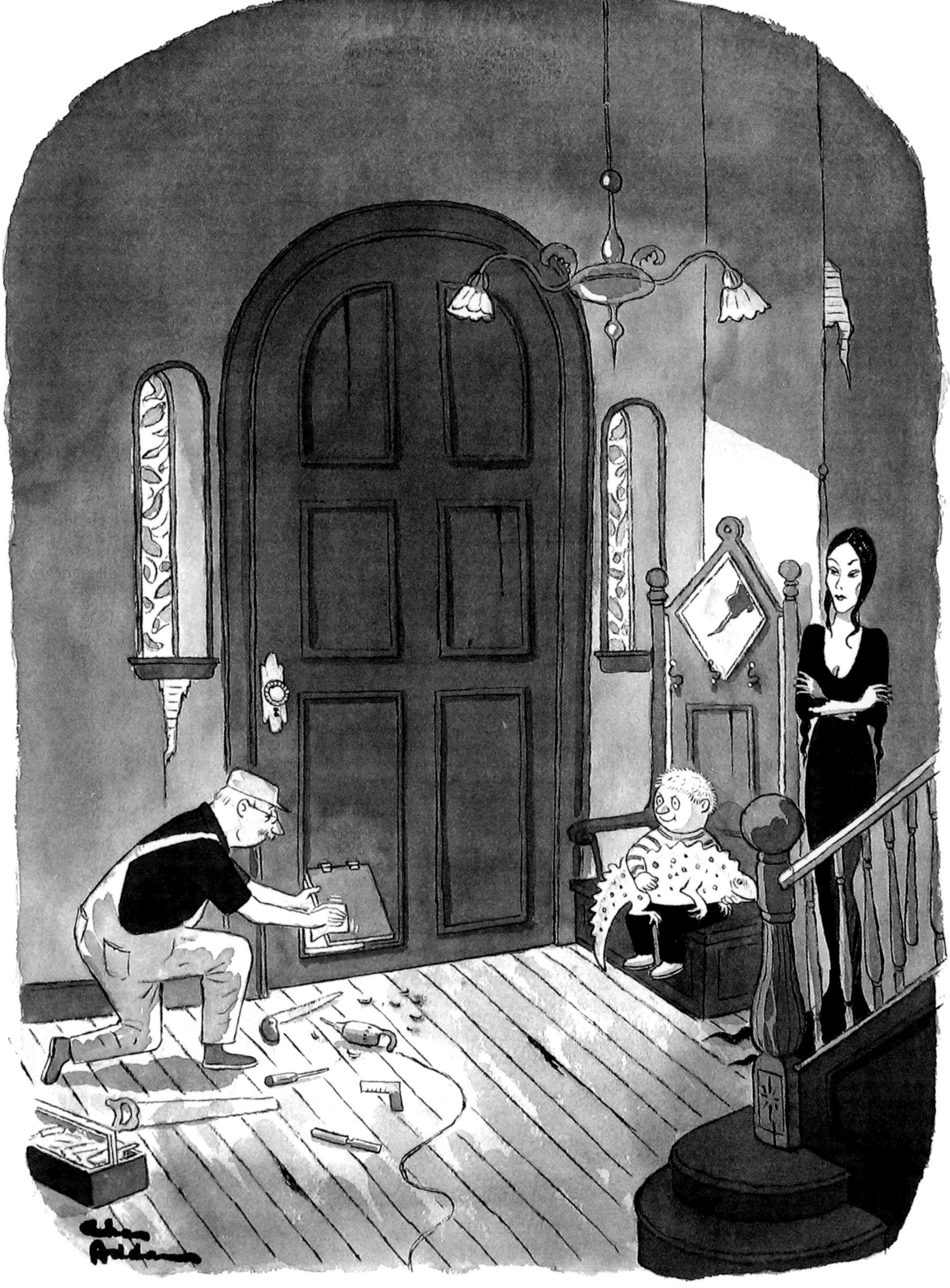

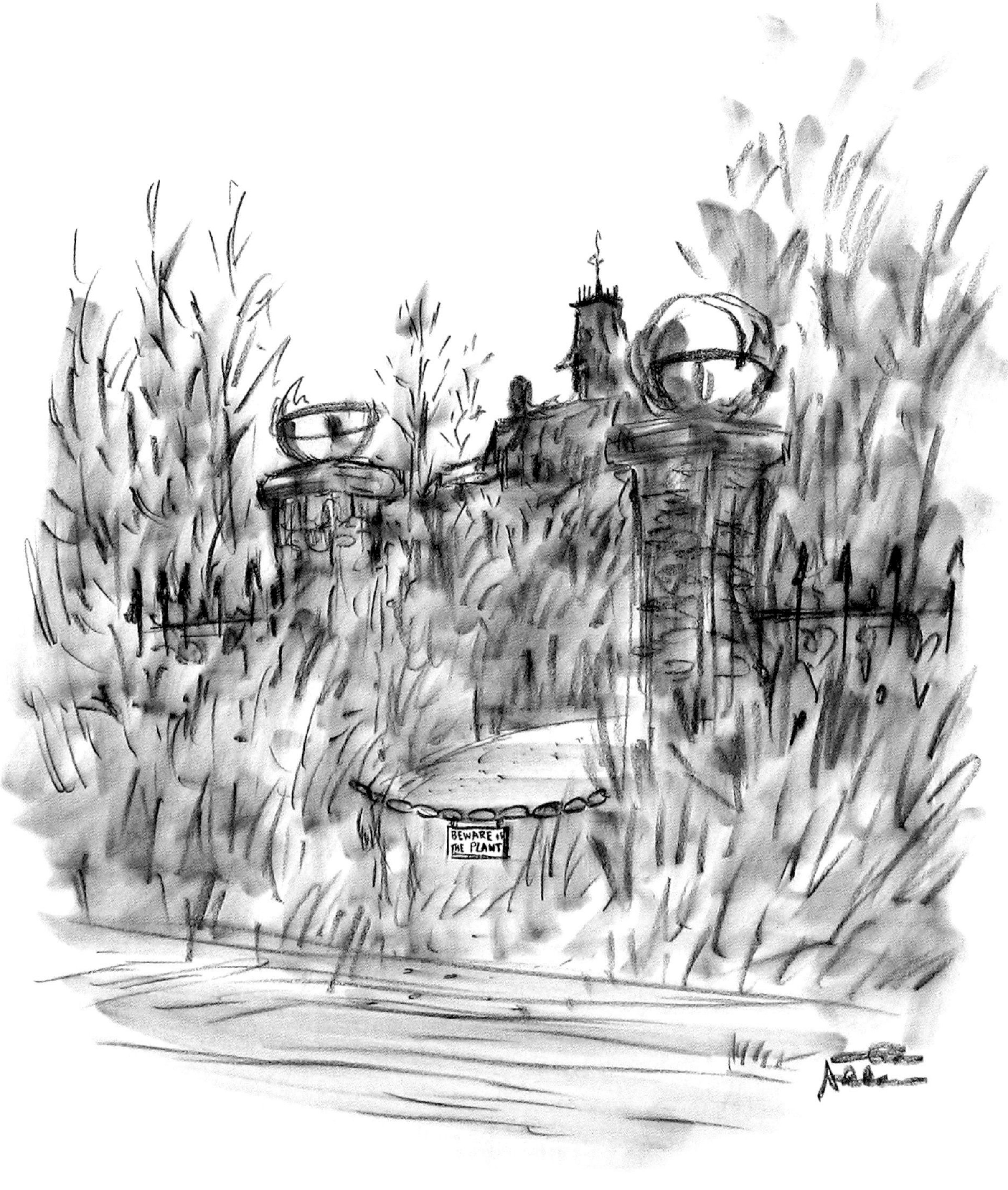
BEWARE
THE PLANT

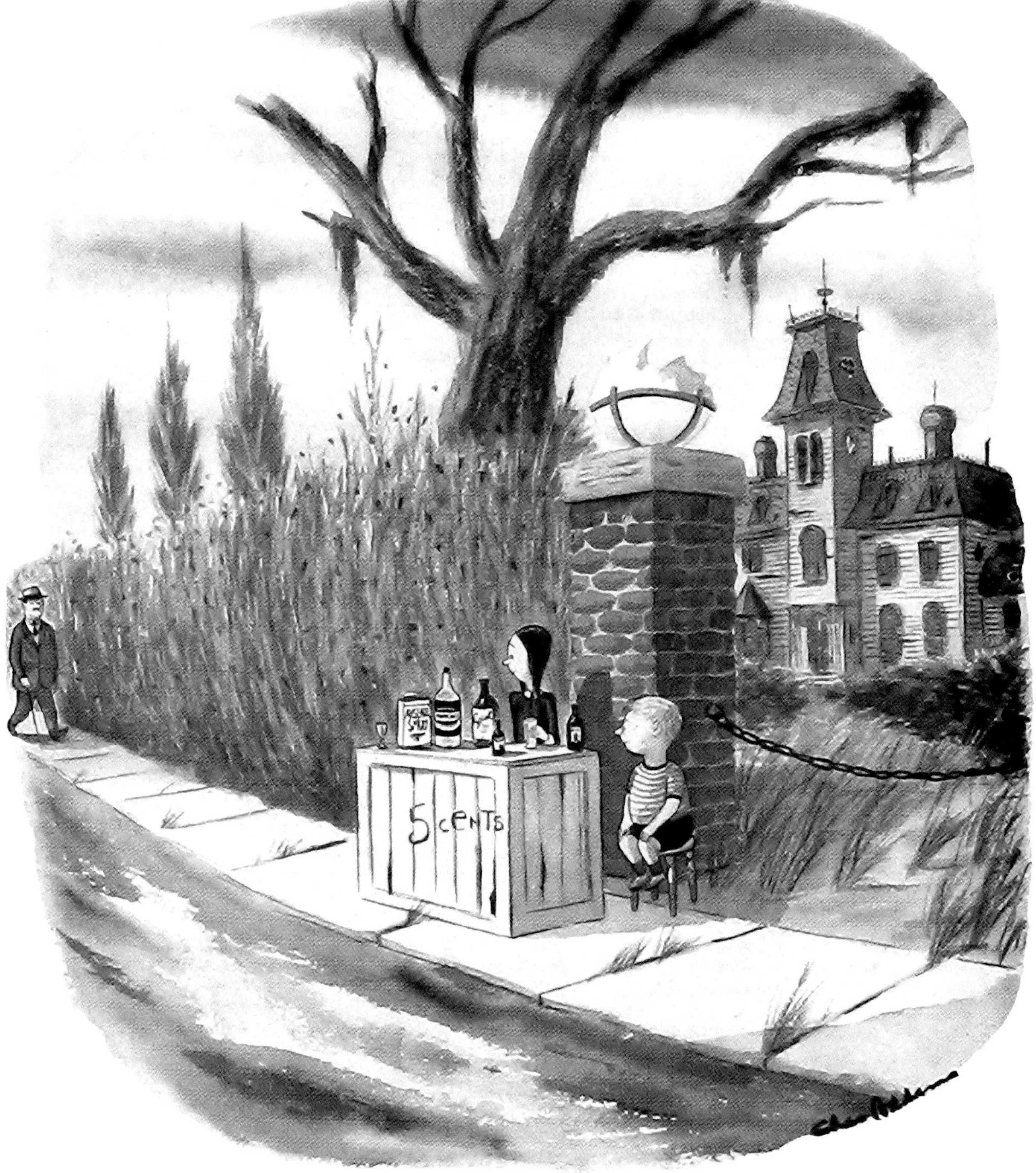
5 cents

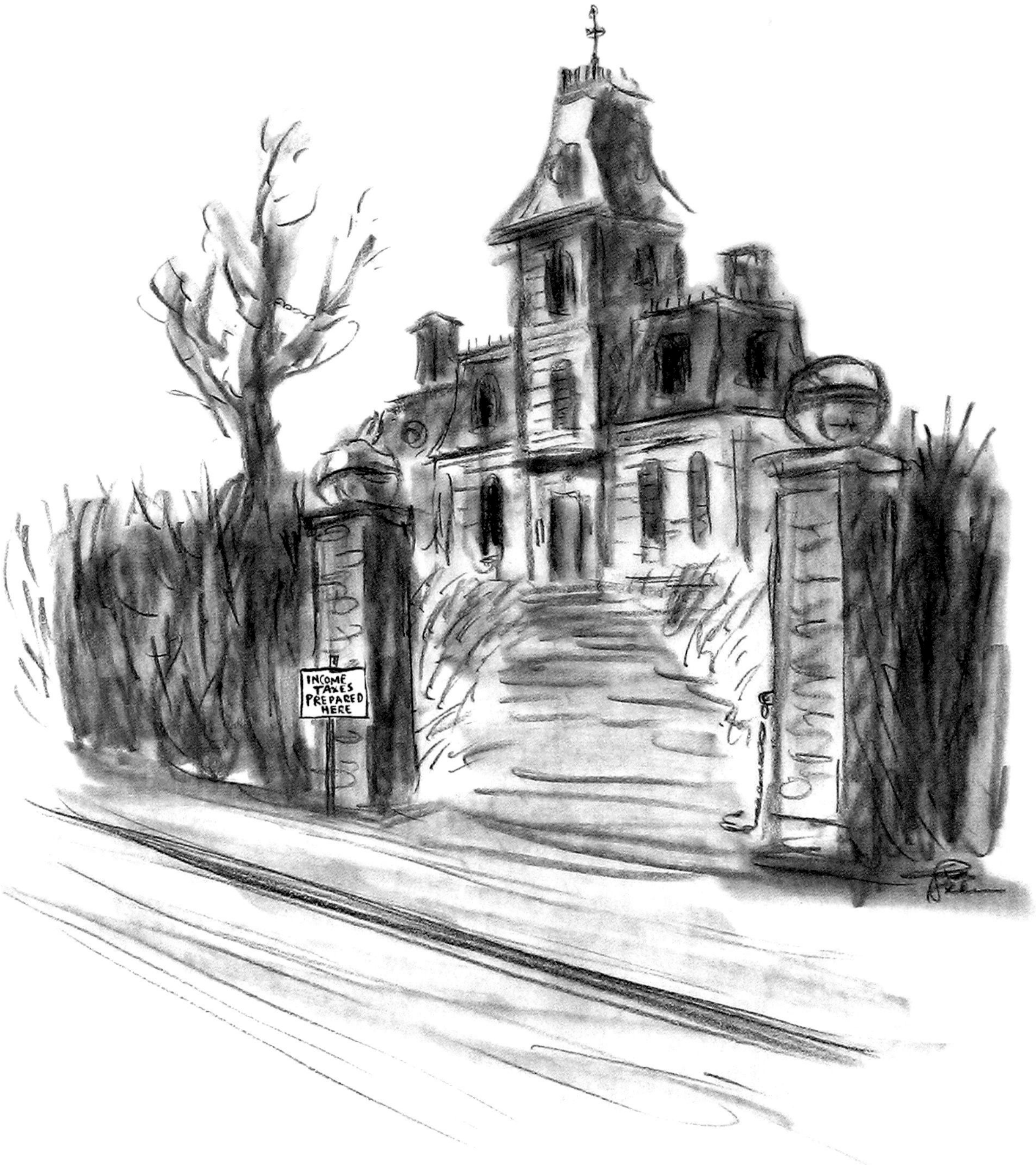
INCOME
TAXES
PREPARED
HERE

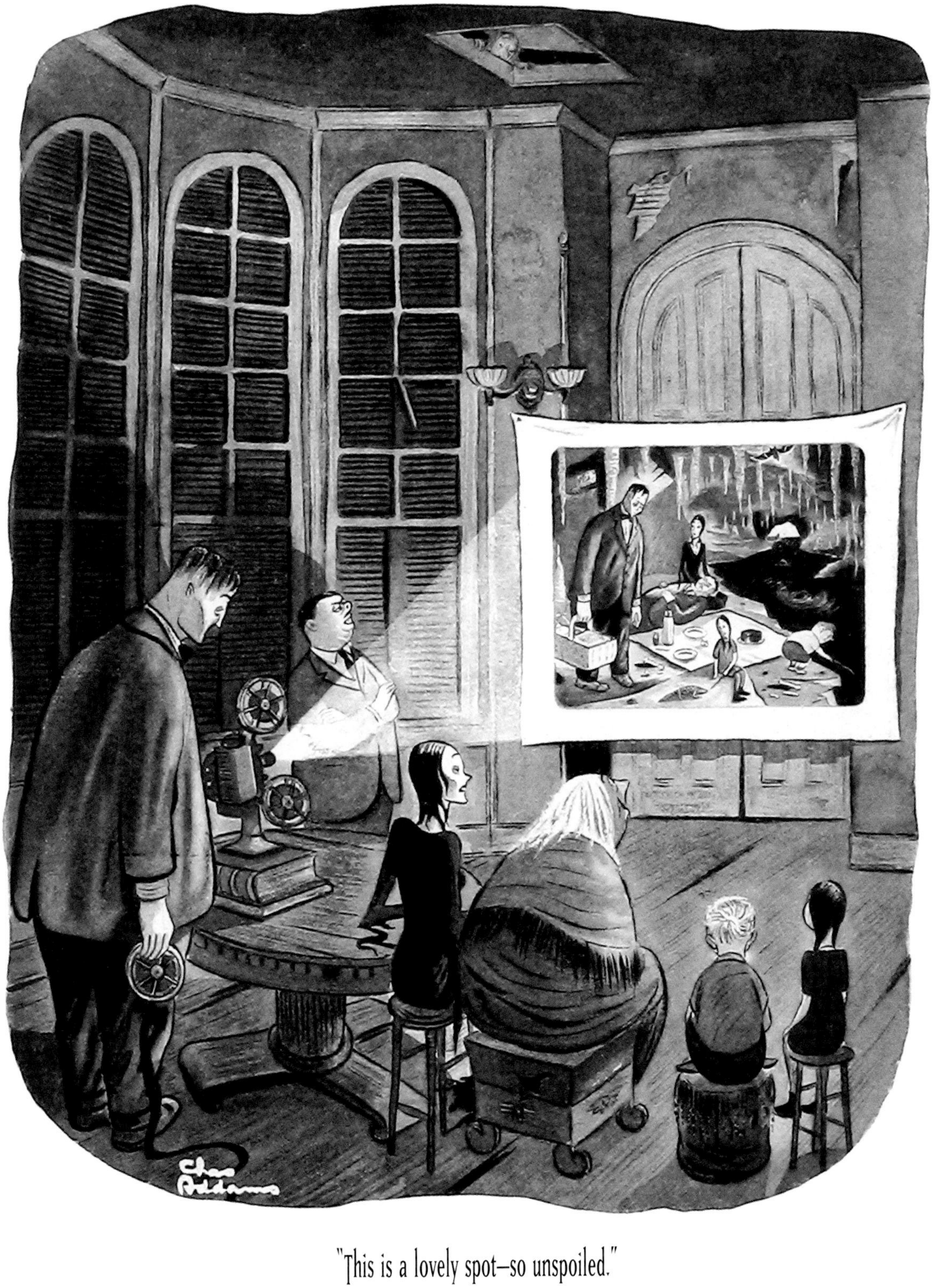
Chas Addams

"This is a lovely spot—so unspoiled."

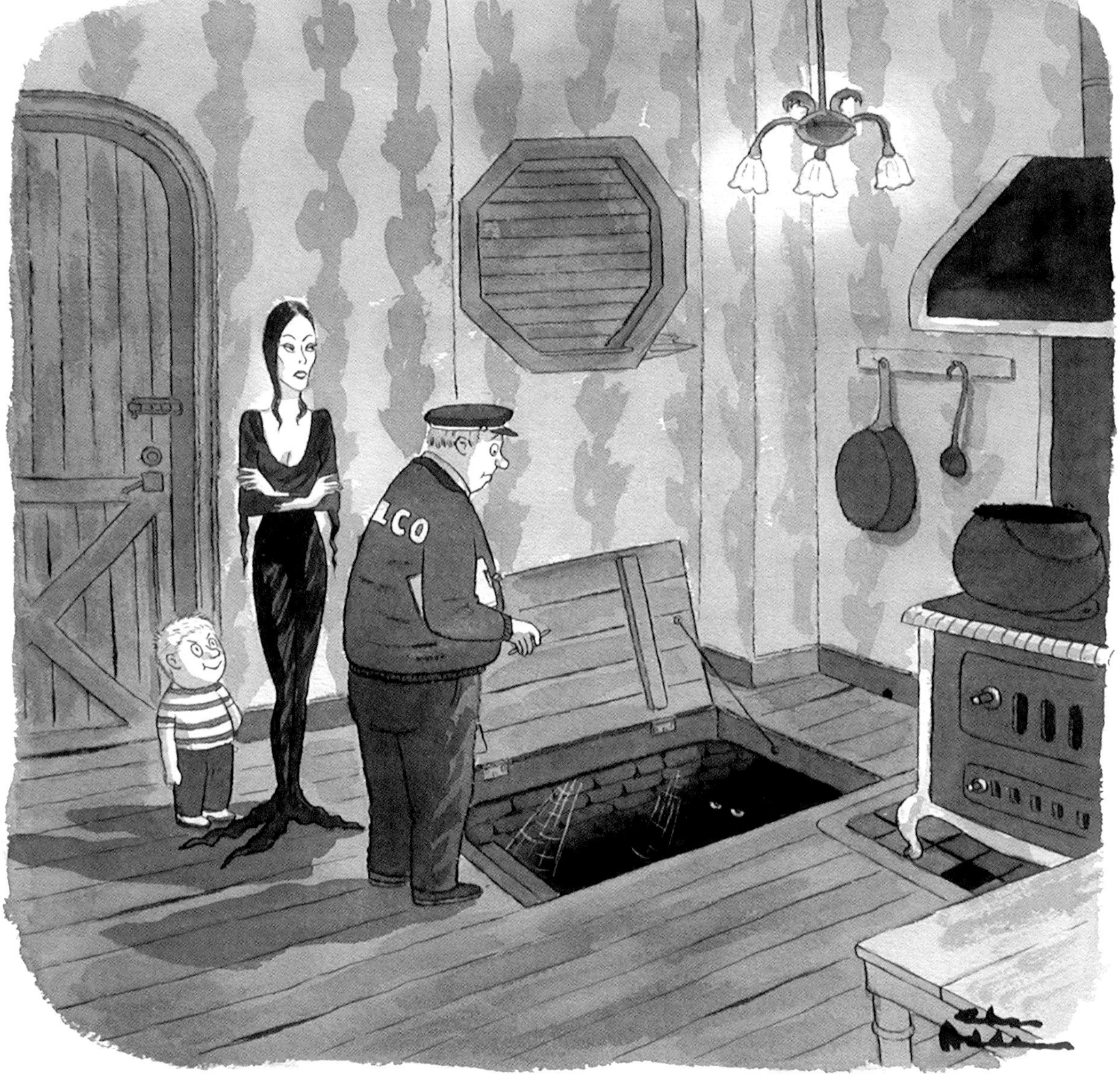
LCO

"At the bottom of the steps, turn right. The meter is on the far wall."

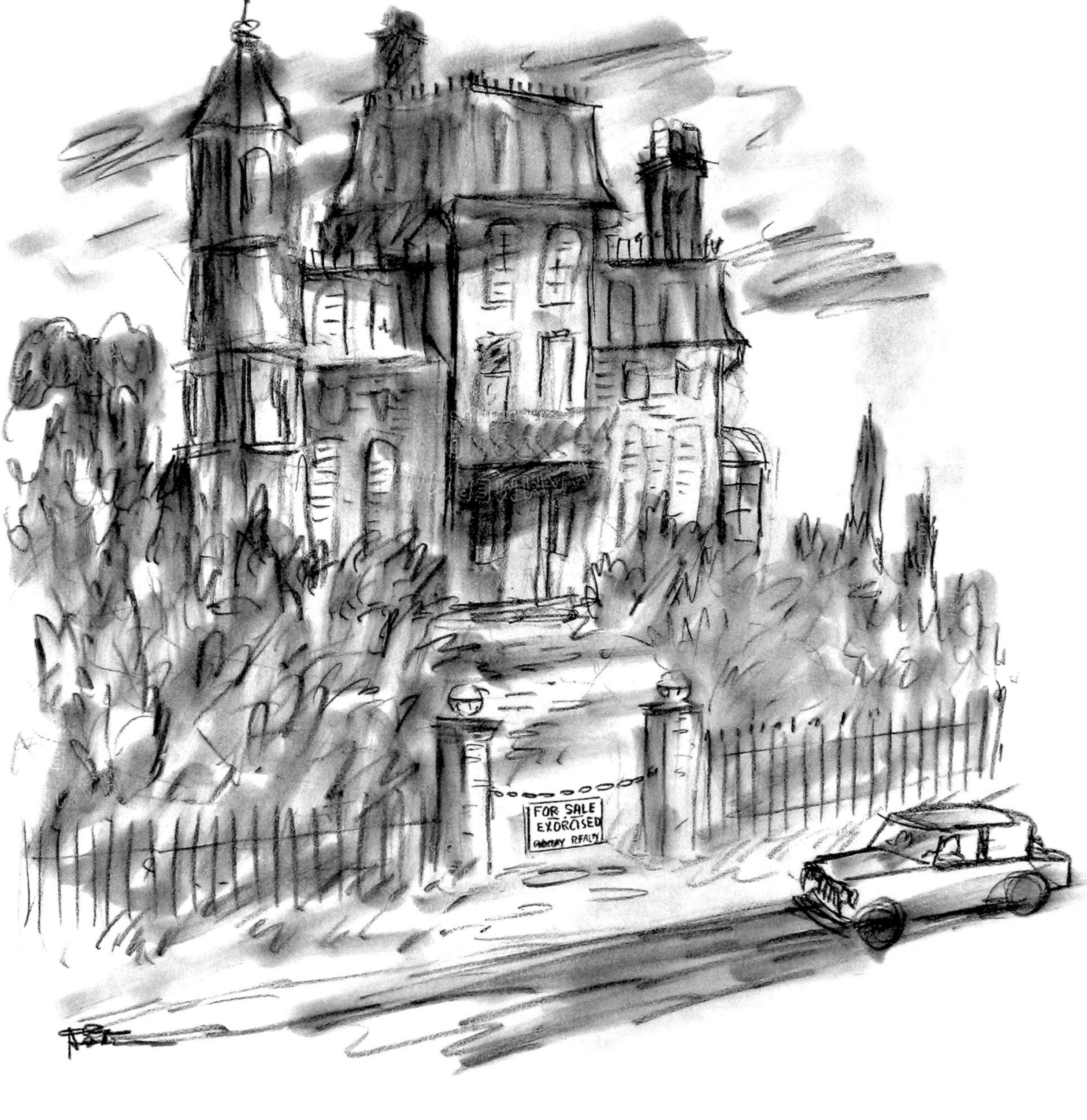
FOR SALE
EXORCISED
REALTY

INDEX OF ILLUSTRATIONS

Unless otherwise specified, the dates given are those of the *New Yorker* publications.

PAGE

Front Cover (jacket)   Exhibition poster, 1986

2   previously unpublished. This is the preliminary drawing for the image that would become the cover art for *Homebodies*.
6   previously unpublished
8   December 15, 1962
9   *Cars and Car-toons of Chas Addams*, exhibition catalogue, 2007
11   *Monster Rally*, 1950
12   previously unpublished
16   *The Groaning Board*, 1964
17   *The New York Times*, October 29, 1982
18   (top) Mobil Oil Corporation advertisement, 1984
     (bottom) *Cars and Car-toons of Chas Addams*, exhibition catalogue, 2007
19   *Road & Track*, December, 1976
20   *Dark Victory: The Life of Bette Davis*, by Ed Sikov, 2007. This is a preliminary drawing of a work used as the Warner Bros. pressbook cover for the 1962 premiere of the film *Whatever Happened to Baby Jane?*
21   *Favorite Haunts*, book jacket, 1976
22   November 4, 1950
23   October 5, 1946
24   *The New York Times*, October 26, 1984
25   *Monster Rally*, paperback cover, 1965
26   *Half-Baked Cookbook*, 2005
27   December 27, 1947
28   *The Groaning Board*, 1964
29   (top) *Playbill*, 1951
     (bottom) previously unpublished
30   *My Crowd*, book jacket, 1970
31   *Publishers Weekly*, cover, August 27, 1973
32   *The New York Times*, May 24, 1979
33   *Page One* (publication produced to honor the Newspaper Guild of New York), cover, May 20, 1949
34   June 24, 1950
35   *The Charles Addams Mother Goose*, 1967
36   previously unpublished
37   *Nightcrawlers*, book jacket, 1957
38   *Addams and Evil*, book jacket, 1947
39   *The Pennsylvania Gazette*, cover, March 1973
40   previously unpublished
42   detail from drawing on page 220
41   *Half-Baked Cookbook*, 2005
43   November 25, 1939
45   August 2, 1941
46   previously unpublished
47   August 6, 1949
48   previously unpublished
49   September 25, 1948
50   February 9, 1952
51   April 14, 1945
52   *Half-Baked Cookbook*, 2005
53   March 13, 1943
54   *Favorite Haunts*, 1976
55   *The Groaning Board*, 1964
56   August 9, 1958
57   *Addams and Evil*, 1947
58   previously unpublished
59   November 20, 1948
60   *Harper's Magazine*, cover, July 1982
61   *Monster Rally*, 1950
62   detail from drawing on page 184
64   November 14, 1942
65   December 27, 1952
66   previously unpublished
67   May 27, 1950
68   March 1, 1952
69   previously unpublished
70   previously unpublished
71   previously unpublished
72   previously unpublished
73   previously unpublished
74   February 12, 1949
75   previously unpublished
76   previously unpublished
77   December 23, 1950
78   July 21, 1945
79   June 26, 1954
80   (top) *Black Maria*, 1960
     (bottom) *The Groaning Board*, 1954
82   *The Charles Addams Mother Goose*, 1967
83   June 19, 1943
85   August 26, 1944
86   August 30, 1947
87   December 10, 1949
88   November 3, 1945
89   October 16, 1954

90	October 8, 1949		133	January 24, 1948
91	April 16, 1949		134	*Half-Baked Cookbook*, 2005
92	previously unpublished		135	January 10, 1948
93	*Homebodies*, 1954		136	previously unpublished
94	previously unpublished		137	*Half-Baked Cookbook*, 2005
95	February 26, 1949		138	previously unpublished
96	August 27, 1949		139	December 22, 1951
97	previously unpublished		140	*Half-Baked Cookbook*, 2005
98	previously unpublished		141	*Half-Baked Cookbook*, 2005
99	May 9, 1959		142	*The Charles Addams Mother Goose*, cover, 1967
100	McClure Syndicate, September 26, 1955		143	April 14, 1951
101	July 8, 1974		144	October 17, 1959
102	June 9, 1951		145	*The Charles Addams Mother Goose*, 1967
103	previously unpublished		146	previously unpublished
104	December 31, 1960, cover		147	January 18, 1941
105	September 5, 1953		149	March 23, 1946
106	previously unpublished		150	November 23, 1946
107	December 24, 1949		151	*Homebodies*, 1954
108	previously unpublished		152	previously unpublished
109	previously unpublished		153	*Favorite Haunts*, 1976
110	November 30, 1946		154	April 9, 1955
111	*The Charles Addams Mother Goose*, 1967		155	previously unpublished
112	(top) previously unpublished (bottom) McClure Syndicate June 25, 1949		156	*Life* magazine, December 11, 1950
113	November 6, 1954		157	*Black Maria*, 1960
114	previously unpublished		158	(top) July 18, 1964 (bottom) October 1, 1979
115	September 11, 1948		159	*Road & Track*, December 1976
116	*The Charles Addams Mother Goose*, 1967		160	previously unpublished
117	previously unpublished		161	*Homebodies*, 1954
118	detail from drawing on page 86		162	April 22, 1950
119	August 6, 1938		163	*Half-Baked Cookbook*, 2005
121	*Drawn and Quartered*, book jacket, 1942		164	September 19, 1953
122	previously unpublished		165	McClure Syndicate, September 2, 1956
123	*Black Maria*, 1960		166	McClure Syndicate, April 9, 1956
124	November 22, 1952		167	*Half-Baked Cookbook*, 2005
125	September 29, 1951		168	March 24, 1956
126	(top) *Cars and Car-toons of Chas Addams*, exhibition catalogue, 2007 (bottom) *The Addams Chronicles*, 1998		169	February 11, 1950
			170	*Black Maria*, 1960
127	previously unpublished		171	previously unpublished
128	detail from drawing on page 135		172	previously unpublished
129	February 8, 1941		173	previously unpublished
130	*Monster Rally*, book jacket, 1950		174	*The Groaning Board*, 1964
131	*The Charles Addams Mother Goose*, 1967		175	McClure Syndicate, January 13, 1957
132	previously unpublished		176	previously unpublished
			177	February 25, 1950

178 *Monster Rally*, 1950
179 January 29, 1949
180 February 17, 1973
181 September 29, 1986
182 detail from drawing on page 119
183 March 20, 1954
184 Mobil Oil Corporation advertisement, 1984
185 November 10, 1945
186 *Dear Dead Days*, book jacket, 1959
187 *Black Maria*, book jacket, 1960
188 August 14, 1948
189 Exhibition poster, 1986
190 January 28, 1956
191 previously unpublished
192 detail from drawing on page 202
193 previously unpublished
194 December 21, 1987
195 October 12, 1963
196 April 12, 1947
197 previously unpublished
198 *Black Maria*, 1960
199 May 26, 1951
200 March 27, 1948
201 previously unpublished
202 February 3, 1951
203 *The Groaning Board*, 1964
204 previously unpublished
205 *The Addams Chronicles*, 1998
206 *Half-Baked Cookbook*, 2005
207 previously unpublished
208 previously unpublished
209 *Black Maria*, 1960
210 detail from drawing on page 125
211 December 21, 1946
212 previously unpublished
213 August 28, 1954
214 previously unpublished
215 September 5, 1988
216 previously unpublished
217 *Monster Rally*, 1950
218 previously unpublished
219 September 30, 1944
220 May 9, 1988
221 previously unpublished
Back Cover *Drawn & Quartered*, paperback cover, 1962

BIBLIOGRAPHY
COMPILATIONS OF CHARLES ADDAMS CARTOONS

Addams and Evil (New York: Random House, 1947).

The Charles Addams Mother Goose (New York: Windmill Books, 1967; Simon & Schuster, 2002).

Chas Addams' Black Maria: A New Cartoon Collection (New York: Simon & Schuster, 1960).

Chas Addams' Homebodies (New York: Simon & Schuster, 1954).

Chas Addams' Monster Rally, foreword by John O'Hara (New York: Simon & Schuster, 1950).

Chas Addams' Nightcrawlers (New York: Simon & Schuster, 1957).

Creature Comforts (New York: Simon & Schuster, 1981).

Dear Dead Days: A Family Album (New York: G. P. Putnam & Sons, 1959).

Drawn and Quartered (New York: Random House, 1942; Simon & Schuster, 1962).

Favorite Haunts (New York: Simon & Schuster, 1976).

The Groaning Board (New York: Simon & Schuster, 1964).

Half-Baked Cookbook (New York: Simon & Schuster, 2005).

Happily Ever After: A Collection of Cartoons to Chill the Heart of Your Loved One (New York: Simon & Schuster, 2006).

My Crowd: The Original Addams Family and Other Ghoulish Creatures (New York: Simon & Schuster, 1970; Barnes & Noble, 2003).

The World of Charles Addams (New York: Alfred A. Knopf, 1993).